Regicide

Book 3 of The Dimensional Wars

Blake Severson

In honor of Debra "Moo" Severson.
April 12th, 1968 – July 7th. 2022
You will always be missed.

Prologue

The Storyteller

Alicia looked at the old man in disbelief. His plain brown robes of sturdy fabric did nothing to reflect the wisdom he contained. His bald head was beaded with a few drops of perspiration in the heat.

"This city used to be called Alem's Crossing? The name of the town from legend?" Alicia asked.

"It was," the old man confirmed.

Shock was the only emotion she could present, so she sat there in silence.

"The Lost Prince renamed this city when he made it the capital of the Kingdom of Fire. They braved a large goblin raid that was orchestrated by some shady figures of the Dark Elves. It was after that battle that our heroes went on an epic journey where the entire party gained their classes." The storyteller recited.

"Are you sure? I didn't think you could do that since class quests are tailored to the person." A young man chimed in.

"Normally not. As fate would have it, their party had quests all in the same general area." The storyteller said.

"Now try not to interrupt," the older man admonished. "For when they returned, a legend was reborn. The Soul Bond was reinstated and Arthur Firebrand joined with Lady Calfuray, the purple dragon."

"Ew, joined with a dragon. That's gross," a younger boy stated.

The old man leaned forward and slapped the young man across the back of his head.

"None of that nonsense, young Jack. You know what I meant."

"Sorry," the boy said.

"Did he ride the dragon?" One person asked.

"Do they really breathe fire?" Another asked.

The storyteller raised his hands for quiet.

"Yes, to the first, although rarely. Also, yes to the second. Now let me continue," the storyteller said, before motioning all the kids to sit and be quiet.

"He dedicated a lot of time to rebuilding the city and turning it into what it is today. We wouldn't have many of the niceties we take for granted without King Arthur."

"Wait, king? Thought he was still a prince," a young girl asked.

"My apologies," the storyteller conceded. "Answering questions out of turn caught me by surprise. After the bond was established, Arthur declared himself the rightful king and established the Kingdom of Fire, centered on Alem's Crossing. He also renamed it Alurian."

"From there, they marched on Seora. The fighting was bitter, but they emerged victorious. Arthur, Allendria, Rayne, and Samson faced off against Lord Preston and defeated him in combat as he was enhanced by the Goddess Isabell's magic."

"This caused a cascade of events and put them on the map, so to speak. The alliance between the evil King Wailyn and the King of the Dark Elves, Gliran, came to the forefront as a delegation of Dark Elves arrived and declared war on Arthur."

"So, he was at war with two nations?" Alicia asked.

The storyteller nodded in agreement.

"How could he beat two enemies at once?" She asked.

"By taking them one at a time. Sadly, the story from here grows darker. Regicide reigned supreme as kings fell. When another enemy emerged, it was almost the end of our world." The storyteller said in a lower voice.

"What enemy?" Young Jack asked.

"Why, the Ar'Tookan, of course," the storyteller said.

Chapter 1

Diplomats

Arthur stood on the battlement of Seora in shocked silence. The guards around him shuffled nervously while he stared at the elf in the field in front of him. This development wasn't unexpected, but he hoped he still had more time. The Dark Elves finally showed their hand and declared war on Arthur and the Kingdom of Fire.

Ambassador Finthra, the leader of the diplomatic party, stood in the field with a smug smile. Arthur couldn't think of anything else to do, so he sent a message to Calfuray, his dragon bond partner, in his mind.

You have any idea where Allendria is?

Last I saw her, she wasn't far from the main gate, working on repairs to one of the grain storage buildings. Balair was with her. Calfuray paused. *Something wrong? You seem a little frazzled.*

A delegation of Dark Elves arrived and declared war on us. I need her at the gates to help me sort through this. He told her in a hurry before changing his focus to Balair.

Allendria with you? Arthur sent to the little drake.

Damn, can't even buy me dinner first? Not so much as a hi, how are ya? Rude as hell. Balair grumbled to him.

It's important! I need her at the main gate as fast as she can get here. He mentally shouted back.

Geez, calm down. I'll tell her. No need to shout. It was less than half a minute later when he sent back another message. *She's on her way.*

Thank you. I'll get you dinner later.

Arthur shifted focus back to the delegation. He needed to delay them for a few minutes until Allendria could arrive to refute their claim.

"Ambassador Finthra, I believe you're mistaken in your assumptions. May I ask what proof you bring of your accusations?" Arthur asked across the field.

"You murdered our ranger squad that was tasked with returning the Princess. Then you murdered our last ambassador and his two companions when they tried the second time." Finthra said with a sneer.

Arthur played along for now. "I believe those accusations are unfounded. I can attest that a party of rangers never came within sight of the village's wall or it would've been reported to me. Are you sure they didn't fall prey to threats in the forest?"

It's technically true. Vana and I killed them before they came within sight of the village.

"I guess I'm supposed to believe that Ambassador Lyrinth and his two guards also fell prey to the forest as well?" Finthra asked.

"I fear I have grave news," Arthur said with all the sincerity he could muster while not bursting into laughter. "A raiding party of orcs and goblins recently attacked our village. We repelled their attacks and chased them from our surrounding area, but I fear they may have gotten to your ambassador and his guards before they reached us."

Ambassador Finthra's purple skin flushed a deep red in what Arthur assumed was anger, while some of his companions wore looks of concern. His sleek black hair waved slightly in the wind and he clenched his fist in anger.

"King Glirin demands the return of Princess Allendria and that you surrender all lands under your ownership to him. He has agreed to spare the lives of any human in what will become his new realm as long as you surrender peacefully," he spat.

Footsteps behind Arthur caught his attention, and he turned to see Allendria strolling up the stairs. The look of anger on her face told Arthur she'd heard at least part of the recent conversation. She stomped up the stairs until she reached Arthur and peered over the battlement. A look of contempt flashed over her face but softened as she took in those assembled.

"Ah, Finthra. How I so dearly hoped Glirin would've killed you by now. I thought he had more sense than that," Allendria quipped with a smile.

"That's King Glirin, Princess Allendria. It's apparent your time in captivity has destroyed what little manners you once had."

"Captivity?" she exclaimed with a laugh as she spun around and examined herself before turning to Arthur and loudly pronouncing, "I imagined there'd be more chains and dungeons if I were in captivity. Are you neglecting your kingly duties in this task?" She asked him with a grin.

"My apologies Princess. I fear I've been remiss in my study of kidnapping procedures," Arthur responded before turning to Finthra. "Ambassador Finthra, could you help me sort out this mess? It seems I've been negligent in my duties for this to classify as kidnapping. Maybe you could show me the proper procedure?"

The Dark Elf's face shifted to the oddest shade of reddish-purple Arthur ever saw before he spluttered, "You brigand. We will leave here with the Princess, and you have two weeks to make your decision on the terms of surrender."

Arthur turned to Allendria and lowered his voice. "Any ideas?"

"The man is a pompous fool and has always been a lackey for Glirin. You'll never change his mind. There's one man in his delegation I trust, though, and I would like to talk to him, even if only briefly. He was part of my father's group when Glirin started his coup."

"How are we going to do that? We want to negotiate?" Arthur asked.

"We can meet them under a flag of truce. I mainly just need to talk to Onrain. If he can spread the word of my safety to those still loyal to my father, it would help keep our people off-balance."

Arthur nodded at the suggestion before turning back to Ambassador Finthra. "Ambassador, Princess Allendria and I would like to accompany you to discuss this matter in person under terms of peace. I'll have my captain of the guard to accompany us. Will that satisfy you?"

"Very well," the Ambassador called back with a wave.

Arthur rushed down the wall and waved at a huffing Samson as he raced for the gate. Someone must've found him and warned him of the danger. Vana came up directly behind him.

"Perfect timing," Arthur told them. "I'm going to go meet with the Ambassador, and I need you and Allendria with me. Vana, do me a favor and take the wall. I know you're a good enough archer to pick them off from here if they try anything."

"I've got ya," the woman said before dashing up the stairs.

Samson stopped and threw his arms over his head as he took a few huge gasps of air. He lowered his arms and stood ready. Arthur nodded. The Paladin strode forward and pushed the door open. Arthur and Allendria followed behind.

Samson strode forward with confident steps, and the elves in the field stood still as they approached. When they were less than twenty feet from the group, they slowed. Arthur began to cast a spell before quickly stopping.

"Ambassador, I'm about to cast a spell to make us some seating. I assure you it isn't an offensive or dangerous spell. I don't want there to be a misunderstanding." Arthur told him carefully.

The elf merely nodded and waved a hand. Arthur used his Earth and Fire Magic to lift chairs of stone from the ground. He placed two of them to the side for him and Finthra, while the others were in pairs to the side. He hoped Allendria would take the chance to grab Onrain and sit with him. Arthur motioned toward the two chairs for him and Finthra, and they took their seats. A glance to the side showed Allendria and Onrain sitting together.

"Ambassador. We both know your purpose here has nothing to do with the Princess and everything to do with the agenda from Isabell you follow." Arthur said, with no more posturing.

"Oh, I'm aware, but I must play to the story. There's nothing you can do to stop us. Wailyn has his supporters and fighters, and we have ours. We are the stronger force. You can't possibly stop us," Finthra said with a sneer.

"You sure think highly of your abilities after your many failures. How's that army of orcs and goblins working out? I sure hope you have far better than them if you hope to succeed against me. Surely you know who I am by now?"

"You think your heritage scares me? Firebrands are nothing more than a relic of a past age. Your power means nothing."

"Apparently, you haven't heard. It's no surprise. You've been on the road for a while to reach here. The Dragon bond is renewed. You'll face a dragon as well."

"It's only one dragon. We've fought them in the past and can do so again. You also forget. The dragons are splintered. You aren't the only one with access to their power," Finthra said coolly.

The insinuation bothered Arthur. If he took the man at his word, the Dark Elves might have a dragon of their own. "Regardless of the options you have, you won't win. You also won't be leaving with Princess Allendria. She will remain here at her own request. I've offered her sanctuary in the Kingdom of Fire. You would've been much better off just trying a surprise attack with your army instead of this tactic. You won't scare me off, and your words won't sway my people."

"We wanted to be fair and declare war officially. You don't stand a chance with your meager forces, no matter how you look at things. If nothing else, it was refreshing to talk to a human for the first time in generations. We'll see you on the field of battle," the ambassador said with a final bow of his head, and he rose to his feet.

Everyone in the clearing immediately stood, and Arthur dismissed the chairs with his magic. The two groups separated, and the Dark Elves turned to leave the city.

"Tell my Uncle I'll be happy to rid him of his head before this is over," Allendria called to Finthra with an uncharacteristic smile.

The Ambassador faltered in his steps for a moment before just shaking his head and continuing his walk. Arthur, Samson, and Allendria turned and headed for the gate.

"You get to talk to Onrain?" Arthur asked Allendria.

"Yeah. I told him about the events that had transpired. He was furious when I let him know that Glirin and his cronies allied with the orcs and goblins to raid the human kingdom. Many of my father's supporters have been silent about their beliefs since his fall, but they don't like how things are going."

"Do you think we could rely on any of them when the time comes?"

"Probably. If I return to remove Glirin, I believe I could rally some to our cause. I don't know how many survived his takeover, though. I mainly wanted to let Onrain know what had happened here so he could spread the word about my safety at home. We didn't have time for him to tell me much about what happened in Calzas." Allendria said.

Arthur looked ahead to Samson. "Samson. We need a plan. Now we have a war on two fronts."

"I hate to be the bearer of bad news, but there's nothing we can do about that right now. If those Dark Elves were smart, they'd have an army right behind them, ready to attack. Based on what I saw at our meeting, I doubt they do. That means we have some time. We still have an extremely long list of things to get done in this city before we worry about much else. The people here aren't faring well. Our improvements help, but it'll take time for them to get back on their feet."

"Guess you're right. Just tired of always having to react," Arthur moped.

"On the bright side, if they attack now, Calfuray can probably roast most of them," Samson said with some brevity in his voice.

Arthur chuckled. "Isn't that the truth? If they approached from the forest, I'd have no qualms about her lighting them on fire. Getting them before they reach the city would be key. I really need to know the mood of the city. We've seen little since we took over and have worked hard to change their minds about us, but we don't know if it's working. I need to find Rayne and talk to him."

"What do you need him for?" Samson asked.

"I plan on having him become my new spymaster. I need him to infiltrate the darker parts of the city and get a feel for the true pulse of the citizens. We need to find out exactly what resources this city has and the attitudes of the populace. With this war looming over us on two fronts, we may need to relocate some of these people to Alurian."

"Is that a good idea? That puts them closer to the front line of the battle with the Dark Elves."

"I plan on taking the ones willing to fight and healthy enough to help. I don't want to throw them into the fighting immediately and back at Alurian would be the best place to train them. We also won't be able to keep up with food demand here for an extended amount of time. There are just too many mouths to feed." Arthur told him.

"That just causes a food issue for Alurian instead," Samson sighed, "It seems neither option is very appealing."

"Won't argue with that, but we have to do something. We'll need fighters and artisans. This city is utterly broke in every version of the word. The buildings are falling apart, there is no market, they have no food, and money is practically nonexistent. Rayne warned me that the treasury here was bound to be empty. He'd snuck into Lord Preston's manor before and found his empty treasury. The city coffers looked much the same."

No one said anything else as they approached the city gate. The gates swung open just far enough for them to shuffle through and closed behind them with a thud. A long metal locking bar slammed into place. Soldiers milled around the area. Many nervously fidgeted or adjusted weapons, waiting on a command.

"Return to your watch for now," Samson called over the group. "I don't foresee any immediate danger. If you weren't already on duty at the gate, you're dismissed back to your previous post."

Sighs of relief passed through the lips of many of the surrounding fighters. They turned and walked from the area and back into the city proper.

"Vana!" Arthur called up and waved for the woman to join them. She scurried down the stairs of the ramparts and joined them at the bottom.

"Did they all leave?" Allendria asked the Ranger as she reached their group.

Vana nodded. "The last of them walked into the trees right before I ran down."

"Good. Now we need to call a meeting to get these issues sorted out. Samson, please gather anyone in the city that has any authority. The leaders of the crafting guilds or merchant guilds would be invaluable. Allendria, could you take a contingent of our guards from Alurian and find any who might have some noble standing in the city to attend? I don't know if any are alive since we killed everyone aligned with Preston. Vana, I need you to find Rayne and have him meet me at Preston's Manor."

They all agreed, and everyone quickly split to go about their tasks. Arthur turned and headed for Preston's manor.

The manor was their unofficial center of business for the city. This place was the quintessential definition of a frontier city. They never created a centralized strong point here. No castle or keep of any kind. A few of the larger manor houses had small stone walls, but they were barely as tall as their original wall in Alurian when the bandits first attacked.

The entire defense of this city relied on the outer wall. If the defenders took it, they had the city as well. Their victory proved that point. It was something they needed to address. Alurian didn't have this central defense either, but it was barely a town. The new Dark Elven embassy in Alurian was a far better fortress on its own than anything currently standing in this place.

Arthur entered the manor and walked to the central living space. He paced back and forth while waiting for Rayne to arrive. The thoughts of everything to do weighed on him. A noise brought him out of his reverie, and he looked up to see Rayne walk into the room. The broad smile from the young man lifted his spirits and dimmed some of his worries.

"Been staying busy?" Arthur asked.

"Relatively. I've been searching for old contacts to see if anyone is still around."

"That makes what I'm going to ask a little easier," Arthur breathed.

Rayne's eyebrow shot up at the statement, "What is it?"

"I need a spymaster," Arthur told him bluntly.

"I agree. Every good king or queen knows the value of information, and it's imperative that you get something established early. Why are you telling me instead of finding one? Do you need recommendations or something? I haven't found many old contacts and don't even know who is still alive."

Arthur smiled at the confused look on Rayne's face. "No. I want you to be my spymaster."

Rayne's mouth fell open for a moment with a look of shock plastered on his face. It didn't take long for his mind to spin back into motion. "I can't do that. I'm far too young to take control of that. There are others with more years of experience than me."

"That's probably true," Arthur agreed, "but I don't care. I trust you. I know your motives, and I understand your position, but most importantly, I know you're a good man. Best yet, you're a good man who isn't afraid to do whatever is necessary. That alone is almost impossible to find. So, will you be my spymaster?"

The young man looked conflicted and stood in silence. His head hung down as his eyes scanned the floor. It took him half a minute before he finally looked back at Arthur.

"I'll do it. What do you need?"

Rayne has accepted the Kingdom level position of Spymaster for the Kingdom of Fire. This position is beholden only to the King and those he specifically appoints. Because of its sensitive nature, this job will never appear on any status screens for the kingdom.

Both men froze for a few seconds as they read the message. Arthur looked at Rayne and just shrugged before answering his question.

"I need you to build a full spy network from the ground up. I'll find any resources you need to make this happen. We don't know what even greases the wheels these days, so to speak. I'd assume that with the extreme problems in the city, food is the number one currency everywhere. Recruit whomever you have to. I leave all the decisions on how to handle the business to you. I just want information on the city itself. How are the people holding up? Are there any dissenters still hiding out here? Are there any hidden stockpiles of goods or food stashed around? Would people be willing to leave if given a choice for a better life?" Arthur explained.

"You considering abandoning the city and taking everyone back to Alurian?" Rayne asked.

"Not everyone. I'd like to take the able-bodied fighters and essential artisans with us. Going to Alurian takes them closer to the battle with the Dark Elves. I am sure they are currently our biggest threat. The human kingdom has dwindled so far because of King Wailyn's stupidity that I doubt they have the manpower to march on us. We took this city with an army that was a joke in terms of size. I have a terrible feeling that Calzas won't be nearly as easy. Allendria planted some seeds with one of the diplomat's party who was loyal to her father. Hopefully, we can convince some of them to join our cause when the time comes to strike."

"I know nothing of Dark Elven society or customs, so we'll have to rely on Allendria for that. I'll start figuring out what we will need to make this work. It'll take time, but I'll start approaching people about the chance to work for the new kingdom instead of against it. Once I figure out the terms of employment, I'll come back to you with the list of resources I'll need access to so we can secure our network."

"Perfect. I also sent the others to go round up any leadership left in this city. We are going to hold a meeting here once they gather everyone, so hang around. It should paint a good picture of what we have to work with and any issues we may need to deal with." Arthur said.

"Sounds like a plan. How are things with you and Allendria?" Rayne asked.

"What do you mean? Everything is fine, as far as I know."

"I figured she'd be mad or upset that she had to come to our rescue the day after you asked for her hand in marriage," Rayne said with a chuckle.

"Luckily, she seems pretty practical and understands this world is harsh. She hasn't expressed much worry. I know Calfuray wasn't very pleased with me trying to get her killed. She's been avoiding me since the battle. Probably for the best. I'd rather her cool off for a while before returning in anger and stepping on me."

They trudged around the room, chatting about mostly inconsequential things before the door opened, and they watched Allendria stride through. Three middle-aged men and an older woman followed behind her. She spotted the two of them as she entered and turned in their direction. Her steps halted when she was ten feet away, and she gave a quick bow.

"King Firebrand, I've arrived with four nobles from the city of Seora, as you requested." She told him formally.

The tone of her voice and the seriousness of the situation stunned him before he realized what was happening. She needed to treat him like an actual king in front of these people. It's what they'd expect.

"Thank you, Princess Allendria. I appreciate your willingness to help with this task," he told her, returning her bow. She smiled at him and winked as he turned to look at the newly arrived guests.

"Greetings, nobles of Seora. I'm King Arthur Firebrand of the Kingdom of Fire. Before we go any further, let me answer the questions I'm sure most of you have. Yes, I'm the son of Tristan and Violet Firebrand. No, I'm not dead. Yes, I'm pretty young for the age I should be, but it's a long and hard-to-believe story about how I've returned. With those items addressed, I ask that you join me for a meeting to discuss the future of the city. More will arrive shortly, and we will begin. In the meantime, I'd like to come by and meet you all," Arthur told them as he walked toward the first man in line. His mind shifted for a moment, and he changed direction and headed for the older lady instead.

"Greetings, my lady. I apologize. I nearly forgot my manners. Proper respect for both a lady and an elder of society are both equally important in a civilized country," Arthur told her with a curt bow.

"Thank you for the consideration," she told him with a wicked grin. "My name is Lady Gemmalin, but I fear I'm a little too old for you, my liege."

"A sense of humor! Lovely. We should get along just fine," Arthur told her with a hearty laugh. She returned his grin.

"Have you retired to your estates, or do you still manage anything in the city?" Arthur asked the elderly woman.

"I'm old, but I'm not dead. Retirement may never be in my future. I managed the textile markets until they disappeared. It's a shame too. We used to make some really fabulous clothing."

"We'll see what we can do to fix that," Arthur told her confidently.

A glimmer of hope and eagerness lit her ancient eyes before Arthur continued to the next person in line.

The next man was tall and lean. He appeared to be in his late thirties with dirty blonde hair. His brown eyes darted to Arthur's hair before looking back at his face.

"Well met. What's your name and title?" Arthur asked.

"I'm Lord Remere Ealin," he said with a hasty bow.

"What function did you serve in the city, Lord Ealin?"

"I was quartermaster for Seora."

"Was quartermaster? How long ago was that?" Arthur asked, intrigued by the man's tone in the statement.

"I was removed from my position almost half a year ago. Lord Preston grew tired of me constantly asking about the shortages and lack of funds for everything he continued to do."

"Good to know. So, you're already aware of the bleak state of the city's funds and supplies, then?"

"I know what they were a month ago, but not sure now. Hard to imagine they could be much worse since there wasn't much to begin with. I've seen no shipments come in for longer than I care to remember."

"Well, let's see if we can fix that," Arthur said with a smile.

The other two introductions continued in the same way. The first of them was an older gentleman with gray in his hair and a short beard by the name of Lord Gregory Trip. His family historically controlled mercantile efforts in the city.

The last man was shorter than the rest and wore finer clothing of better make. His jet-black hair hung to his shoulders, and Arthur caught the shimmer of a bracelet from under one sleeve of his long tunic. His name was Lord Joseph Nealan, and his family managed the different guilds at the city level.

"Thank you all for coming," Arthur told them. "Let's go find seats in the formal dining area and wait for the rest of our guests to arrive."

Chapter 2

Decisions, Decisions

Arthur pinched the bridge of his nose. It took a while for the entire group to assemble. Rayne and Samson reappeared with representatives from the city. There were eight of them in total. Allendria sat in on the meeting with them, but she was careful to sit near the edge of the room and not at the table. Her royal upbringing made her all too knowledgeable about propriety.

She wasn't actually a part of this kingdom yet and still served in an ambassadorial function for the Dark Elves. After they announced her official betrothal and wedding, she would gain a small measure of authority in this kingdom. Until then, Arthur was thankful she excused herself and just remained a silent observer.

The noise from everyone talking in the room caused his head to ache. He stood to his feet to address the crowd.

"Ladies and Gentlemen, welcome. For those who don't know, I'm King Arthur Firebrand. I've asked all of you here so we can plan the future of this city. Seora has seen rough times of late. It's painfully obvious with a quick inspection. Our goal is to figure out how to fix this."

The room exploded into people talking. Everyone tried to yell their opinions over the others in the room. Arthur raised his hands at the onslaught.

"Everyone be quiet!"

The voices in the room drowned out his statement. In frustration, he employed the same trick he did during the battle over the city and amplified his voice with Air Magic.

"I said be quiet!" His voice reverberated around the room. All those in attendance fell into silence, and many of them clapped their hands to their ears.

"Let's make this process a little easier. We'll divide it into sections. For now, let's address one of the major concerns. Food. Any here that has an affiliation with food production or distribution in the city, please stand. The rest of you remain seated." Arthur told them.

Lord Ealin and Lord Trip both stood up while two others from the newly arrived group joined them.

"I recognize Lords Ealin and Trip. You two," Arthur said as he gestured at the new figures, "what are your names and function in the city?"

They looked at each other before one finally answered. He was a man that looked to be in his late forties with gray peppering his mustache. His broad shoulders and muscular figure made Arthur picture him as a soldier more than anything else.

"I'm Theo Loore, Your Majesty. I'm the leader of the Merchants Guild."

Arthur nodded at the explanation, and the second man took up his introduction.

"I'm Clinton Weer, Your Majesty. I worked with Lord Ealin and handled storage and distribution of grains and food within the city."

"Pleasure to meet you both," Arthur said as he scanned the room one more time. No one else stood. *Who grows the damn food?*

"Now, gentlemen, we have four people here who dealt in distribution and storage, but I have yet to see a single person here to represent the farmers."

They all looked at each other in confusion. Lord Ealin was the first to put their confusion into words.

"The serfs, Your Majesty? They don't have guilds or representatives. They are subjects of the city and grow food as their duty."

Serfs? I vaguely recall that from history. I think they were essentially slaves.

"Are any of these serfs still alive and within the city? Did they flee their farms during the struggles?"

"Some remain, although I doubt there are many left. Lord Preston had a lot of them executed when they fled the raids of bandits in the countryside. He blamed their cowardice for our lack of food." Lord Trip told him grimly.

So, not many farmers left, then? Guess it's the perfect time to change the status quo.

"Does anyone in here know of any seed stock left anywhere in the city? Don't fear reprisal for hoarding anything. If you hid it to keep it from the corrupt lords, I don't fault you. This is a new day, though, and we have to get this city back to health. I offer a period of grace and promise not to punish any who come forward. If I find out people are hoarding resources after today, there will be repercussions." Arthur stressed.

The assembled people cast nervous glances around the room and jumped from face to face. Arthur noticed Lords Ealin and Trip staring at each other before they both resolutely nodded and turned to face him.

"Your Majesty. Lord Trip and I have a small stockpile of seeds we stashed away. When I noticed the falling crop yields and the baffling mismanagement from the previous lord, I contacted Lord Trip, and we worked on a plan to hide some. I'm not aware of any more anywhere in the city." Lord Ealin said.

"I appreciate your honesty and dedication. It'll be imperative to check this stock and plant crops as soon as possible." Arthur responded.

"Your Majesty," Theo said tentatively, "We don't have the serfs to plant crops. It may take some time to find some."

"I'll put out a call to people in the city. I'm sure I can find people to volunteer to grow food," Arthur said with a dismissive wave.

"I don't think it will be that easy," Lord Trip chimed in. "Most people won't willingly become serfs."

"I don't plan on asking them to be serfs. I plan on naming freeholders and allowing them to set up freeholds within the kingdom for farming."

The gathered crowd was silent before they all erupted into conversation again. Sound assaulted his ears, and the headache that had finally ebbed flared back to full life. He wasted no time and infused his magic into his voice.

"Enough!"

Arthur looked around as the crowd finally settled back down.

"I swear I will start throwing people out of this meeting if you can't act like adults and have a rational conversation without yelling over each other," Arthur told them with a growl. "Now, let's make this easy. Lady Gemmalin, do you have a comment about this?"

The older woman stood and looked around. "I don't object to the freeholds. I am concerned it will fight against your goal. Setting up freeholds for the farmers is a noble effort to help the repressed people, but the time to establish these freeholds will make it almost impossible to get the crops growing. The freeholders will want to prioritize their housing over actually preparing fields and planting."

Arthur watched the rest of the people in the room nod in agreement.

"I agree with Lady Gemmalin, Your Majesty. The time it would take to set these up would defeat the goal of getting the crops going. If we forced the growing or planted within the immediate area around the city, we could start growing sooner."

"I'm not concerned with that. I plan to use magic," Arthur said as he waved his hands in wild motions. The others in the room looked at him as though he lost his mind, and he heard Allendria chuckle near the edge of the room.

Humor here seems half dead.

"I know many of you haven't seen our magical construction techniques. I plan to employ our methods to establish these freeholds with the basic amenities they need. We can quickly prepare the fields and let the freeholders concentrate on planting. We will also recruit people for magical service. Ideally, I'd like to ensure each freehold has a resident mage who can help keep the crops watered and repair any buildings as needed." Arthur explained.

"You can do that? How long would it take to establish a freehold?" Lord Trip asked.

Arthur looked up in thought as he paced near his chair. "I think if I can find a small supply of iron, we could build a freehold each day. It would depend on the size of the hold and the number of families that'll live there."

Mouths hung open in disbelief around the room.

"I want to look for volunteers today for every role we need to fill. Before we get to that, let's talk about the immediate food supply. Getting the crops up and running is of vital importance, but those still take time to grow. Until then, we need to provide food for the people here. Is there a guild of rangers in the city?"

"No, Your Majesty. There used to be a city post for a ranger, but they executed the previous one." Clinton told him.

"Executed? What did he do? Did he commit murder?"

"No. He wanted to hunt to increase the food supply for the city and not just feed the nobles. Lord Preston had him executed when he found out the man snuck some of his extra kills to the general populace." Clinton said with his head hung low.

"Of course he did. Was there anyone who hunted with him? A group of archers with experience? If so, I want to meet with all of them. We need to establish a hunting party, and I plan for our forces to take volunteers to learn the craft into the woods."

"There were a handful. I'm not sure how many remain in the city, but I'll find them for you." Lord Ealin told him with confidence.

"Thank you," Arthur said. "We could go on for days about food, but those are the two priorities for now. When we get food into the city regularly, we can discuss the exact logistics and market for the goods. Until then, let's move to the next topic. Military. How many military forces are available in the city, minus the ones I brought?" Arthur asked Samson.

"We have roughly three-hundred soldiers on the city roll after weeding out the corrupt followers of Lord Preston," Samson answered in stoic fashion.

"We need to put out a call for soldiers as well," Arthur told them.

"Your Majesty," Lady Gemmalin began, "the people here have seen nonstop famine and strife. I don't think they will be very receptive to joining your army for conquest."

Arthur smiled at the kindly old woman. "I agree, Lady Gemmalin. I don't plan on recruiting any for my forces unless they volunteer for that on their own. We will ask for people to train as guards for the city. We also need a few trained soldiers at each freehold in case of emergencies. I will ask none of them to come with me to war. I will allow those that wish it to accompany me, though."

Lady Gemmalin looked relieved at the statement and sat back down with a polite nod.

"Anyone have any objections to that?"

"Your Majesty. I hate to interrupt these plans, but how is the kingdom going to afford these services? Guards cost money to maintain, and the city is broke." Lord Ealin said with a tremor of nervousness in his voice.

"I understand the concern, Lord Ealin. The early period of rebuilding will be difficult, and much of this will rely on people helping each other and food being provided for service. As we yield crops, the markets can return and commerce with it. The transition will be rough, but I know people will work for the food they need to survive until we can get to that point. That brings us to the next topic, though. Lord Trip and Lady Gemmalin. What major industries was this city known for?"

"This city boasted a large textile market," Lady Gemmalin began before she paused and looked at Lord Trip. He waved for her to continue. "It housed many of the industries any city this size needs, such as blacksmiths, tanners, and cartwrights, but our major exports were fabric and leatherwork."

"Well, the leatherwork shouldn't be hard to jumpstart since we'll be doing an abundance of hunting. The textiles will be a little more difficult. Is there any seed stock left for the textile plants? Any flax seeds? Cotton seeds?" Arthur asked.

"We have a storage silo of flax seeds in the lower district. No one has touched them since they aren't worth eating. Why would you want cotton seeds, though?" Lady Gemmalin asked in confusion.

"Where I'm from, cotton is woven into fabric that is both sturdy and comfortable. It's comparable to wool but much lighter and cooler."

The old woman's eyes flashed in excitement, and Arthur watched the gears in her head turn.

"I'd be very interested in hearing of this method. If we can replicate the process here, it might be a good chance to start a new market here in the kingdom and bring this city back to its glory." Lady Gemmalin said with conviction.

"I'll see if we can find some in the surrounding forests. I have seen little since I arrived. Industry will be important, and I plan on establishing at least one freehold for the growth of the flax. We can do more for cotton as we get to that point. None of those industries will gain much popularity until the food issue has stabilized and trade resumes, so we have time. I'd like to ask that all three of you resume your previous posts within the city. Lady Gemmalin, I'll have you oversee everything textile."

The older lady nodded in eagerness before Arthur continued.

"Lord Ealin, I'd like you to resume your duty as quartermaster, and Lord Trip, I'd ask you to take up the mantle over the mercantile efforts."

"Yes, Your Majesty," both men said in unison.

"I know most of you won't have much to do but monitor in the short term, but as soon as goods and crops come in, everything goes through you three. Feel free to recruit the guilds to your service as needed," Arthur said as he gestured to those gathered in the room.

The nobles all nodded in agreement.

"Any other major concerns?"

"Your Majesty?" A quiet voice from the tradespeople's group spoke up. Arthur scanned the crowd and found a young man, probably in his twenties, staring at him with a nervous look on his face.

"Yes?"

"We've heard rumors," he started slowly. "Can we really travel to Alem's Crossing and live there instead?"

"What's your name?" Arthur asked.

"Pamin, Your Majesty."

"Well, Pamin. I will allow those who want to go to Alem's Crossing to make that journey, although it is now known as Alurian. I require that they be physically able to make the trip and contribute to the town. This kingdom is at war with the Dark Elves, and they are closer to Alurian. I'd prefer those who can't protect themselves to stay here."

Faces nodded in agreement around the room at his pronouncement.

"Time to get to work. Put out the word and find us some recruits. Our number one priority is volunteers as freeholders and guards. I want crews ready to go in two days. We can do some combat training on the trip."

"I'll work with the local leaders to help round some up," Samson said.

"Lords Ealin and Trip, please arrange for the seeds to be loaded and ready for transport and planting. If we can scrape up any tools that may prove useful, do so. Clinton, if you can locate any of those rangers, send them to me. The rest of you," Arthur said with a gesture at the surrounding city folk, "help get the word out. Organize our artisans and get them ready to receive supplies. I want the blacksmith shop, tannery, and leatherworking craft workers on standby and ready to work."

A small mumble of excitement filled the room as people began shifting in place in anticipation.

"Finally, make it known that I'm offering magical training for people willing to be stationed as guards and helpers in the freeholds. They will be under the employment of the city but posted on rotations. Minimum service requirements will apply for that training."

Everyone began stirring until his offer of magic came out. They all froze in shock at the news.

"Truly, Your Majesty? You offer magical training for service? No special school? No overpriced fees?" Clinton asked in disbelief.

"I only require two years of service to the city. After that, you can use your talents as you wish. While under the employment of the city, you can still pursue personal projects with your magic as long as it doesn't interfere with your primary duties." Arthur confirmed with a nod. "Everyone is dismissed."

The group stared with open mouths for a short time before the chattering began, and they made for the doors. Each of them displayed a fair amount of pep in their step. Much more than Arthur had seen from them upon their arrival.

"I appreciate what you're trying to do," an old voice mumbled.

Arthur turned and locked eyes with Lady Gemmalin.

"Ah, Lady Gemmalin. I appreciate you taking up your old post. I fear I have no skill with textiles or much knowledge of their market," Arthur told her with a genuine smile.

She reached up and gently touched his cheek, "You truly have the legendary fire and charisma of a Firebrand. Let's get this city back on its feet. Shall we?"

Arthur smiled and nodded as she shuffled out the door. Her pace moving quicker than he expected of someone her age. Arthur sank into the closest chair when the last of the guests left. Samson, Rayne, and Allendria remained behind.

"Need anything else from me, or should I start the search for volunteers?" Samson asked.

Arthur sighed. "I wish the answer was nothing and we could just relax and live a normal life. Sadly, it's not the case. I need soldiers, Samson. Actually, I need guards. We have to get crops in the ground and have to do it quickly. I meant what I said. I want us to be on the move in two days. Start putting together a massive hunt. I want every guard and soldier we can spare marching with us. We will use it as a training exercise for the new recruits and a much-needed trip to restore our supplies. I also intend on making stops to rest and build the freeholds."

"I'll get to work," Samson agreed with a nod.

"Allendria, I want you with me. We can spend the next couple of days working on renovating parts of the city with our magic. I want us to focus on combining our spells together and sharing my magical reserves. We should be able to get the process down so we can get these freeholds built fast."

"Of course. What are your plans for magical training?" She asked.

"I'd appreciate it if you could take care of some of that. I'll help you, of course, but I usually get busy during trips like that. You may check with our construction crew and see if any of them would take on a job as an instructor," Arthur suggested.

She looked up in thought for a few moments before nodding. "I agree. I think I know just the person."

"Finally, Rayne, get to work on your network. Us four," Arthur said with a wave at the assembled friends, "are the only ones who will know of your position. If anything comes up, approach any of us for help."

"I'll take care of it," Rayne agreed. He bowed slightly and left the room.

Allendria rose from her chair at the edge of the room and sat next to Arthur. She ran her fingers through his hair.

"It's a lot to do, but we'll make it work," she reassured him.

"I'll be on my way if you need nothing else," Samson grumbled.

"Go on. You've more important things to do."

"Care to take a walk?" Arthur asked Allendria. "I need to clear my head a little and get away from the activity for a bit."

"Let's go," she said as she latched onto his arm and yanked him to his feet. He chuckled at her enthusiasm, and they scrambled out the door and into the courtyard. A few of the people from the meeting gathered in the area in conversation. Arthur and Allendria turned and headed for the main street of the city.

Hey, Calfuray. You anywhere near?

Yes. What's going on?

Could you do something for me?

That depends on what you want. Arthur detected a hint of annoyance in her response.

Could you and Balair do a little scouting while out hunting? We want to get a big hunt together in a couple of days and would appreciate it if you could point us toward groups of animals.

A very unladylike grunt quickly followed.

Still not sure how she communicates those over a mental link. Arthur reflected.

I suppose I'll do it. You anywhere close, little rat?

I'm hurt, Lady Calfuray. Is that any way for nobility to act? Balair sent into the link with a hint of mockery.

Arthur, can I just eat him and send him back to his plane?

Play nice, you two. The more info you can get, the better. We will adventure out with a decent size party. We'll make stops along the way to set up new homesteads for farming. If you see easily defensible areas around here that would be ideal locations, please let me know.

I'm not sure what is suitable for you humans, Balair grumbled into his mind.

Just do your best and let me know.

Uh. You could try Giliad's Rise. A soft voice interrupted their thoughts.

Arthur's steps faltered, and he came to a stop. His gaze swept around the area, trying to find the source of the voice before he realized it must've been in his head.

Who was that? Both Balair and Calfuray asked at the same time.

"Arthur, is something wrong?" Allendria asked.

He turned and saw she'd stopped with him and stared into his eyes with a look of concern.

"Someone just interrupted my mental conversation with Balair and Calfuray," he told her softly as he scanned the area.

"Who was that?" Arthur asked in a loud, gruff voice.

People near them looked around in confusion at each other.

Who are you? Arthur asked quietly into the mental communication.

No answer echoed back, and Arthur stood in silence. Movement drew his attention to a young woman near the wall in the courtyard. Red flushed her cheeks, and she looked downward as though trying to hide. Her footsteps scurried along like a nervous rabbit avoiding prey.

With a nod toward the woman, they both walked toward the entrance of the courtyard to cut off her retreat. They came to a halt directly in her path and waited for her arrival. When she closed the distance, she finally picked her head up and stared at him. Captivating green eyes stood out with a shock of dark brown hair. It looked slightly disheveled, but still clean.

"Was that you?" Arthur asked.

She stared back at him without responding.

A voice echoed through the clearing as Calfuray swooped down low. "Is that her?"

Those around scurried back to their tasks or shied away from the clearing. The loud voice of the dragon scaring them away. The young woman never even shifted and didn't cringe at the sound.

"It's okay. You can talk to us. Who are you?" Allendria asked the young woman.

Her eyes remained fixed on Arthur, and she never turned her attention to Allendria when she spoke. The situation didn't sit right with him. *How could she show absolutely no reaction to them? It's almost like she couldn't hear…* and the thought crashed into his awareness.

You can't hear us speak aloud, can you? Arthur asked into their mental space.

Her eyes shifted to meet his at the question, and she shuffled from foot to foot.

I can't. She finally confirmed as she dropped her gaze to the ground.

I apologize for being blunt about this, but did you lose your hearing, or were you born without it? Calfuray asked as Arthur watched her shadow pass over them again.

I lost it when I was young. After recovering from a sickness that nearly killed me, it was gone. I'm sorry to bother you. I was just happy to hear a conversation for the first time in a long time.

How long has it been since you last heard someone? Arthur asked, intrigued.

Over a year.

Chapter 3

The Magic of Familiars

"What's wrong, Arthur?" Allendria asked. Arthur turned to see a look of concern etched on her face.

"She's been all alone. She hasn't heard anyone else talk in over a year," he told her softly.

Allendria's hand flew to cover her mouth as she gasped.

"Is she still sane?" She asked cautiously.

"Appears to be fine, but I can't tell for sure."

Balair swooped down from the sky and landed in front of the woman.

What's your name, young lady? Balair asked.

Zoe. She said as she backed away.

It's good to meet you, Zoe. I have to admit, I'm not sure how you can intrude into this conversation. It makes me a little uneasy about our safety. Arthur said as he turned his attention back to the woman.

You needn't worry. It's the magic of the familiar bond. Something happened when I lost my hearing, and now I can access mind speech. It only seems to work with familiars.

I guess that's good to know, but how is it you figured that out? Calfuray asked.

I didn't. My old master did. She had a pet raven she would speak to. I ran into her one day while wandering town looking for work. Much like you, I interrupted a conversation she was having with her familiar. She took me in, and in return, I worked for her.

What did she do, if you don't mind me asking? Arthur asked.

She was an herbalist with a touch of skill in Alchemy. I helped her tend to a small herb garden and brew basic recipes to cure minor ailments. Her name was Elle, and she passed away a year ago when things started taking a turn for the worst here. I've been tending her small cottage since.

A hand touched his shoulder, and he looked to see Allendria's face creased with what appeared to be a motherly concern.

"Is she okay? Does she need help with anything? Can you do something with magic to fix it?" Allendria asked.

Arthur gazed at her for a moment before shaking his head. "Fix her with magic? I doubt it. I only know the one fairly basic healing spell, and I doubt it could fix an issue this severe. You would know better than me if there is anything that could help her. Your people are the ones far better versed in magic."

"One of our elders may know something that might work, but healing magic isn't my specialty either. I doubt I could burn the problem out of her," she said with a smirk.

"What's the right choice, though? I hate the idea of leaving her alone because she can't talk to anyone else, but there's nothing I can do for her." Arthur whispered to Allendria.

"We have to help her somehow. While her loss of hearing is a problem, her gift of intrusion into your mind speech is even more intriguing. I've never heard of another capable of doing that. Just think. If we had an enemy with a familiar, she could even eavesdrop on them."

Arthur nodded along with her reasoning. Allendria had a good point. This woman could be an incredible tactical advantage. Her handicap might make it difficult for her to be useful. To spy on enemies using her talent, she would need to be near the battle. That meant she needed the ability to defend herself. While possible to fight without hearing, it was much more difficult. Sound played a large part in defending yourself. You needed to hear someone sneaking up on you. In a larger battle, attacks could come from all sides, and hearing was the best method to pinpoint those attacks.

He was getting ahead of himself, though. This woman may have no interest in fighting. It was possible she was a peaceful soul.

Zoe. My name is Arthur. I'm the new king here. This is Allendria, Arthur said as he pointed at the Dark Elf, *and that is Balair.* *He* continued as he gestured toward the drake. *Calfuray is the majestic dragon flying overhead.*

Zoe nodded her head, but looked nervous. Arthur couldn't tell if it was because of the small dragon staring at her from only a few feet away or if it was his title that made her nervous.

I'd like to help you, but I'm not sure how. Arthur told her cautiously.

Her eyes widened in surprise. *Can you do miracles, your, uh, majesty?*

Arthur chuckled. *No, Zoe, although I can do magic, which can sometimes resemble miracles. Just call me Arthur, though. No need for silly titles.*

I don't think you can help me then. Elle had a few people with magic try to help me, but nothing ever worked. I think I'm just cursed for the rest of my life to this mundane existence.

I don't want to see you resigned to loneliness again. Do you have any useful skills? I might find you a place to work with Allendria and me. If we keep you around, you will at least have someone to talk to.

Zoe looked down at her feet and shuffled nervously. *I am a decent cook. My old master had me prepare her meals and do some gardening for her. I have the minor skill in Alchemy I mentioned before, but not enough to warrant it as a profession.*

"Care to hire a cook?" Arthur asked Allendria.

She sighed as she looked into his eyes.

"I said we needed to help her, not adopt her," she told him with a crooked smile.

"So, that's a yes?" Arthur asked with a smile.

"Sure. I don't want her all alone on her own again. Maybe if we keep her close, she will be of use," Allendria agreed.

Zoe, would you like to become my household cook? We could use someone that can help with the task, and it would give you a good reason to stick around and have someone to talk to.

I don't know. The young woman began. *I have a house to take care of here that Elle left to me. It isn't much, but I feel wrong just leaving it behind.*

Balair moved toward the woman and lifted his head to snuggle against her hand. She jumped at first before she looked at the dragon and smiled.

Join us, Zoe. I need someone to talk to who isn't a moron and doesn't threaten to eat me daily. Balair told her.

Hey! Arthur complained while Calfuray let out a low rumbling chuckle as she passed by overhead.

Small tears formed in the corners of Zoe's eyes before they trickled down her cheek. *I'd like that.*

Let's go find you a place to stay for now. Allendria and I have some business to attend to, but I'll get you set up in the manor until we can work out the details.

Arthur informed Allendria of the decision, and they turned to walk back toward the manor. Once inside, he found Samson congregating in the main hall.

"Samson, can you do me a favor?" Arthur asked.

"Of course, My Liege," he said with a bow.

Arthur rolled his eyes at the man's behavior but ignored it.

"Can you take Zoe here and show her to the kitchens and get a place sorted out to stay? We've hired her as a personal chef for the household. She can't hear, though, so you'll have to direct her through motions." Arthur told him.

"Uh, not to be indelicate, but how much use is a deaf cook? Can she read and write? Otherwise, I don't know how she might perform her job efficiently."

"She'll be fine. I can communicate with her without a problem. Just see her taken care of, please?"

Samson quirked an eyebrow before nodding
and turning to the woman. Arthur explained who
he was and told her that Samson would show her
around. She thanked him and followed the
paladin out of the room.

"Back to our stroll?" Arthur asked
Allendria.

She wrapped her arm through the crook of
his and held on tight. "Let's go."

They walked back out into the courtyard and
exited through the small gate in the wall. The
roughly cobbled streets greeted them, and
Arthur nearly tripped over a broken stone.

"This place needs a lot of work," he said
with a sigh.

"Nothing some magic can't fix," Allendria
said with a sniff. "With the mana you have at
your disposal, you should be able to take care
of it quickly."

"I guess I could burn some mana while we
walk," he agreed.

Arthur found his old Raise Cobblestone
Street spell and started the cast. It took
hold, and the stretch of road in front of him
transformed and shifted as the cobblestones
changed and flattened. The entire street
elevated another inch to match the parameters
of the spell. Before long, a perfectly level
stretch of road roughly thirty feet wide and
ten feet long sat in front of them.

*You have gained 80 experience in Earth
Magic and Fire Magic for successfully casting
Combination Spell: Raise Cobblestone Street.*

He stepped onto the path and continued
walking. When they reached the end of the new
stretch, he cast the spell again. It became
monotonous as they continued forward.

"I understand the idea behind your plan
with these farmsteads, but how do you plan on
making it work?" Allendria asked as they
walked along the freshly raised street.

"What do you mean? It shouldn't be too hard
to raise a quick farmstead. With our mana and
the mana from the construction crew, it should
be a quick affair. A few small cottages, a
basic defensive wall, and some quick work
tilling the ground will make it simple for
them to plant and start growing food."

"I understand that, to a degree. But that
doesn't fix the weather."

"The weather? What are you talking about?"
Arthur asked.

"Uh, winter. It's not far away. Most of the
plants they have seeds for are warm-weather
plants. They won't survive the winter, even if
it is relatively mild in this area."

"Shit," Arthur muttered to himself.

Allendria laughed, "I guess you weren't
aware since you arrived right when spring
started."

"Yeah, I forgot all about the seasons. I
don't even know how they work here. That
causes an enormous problem. I guess we could
whip up some magic to make it work. If we
could devise a way to grow food year-round,
that would fix a lot of problems. Maybe build
a greenhouse or something."

"What's a greenhouse?" Allendria asked.

"It's a building made of clear materials
that regulates the temperature inside but
allows the heat from the sun to come in. It
allows you to grow things year-round that
can't hold up to the cold. I don't suppose you
have a ton of glass hidden anywhere, huh?"

Her exasperated look answered his question.

"Didn't think so. Maybe make some
temperature controls and litter the fields
with them?"

"That might work, but it would require a
lot of constant recharging. It would be
tedious."

Arthur considered the issue as he wiped
sweat from his brow. "I've had an idea
inspired by my home, but not sure how to make
it work. If we could, it might prove to be the
answer."

"What's the problem?"

"Well, back in my world, we have wires that
run through our houses and send power to all
the different devices. All the power comes in
one central location and is fed to the places
as needed. If I could create a central power
storage and then connect it to all these
controls in the field, the workers could just
keep the power storage full, and it would keep
them from trying to recharge them
individually."

"That sounds amazing. How do we do that?"

"That's the part I don't know. I'm
confident I can do it, but not sure how to
connect them. I guess I could try wiring them
together with thin copper wire. If I forge the
wire with magic, I should be able to include
tiny symbols for enchantment. It might allow
them to direct energy from a central point. It
would require a lot of copper, though."

"Why not use stone?" Allendria asked.

"Because stone doesn't conduct…," Arthur started before trailing off, "I was stuck thinking of it like my world. Stone can't conduct electricity, but I can enchant it with magic with no problem. If we just create pathways of stone, that might work. We could use them as dividers for sections of the fields. I think I can use my Mineral Compression to make decent-sized gems for energy storage. We just need to experiment with the idea to make it work."

"Let's try it out then," Allendria suggested.

Arthur glanced back and noticed he'd made significant progress with the new street. They walked to a vacant lot near the road, and Arthur began his work. He used Flatten Earth to level everything out and then cast his Stone Building Wall spell. Since this was just a proof of concept, he didn't make the foundation very large. The stone slab was ten feet square and two inches thick.

"What do you think is the best option? Do I need to raise the walls and then create a separate channel of stone in them with the enchantment?"

"I think you're getting ahead of yourself. What enchantment do you think will work? I also think you're overthinking it. Why not just enchant all the walls? That way, if one is damaged or cracked, the power can still flow through the rest." Allendria suggested.

"That's even better. It'll prevent minor damage from messing up everything. Now to figure out the enchantment."

Arthur used his magic to raise a small chunk of stone on the ground. He sat down in front of the block and thought about the problem. It took him a few minutes, but he finally decided on a stylized symbol. He tried to find something similar to 'conduct' but it didn't exist. Instead, he tried one that meant 'flow.' Using a careful stream of Fire and Earth Magic, he slowly carved the symbol into the stone. When it was complete, he poured mana into the rune.

Congratulations, you have successfully enchanted Stone Block. You have gained 35 experience in Enchanting.

"What symbol is that?" Allendria asked.

"It means 'flow.' It was the closest I could find that I think will work."

She stared at the stone for a few moments before nodding. "That might work."

"Now to make the other pieces to test it," Arthur said.

He gathered a handful of loose stones and dirt from the surrounding area and cast Mineral Compression. The materials were low grade and wouldn't produce anything overly useful. Power swirled as the matter combined, and a tiny gem the size of his thumbnail rested in his palm. It was an oval-shaped stone with a gray color. The description listed it as a Smoky Quartz Shard.

"You wouldn't have any ink on you, would you?" Arthur asked Allendria with an innocent smile.

She gave him a blank stare.

"Yeah, didn't think so."

Arthur pulled a waterskin from his inventory and mixed some water with a small bit of dirt. A small stick nearby worked as a crude pen, and he used the muddy dirt to create a small symbol for 'storage' on the gem. The influx of mana that followed burned the symbol into the gem and activated the enchantment.

Quickly sorting through his inventory produced the items he needed for a magical temperature control. He wasted no time using his Arcane Smithing skill to create the item.

With the temperature control, the storage gem, and the enchanted stone all complete, he needed to combine them. He feared this would be the most troublesome part. To his surprise, it was actually the easiest. When he touched the storage gem to the stone block, he received a message.

Would you like to combine the Enchanted Smoky Quartz Shard with the Enchanted Stone Block? Yes/No. Warning: the gem will be permanently affixed to the stone. You cannot remove it or replace it without destroying the gem.

Arthur selected *Yes*, and the gem melded into the surface. Nothing more happened, and a quick glance at the stone showed it was no different. The stone and the gem both registered as separate items. Not sure what else to do, he set the temperature control on the top of the block. He changed the dial to activate the device, and the surrounding area warmed.

"Does it work?" Allendria asked while they stared at the device.

"Not sure. We need to give it a few minutes
until some of the mana in the temperature
controller dissipates."

Arthur continued their stroll and used the
time to cast a few more of his Raise
Cobblestone Street spells. The more of the
streets he could repair now, the better off
the city would be in the end. He knew their
magical construction team was already working
around the town. They listed all the storage
and administration buildings as top priority.
The crews inspected and then magically
reinforced each as needed. Many of the granary
silos were currently empty, but he wanted them
in pristine shape before the crops flowed in.

When they finally returned to the enchanted
stone, he looked at the controller.

Item: Intricate Mage- crafted Steel Temperature Control (Sapphire Storage)	**Durability:** 100/100 **Rarity:** Rare **Quality:** Well Crafted **Weight:** 0.04 kg **Slot:** Crafting Item **Charges:** 2,794/2,800 ***Area of Effect:*** 20 feet in all directions **Traits:** A device that allows you to adjust the temperature of the surrounding room for up to twenty feet in any direction

	Enchantment: • Charges only deplete when temperature is far outside of the desired range. Once the temperature has stabilized in the given area, charges deplete very slowly to maintain.

"I don't think it worked. It isn't at full charge anymore, but the storage gem is," Arthur said.

"How did you link them together?" Allendria asked.

"I didn't," Arthur told her, "I don't know how to."

"Try using the storage gem. You haven't touched it since you placed the temperature device on the stone." Allendria suggested.

"Can't hurt to try," Arthur agreed.

He bent over and touched the smoky gem. A smile split his face as a message appeared.

Do you wish to allow Intricate Mage-crafted Steel Temperature Control (Sapphire Storage) access to the stored power in Enchanted Smoky Quartz Shard? Yes/No.

He selected *Yes* and looked at the temperature control again. This time, it showed full charges, and the mana storage gem was depleted by the same amount.

"Perfect!"

"It worked?" Allendria asked.

"Sure did. Even better, the recharge ratio is one-to-one. I was afraid it would take more than one charge of the storage crystal to restore a charge on the temperature control."

"Hmm," Allendria murmured, "That might be the case as you expand the design to cover a larger area. The farther the energy flows, the more it may lose potency. But I could be wrong. It may work perfectly no matter the distance connected."

"Hopefully, luck will hold out, and it will stay an even ratio. If not, I'll think of something that can offset it. The good part is we can now create the farms we need, and the time of year won't matter."

"So, now that you have a working model of the solution, what is the final layout going to look like?" Allendria asked.

"I don't know. I was envisioning a few standard houses similar to the basic ones we've made in Alurian. Creating a well in each small homestead will help provide water for the people and for the crops. We could even implement indoor plumbing in the houses. We want the people to have a comfortable life at home so they will be efficient in their food production."

"No objections here. If you're done playing in the dirt, are you ready to head back toward the manor?" Allendria asked.

Arthur agreed. They took a circuitous route back to the manor so he could continue improving roads along the alternate path. When they entered the manor, Sampson greeted him.

"Welcome back," Samson said. "Are you done wasting time in town?"

Arthur smiled, "For now."

"Good, because we have a lot of work to take care of," Samson told him as he motioned toward a small mountain of paperwork on a nearby desk. He was suddenly less enthusiastic about them having easier access to paper.

Samson took a seat at the desk and motioned for Arthur to join him. Resigned to an afternoon of tedious work, Arthur looked at his gains in experience for the work in town.

You have gained 1,450 total experience in Earth Magic.

You have gained 1,190 total experience in Fire Magic.

You have gained 205 total experience in Enchanting.

You have gained 180 total experience in Jeweler.

You have gained 80 total experience in Arcane Smithing and Blacksmithing.

* * *

Rayne crept through the alleyway. Dirt and debris littered the surrounding walls. Broken and rotted crates adorned the sides and restricted the space available to traverse. A small, furry creature darted across the path and disappeared under a pile of wood.

A glint of light ahead caused him to freeze. On instinct, he pressed against a nearby wall and activated his Stealth ability. The light patter of boots on stone echoed down the path as he kept watch ahead of him. The outline of a lithe figure emerged from the shadows.

Twenty feet from him, the person stopped. Their hood obscuring their identity.

"You can come out now," the figure stated as she threw her hood back and stared at him. Her auburn hair hung down in curls to her shoulders. Crystalline blue eyes shimmered in the faint moonlight.

He remained still for a few moments before sighing and walking into the middle of the alleyway, breaking his stealth.

"See, that wasn't that hard," she quipped.

"Do I know you?" Rayne asked.

"Probably not. But I'm pretty sure you're looking for me."

Rayne's eyebrows shot up at her statement. "I'm looking for you, huh?"

"Well, based on who you keep as friends and what we have observed of you, I assume you're looking for the criminal empire in the city. That would be me."

Rayne eyed her carefully as she stood perfectly still and kept her gaze locked directly on him. Nothing in her demeanor told him she was lying, but he couldn't tell for sure.

"How about a name?" Rayne asked.

"I'm Scarlett," she told him.

"Well, that's awfully convenient. Little leery of the fact you found me first."

"I like to stay informed. Although, I am curious what the king's lackey needs from me."

"I'm not his lackey," Rayne huffed defensively. "He's a friend."

"Kings don't have friends, only subjects."

"This one's different."

"Let's say I believe you," she started as she grabbed a stray strand of hair and tucked it behind her ear, "you still haven't answered my question."

"I'm recruiting for a spy network. We need eyes and ears in town to keep everything on track."

"I can't give up my business to take a job with the king. What exactly are you proposing?"

"You can have your fun little club of criminals," Rayne began with a dismissive wave. "We don't care about petty theft or underground tax evasion. I want you to feed me information in return for the local authorities turning their eye from petty crime within your organization. We will not tolerate serious crimes or anything that disrupts the well-being of this city."

Scarlett lifted her hand to her chin and looked thoughtful. "An interesting idea. I'll have to discuss it with the rest of the leadership."

"I thought you were the leader?" Rayne asked.

"I am the leader. That doesn't mean I make all the decisions on my own. That's how mistakes are made, and businesses fail. I take the opinions and guidance of my fellow leaders seriously."

"Fine. I'll be leaving the city shortly for a trip to scour the surrounding area. You have until I return to decide. Just know that if you decide to refuse this offer, there will be no protection for you. Our new king doesn't care much for crime of any kind, even petty crime."

"Thanks for the warning. I'll seek you out when you return," she told him and slowly backed away, keeping her hand out and visible. She continued for half a dozen steps and then turned and walked away with a casual saunter. It wasn't long before her form faded into the shadows.

"That was awfully strange," Rayne muttered to himself before leaving the alley and heading back toward Lord Preston's old manor.

Chapter 4

Farming

Arthur stepped to the side as an arrow whizzed by his head.

"I swear to all that is holy, if someone shoots me again, you will not like the consequences," he yelled over the action.

"You heard him." Samson bellowed over the group, "Pay attention to where you're shooting. I'm pretty sure shooting the king is punishable by death."

Arthur grinned at the uncomfortable look on some of their faces. He wouldn't put someone to death over that, but most of them were new recruits and didn't know him. The memory of his first encounter with Paul flashed through his mind, and he chuckled under his breath.

One of their new volunteers launched an arrow, and it thwacked into the side of a big boar. The creature squealed and started dragging its back legs, now paralyzed from the arrow in its spine.

"Someone please put that creature out of its misery," Samson told the group, and a few more arrows took the pig down.

A short wall rose from the ground. It was only a foot tall and seven feet wide, but it was directly in the path of a large group of the stampeding animals. Crunching noise filled the air as leg bones smashed into the stone and the boars face-planted into the dirt. A few Fire Arrows sizzled into the downed animals, sending the smell of burning fur through the clearing.

The space was a dance of controlled chaos. Eighty men and women stood and fought. Twelve of them were newly made mages, training their Earth and Fire Magic. They stood near the flank of the main group and cast spells as they were able. Fifty people made up the bulk of the force. The tank style stood at the front of the formation and tried to stop the beasts as they charged. Behind them was a row of people wielding spears. They thrust the tips through gaps in the shields, slowly bleeding the pigs dry.

Vana stood near the rest of the force, newly assigned rangers, and instructed them on Archery. When one of her subordinates made a bad shot, she walked up to correct them. Usually, it was something simple when she did. Pushing their feet farther apart, correcting their grip on the bow or the string, or fixing their posture while firing.

A group of three large boars broke from the main body and veered off into the trees. Arthur activated Weak Haste and fished throwing knives from his belt. They covered the distance in a flash and sunk into the throats of all three. Blood spurted from the wounds as the animals collapsed to the ground, kicking and thrashing as they died.

You dealt 50 damage to Boar (Level 4) with Throwing Knives.

You dealt 50 damage to Boar (Level 4) with Throwing Knives.

You dealt 50 damage to Boar (Level 4) with Throwing Knives.

Typically, he wouldn't bother with these low-level animals, but the city and the new farmsteads needed all the food they could get. He also didn't want them escaping and scaring off nearby wildlife as they fled.

"Great job, fighters," Samson told them.

The paladin walked among the assembled people. He bent down to help a young man up from his spot on the ground. The fighter was panting and covered in sweat. A small trail of blood marred the side of his face. The edge of his shield sported a nasty rent.

"Go get healed up," Samson told him and pointed toward a group of three casters near the edge of the clearing. They were the new medical corps for the small army. These specialized in Water Magic, and Arthur taught each of them his Minor Heal Spell. They were diligently practicing their skills during the hunt to level up their Water Magic.

Arthur organized the uninjured fighters and scavenged the battlefield. As usual, anything of use went straight into a dimensional space. They already had two of his 'closets' full of animal carcasses. While it sounded like a lot, they had an entire city to feed. Much of this would go to stocking the farming villages and feeding their traveling group.

A light touch on the back of his neck broke him out of his trance. Soft fingers ran up the back of his head and tickled the little bits of hair under the edge of his helmet.

"That was almost boring. I only got to kill a few of them," Allendria grumbled.

"We are here for them to gain experience and level their skills. These are far too low level for us, anyway."

"I know. Still makes it boring."

"We have more than enough fighting ahead of us," Arthur said.

"How do you plan on tackling that?" Allendria asked.

"Hell if I know. I'm still making most of this up as I go along. Between Wailyn and Glirin, I don't know what the best course will be. I'm leaning toward Glirin first since he's so close to Alurian, but I also know he's probably stronger in terms of military force."

"Without a doubt." Allendria agreed, "Our warriors are superior to those Wailyn commands, and most of the Dark Elves are versed in at least basic magic."

"I'm surprised they haven't taken over the kingdom already."

"We have discussed it. We even tried it two different times throughout history. Both times we lost. You humans were much stronger in the past. That and you have an annoying knack of stubbornest. You just won't die," she said with a smile.

"We are like cockroaches sometimes."

I don't see any other large groups of animals until you reach the proposed site for your new farming shack. Calfuray said.

Farming shack, huh? It will be a small farming village or even a homestead. Arthur mused.

All the same to me. She harrumphed. *You silly humans wanting to live in wood and stone boxes. I'll take the stars and an open sky any day.*

Arthur just laughed and mumbled to himself, "We don't have scales and aren't the size of a house, either."

"Calfuray talking to you again?" Allendria asked.

"Yep. Told me there isn't much left to hunt between here and the proposed farming village location. Guess it's almost time to crank up the magic."

"About time," she said as she stretched her neck from side to side. "I need some kind of challenge."

Samson directed the fighters back into formation, and they marched to the nearby road. The rest of their party waited for them on the road. All the noncombatants remained out here during the fighting. They practiced just as diligently as the warriors, but were using it to improve their other skills.

The road from Seora had undergone vast improvements during their march. Arthur spent his time and excess mana casting spells and converting the roads to cobblestone. It also proved useful as an instructional tool for their new mages. Each of them would be responsible for the upkeep and defenses of the new villages and needed to raise their skill levels. It was a slow process for many of them since they didn't have Arthur's mana reserves nor his regeneration rate. They rotated through each of them and cast the spell as often as possible to create the cobblestone street. When all of them were waiting for mana to regenerate, Arthur took over and continued the work.

To save himself some time, he created a scalable version of the spell. He could now make a section of street that was nearly forty yards. Unfortunately, even with his new magic corps and his prestigious mana, they couldn't cover every section of the road. There were spots that were still plain dirt trails. Arthur could have continued pouring magic out in these places, but he didn't want to dip into the mana reserves of his items. They were sections that could be addressed later. For now, a good portion of the path was much easier to navigate.

Many of the new members made great strides in their magic levels, and most were nearing level ten as they finally arrived in front of Giliad's Rise. The rolling grassland made for a picturesque scene in front of him. The rise itself was easy to spot. A large plateau rose thirty feet off the ground. The jagged edges of the walls left no doubt about how steep the incline was. From this side, only one small slope led to the top. It made for a perfect natural defense. A quick stone fortification across the opening would be easy to accomplish.

It looks like a large platter from up here. Balair sent to him.

Is this spot in front of us the only ramp up, or is there another on the other side? Arthur asked.

There is one on the opposite side as well. Calfuray confirmed.

Arthur turned to Allendria. "This place looks perfect. There is one access point on each side. The rest is sheer walls that make for excellent natural defense. With a little magic, we can make this place a verifiable fortress."

"You think the cliff is high enough? A determined person could climb that handily," she said with skepticism lacing her voice.

"I'm more interested in the inhabitant's safety from animals and predators. It will make for a formidable defense against an army as well, but I don't expect them to hold against that. The ramp on the other side will give them an escape route in an emergency."

"Fair enough, I guess."

The group proceeded up the incline until everyone settled on the flat top of the plateau. A rolling field of bright green grass covered the platform. The stalks brushed against Arthur's legs as he stood and surveyed the location. He turned to address the group of travelers.

"This is our first stop, ladies and gentlemen. Paladin Samson," he said, turning to the man, "have our fighting force spread out and check every inch of this proposed site. Do not leave the plateau itself for now. Have a party cover both of the inclines on rotating shifts."

Samson saluted and bellowed, "It will be done, Your Majesty."

"Everyone else, it's time to get to work. Construction crew, start preparing the foundations for the buildings and staking out our fields. We will keep everything on top of the platform for now and look at expanding out as needed. Anyone not in the magical construction corps, assist with clearing out the place and start cutting this grass to a manageable level. Princess Allendria and I will work on the fortifications to the two entrances of the plateau."

Everyone stood around for a few seconds before Calfuray settled on the ground with a slight rumble. Her landing startled the group, and everyone scattered to make themselves useful. Arthur only chuckled and turned to the dragon.

You did that on purpose, didn't you?

Possibly, she told him with a toothy grin.

Think you can stay out of trouble while we work? Arthur asked.

She stretched her legs out like a cat and slowly curled up on the grass. *I'm going to take a nap.*

I'll take that as a yes.

Arthur surveyed the area and picked his starting point. His selection of spells for stonework was lengthy, but very specialized. Instead of piecing together previous spells, he made a new spell that would create an entire section of wall from top to bottom all at once. He had enough mana, so there was no reason not to.

Threads of red and brown energy danced over his fingers as he concentrated on the space and drew on his power. The dirt flowed like water as the power molded the ground. Layer upon layer rose and solidified into a solid sheet of smooth stone.

The structure rose higher as the magic continued to build. A flat surface formed on the back of the wall to use as the walkway, while the front stretched higher into crenelations. When the spell was done, he looked at his notifications.

Congratulations, you have discovered the Combination Spell: Raise Advanced Wall Segment. You have gained 250 experience in Earth Magic and Fire Magic for discovering a known spell.

You have gained 550 experience in Earth Magic and Fire Magic for successfully casting Combination Spell: Raise Advanced Wall Segment.

Raise Advanced Wall Segment	
Requirements: Fire Magic and Earth Magic Mana Cost: 300 MP Cast Time: 14 seconds	Description: Creates a 20-foot x 26-foot x 80-foot wall of stone from the ground.
Mastery Level: 1	

Ah, feels good to create a new spell. It's only slightly concerning that these are classified as discovered spells. How has this world fallen so far?

Fingers danced along his shoulders, and he turned his head to see Allendria pressing up against him.

"Good work. Wanted to do it all at once this time?" She asked.

"Yeah. Figured it'd be easier long term. I can use this for future villages as well. One standard template is easier to manage."

She nodded along and then laid her head on his shoulder.

"Want to try working together on it?" She whispered in his ear.

Chills ran up his spine from the breath in his ear.

"Let's give it a shot."

Her fingers crawled down the front of his armor and rested against his chest. Warmth flowed from her hands as the mana permeated his body.

Arthur turned his focus back to the landscape and pictured a new wall section connected to the other. He pushed power and activated the spell. The strain on his mana was lighter as he felt Allendria's power joining him.

Her power was almost intoxicating as it flowed through his body and mixed with his. The stone wall rose and locked into place, but it did it in nearly half the time. The added power from Allendria offset some of the mana cost, but the speed also increased.

Arthur considered the implications. If the issue were one of casting speed, this would solve beating that time. In terms of efficiency, it was about the same. It cost him almost half the normal mana for this spell. He was sure it cost Allendria about the same.

"That works pretty well," Allendria said.

"It's good to cast some quick reaction spells. Doesn't seem very useful for this type of work. It cost you about 150 mana, didn't it?" Arthur asked.

"Almost exactly," she agreed.

"So, the spell still cost the same between the two of us and did the work in almost half the time. On the flip side, if both of us just cast the same spell, we could have two sections of wall built in the time it would take us to cast two sections together."

"That's true, but you're forgetting one thing," she told him. She lifted off his shoulder and walked to his side. A grin plastered her face.

"What is that?"

"It teaches the other person the spell."

"For real?" Arthur asked.

"Yep. I now know Raise Advanced Wall Segment."

"So, I can teach people by casting together with them instead of using my limited transfers of skills with my Teacher ability?"

"Pretty much. Should help the construction crews a lot. Learning the exact spells can be a pain for some of the newer ones. Spells like this one would still be a challenge for them since they are so mana intensive for normal people." Allendria reminded him.

"How about you get that sexy ass to work, then?" he told her with a light slap on the butt.

"I guess I can, Your Majesty," she said with a quick bow. She glanced up, and he saw the grin on her face before she turned and walked away. He swore she was putting a little extra emphasis on her hip swing.

The two of them worked diligently to span the entire entrance to the plateau. It took most of the day to finish the wall sections. As the sun slowly sank and the horizon blazed orange, the two of them combined their power and created a gatehouse. The structure loomed in front of them, and the opening perfectly surrounded the setting sun.

They turned together and traveled back to the main encampment. People scurried across the area, taking care of different tasks. Some carried buckets of water, while others touted food supplies. The area itself had transformed. Fresh housing plots stood bare on the ground with stone foundations already in place. They mapped out roads and had already cleared the ground for them. The magical crews had been hard at work.

"Enjoy your brief vacation together?"
Samson asked.

"I love the smell of fresh dirt and sweat,"
Allendria drawled.

Arthur grinned at her antics before turning
to Samson. "On the plus side, the wall is
complete. The only thing left is to hang doors
on the gatehouse. Think you can get some
people to handle that tomorrow?"

"I'll see to it. Are you going to complete
the other side tomorrow?" Samson asked.

"That's the plan. We also discovered a bit
of a trick for teaching people spells. Once we
get this place in order, I think I'll work
with some casters during our trip to the next
settlement site."

"Would be really helpful," Samson agreed.
"Our magic users have done a great job on the
initial work, but they are using base-level
spells and burning through mana fast. If you
could teach them some of the larger spells, it
would probably make the place sturdier and
more uniform. With people teaching themselves
spells, a lot of the roads don't match in
design. They are still functional, but it
looks strange with all the random patterns."

Arthur grimaced and looked around. He
spotted what Samson mentioned. The Raised
Cobblestone Streets looked sturdy enough, but
they each had random patterns. Some were
slightly wider or taller than others, causing
small gaps and bumps. Implementing a standard
one with them learning his exact spell would
imprint the same dimensions on everyone.

Allendria sighed. "We had similar problems with the construction crews while building the new homes in Alurian. It took time to work with each person and ensure they created the spell to the same dimensions. We didn't consider controlling the spells on the roads as well."

"Change in plans then, Samson. We will finish up the wall on the other side tomorrow. Don't let any of the construction mages work on roads. They can clear the pathways and get them ready, but no raising streets. Have them focus on the buildings and fields instead. The day after tomorrow, I'll work with a few dedicated people to be on road duty and make sure they all know the same spell." Arthur told him.

"Sounds like a plan. I have a handful of scouting and hunting parties out. Each of them also has an herbalist with them to locate any useful plants that we may wish to cultivate. Give the fighting group a little something to do other than stand guard all day."

"You're in command. Whatever you think is best. I'd suggest stationing guards on the wall who will end up permanently stationed here. Get them used to standing guard on their future home."

"Already have it planned. I figured you two would have it done, so I already set the rotation. The first group should report to the wall any minute now."

"Any idea where we can find some food?" Allendria asked.

"Communal meal over on the slab where the town hall will be," he said as he gestured to a foundation behind him.

"I'll race you there," Arthur said as he smiled and dashed off.

"Hey, that's not fair!" Allendria yelled as she sprinted to catch up.

Arthur barely heard Samson mumble, "Kids these days," before he was out of range and Allendria was gaining on him.

The two scarfed down a helping of a thick stew. Arthur rose and stretched his arms overhead. The stars were bright along the cloudless sky. A fresh breeze ruffled his hair, and the temperature was perfect. *This would be a perfect night to sleep on a trampoline.*

With that bit of inspiration, he went digging through his storage space. He had nothing remotely close to a trampoline, but another idea took over. He found a decent-sized canvas sheet and went to work. A few bundles of rope and the perfect set of trees later, Allendria walked up beside him.

"What is it?" she asked.

"A hammock," Arthur said excitedly. "Made it big enough for two."

"That's a bed?" she asked.

"Kinda. I want to sleep under the stars tonight. It's nice out here."

"Silly humans. I thought you loved your buildings too much to sleep with nature."

"Typically. Sometimes inspiration pops up, and we want a change in scenery. Would you care to join me in my luxury hammock?" He said as he waved toward the contraption.

She walked over and sat down on the hanging canvas. She wobbled a bit before gaining her balance.

"Doesn't seem very sturdy. Feel like I'll fall out."

"It's always a little tricky getting in and getting out. After you settle in, it stays nice and steady."

Arthur helped her lay out flat and slowly slipped in beside her. The sides folded up and held them firmly. Her hair smelled like a mix of dirt and lavender. He wasn't sure where the lavender smell came from, but wouldn't complain. They drifted off to sleep together.

* * *

A loud noise startled Arthur, and he jumped to his feet. At least, that was what he tried. His body wobbled, and his legs got tangled in the hammock. Tripping forward, his face hit the dirt with his legs still caught in the canvas and up in the air.

Laughter drifted to his ears, and he looked up to see Allendria, Balair, and Samson staring down at him. A soft chuckle came from Samson while Allendria looked on the verge of tears. The little drake's eyes looked devilish, and Arthur heard a loud laugh echoing in his mind.

"Very funny," Arthur huffed, and everyone's laughter increased. Even Samson's turned into a deep belly laugh.

It took him a few minutes to extricate himself from the hammock, and they grabbed some food. Allendria joined him as he walked toward the second entrance to the plateau. They used the same spell from the previous day and created an almost identical wall in this gap.

More out of habit than anything, the two joined their power to create the gatehouse. They stood back and admired their work.

"This side went a little faster," Allendria noted.

"We already knew the spells, so we didn't need to waste a sizable chunk of mana creating new ones. This side is also slightly shorter than the other. Gives us some time to help around the village."

Allendria interlocked her arm with his, and they walked back to the main village.

The place was a beehive of activity as magic raged everywhere. Walls of stone rose on foundations, and people walked around, checking the status of the work.

"I better find someone in charge of construction around here and get together a group of road workers," Arthur said.

"Good luck. I'll go see if there is anything I can help with."

The two split ways, and before long, Arthur stared at four different people from the crews.

"I'm going to show each of you the same spell for the roadwork. We want everyone using the same one, so the roads match up, and all seamlessly blend," Arthur said.

He explained how to combine their mana together to cast spells. They looked apprehensive but nodded along. None of them would dare question the king. He took each of them to the side and had them channel their mana into him and pay attention as he cast the spell. Each of them learned the spell, and all had shocked looks on their faces.

Arthur turned to them as a group and addressed them. "Keep in mind, this technique is not one you may use to teach anyone not under contract with a city of the kingdom. If I hear word of anyone teaching spells in this manner to anyone outside of your contracts, you will not like the consequences."

They looked suitably cowed, so he nodded
and moved away. Lost in thought, he looked
over his experience gains since yesterday.

*You have gained 150 total experience in
Throwing Knives.*
*You have gained 1,350 total experience in
Dimensional Magic.*
You have gained 380 total experience.
*You have gained 15,870 total experience in
Earth Magic.*
*Congratulations, you have reached level 24
in Earth Magic. Earth Magic spells now have a
69% increased effect. You seriously need to
get a life.*
*You have gained 15,870 total experience in
Fire Magic.*

A young man ran up to him.

"Paladin Samson is looking for you, Your
Majesty."

Instead of bugging the messenger, Arthur
just nodded and told him, "Lead the way."

The young man led him through the
construction work in winding patterns until
they came up on Samson. He had a grim look on
his face, and Arthur's attention immediately
sharpened.

"What's wrong?" Arthur asked in a low tone
as he came face to face with the paladin.

"Enemies have been spotted, and they are
headed this way."

"How many?"

"Looks to be a few dozen at least."

"So not enough to be an actual threat to
us. Are they bandits?" Arthur asked.

"Kind of. They are one of the lost bands of
goblins."

"Looks like it's time to see how well the guards can defend this site."

"I have people hanging the second set of gates on the gatehouse you finished earlier today. At least we have a solid barrier on both sides."

"Round the men up. Let's get started." Arthur told him.

Chapter 5

Raiders at the door... Again

Arthur surveyed their forces. Samson marched up and down the line of guards as they formed up in ranks. His steely glare made a few of them shift on their feet. He stopped in front of the man on the far end and came to attention.

"Guard Captain Kinny, report!" Samson called.

"All present and accounted for, sir!" Kinny responded with a fist to his chest.

"You've had some very basic training in fighting over the last few days. Don't do anything stupid on the wall. That said. The King wishes to speak to you," Samson told them and waved for Arthur to come forward.

The guards stood straighter as Arthur walked to stand in front of them. "Men and women of the Kingdom of Fire. An enemy stands outside of your new farming community. Make no mistake, these are the real deal. Training is over quicker than we hoped. While we have a large force here that could easily wipe them out, I am forbidding them to interfere."

Some guards looked around in disbelief, unsure they had heard his words correctly. A few started mumbling to each other.

"Keep your mouths shut while the King is addressing you," Samson snapped at the assembled forces. They went silent as Arthur continued.

"This isn't some odd punishment. I have every confidence you will make this place proud. Only the members of the guard force who will stay here for permanent duty will man the walls for this fight. All other forces are to act in reserves behind the walls. These are the kinds of challenges you will have to protect yourself and your fellow citizens against when the army is no longer here. You have fresh battlements to work from. I want to see you protect what is yours. Princess Allendria, Paladin Samson, Ranger Vana, and I will join you on the walls, but primarily to keep people from dying. We will not directly intervene in the fight unless absolutely necessary. Make the kingdom proud." Arthur called with a final salute to the guards.

The guards let out a cheer. They split into groups, and the Giliad's Rise guards walked toward the battlements. Samson walked up to Arthur.

"Are you sure you should be up on the wall? I don't think either of you should be up there." The paladin said while looking at Arthur and Allendria.

"Come on now, Samson. You know these goblins are no danger to us. Any of us three could probably beat the entire group by ourselves. I just want us to be up on the wall to ensure the guards know their job and don't shoot each other instead of the enemy."

"I guess so," Samson grumbled, "but it just takes one stray arrow you don't see to end you. Then where would we be?"

"We'll be fine. This is a glorified training session more than anything else." Allendria sighed as she walked up and placed a hand on Samson's shoulder.

"It's a shame I won't be able to compete for a kill count this fight. Sometimes it sucks letting others have all the fun," Vana quipped as she rested her hand on Samson's other shoulder.

"Fine. Let's do this then." Samson agreed.

"I see all the guards walking to the eastern wall. Is anyone manning the western wall to look for surprises?" Arthur asked.

Samson put his hand on his face and sighed. He stomped toward Guard Captain Kinny. "Captain, where do you think you're going?"

Arthur smiled as he heard Samson dress down the guard captain before a few of the fighters changed direction and ran for the western gate.

Balair and Cal, can you two monitor this force of goblins headed toward us? Don't engage them, but make sure they don't sneak around us or climb the cliffs.

Damn, dude. I had an epic nap planned for this afternoon. Balair complained.

I can take the skies. Let the worthless rat sleep. As ugly as he is, he needs all the beauty sleep possible. Calfuray sent back.

Listen here, you overgrown lizard! I'm clearly the better choice. As fat as you are, they'll see you in the sky without even trying.

Fat! When I catch you, I'll eat you, you little toothpick.

Arthur watched a flash of fire in the sky and laughed. *You two stop. You will give yourselves away. Both of you need to be nicer to each other.*

They huffed in agreement and flew toward the approaching force.

"They bickering again?" Allendria asked.

"Always. You ready to watch a fight?"

"I guess so. Is it bad that I agree with Vana? So boring just standing by and watching and not getting to fight."

"Not really. I feel the same way, but if this kingdom is to survive and thrive, we have to make sure the people can take care of themselves. We can't have one of us live in every village for protection."

She took his hand, and they walked toward the wall. At the gatehouse, they split, and each took a side of the gatehouse and climbed the battlements. Samson stood with Arthur, and Vana was with Allendria. The group watched as the guard force held positions. Anxiety plastered on their faces.

All of them had their bows out, and each fiddled with an arrow. Some had them resting on the bowstrings while others held them down by their side and ran their fingers along the feathers.

Five-hundred yards away, the trees shook. They all readied themselves for the enemy. Their anticipation built only to see a pack of deer and a score of wild hogs rush from the forest and scatter. A few nervous laughs echoed over the battlements as the group calmed down.

It wasn't long before they spotted movement in the trees again. This time, a couple of goblins popped out and looked around. It was hard to tell exactly what they were doing from that distance, but they slowly continued onto the grassland as more emerged from the trees behind them. The initial estimate was slightly off since this looked closer to four dozen goblins.

The goblins moved at a steady pace. They marched straight for the wall while beating their crude weapons on wooden shields. Two animal skin war drums thumped in the back of the group. When they were within a hundred yards of the wall, they stopped. The drum beat picked up and started building speed. When it hit a fast enough pace, the goblins yelled, and all rushed forward in a mad dash.

"Not very bright, are they? Charging a stone wall with no way to climb it." Arthur mused.

"Not the most intelligent of creatures, to be sure," Samson agreed. "Barely a step up from animals."

"Guards! Knock arrows and make ready!" Guard Captain Kinny called over the roar of the charge. Up and down the wall, the fifteen guards nocked arrows and brought their bows up to a ready position.

The charging force gained ground quickly, and Captain Kinny called out again, "Draw!"

When the force was only a couple dozen yards away, he gave the final command, "Fire at will!"

Arrows flew from the battlements. Arthur grimaced as maybe three of the fifteen arrows hit a target. The archers were already fitting another arrow into their bows and quickly let loose another batch of arrows. This time eight found their marks, and the injured goblins fell under the stampede of their fellows. Most of the wounds themselves wouldn't be fatal, but falling under that trampling mess would almost guarantee their death.

The goblins hit the wall with a thud as they tried to scrabble up the smooth surface with their hands and crude weapons. The guards kept firing arrows as fast as they could fit them onto their bows. Arthur watched the fight with passive interest. A flash of red caught his eye, and he turned to see a small wall of fire blossom along the outer edge of the stone and scorch several of the goblins. The odor of burned flesh drifted on the wind, mixed with the coppery stench of blood.

Arthur was about to yell at someone for disobeying orders when he caught sight of the mage. They were dressed in normal clothing and had no armor on.

"Did I miss something?" Arthur asked Samson.

"Possibly. Why do you ask?"

"Why is there a mage on the wall? Weren't our people supposed to wait in reserve?"

"Our people are waiting in reserve. He is one of the village's dedicated mages. As such, he is here to help defend as well."

Arthur felt stupid as soon as Samson reminded him they assigned dedicated magic users to the farming settlements.

"Can we at least get them some sturdy armor? If nothing else, a decent helmet and leather chest piece to protect them from basic arrows?"

"Not a bad idea. We can keep the equipment in the guard shack by the wall once completed."

The two continued to watch the battle unfold. A few of the goblins climbed on top of their fellow fighters and jumped up to grab the top of the wall. Their short stature made it very difficult to reach the top. None of them survived long. They either became the new primary target for the archers, or the guards just walked up and bashed their hands with their weapons. The unfortunate targets lost their grip and fell back into the crowd.

The green-skinned creatures fell under the onslaught until only a dozen remained. They finally gave up the relentless pursuit and fled from the wall. Arrows chased them across the grassland until they were out of range. A cheer came up from the defenders.

Guard Captain Kinny approached and saluted Samson. "Should we pursue them, sir?"

"How would you pursue them?" Samson asked.

"March out and charge after them?" Kinny said, obviously unsure of the answer.

"Do you think that is the best course of action for chasing a fleeing enemy?"

"No, sir. Ideally, I'd have cavalry chase them down and finish them."

"Very good," Samson agreed. "That would be ideal, but we don't have any cavalry. What's your next best option?"

The guard captain looked unsure of himself before he finally answered. "Do nothing. Let them run."

"That's the answer I wanted to hear. Chasing them into that forest can easily lead to your doom. Your number one job is to protect this community and these walls. If you had a mounted force that could wipe them out, I'd tell you to go for it. Letting them go can keep others from trying the same thing. On the flip side, they may bring more with them and come back. That's why I don't enjoy taking chances."

Just as Samson finished that, Arthur saw blasts of fire on the plains and turned toward the light. The fleeing goblins ran into the jaws of hell. Both Calfuray and Balair were on the ground, ripping them apart with claws and blasts of flame.

"Even more ideal than cavalry is dragons," Samson said with a grin.

"So much for the cleanup. Guess we can go back to the business at hand. Have those who didn't take part in the fight police the field and gather useful materials. We can pile the bodies up near the trees, and we'll incinerate them. I want to talk to the local guard group. Have them head back to the village. I want them assembled near the new inn." Arthur listed out.

Samson saluted and began yelling orders. The assembled reserves grumbled when they heard they would have to do cleanup. A few cheers came from the fighters on the wall until Samson turned glares their way. That caused them to quiet down and immediately avert their eyes.

Arthur and Allendria walked back toward the village site. When they neared the shell of the new inn, they stopped and turned to wait. A thump sounded beside them, and they turned to see Balair strutting across the ground toward them.

Did you see me roasting those goblins? He sent to Arthur and Allendria.

Ever so brave of you. Didn't know your fire breath was that advanced. Allendria agreed.

It's not. Calfuray snickered into their minds. *He was trying to hide his pathetic fire breath in mine.*

Balair bristled beside them as he arched his back like a cat.

How dare you! I'm a fine specimen of my kind and can breathe fire like a champ.

Arthur could only shake his head and smile as he drowned out the two bickering in his head. The guard forces from the wall approached in a loose formation and stopped in front of Arthur and Allendria. Vana and Samson walked up to join them and stood nearby.

People from the village saw the approaching force and trickled toward the gathering to hear the news. Many looked anxious, and some clutched children in their hands. They gathered behind Arthur and his group.

Arthur stepped forward, "Men and women of Giliad's Rise, you have done this village proud. You stood toe to toe with the enemy and protected your charge. We can find no greater honor than protecting innocents from the evils of this world."

The fighters stood straighter. A few of them gathered a little moisture in their eyes at the praise.

"You've shown the true power of our kingdom today. If a threat comes in the future, remember this. Remember how so few of you defended against a large group. I don't expect to see many goblins roaming around these parts, but if they come, you can drive them off. You've earned the rest of the day off. Mingle with friends or family. If you decide to chip in with the building work, I won't object, but the day is yours."

The group responded with a uniform "Kingdom of Fire" call, and Samson dismissed them.

"Must be nice to have the day off," Vana grumbled.

"Shouldn't you be scouting or something?" Arthur asked with a grin.

She punched him in the shoulder. "Ass."

"Guess we should get back to work too," Allendria told him.

"You just had to ruin the moment. Can't I just go take a nap?" Arthur complained.

"I don't get a nap, so neither do you." Allendria shot back.

"I mean, no one is saying you can't…" Arthur mumbled before trudging along behind her.

"I need to get my scouts out," Vana said.

Arthur turned and saw her with a hand on Samson's shoulder as she whispered into his ear. He wasn't sure what she said, but Samson's cheeks flushed red. Arthur grinned at the flustered response from the stoic paladin.

I guess women can do that to anyone.

Balair interrupted his thought. *You two have fun. I'm going to go investigate the shade under that fine oak tree over there.*

"Oh, so he gets a nap, but I don't?" Arthur whined.

"No one expects anything from him. We all know he's worthless." Allendria said.

At least she understands. Calfuray grumbled to them all before flying away toward the trees.

Arthur and Allendria wove through the budding village. Stone rose from flashes of magical power as the construction crews worked to create building walls. The two of them found an empty foundation with no one around and stepped up onto the smooth stone.

"This is supposed to be a standard two-bedroom house. Care to do this together?" Allendria asked.

"Sounds good. Won't hurt to practice sharing the power."

The two held hands and fed power into the surrounding stone. Arthur used his pre-made spells to create the standard building they'd developed. Allendria fed her power to him as he guided the spells and lifted the walls.

The process sped by as they focused solely on the work. In no time at all, the building stood complete, minus the few interior upgrades. Some of the construction workers would come in with the final touches. The comforts of basic furniture, a cooking pit, and temperature control devices for the air and water would finish out the space. Anything else would be up to the new tenets to provide.

One recent addition to these base houses was food storage. The original housing in Alurian didn't include any spaces for that. Mainly because food was almost nonexistent, and they used the inn as a base for all food storage and preparation. Here, the residents would need to preserve their own supply of food. To accomplish this, each house had a cold storage cellar similar to the one he built at the inn in Alurian. These were smaller but could still hold a generous supply of items.

The ability to keep food cold was an incredible benefit. Things like milk were almost impossible to keep around for use without proper storage. Between the climate-controlled rooms and hot water, some nobles would consider these houses a luxury.

Allendria and Arthur stood outside and laid eyes on their creation. It looked identical to the other buildings nearby, except they completed theirs. The normal crews didn't have the mana pool the two of them did, so it took them longer to wait for the mana to regenerate.

"That was quick. Think I can take over for the next building?" Allendria asked.

"Sure. How about we walk out to the wall and make one of the guard barracks?" Arthur suggested.

"That should be fun."

The two walked together back toward the eastern wall. Soldiers still milled about and flowed in and out of the gates. Some brought back scraps of metal from salvaged weapons and armor. Others came back dirty with blood on their boots as they took a break to grab some food.

"What size were you thinking about for the barracks?" Allendria asked.

"Hmm. I originally thought of a small building. Just enough for a few people who were on watch shift. Now that I look around here, though, I wonder if we should make it larger to accommodate a force that might have to hold out against a siege?" Arthur mused.

"Paladin Samson! Can you come down here for a minute?" Allendria called to the armored figure on top of the wall.

The warrior looked at them and nodded. He set a quick pace as his feet met the nearest set of stairs. In a matter of moments, he stood in front of them.

"Wasn't expecting to see you two here again. Thought you were working in town?"

"We already finished a house and figured we'd come build the guard barracks. Wanted to get your feedback on the design." Arthur told him.

Arthur explained what he'd told Allendria about the size of the building and asked Samson for his thoughts.

"It's only a difference in mana for us, right? No other actual building costs?" Samson asked.

"Essentially. It will take more of the temperature devices to control the building as it grows larger, but otherwise, the same cost."

"In that case, the bigger the better. I'd like a full-service barracks if you can manage. A cooking and food preparation space, living quarters, an armory, sleeping space. I'd also request a separate section with the same amenities but a larger sleeping space."

"Why two different areas?" Allendria asked.

"Refugees," Samson answered. "In case of an attack in the surrounding area, we may have refugees show up for shelter. I'd prefer not to let newcomers into the village proper. If we can quarter them in the adjacent building, it will let the guards monitor them and ensure there aren't any misunderstandings."

Arthur considered the proposal before answering. "I like it, but doesn't that put them really close to our defenses? If you're worried about some kind of sabotage, wouldn't it be easier for them to betray the village defenses when right next to them?"

"That's partially true, but we also have the chance to keep them under guard. I'll make sure they place heavy doors on the building so we can keep them confined if the need arises."

"You're our military commander, so I'll use your recommendation."

"Does that mean I can go back to work?" Samson asked. "I'm sure the forces outside the wall have been slacking since I left my supervisory spot."

Arthur and Allendria both laughed before they waved for him to continue.

"He needs to loosen up a little," Allendria said.

"I would say that's not possible, but I believe Vana may break him out of his shell," Arthur added.

Allendria raised an eyebrow at him. "Oh, really?"

"Yeah, I think it would be good for both of them. Vana might loosen him up a bit, and Samson might rein some of her wild side in."

Allendria burst out laughing at that. "Good luck with that. No one will tame her. I swear she's half beast herself."

"You've got a point." Arthur conceded. "You care to get started?"

She nodded, and they grasped hands. Arthur fed power to her this time, and she directed the magic. The feel of the magic flowing out of him was strange. It took some time for him to figure out why, though.

When he cast spells, he could feel the different elemental power as it built in his body and flowed from him. When sharing power with Allendria, it flowed from him as pure, unattributed mana. No elemental force was present in the flow. He shifted his focus to her and watched the mana enter her body and wrap around the already-formed threads of her power. As it wrapped, it changed and melded to match the mana that Allendria commanded.

So our magic is naturally neutral, pure mana, and we transform it into the elemental attributes…

It didn't take him long to realize this was a very boring process. After his revelation about the mana, the rest of the task was an exercise in patience, something Arthur severely lacked. His mind wandered as he almost subconsciously fed mana to Allendria.

As his mind drifted, an idea came to him.

I wonder if I can practice some of my other magic while feeding Allendria my pure magic?

The idea sharpened into focus, and he concentrated on his new task. He built Dimensional Magic in his right hand while feeding his pure mana to Allendria through his left. The power formed in his right, but the mana in his left collapsed and trickled to nothing. Allendria's face twisted in concentration as she finished her spell using only her own mana.

"Can't stay focused when it's my turn, huh? I did it during your time, even though I'll admit it was boring," she huffed.

"Sorry. Was trying to do something else," Arthur said with an impish grin.

"What were you up to?"

"I'm trying to see if I can cast a spell of my own while channeling mana to you. It could allow me to still grind experience while supplementing your spell-casting."

"That'd be neat if you could pull it off. It would be even better if you had warned me so I was prepared if the power shut off. I almost lost control of that spell because losing your power surprised me. That would've hurt with the backlash."

Arthur grimaced at the idea of the spell backlash. That much built-up power could cause actual damage.

"Sorry, hun. Mind if I keep trying?"

"Go ahead. Now that I'm aware of it, I'll keep a stronger focus."

Arthur kissed her on the cheek and started funneling mana back to her again. Like the last time, he focused on moving Dimensional Magic to his right hand. When he felt the power slipping from his left, he stopped the flow to his right and picked up the power output to the left. This started a never-ending cycle of magic trying to spiral out of control on both sides. It took a fair amount of juggling back and forth until he had enough Dimensional Magic built up, where he felt confident enough to activate his Rift spell.

The built-up power expanded out, and Arthur shifted his focus to feeding mana to Allendria while he let the ability take over and create the rift. It was why he used an already-learned spell instead of trying to create something new. The power snapped into place, and he received a notification that made him grin.

Congratulations, you have learned Dual Casting for a 100 experience bonus. You can cast two spells simultaneously. The second spell costs an additional 50% mana to cast.
You have gained 75 experience in Dual Casting.
You have gained 160 experience in Dimensional Magic for casting Dimensional Rift.

Now that is fantastic.

Chapter 6

Leaps and Bounds

The revelation about his Dual Casting drove Arthur into a frenzy. He used that chance to let Allendria take over and just fed her mana while he pumped out Dimensional Magic spells. His focus could be on any area of magic, but this was the one he wanted to level the most.

Since he discovered Dimensional Magic, he'd dreamed of a special type of spell using it. His only hope was the special ability he gained at level twenty would fill in the last details he needed to make his dream a reality.

Until that time, he would hunker down and burn through mana. It also had the added effect of leveling his Dual Casting ability and eventually unlocking the talents for it.

They spent the rest of the day working on building up the large barracks building. Allendria took control of the project and Arthur followed numbly behind, like a lost puppy. Small rifts of power appeared and quickly winked out near him as he pumped out spells. The draw on his mana concerned him, though.

He was so excited when he first learned of the ability that he hadn't noticed the bad part. When he cast the additional spell, it also cost fifty percent more. Instead of 160 mana per cast, his rift spell now cost 240.

This higher mana cost forced him to pull heavily on the mana stored in his items. His total mana storage sat at 14,580. That included his base mana pool and the extra storage in his sword and amulet. His mana regeneration rate was high, but it couldn't outpace that amount of mana use. The items only regenerated if he refilled with excess mana from his own mana pool.

As the sunset faded over the horizon, Allendria cast the last spell to finish the barracks. Arthur's mana feed failed during the cast, but she stabilized the spell quickly and completed it. They'd needed to take a few breaks for Allendria's mana to regenerate, but she had her own mana storage items to help bolster her total mana. Even with the dual casting, Arthur completed fifty casts of his rift spell. The experience gains were impressive.

You have gained 3,750 total experience in Dual Casting.

Congratulations, you have reached levels 2, 3, 4, and 5 in Dual Casting. Decreases the mana draw of dual-cast spells by 8%. Holding a pretty girl's hand, and you're more interested in making portals?

You have gained 10,120 total experience in Dimensional Magic.

Congratulations, you have reached level 13 in Dimensional Magic. Decreases the mana draw of dimensional spells by 36%. Have some high hopes for this magic, huh?

Arthur and Allendria headed back into town and settled down for a good meal. The gymnastic event that took place getting in the hammock finally ended with the two of them asleep in each other's arms.

When the sun rose, they were back at work. The little village was close to completion now. Their progress quickly disproved his original statement of building a village a day. A lot of that had to do with the complexity of these freeholds. If they were just showing up, tilling up some fields, and building basic stone houses, they could easily finish it in a day. He wanted the lifeblood of this country to live decent lives in relative comfort. Engineering the fields to grow year-round also took time.

Allendria and Arthur spent the morning building a barracks near the western wall. This one was half the size of the one on the east. They didn't think the extra space was necessary.

While they walked around the proposed site, Allendria created the foundation. Arthur looked over his talents for Dual Casting.

You have 2 unused Talent Points.

Tier 1	
Rapid Fire (0/15)	*Increases the casting speed of both spells by 1% per point.*
Mana Overload (0/10)	*Increases the casting power of dual-cast spells by 2% per point.*

Focused Core (0/10)	*Learn to focus your power and increase your mana efficiency. Reduces the casting cost penalty of dual casting by 2% per point.*

Hmm, all pretty standard percentage boosts.

Arthur put both points into Focused Core. The extra casting cost was the part he liked the least, so fixing it made him feel better.

Like the day before, their process became monotonous. This time, Arthur optimized his experience gain some more. Instead of casting Dimensional Rift for 237 mana and getting 160 experience, he cast four Dimensional Access spells for 148 mana and netted 200 experience.

This optimized casting allowed him more experience for less mana. It required him to cast a lot more spells, but casting speed wasn't his problem. The total experience per hour was better. It also meant they needed fewer breaks. The lower mana cost of the spells and the increased number he cast allowed more regeneration. They still had to dip into their items' mana pools, but they didn't fully deplete them. A couple of breaks helped ensure they had some mana to spare as they lay the last spell on the new barracks.

By the middle of the day, Arthur felt better about his experience as they headed to the village center in search of Samson.

You have gained 5,000 total experience in Dual Casting.

Congratulations, you have reached levels 6 and 7 in Dual Casting. Decreases the mana draw of dual-cast spells by 12%. Priorities, dude!
You have gained 13,000 total experience in Dimensional Magic.
Congratulations, you have reached level 14 in Dimensional Magic. Decreases the mana draw of dimensional spells by 39%. Pay attention to the lady!

Everyone seemed in high spirits as they passed people clearing construction sites and moving furniture into the new buildings. The air nearly buzzed with magic as it permeated the ground and lifted stone into place.

"Samson," Arthur called as they approached the paladin.

"Productive morning?" he asked.

"Finished the barracks on the west side. What's the overall progress here?" Allendria asked.

"Construction is moving along nicely. We should finish the place and move on in the morning."

Arthur looked around at the buildings. "Really? That's not half bad."

"There will be a handful of things that still need fine-tuning, but that is why each of these villages will have its own magic users to deal with day-to-day stuff. They can do a little construction work and make tweaks for the people who live here." Samson reminded him.

"Any word from Vana?" Allendria asked.

"Her team is out hunting right now and plans to be back by nightfall. She has a group with her who volunteered to stay in this village to supply meat. They will also act as scouts and advanced messengers should anything threaten the area."

"Great thinking. Let's plan on having a last dinner here tonight and then heading out tomorrow morning toward our next destination." Arthur said.

"It'll be done," Samson agreed.

* * *

Shadows danced along the walls as Rayne strolled down the alleyway. The darkness almost felt welcoming to him as he walked without apparent care. He wore his normal armor, but covered it with a layer of finer clothes. A garish ring with a large ruby faintly glimmered in the moonlight as he traveled.

A noise caught his attention, but he did his best to focus straight ahead. He knew exactly where the sound came from. Using his One with the Ground spell, he saw the footfalls of the two people slowly creeping down the alley behind him.

Their movement patterns were erratic. They tried their best to cover their noise as they moved, but they were obviously amateurs. A small grin tugged at the corners of Rayne's mouth. *The trap is unfolding nicely.*

A glimmer of light ahead of him made him step to the side, and a flash of metal passed beside him through where he previously stood. The blade clattered to a stop on the stone behind him. Both of his pursuers looked startled. Faces plastered with surprise, they stared at him in disbelief before shaking off the feeling. In a mad dash, they charged Rayne with daggers drawn.

The darkness seemed to move around Rayne as he slowly released his passenger. Purple energy swirled to envelop him, and he vanished from sight. The two thugs in the alley stopped in confusion and looked around.

Rayne never sped up his movements. He walked with a slow, deliberate pace and stood behind one of them. His stiletto dagger lashed out and caught the man in the kidney. Screams never followed because Rayne's hand had an iron grip over the man's mouth. Energy flowed from the would-be assassin into Rayne as he fed on the soul energy. The flow of power stopped when the man went limp, and Rayne lowered him to the ground.

You have dealt 170 HP damage to Pickpocket (Level 10) with Enchanted Mage-crafted Steel Stiletto Dagger (Critical Hit) (Mortal Blow).
You have absorbed 120 Spiritual Power from Pickpocket (Level 10).
Pickpocket (Level 10) has died.

Still wish I knew how much power it took to advance to the next level of my Soul of Shadows.

The second man backed away with fear in his eyes. His dagger trembled in his hand and his knees shook. Rayne smiled.

"I told you this city was off-limits for your kind. If you don't have an agreement to operate with me, you're as good as dead."

The pickpocket gulped and dropped his blade as he turned and ran. Rayne took two quick steps, and his hand latched on with an iron grip. The man struggled to escape, but the difference in power was impossible to overcome. A quick flash of his blade allowed him to drain this man as well.

You have dealt 170 HP damage to Pickpocket (Level 10) with Enchanted Mage-crafted Steel Stiletto Dagger (Critical Hit) (Mortal Blow).
You have absorbed 120 Spiritual Power from Pickpocket (Level 10).
Pickpocket (Level 10) has died.

Rayne wiped his dagger on the shirt of the second man and put it back in its sheathe. He stood up and looked toward the end of the alley he first traveled.

"You can come out now. Sneaking up on me may cause me to wonder if your earlier offer was genuine." Rayne said.

Bright blue eyes appeared in the moonlight as a woman emerged from a shadow. Curly auburn hair framed her pale face. She wore a skin-tight suit of leather armor. Like Rayne's own armor, hers covered up any metal buckles and fasteners to prevent reflections.

"Come now, I had nothing to do with those two. I'd never sully myself with people that unskilled," Scarlett scoffed.

"I thought you were leaving town?" She asked.

"Decided I was of more use here than roaming the countryside."

Rayne watched her as she approached, but he didn't detect any threatening movements. Her words rang true with him as well. The leader of an underground group didn't mingle with lowlifes like this. She could have hired them way down the food chain, but he couldn't dwell on small things in the criminal underground.

"So, was a decision made?" Rayne asked.

"We accepted your proposal," she grumbled.

"You don't sound too happy about that?"

"Not the ideal situation, but we understand times change. If you truly mean to allow us to operate untouched, then we will feed you the information you need."

"I'd like to clarify the untouched part. Major crimes are off-limits. Other than that, we will allow you to operate freely."

"Yeah, yeah, I remember."

"In that case, here," Rayne said as he took a step toward her and held out a small metal pin. "I have more of these," he added as he handed over a pouch filled with them.

"What are these for?" Scarlett asked.

"Consider them free passes. Have your thieves wear them, and they will be safe. The city guards all know this pin and will leave any wearing it alone."

Scarlett rolled the pin around her fingers as she examined it. "Nothing magical on it. Just a plain symbol."

Rayne didn't bother correcting her. He knew it actually had some magic in it to prevent it from being duplicated. It wasn't enough to change the grade on it, though.

"Well, in that case, you should know that a group of people are banding together in the warehouse district, intending to raid what few supplies remained. They plan to flee the city before the king returns. Another faction has risen in the merchant district and is considering staging a coup and overthrowing the government here. I'm not sure how they plan on doing that when the guards are loyal to the king, but I figured you needed to know."

"Thanks for the heads up. It sounds like I need to get back to work," Rayne said with a smile.

Scarlett reached up, and Rayne flinched back. She froze with her hand in mid-air, and Rayne watched her. Her hand slowly moved forward again, and she brushed the back of her nails down his cheek.

"You are rather handsome when your anger comes out," she mused before she turned and walked back into the shadows.

Rayne let out a deep breath he hadn't realized he'd been holding. "Women."

* * *

The next village location is up ahead. Calfuray sent to Arthur, Samson, and Allendria.

Thanks, Cal. Arthur answered.

They crested the next rise, and the location came into sight in the afternoon sun. It had taken three days of travel to get here. The locals called this location The Cliff. Not very imaginative since it seriously was an enormous cliff with a flowing grassland at the base. A small waterfall splashed down from the top of the stone edifice. Rainbows flashed in the water's mist.

The land was relatively flat, and this rock face stood over eighty feet tall. Even better, the archipelago itself sported a sheer rock face all around. Calfuray and Balair flew over it to verify. With no easy way to the top, it meant people couldn't sneak around the back and fire down into the place. It also made for a natural defensive barrier on one side. Instead of being able to build the two short walls like they had last time, they needed to build a solid half-circle wall around the face of the cliff.

"Almost time for some proper work again," Arthur quipped.

"I agree. All this nonstop hiking causes chafing in this armor." Samson grunted.

Vana slid up beside him and whispered in his ear. Arthur wasn't sure if she did it on purpose, but she was a little too loud, and he heard what she said.

"I could rub something on it to help."

Arthur stifled his laugh as Samson turned bright red. Allendria stood next to him, and looked like she was fighting the urge as well. Her hearing was usually better than his, so he was sure she'd heard.

"Ranger Vana," Arthur called out loud enough for all nearby to hear, "take a group of scouts and inspect our campsite ahead of our arrival."

"Yes, Your Majesty." She told him with a bow. Lifting her head just enough for him to see, she winked at him. After a few moments, she spun around, called out for her scouting team, and led the charge forward.

"Paladin Samson," Arthur yelled out, "Assemble the fighting forces and make sure everyone is on alert. When we arrive, I want you to secure the area for the civilians to begin their work."

"Yes, Your Majesty," he said with a salute.

Everyone scattered to organize their people. The noncombatants grouped together, and all moved to the center of the formation. Guards took place at the front and back.

A purple streak across the sky heralded Calfuray as she settled onto the grassland near the cliff. The red and orange form of Balair was close behind.

When finally at the site, everyone scattered to begin their work. With the first village complete, they already knew the process and started immediately. A small table came out of one of Arthur's storage spaces, and they drew the layout for this village on it. Everyone used this as the primary reference to begin work.

Samson made sure his armed forces set guards out along the perimeter. Everyone else began clearing roads and marking off foundation sites. The design here would be very similar to the first location in terms of layout.

As with the first village, they spent the rest of that first day clearing out proposed roads and the surrounding area. Camp was set, and everyone settled down for well-deserved rest.

* * *

The morning came with a bright orange sunrise on the horizon.

Event Quest: Save the Bard!	
Requirements: None. Rewards: 38,000 experience, Neutral Standing with Dwarves of Gideon.	Description: A weary bard is under attack by a band of orcs. Come to his aid.
Will you accept this quest? Yes/No.	

"What's going on?" Arthur asked as he slipped from the hammock.

He turned in circles to see only him and Allendria sleeping nearby. He grabbed his sword and jogged toward the village center in search of Samson. The stalwart paladin directed armed men and women and arranged them into formation.

"You get the quest notice as well?" Arthur asked.

"Yes, Your Majesty. We are organizing to march as we speak.

"Good. Let me know when you are ready."

"Of course," Samson agreed.

Arthur looked over his gear. Sleeping in his armor was common in the field, even though he despised doing it. His dagger was in place, and he secured his sword on his belt.

You guys see anything that looks like someone fleeing orcs? Arthur asked into his mental communication.

Why so loud? It's too early in the morning to be awake. Balair grumbled.

I see nothing specific, but a flock of birds lifted from the group of trees south of the city. Something spooked them. Calfuray said.

Can you get a closer look?

On it.

Arthur saw her purple form streak through the morning sunlight as she dove toward the mentioned trees. Footsteps approached, and he turned to see Allendria. She wore a frown as she looked at him.

"Why didn't you wake me?" Allendria asked.

"Sorry. Was startled by the quest and ran to Samson to find out what was happening."

"So, you would just leave me asleep in a hammock during a fight?" She asked in a half-teasing tone.

"Of course not," Arthur attempted to placate her. "I didn't want to wake you until I knew it was something important."

Her eyes narrowed. "Nice try, but not falling for it."

She huffed and stomped by him, headed toward Samson.

A winded Vana ran toward the paladin, and Arthur rushed to hear the conversation.

"The dwarf in question is on a wagon, loaded with barrels, headed toward us from the trees in the south. From our quick glance, it looks like a score of orcs follow him." The ranger summed up.

"Militia! Form up," Samson called as he watched the last few members stumble into their columns. "Move out!"

The Paladin led the procession toward the south, and Arthur and Allendria followed. Arthur accepted the quest, and they moved at a quick pace toward the identified target.

Blades of grass snapped under their feet as the column stomped through the field at a fast march. The fighters looked nervous as they traveled.

"Where are all these enemies coming from? I thought we drove out the orcs and goblins?" Arthur asked Samson.

The big man laughed. "We don't have anywhere close to the military power to drive them all out. These bands of raiders are all over the countryside. We don't have enough people to hunt them all down, nor the training to do so with our forces."

"Another item to add to the list?" Arthur asked.

"Absolutely," Samson said with a nod.

A bestial roar filled the area as two men ran from the trees at a dead sprint. It didn't take long to see why, as a force of a dozen orcs broke from the trees and ran for the fleeing humans.

"Shields to the front. Hold the line. Spearmen, take position in the gaps!" Samson ordered.

The men rushed to obey the commands and arrayed themselves in a solid line. Shields slammed into the dirt to hold their ground, and spears rested in the gaps, ready to thrust.

Arrows flew from their line and picked off the orcs closest to the fleeing people. Arthur looked to his side to see the archer in question. Vana held her bow up high and launched shaft after shaft into the charging orcs. Every arrow hit flesh, although not always a deadly shot.

The humans reached the shield line, and they opened small gaps to let them through before immediately snapping shut. Only eight orcs remained on their feet, but they hit the wall in a rush of fury. The fighters braced as well as they could, but the shield line was pushed backward by the overwhelming size of the monsters.

Spears jabbed forward, and blood pooled on the ground from the attackers. Allendria stepped up beside him and launched her miniature beams of fire into the enemies, cutting them down one by one. Arthur didn't want to attack with spells since his favorite ones were AOE.

A final spear thrust ended the life of the last standing orc, and it fell to the ground. Everyone let out a short cheer. Two fleeing humans converged on Vana and rushed to her side. Arthur hurried over to hear what they said.

"… right behind us. Another force is pursuing him as well." One of them said.

"Vana?" Arthur asked.

"Two of my scouts," she said as she gestured toward the men. "I had them searching for the dwarf. They found this group of enemies sitting in ambush, waiting for him to arrive. They attacked and lured them to us. The dwarf should be out soon, followed by a larger pursuit force."

"Great," Arthur groaned. He turned and rushed for the fighters. A few of them had minor injuries, so he cast his Minor Heal on each, bringing them back to top shape.

"What do we do about the dwarf?" Samson asked in hushed tones as he walked over to join Arthur.

"What do you mean?" Arthur asked, confused by the question.

"Do we care about the quest, or are we just going to drive away the orcs?" Samson asked.

"Samson, our job is to protect people. As a Paladin, I'd expect you to adhere to that. This dwarf needs our help and is in our kingdom. It's our job to offer that help." Arthur said.

The paladin looked at a loss before his mouth firmed into a line, and he nodded in agreement. The armored man turned and shouted orders to his forces.

"Get ready for a charge. Ranged attackers do all the damage you can before they arrive. Do not attack the dwarf. Our job is to help him and get him back behind our forces!"

His words rang over the crowd, and everyone stood straighter. Their shields locked back into the dirt, and they prepared for an assault. In a moment of inspiration, Arthur ran in front of the line and started casting spells. He used their respite to conjure up short stretches of wall with an opening in the middle. Many of the armed forces climbed the wall and readied spears. A group of soldiers with swords and shields held the opening in the center.

Arthur fidgeted in place and took a quick look at his stat gains so far.

You have gained 3,600 total experience in Dimensional Magic.

Congratulations, you have reached level 15 in Dimensional Magic. Decreases the mana draw of dimensional spells by 33%. You shouldn't keep so much stuff in your closet.

You have gained 2,100 total experience in Water Magic.

Congratulations, you have reached level 11 in Water Magic. Increases the effect of your Water Magic spells by 21%. Now you're a nurse! Great…

You have gained 3,410 total experience in Earth and Fire Magic.

Knowing he still had some time, he looked at his overall Dimensional Magic Talent Tree.

You have 2 unspent Talents Point.

Talent	Description
Tier 1	
Bend it to Your Will (0/10)	Increases spell power with Dimensional Magic by 4% per point.
Dimensional Drawer (1/1)	Teaches you how to create a Dimensional Drawer. This anchors a small, empty space, for you for use as storage that is accessible from anywhere.
Power of the Void (0/10)	Reduces the mana needed to cast Dimensional Spells by 4% per level.
Tier 2	
Spatial Work (10/10)	All spells that deal with creating spatial pockets are now capable of 5% more size per point in this skill.
Unlock Portals (0/8)	Portals are complex things that require a lot of knowledge. This skill will teach you how to summon small portals within 100 feet of yourself that connect to each other upon investing all 8 skill points.
Tier 3	

Dimensional Disposal (1/1)	Opens a dimensional portal that will remain until dismissed. Anything placed in the portal will be lost to the void.
Through Time and Space (0/10)	Grants understanding of basic dimensional transport upon investing all 10 points.
Expansion (7/10)	Increases the maximum size of your dimensional spaces by 15% per point.
Enchantment Weaving (1/1)	This talent teaches you how to use Dimensional Magic on Items and Accessories.

With no new options, he put two points into Expansion. With those out of the way, he turned toward his Water Magic talents.

You have 2 unused Talent Points.

Talent	Description
Tier 1	
Flow With It (0/10)	Increases spell power with Water Magic by 3% per point.
Purify Water (1/1)	Teaches you the spell to purify any water source and remove contaminants.

Conserve to Preserve (0/10)	Reduces the mana needed to cast Water Spells by 3% per level.
Tier 2	
Summon Basic Water Elemental (0/1)	Summons a small water elemental that can be used as seen fit. Helpful for routing water flow and cleaning.
Waterlogged (10/10)	Each point increases Water Magic Spell power by 2% and every 2 points increases your base Intellect by 1.
Irrigation (0/10)	Water Magic spells cast for plant growth have a 5% greater effect per point invested.
(Hidden Ability) Water Enchantrix Matrix (1/1) This ability will only become available if you have the following prerequisites: • Water Magic > Level 5 Enchanting Skill > Level 5 Have created Enchanted armor that resulted in	Gives you the knowledge to create an Enchantrix Matrix for the water element. This is the basic structure for advanced Enchanting patterns.

a set bonus	
Tier 3	
Soothing (0/10)	*Water Magic suffuses your body and constantly improves it. Every point grants 0.5 HP and 0.5 MP regeneration per second. Every 5 points increases all your stats by 1.*
Healing (0/10)	*Each point increases the spell power of healing spells by 5%.*
Weather Mage (0/5)	*Increases the spell power and area of effect for any weather-based spells by 5% for each point.*

Any talent that improved base stats usually went to the top. Since he already maxed out Waterlogged, he put his 2 points into Soothing, granting himself 1 HP and MP of regeneration every second. It didn't sound like much based on the percentage, but sixty HP and mana a minute was a lot. By the time he maxed out the talent, it would earn him around three hundred of each a minute. *That talent must be a very rare one since it is so powerful.*

Noise at the tree line drew his focus, and he shifted his feet. A quiet tension spread through the field as everyone gripped weapons and prepared. When the man on the cart burst through the foliage, Arthur was not prepared for what he saw.

"What in the hell?" he mumbled.

Chapter 7

A Bard of a Different Color

Arthur had seen many examples of bards over the years on Earth. D&D and a plethora of video games featured them in one form or another. The person he saw standing on the wooden cart didn't fit any of his expectations.

An exhausted-looking mule thundered ahead, pulling said cart. Barrels, stacked in the back, bounced slightly from the jostling. But none of that drew much attention from the figure at the front. A short man, probably a little less than five feet tall, stood on the driver's seat. He wore finery that Arthur hadn't seen yet on Dravincia. It looked like a full three-piece suit. Not only that, it appeared perfectly tailored to fit the man. While short, he was stocky as well. It didn't look like the flab of fat but the thick muscle of a workman. The biggest surprise was the hair.

When Arthur heard it was a dwarf, he expected an enormous ball of fur to come trundling out with a beard hanging low and frizzy hair flowing down his back. This man was clean-cut and short-cropped on top. It reminded him of a high and tight from his military buddies, but with a lower fade. He trimmed his beard into a neat goatee and also kept it reasonably short.

To add to the shock of the scene, the bard was playing an instrument while also fleeing. Arthur never expected to see the instrument in person. The only time he'd ever seen one before was in a picture in history class when discussing the Renaissance era. The dwarf held what looked like a guitar, but the neck of the device sat on top of the body. Strings attached to one side stretched over a large disc and then continued down the neck. Keys on the side allowed the user to push and change the tension on the strings. It sounded similar to an old violin.

Arthur could feel the sound vibrate through his body as the man approached. As the music filled him, he received a notification.

You are under the influence of Strings of Speed. Your movement speed is increased by 10%.

Hmm, so he buffs. Sounds like a bard to me.
The cart trundled across the landscape as it approached his forces at high speed.

"Fire at his pursuers!" Samson called.

Arrows flew from the soldier's lines, and they launched a few minor spells. Hulking orcs approached, armed with wooden clubs and a scattering of crappy-looking metal weapons. Scraps of leather covered some of them, while others had all of their body parts flopping in the breeze.

Arthur condensed power in both hands and dual-cast his Fireblast spell. The twin vortexes of flame compressed into his hands until swirling balls of liquid fire remained. Using every ounce of his strength and a slight push of Air Magic, he launched them into the approaching enemies.

The power struck the leading forces and exploded into swirling domes of flame as skin blistered and melted under the intense heat. Dozens of enemies fell to the flame, and his notifications piled up. He condensed it down to total damage instead of seeing it all individually.

You have dealt 3,810 total damage with Fireblast.
Orc has died. (x18)

When the bard reached their shield wall, Arthur's forces pulled the same maneuver from before and opened the line for the cart to squeeze through. In a snap, they were back in place and ready for the enemy.

Orcs collided with his defenders in a screech of steel. Dirt flew up from the impact as they pushed the shields backward. Arrows punched into the green flesh, but the orcs kept pushing into the line. It buckled inward until their paladin took the field.

Samson walked into the buckling part of the line with his shield in front and his blade down and ready. The men near him perked up when they saw him and firmed up their part of the line. The paladin approached the biggest, nastiest-looking orc and smashed his shield into its face.

Even from his relative distance, Arthur swore he saw the creature's eyes roll back in its head as Samson continued to the next in line. Another clang of his shield, and the next one fell while the paladin took the time to stab the first in the throat as he passed. With Samson in the lead, the line pushed back outward.

Arthur started walking toward the fight when the air itself shifted. The tune from before faded, and an unfamiliar sound replaced it. This one was deeper, and it felt thicker somehow. He couldn't even explain the feeling himself.

You are under the influence of Cadence of Force. Your Defense and Hit Points are increased by 15%.

That's awesome!

With Paladin Samson leading them and the new buff bolstering their confidence, they pushed forward.

Arthur ran into the fray and pulled out Ember. Activating Weak Haste, his speed and perception increased. Orcs were big and strong but not really known for their speed. He danced between the brutes, landing hit after hit, opening arteries and clipping tendons to leave them bleeding out and immobile.

Arthur felt as much as heard footsteps behind him and spun with his weapon up to block an attack. The orc behind him froze mid-step as an arrow sprouted from its eye.

"What are you doing down there? Are you crazy?" Vana asked over the roar of combat.

"Warming up?" Arthur answered.

"We haven't even been married yet. If you die before then, I'll resurrect you just to kill you myself," Allendria added.

With a grumble, Arthur disengaged from the fight and backed out of the cluster of bodies. He took the time to cast his Minor Heal spell on those who needed it as he pulled back. Flashes of flame lit up both sides of the attacking orcs as Balair and Calfuray attacked. Calfuray's flame was much larger and killed more orcs, but Arthur wouldn't rub that in Balair's face.

The fighting continued, but Arthur couldn't sit around and do nothing. Instead, he ran up to their hastily raised wall and launched spells into the fray. He spun up a dual-cast Fireblast spell again since it was off cooldown and launched both orbs into the monsters. Just like before, the damage was impressive.

You have dealt 4,640 total damage with Fireblast.
Orc has died. (x23)

From there, he launched Fire Arrows with wild abandon. He had more than enough mana, so there was no point in not using it.

You have dealt 1,380 total damage with Fire Arrow.
Orc has died. (x6)

Beams of flame burned holes through orcs as Allendria took her careful shots. In a flash of inspiration, Arthur smiled and ran down the short stretch of the rampart to her. He placed his hand on her shoulder and joined his mana with hers.

"Can you launch another of those fire beams?" He asked, "I'd like to learn the spell."

She said nothing, but fire blossomed in her hand and then slowly condensed. Arthur could tell she was deliberately slowing down the process to show him. He'd seen her cast this spell at great speed in the past. The energy launched from her hand in a pinpoint attack and punched another hole into an enemy. Blood sprayed from the puncture upon impact, but the flame seared the walls of the wound shut again.

Congratulations, you have learned the Fire Magic Spell: Searing Beam for a 250 experience bonus to Fire Magic.

Spell: Searing Beam	
Requirements: Fire Magic Mana Cost: 30 MP Cast Time: 1 second	Description: Create a beam of fire energy that burns holes through targets and causes the following damage: • Organic targets take 40 base health damage. • Inorganic targets take 40 durability damage. Afflicts burn on combustible targets.
Mastery Level: 1	

Armed with the new spell, Arthur began casting it rapid fire. The power came easily, and he burned holes through green skin as fast as he could pour in the mana.

Samson pushed outward with his melee fighters, gaining ground and putting down more of the creatures.

The fight quickly became monotonous, so Arthur switched it up. To add some difficulty, he began casting rifts into the battlefield and slicing through the enemies with his sword. A rift opened, and a slice cut into a neck before Arthur withdrew his sword and burned a hole through another with a Searing Beam. He alternated back and forth, raining destruction through the group until everything became still.

Fighters on both sides continued their melee. Samson and his group barreled through orcs with swords and shields while rangers and mages manned the walls to launch projectiles into their foes.

The nearby soldiers looked at Arthur with fear and awe in their eyes. Carnage laced the battlefield, and his sword still dripped with blood by his side. He heaved in breaths in rapid succession from his exertion.

"I think that's all of them," Allendria said as she laid her hand on his shoulder.

"Sure hope so," Arthur said as he looked at his mana. "Nearly out of mana myself. Even drained most of my sword and necklace."

"Stand down. Unit one, post a watch on this fortification and watch for stragglers." Samson called over the group.

Sighs of relief intermixed with groans. Arthur assumed the groans came from those in unit one who now had the distinct 'honor' of standing watch. He hopped down from the wall and headed for the gathering around the strange figure and his cart. The man finally lowered his instrument, and Arthur saw a notification pop up.

Cadence of Force buff has ended.

Arthur came to a stop near the cart. "Well met, sir bard."

The dwarf looked up and locked eyes with Arthur. "Thank you, uh, my lord?"

"That's, Your Majesty, dwarf." Samson rumbled.

"Majesty?" He began as his eyes bulged. The bard scrambled down from the cart and bowed at the waist. "My apologies, Your Majesty."

Arthur gave Samson a dirty look before he turned his attention back to the dwarf.

"None of that," Arthur said with a wave. "Not a fan of being very formal myself. What's your name?"

"Wesley, your Majesty." The dwarf said as he stood straight and tried to avoid eye contact.

"No need to fear, Wesley. I hope I'm not rude, but I expected your accent to be different." Arthur said.

"Different, Your Majesty? We have a few different clans of dwarves around. Most of the mountain clans talk normal, like me. The hill dwarves sound Scottish, and the swamp dwarves sound Australian." The Bard told him.

Arthur nodded along with his explanation and was about to respond when he paused. *Scottish and Australian?*

"What do you mean, Scottish and Australian?" Arthur asked.

The bard went pale for a moment before he stuttered, "Sorry, Your Majesty. Names from my home. I doubt you would know them."

Arthur chuckled at that. "You'd be surprised. When did you arrive in Dravincia?"

"How did you know…?"

"You're not the only one," Arthur said and looked around. Everyone looked at him with interest. He raised his voice. "Everyone back to work. Samson, Vana, and Allendria, can you join us?"

The gathered soldiers dispersed, and Arthur led Wesley and the rest of their group off to the side. "Now we are away from the nosy crew. I'm from Earth as well. Texas, to be exact. How about you?"

"Really? Dang, man, didn't know there was anyone else here. I'm from Sydney. I still don't know how I got here. We were playing a D&D game at a costume party. I was dressed like this as a joke," he said, pointing at his formal attire.

"That explains the odd choice of dress for a bard in this world." Arthur laughed. "Although I confess, I really haven't met a bard yet. Surely you could've replaced them as long as you've been here?"

"Was a bit of an odd class. Took a while to get the skills for it. You know how hard it is to raise your singing skill? Damn pain in the ass for sure. As for the clothes, I find that bards do best when they stand out. I quit wearing these for a long time when I first arrived but finally started again after I gained my class."

"I was never any good at singing myself, so I can only imagine. Why a hurdy-gurdy?" Arthur asked.

The bard looked down at the instrument in his hands. "Surprised you knew its name. Few that I knew back on Earth even knew what this was. I was a music teacher and liked to restore classic instruments. The hurdy-gurdy was an instrument that was sophisticated in the amount of sound it can produce but also relatively easy to make with the resources available here."

Arthur was about to continue the conversation when he noticed the looks of his friends. "Sorry, Wesley, but it seems I forgot my manners with the excitement of the situation. This is Paladin Samson, Ranger Vana, and Pyromancer Allendria, Princess of the Dark Elves, and my fiancée."

The dwarf's eyes grew wider with each title until he grinned at the fiancée. "Didn't take you long to hook one. Nice work."

"I'd be careful with your words. You remember her class title, right?" Arthur said as flames danced along Allendria's fingers.

"Uh, sorry," Wesley said with a quick bow toward Allendria.

"I guess that leaves us at the pressing issue of what a dwarf is doing out here, anyway?" Arthur asked. "I haven't seen one since I arrived."

Wesley looked down at his feet and shifted from side to side.

"They respect bards in dwarven society, so they commonly employ us as primary resources for establishing trade relations with the outside world. I'd like to say they sent me out with the noble intention of setting up diplomatic relations with a country, but I'm afraid they just wanted me gone. I was a bit too strange for them with my odd speech and customs. They didn't understand how I wasn't an expert in their culture by my age."

"That would be tough," Vana agreed. "What's in the barrels, then?"

"Oh, dwarven ale. Not the best of the brew, but fine enough."

Samson perked up at that. "You truly have ale? We've seen little of that in years. No one could afford to waste time growing hops and barley when people were already starving."

"I've heard of the struggles up here. I didn't know it was that bad and expected a lot to be rumors." Wesley admitted.

"The elves keep a stash of wine that we make ourselves, but we also ran out of ale years ago. It's fascinating that the dwarves have kept on top of the trade." Allendria added.

"It's only possible because the hill dwarves and the mountain dwarves came to an agreement. The hill dwarves grow the crops needed, and the mountain dwarves trade them metal tools and armaments for it. It's been a fruitful arrangement so far."

"I tell you what, Wesley. I'm interested in establishing trade for ale in my kingdom. What are the dwarves wanting in return? Is it purely coin? Certain materials?"

Wesley took on a contemplative look. "I'm honestly not sure. They are always looking for food under the mountain. Living underground limits our options. Coin spends there as it does everywhere else. Clothing is good for trade, and so is leather."

"Not very good at this, huh?" Allendria asked with a smile.

Wesley gulped before he answered, "First time."

"I'll tell you what. I'll buy the barrels you have on you now for coin, and then you can return to the dwarves and ask what they want for a permanent trade. We will offer coins, leather, food, and eventually cloth. We are just setting our farming and textile trade back up, but it shouldn't take long for the industries to pick up."

"I'm sure that would work," he nodded in agreement.

Arthur waved to the side and activated his Access Dimensional Storage spell. The black door in space appeared, and Wesley yelped in surprise.

"Just one of my spells. No need to fear." Arthur explained before walking inside. He shuffled through some of the wooden crates before finding a quill pen and some parchment.

"Forgot to ask. What's the name of the dwarven kingdom or clan you're from?" Arthur asked.

"The Flintforge Clan from the Dwarves of Gideon."

Arthur poked his head back out of the doorway and looked at the bard. "Not related to Flint Fireforge, I suppose?"

"Sadly, no. I asked as well, and they looked at me funny."

"Such a shame," Arthur said with a shake of his head before he returned his focus to the parchment. A bit of careful pen work, and he had a neat letter penned in front of him. It was an offer of trade between the Kingdom of Fire and the Flintforge Clan.

"What do I owe you for the ale?" Arthur asked.

Wesley looked at the ten barrels standing up in the cart. "I can do five gold each for this batch. I can't guarantee that price for future arrangements, though."

Arthur nodded as he stepped out of his storage and closed the portal. He walked over to Wesley and extended his hand. The dwarf smiled and shook it.

"Done. Care to take this back to your clan for consideration?" Arthur asked as he extended the note. He noticed it now had a name and an item description.

Item: Proposed Trade Agreement	**Durability:** 100/100 **Rarity:** Unique **Quality:** Good **Weight:** 0.03 kg **Traits:** A trade treaty proposal from the Kingdom of Fire to the Flintforge Clan.

Arthur also noticed another notification. All of his experience notifications from the battle were still there, but he glossed over them for now and looked at the newest ones.

You have gained 1,800 experience in Barter.
Congratulations, you have reached level 4 in Barter. All trading agreements will favor you with 6% more value for your goods. About time you learned some trade.

"I encourage you to stick around for a little while before you run off. We are setting up a farming village at this location, and you should at least stay until tomorrow to make sure there are no more orcs in the nearby area. Vana can send out her scouts to look around." Arthur said.

Wesley looked around. "Setting up a village? All I see is that cleared-off area over there."

"That's the place. We just got here yesterday."

"Guess I can stick around then. If you just started, you'll be here for a while."

"Yeah, we should be done in a couple of days and then moving on," Samson said.

"A couple days? How is that possible?" Wesley asked.

"Magic," Arthur said while waggling his fingers.

"You know, that's a lot funnier when magic doesn't exist," Wesley said with a grumble.

"Cheer up," Vana told the bard. "You'll be the favorite person of everyone in the village after the ale."

The party laughed as everyone walked back toward the village site. Arthur sifted through his experience gains from the fight on the way back.

You have gained 2,210 total experience.
You have gained 1,250 total experience in Dimensional Magic.
You have gained 1,800 total experience in Fire Magic.
You have gained 620 total experience in Earth Magic.
You have gained 1,580 total experience in Swords.
You have gained 350 total experience in Water Magic.

A heavy thud beside him drew the group's attention. Wesley squealed before he yelled, "Everyone run!"

The group all laughed and told him to calm down. He skidded to a halt after a couple of steps. Arthur walked up next to him.

"Wesley, meet Calfuray. She is my bondmate. The little red and orange one is one of my summoned friends."

Who are you calling little? Are we really going to hash this out again? Balair grumbled as he shifted back and forth.

"Dude, you have a dragon? That's awesome." Wesley blurted.

"You remember that conversation about Allendria?" Arthur asked.

Wesley calmed down and nodded. "Try to remember that before you say something. Calfuray is a friend and doesn't belong to me. The little shit kinda does, but he's still a friend, anyway."

"Sorry. Still bad at all this."

Everyone arrived at the construction site and got to work. Arthur and Allendria headed off toward the edge of the village. They began working on the fortifications around the perimeter. Since the village was up against a cliff, they had to build a half circle away from the wall to cover the housing and farming areas.

After more repetitive stonework, Arthur challenged himself some more. With his extended mana pool, he needed to put it to better use to grind experience. It took a few more breaks since he had expended a lot of his excess during the fight. He spent the first chunk of time dual casting his wall spells. Gaining experience in three skills at once was an easy decision.

He continued this work for a couple of hours before switching it up. Being able to split his focus like he did while working with Allendria allowed him to do something he hadn't expected. With a little trial and error, Arthur could dual-cast two different spells. With this new split, he started casting stone walls at the same time as his Access Dimensional Storage spell.

The work continued into the evening and eventually ceased when Arthur's spell-casting drained his mana completely. The sun was falling below the horizon. He wasn't sure running himself dry was a good idea shortly after a battle, but he got caught up in the work. The flash of experience rolling in was like a drug as he watched the messages flow in.

His trip back to the village was uneventful, and he met up with Allendria, Samson, and Vana on his return.

"Fun day?" He asked them.

"Of course," Allendria huffed. "I got about half of my side complete for the wall."

"That's good news. I almost finished my side. We can wrap it up tomorrow and build a few turrets and the gate. How's the morale of the guards?"

"Running high. The victory helped bolster them. On a stroke of pure luck, we didn't lose anyone. A few required magical healing to stabilize, but I expect them to make a full recovery. The bard has also been helpful. His singing brightens the mood of those nearby. I've even noticed he has a buff that increases casting speed and regeneration that he's been using to help with the construction effort." Samson said.

"Good to know he's putting in the effort."

"Are you sure we should trust him? We know nothing about him." Allendria said.

"Not completely. I understand some of how he feels right now. We have no reason not to trust him." Arthur said before turning to Vana. "Can you assign someone to monitor him? From a distance. Don't interfere with him. Just make sure he isn't doing anything suspicious."

"Can do. The scouts also returned. We have no enemies near us. They combed through the woods and surrounding fields. All the orcs were killed or fled the area completely." Vana said.

"That's even better news. I think it's time to raise spirits some more. Samson, roll out two of the ale barrels and pop them open. The village can have some fun and drink tonight. Watch the guards and make sure they ration themselves. I don't want drunk people falling asleep on watch."

"Sounds like a great idea."

Samson hurried off and grabbed a couple of guards. It took them no time at all to drop the barrels down and roll them to the center of the village inn's foundation. As soon as the barrels were open, the party began in full. Wesley filled the area with music, and the crowd began dancing. Drink flowed all around, and a sense of merriment filled the air.

"Not going to join them?" Allendria asked.

"Never been much of a drinker," Arthur said with a wave.

"How about a dancer?" she asked with a smile.

Arthur stood and grabbed her hand. He couldn't deny her some fun. They joined the group on the floor and launched into an impromptu dance that reminded Arthur of a two-step.

Arthur spotted Balair slinking around the edges of the slab and snatching mugs of ale that were left unattended. He considered saying something and stopping the little drake, but he let him have some fun. The night ended as Arthur and Allendria collapsed into a now familiar hammock. He spent a few moments glancing over the experience from the construction and dual casting before falling asleep.

You have gained 5,850 total experience in Dimensional Magic.

You have gained 4,400 total experience in Earth Magic and Fire Magic.

You have gained 2,120 total experience in Dual Casting.

Chapter 8

A Drunk Drake

Arthur jolted awake because of a yell and scrambled out of his hammock. It took him a few moments to orient himself and to let the haze of sleep fade.

Help!

Arthur snapped into alertness in an instant and felt for his bond. Balair wasn't far away toward the center of town.

Oddly enough, close to where the yelling is coming from. Arthur groaned and ran toward the noise.

He came to an area in the small tent city with a clearing. Wooden crates of supplies surrounded the circular space on two sides, with random tools lying amongst the boxes. A group of people milled around the area, fixated on something going on in the middle.

"You little bastard, when I catch you, you're gonna regret it." A woman yelled as she chased Balair around the clearing with a wooden rod. She swung wildly, and Balair barely dodged, causing her weapon to smash through a wooden crate.

The miss didn't discourage her, and she continued chasing the drake around the area. Arthur saw Balair stumble, and the woman's face lit up with glee as she landed a solid *thunk* on his head.

Ow. Dammit. Help me. He mewled through their bond as his eyes finally caught sight of Arthur.

It took Arthur a few moments to stop laughing before he finally called out over the crowd. "What's going on here?"

"Your flying rodent over there pissed on my tent and the shoes we left outside last night." The woman said as she stabbed the rod in his direction.

"Balair, what the fuck, man? Did you pee on their stuff?" Arthur asked.

Absolutely not. The drake huffed as he shook his head.

"You lying little shit," the woman started as she dashed for him again.

"I said hold up!"

The woman stopped dead in her tracks and her eyes grew wide. Arthur assumed she finally realized who was addressing her through her rage.

"Now. Miss…" Arthur dragged out.

"Tilly, Your Majesty." She said.

"Good. Miss Tilly. What happened?"

"Well, I woke up this morning and noticed the side of our tent was wet. I thought it might've rained outside, but the smell was something awful. When we got out of bed, our shoes and work clothes we left outside were also wet and stunk. It's only that one side of the tent that was affected, and it smells like that rotten lizard's pee." She finished as she poked a finger toward Balair.

"Show me," Arthur said, and she turned and led him away from the spot. Arthur saw Balair standing still and gestured for him to follow.

They arrived outside of the tent, and Arthur saw the large stain on the side. Judging by the smell, it was definitely Balair. Drake's piss had a hint of sulfur in it.

Arthur turned toward Balair after she waved toward the damage. "I thought you told me you didn't do this?"

I didn't. He answered.

"Well, I know it wasn't Cal, so you're the only other person it could be."

Nah. Drunk Balair did that.

"That's you, dipshit!" Arthur yelled.

Nope. Drunk Balair is an asshole and doesn't care about anyone's stuff. He also has a grudge against Sober Balair.

"For fuck's sake," Arthur grumbled as he ran a hand across his face. "It's too early in the morning for this nonsense."

"Miss Tilly. I'm sorry about this. Speak to the logistics manager and have them issue you a new tent and a set of work clothes. I'll take care of the drake problem for you." Arthur explained.

She thanked Arthur and rounded up the soiled supplies. Arthur turned and walked toward the perimeter of the village.

Get over here. He growled at Balair.

While Arthur waited for Balair to lumber down the path to him, Allendria walked up beside him.

"Bit of trouble?" She asked.

"Of the small Drake variety, yes."

Balair approached with his head downcast as he trundled along the path. When he arrived, he sat in front of Arthur.

"I saw you sneaking drinks from the people last night during the party and wanted to let you have a little fun. I didn't think it'd turn into this. From now on, no more drinking without permission. Understand?"

Okay. But I have one question.

"What?" Arthur asked.

Did a cat shit in my mouth last night?

Allendria and Arthur burst out laughing at the question. The two of them continued while Balair slunk away. When the laughter finally subsided, Allendria turned to Arthur.

"So, he got drunk last night? What did he do?"

Arthur gave her a quick summary of the events.

"And you didn't come to find me, so I could see it?" She pouted.

"I woke up to yelling and didn't know what was happening. You were up and out early this morning."

"Wanted to get a head start on some of the building. Ran into Wesley, though, and ended up listening to him for a while. He was preparing to head out with his cart. Now that it's empty, he said his trip back would be quick. Funny enough, he arrived about the same time you did here. Not sure how that is possible."

"Hmm. I'm not sure, either. Hopefully, there isn't another god trying to stir up trouble."

Allendria frowned at that thought.

"I guess we can only hope. Ready for work?" She asked.

"Might as well." Arthur agreed.

The two walked back to the perimeter and began their work on the village wall. Arthur watched Wesley's cart bounce along the dirt road in the distance, headed back to his clan.

The makeshift fortification in the distance drew Arthur's attention, and he saw soldiers still working at disposing of the corpses. A mage walked from pile to pile, feeding flame into the creatures to turn them to ash. The smell of burned flesh drifted in the wind as a nasty reminder of the bloodshed the day before.

Arthur's nose crinkled at the smell, so he used his Air Magic to blow the stench away from their camp. After that, Arthur focused on his magical training.

Like the day before, he spent time dual-casting opposing spells. He stuck with his Access Dimensional Storage spell since it was a decent experience for a low mana cost. There was nothing he could currently do about the cost of his wall spell. He already upgraded it through his talents.

The sun sped across the sky as he continued his work. It was the middle of the afternoon when Allendria finally drew close. Their walls finally met, and they both breathed a sigh of relief. She looked far more drained than Arthur felt.

"You okay?" He asked.

"Of course. That's a lot of magic to pour out in a day. Even taking breaks it is exhausting."

Arthur nodded at her explanation, and they walked along the wall. On their trek, Arthur stopped from time to time and lifted a small tower at gradual intervals. Each tower lifted another ten feet from the wall and featured a triangular roof and a short parapet around the platform. When the final tower was completed, they set to building the gatehouses.

Their original design was for a single gatehouse, but Arthur realized they needed at least one other exit from the place. There was no road leading through here, so they made a gate closest to the main dirt path that led to this area. The people who lived here could work toward raising the road out to intersect with the existing trail. With that gatehouse done, Arthur also created one closer to the rock wall so it could evacuate citizens if an attack came.

With the work complete, they walked back toward the village.

"I'm surprised you didn't take more time to talk to Wesley," Allendria said.

"I considered it but didn't want to overload him. It was overwhelming for me to find someone else from Earth. I'm sure he felt the same. I also don't want to get my hopes up just yet. This world is a dangerous place. If he can find us again after he proposes our trade agreement, I'll spend some more time with him." Arthur told her.

"Reasonable enough. I wonder how Zoe is getting along?"

"I hope she is fine back at the castle. Rayne is checking in on her. I asked him to make sure she didn't need help with anything. I'm sure the situation is difficult for her as well." Arthur said.

"Rayne's a good man. He'll take care of it." Allendria agreed.

* * *

Rayne walked down the hallway in Lord Preston's old manor. They had officially renamed it to the City Manor since it was primarily for government functions now.

Tapestries decorated the once bleak walls. They were a little threadbare and sported a few small holes, but they definitely livened the place up. The scent of soap now filled the halls from workers scrubbing the floors and walls clean.

The smell of food drew his attention as he approached the kitchen. Peeking in the doorway, he spotted Zoe flipping chunks of meat in a skillet. Meat was still scarce in town, but the hunting parties that Arthur set up were bringing in more daily. Rank had its privileges, so the City Hall could always scrounge up some. With Rayne being nominally in charge, that meant a better food selection.

Rayne approached and made sure he stood in her line of sight. She looked up and smiled at him.

He waved back to her. "How are you doing?"

She kept smiling, but she nodded as though she were fine. He still wasn't used to her not being able to hear. This led him to discover she could partially read lips.

"Do you need anything from me?"

She shook her head no.

Rayne waved to her and left the room. His thoughts drifted back to his sister in Alurian, and he idly wondered how she was doing. When he'd left, she seemed happy with her job at the inn. Hopefully, that hadn't changed in the time he was gone.

A small group of people chatted amicably in the main hall as he walked in. An older lady spotted him, separated herself from the group, and headed toward Rayne.

"Good morning, Lady Gemmalin," Rayne said with a quick bow.

"Why, hello young man. How goes the mission to build the freeholds?" She asked.

"I haven't received word from King Arthur yet. As soon as I do, I'll update the impromptu council. Any word on the restructuring of the textiles?"

"I've got the ladies arranged. Everyone is ready to get to work as soon as the supplies come in. We need cloth and leather before we can begin."

"I understand the dilemma. The hunters are bringing in what they can, but I'm sure Arthur will have a load of leather when he arrives. Are there enough tanners in town to handle the surge that will arrive?" Rayne asked.

"I arranged extra hands to be available. They are working to expand some tanks to handle more hides at once."

"Looks like you have everything in order," Rayne said.

She raised her hand to his cheek. "The key to old age is just acting like you have everything under control."

Rayne laughed. "I'll trust in your wisdom, then."

They said their goodbyes, and Rayne left
the manor house. Clouds covered the sky, and a
gray cast spread over the city. The dingy
light sucked the will out of him as he walked
the streets. He scanned his surroundings for
people before ducking into an alley.

Trash still littered the area, but it
wasn't nearly as dense as before. The
construction crews were doing their best to
clean up the roads as they fixed structures.
Rayne grabbed a throwing knife from his belt
and launched it into a shadow. A squealing
noise punctuated the area, and Rayne walked
over and pulled the knife from a dead rat.

*You dealt 25 damage to Rat with Throwing
Knife.*
Rat has died.

"Picking on the vermin now?" A woman's
voice drifted from the darkness further down
the alley.

"More like cleaning up the filth. All they
do is spread disease." Rayne shrugged.

"Is that what you're trying to do with us
as well?" She asked as she walked from the
shadows. Her curly hair perfectly framed her
face as she walked toward him. A tight leather
outfit hugged her curves, but he noticed
patches of fabric on the more mobile areas. It
not only looked great, but Rayne bet it also
masked some of her noise while moving.

"Have something for me, Scarlett?" Rayne
asked.

"A few of my little birds by the northern gatehouse heard some guards talking about a change in leadership. Sounded like they were planning on filtering in loyalists to their group and then making a move on the leadership. Might be worth checking out."

"I'll do that. Thank you for the information. Guess it's back to work for me." Rayne said as he turned to leave.

A hand grabbed his shoulder before he could walk away. He tensed at the contact, but it quickly lifted from him.

"Are you sure you can handle it by yourself?" Scarlett asked.

"Oh, I'm absolutely sure. I appreciate the concern. Take care, Lady Scarlett." Rayne said as he walked back out of the alley.

I sure hope she's right about this plot. I'd hate to end our agreement with her. She is quite pleasing to deal with for a thief.

* * *

Arthur and Allendria strolled out in front of the caravan. The city of Seora was visible on the horizon. Their trip had taken weeks, but it was fruitful in the end. The kingdom now had four fully functional farming villages producing food and one additional farming village for textiles.

The state-of-the-art villages were all
equipped with temperature-controlled fields.
Each house sported its own controls to keep
the place comfortable, and the inns had large
freezer spaces for storing food. Arthur also
took the time to make an additional cold
cellar in each village to store any root
vegetables. The work also resulted in enormous
boosts to his skills. He spent every bit of
time he could focus on his Dual Casting and
his Dimensional Magic.

*You have gained 11,290 total experience in
Dimensional Magic.*
*Congratulations, you have reached level 16
in Dimensional Magic. Decreases the mana draw
of dimensional spells by 36%. Too monotonous
to even bother with.*
*You have gained 9,650 total experience in
Earth Magic and Fire Magic.*
*Congratulations, you have reached level 24
in Fire Magic. Fire Magic spells now have a
69% increased effect. Can you please light
something on fire? Just for me?*
*You have gained 4,440 total experience in
Dual Casting.*
*Congratulations, you have reached levels 8
and 9 in Dual Casting. Decreases the mana draw
of dual-cast spells by 16%. You are such a
bore.*

A check on his Dual Casting Talents helped
him drop in his points. He used all his points
to max out Focused Core.

Focused Core (10/10)	Learn to focus your power and increase your mana efficiency. Reduces the casting cost penalty of dual casting by 2% per point.

It had been so long since he'd seen his Fire Magic talents that he pulled up the full sheet.

You have 2 unspent Talent Points.

Talent	Description
Tier 1	
Furious Fire (4/5)	Increases effectiveness of Fire Magic spells by 5%
Superheating (3/3)	Decreases the base mana cost of Arcane Forging spell by 5 mana per rank.
Flame Blade (0/1)	An ability that creates a blade of pure fire that is two feet long for 30 seconds. The blade deals damage based on Intellect. (Base damage = 0.75 x Intellect) Cost: 25 Mana Cooldown: 2 Hours
Tier 2	

Power of Flame (6/6)	*You gain a deeper knowledge of the Flame. This ability decreases the required mana for your fire spells by 5%. For every 2 ranks, you also gain 1 Intellect.*
Fan the Flames (0/5)	*This ability increases damage done by your offensive fire spells by 5% per rank.*
Tier 3	
Molten Fury (10/10)	*Increases the power of combination spells between Earth and Fire Elements by 3% per point.*
Flame Efficiency (4/10)	*All enchantments with the fire element cost 3% less mana per point.*
(Hidden Ability) Summon Crimson Whelp (1/1) *This ability will only become available if you have the following prerequisites:* • *Hidden*	*Allows you to summon a small crimson dragonling become your familiar. Your familiar will be summoned as a level 5 creature and can level up and learn skills. familiars stay until the summoner dismisses them or they are killed. If your familiar is killed, it can be resummoned after a 6-hour cooldown.*

	Cost: 150MP
Tier 4	
Power of Light (8/10)	Each point in this skill deepens your knowledge of fire magic and how it relates to light magic. You are required to have all 10 of these points to unlock light magic.
Flame Shield (0/5)	The first point in this talent unlocks the spell fire shield. Every point after the first increases its effectiveness by 5%. Fire Shield Summon a disc of fire that protects you from 40 ranged damage. Cost: 25MP Cooldown: 2 minutes
Familiar Growth (2/10)	Your familiar is a creature of fire. Each point in this ability will increase his size by 5%, attack by 3%, and Armor by 3%.

He was torn by his decision here. He only
had two points to spend, and these were
becoming more and more precious. On one hand,
he could beef up Balair some more using the
Familiar Growth talent. Balair was always on
his side and could use the stats. The only
thing holding him back was the Power of Light.
Two more points, and he could learn the
intricacies of Light Magic.

The debate warred in his head before he
decided the Light Magic was far more
beneficial. Especially when combined with his
other skills, such as Enchanting. He put his
two points into Power of Light.

*Congratulations, you have learned Light
Magic.*

*Congratulations, you have gained 250 bonus
experience for learning the spell Shine.*

Spell: Shine	
Requirements: Light Magic Mana Cost: 10 MP Cast Time: 0.2 seconds	Description: Emits a quick flash of bright light. Best used for distraction.
Mastery Level: 1	

I definitely need to level that skill up.
That reminded Arthur to dig through his
experience gains during their fighting. On
their trip, they'd run across numerous packs
of animals and used that chance to add to
their stores. The normal experience wasn't
much since the animals were much lower level,
but it greatly improved his skills.

You have gained 4,810 total experience in Throwing Knives.

Congratulations, you have reached levels 5, 6, and 7 in Throwing Knives. You now have 18% increased accuracy with Throwing Knives. You should try to hit an apple off someone's head.

You have gained 2,150 total experience in Swords.

You have gained 1,980 total experience in Small Blades.

You have gained 2,190 total experience in Dual Wield.

Congratulations, you have reached level 8 in Dual Wield. Accuracy penalty with off-hand weapons decreased by 21%. Your coordination sucks.

You have gained 1,245 total experience.

"When we get back to Seora, we need to consult with the lords and make sure that caravans are prepared to go pick up the food and transport it into town," Allendria said.

"Hopefully, they can do that without screwing things up. We'll need to make sure they have some way to do it. Last I checked, there aren't any beasts of burden there. They can't exactly pull wagons to and from the city." Arthur said as he looked at the sky.

"There are many ways around that. We could domesticate some wild animals?" She suggested.

"I'm sure we could, but that would take too long. I could create more golems as I did for our war supplies, but they won't last long enough, and I can't babysit every trip. Guess it's time to whip out some more magic."

"Magic?" she asked with a raised eyebrow.

Arthur smiled at the response and waggled his fingers. She laughed before lightly slapping his cheek. "That eventually gets old."

"You still laughed, didn't you?" He asked.
She grumbled at him, "I suppose so."
"Then it hasn't gotten old yet."
"Alright. But the magic?"
"Dimensional Magic. I can use it with my Enchanting. I'll just enchant Bags of Holding. The couriers can carry them, and it will help preserve the food, no matter the weather or conditions."

"You really want to entrust items that rare to regular people here?"

"Want is such a strong word. Necessity sometimes wins out."

"There has to be some way to limit their use. Can you Soul Bind the items? That way, only those assigned to the job can use it."

"I guess it might be possible. I'm not sure if it's the best idea. If I force them to bind the bags and someone wants it bad enough, they'll just kill them for it. Can't be bound to a dead person."

Allendria placed her finger on her chin in thought. "I haven't seen one personally, but I remember there is a distinction between how they work with Soul Bind. The best thing is to bind them to your head of commerce or whomever you have in charge of this endeavor. They can lend the bags to the couriers, and if anything happens to them, the bags reappear with them. There was a clever use of this a couple of decades ago. A courier was captured by an army approaching one of our villages undetected. They slipped in a note of warning and relinquished their hold over the item. It immediately returned to the owner, and they found the note. It saved a lot of lives."

"That's a great idea. We could even use them as instant messenger bags in the army. If I make a surplus, our scouts can take them and drop in notes. When ready, they relinquish control, and we instantly have them instead of having to wait on the round trip. Guess it means I'll need to keep hold of a large bundle of the leather for my use."

Allendria frowned at him. "You really think you have the time you need to make those bags? Enchanting them will take you long enough. I'd suggest you let the crafters do that work. Pay them to make the bags, but leave out the last of the stitching. You can apply the Enchantments and finish it up. They get paid for the work, and you can use your time more wisely."

Arthur leaned over and kissed her. "You always have the best ideas."

"Someone has to think around here."

Chapter 9

Sorting Seora

Arthur and Samson led the force toward the walls of Seora. Their remaining hunters and fighters were all coated in a thick layer of dust from their travels. Vana and Allendria walked forward to join the line at the front, and Arthur and Samson nodded to them both.

"Paladin Samson, care to announce us to the city? We return triumphant thanks to your leadership."

Samson glanced at him in a way that told Arthur he was trying to decide if he was being patronizing before he smiled and agreed. The force slowed their march while Samson took longer strides to gain distance. When he was a few dozen yards from the gate, he bellowed, "King Arthur Firebrand and company returning to the city!"

The guards on top of the gatehouse saluted before one turned and yelled at someone behind the wall. Within a few seconds, the gates slowly opened. The groaning of metal and timber punctuated every movement as the cumbersome doors spun and revealed a row of guards on either side. All of them faced the center of the road, and all stood at attention.

Samson stopped and waited for Arthur to approach and then matched his stride at his side. Allendria and Vana joined them, and the party of four walked through the doorway. The guards on the road all saluted as they passed. Arthur glanced backward and saw the other people with them straighten their backs and stand taller at the ceremonial greeting. At the end of the line of soldiers stood two familiar faces.

Rayne waited with Zoe in the middle of the road. He stood with his weight shifted on his right side, lightly tapping his toe. The dark leather somehow blending with the surroundings. Zoe stood by his side in a simple gown. Arthur wasn't sure where it came from, but wouldn't complain. The party stopped in front of the young man.

"Greetings on your return, My King. I trust everything went well?" Rayne said. His voice was a little shaky, and Arthur could tell he was slightly nervous in front of the crowd with this formal greeting.

Instead of dragging out his misery, Arthur stepped forward and clasped wrists with Rayne before pulling him in and wrapping an arm around his shoulder. After the quick embrace, he stepped back.

"It's good to see you, my friend. I trust everything is still in one piece since we left?" Arthur asked.

The stress dropped from Rayne's shoulders, and his posture relaxed. "I'm glad you're back. Things here are in order. How'd the trip go?"

"You missed all the fun," Vana chimed in. "We got to kill a boatload of orcs and even met a dwarven bard. Was a rather interesting trip. Oh, and we set up a handful of villages and killed a lot of animals for meat."

Rayne's face fell at the news. Arthur was sure it was because he missed out on the action. A loud thump punctuated the space as Balair landed next to them.

I'm done flying for now. I think it's nap time. He sent to the group.

"Lazy drakes. Almost worthless," Arthur said with a shake of his head.

The group laughed lightly before Arthur turned to Zoe.

How have you been since we left?

It's been refreshing having food. Rayne has done his best to check on me whenever he can.

That's great. Do you need anything right now?

No Sir. Dinner will be ready for you and Lady Allendria this evening. I've been practicing some simple dishes. I hope you like it.

I'm sure we will. I look forward to seeing what you can do.

The quick conversation ended, and Arthur saw Allendria, Vana, and Samson all greeting Rayne.

"Let's head back to the manor. We have some reports to make and a lot of supplies to unload. Can we send messengers out to gather the city leaders?" Arthur asked Rayne.

He nodded and walked to a nearby man. Rayne spoke a few quick words, and he scurried away. Arthur turned to face the rest of the group that had traveled with them through the trip.

"I thank every one of you for your hard work over the last few weeks. All showed bravery and courage in your fights, and your actions will be what helps the city of Seora get back on its feet. You are all dismissed and have the rest of the day and tomorrow off of duty."

The last statement sent smiles through the crowd, and many hooted in agreement before they all separated and found people in the crowds. Many embraced loved ones or found groups of friends to visit with. Arthur and his group left them all to their reunions and walked back toward the city manor.

I'm heading out to do some real hunting. Not interested in your boring meetings. Cal sent.

Can you take me with you? Arthur asked.

Good try. Have fun, Your Majesty. She sent with a smirk.

Think I'll join her. Then I'm going to find a pleasant spot for a nap. Balair added.

Arthur walked into the newly appointed City Manor and looked around. The dingy feel of the place was gone. People had worked hard to scrub everything clean. The old soot stains on the walls and even the ceiling were gone. The stone floors were almost shining. Even the seams in the stone were clean of excess debris.

"Place looks great," Arthur remarked.

"Much better than how run down it looked before." Vana agreed.

"I had a lot of extra hands around the city and little for them to do. I offered food in return for labor, and many jumped at the chance. The handful of hunters we scrounged up do a passable job at bringing in food. Not nearly enough to supply the city, but more than enough to supply this place and its labor force." Rayne told him.

"Sure you don't want to be a city administrator instead?" Arthur asked as he turned to smile at Rayne.

"No chance in hell. Much rather stick to the shadows."

"Good call." Arthur sighed. *Zoe, can you please excuse us? We have some private business to discuss prior to the city meeting.*

Of course. I'll start preparing for the meal.

Arthur lifted his hand to stop her. *Hold off on that. As much as I look forward to trying what you've come up with, I think we may host an impromptu feast tonight for the city. Care to plan that dinner for tomorrow?*

That works for me. She answered with a short curtsy and walked toward the back of the manor.

"She really has been working hard," Rayne said as he watched her walk away.

"It looks like it. I asked her to wait until tomorrow for that meal." Arthur said as his gaze rested on Allendria.

"She wasn't upset, was she?" Allendria asked.

"Not that I could tell. I told her we would probably host an impromptu feast for the city tonight. She seemed to understand the situation."

"So why send her off?" Samson asked.

"I wanted Rayne to tell us how his work has progressed in the city, and only the four of us are privy to that information," Arthur told him.

"Not to be indelicate, but she can't hear us…" Samson trailed off.

"That's correct, but I know she can passably read lips. Rather not take the chance." Arthur said.

"I can confirm she can read lips." Rayne agreed.

"Very well," Samson said.

"So, Rayne. How have things been since we left?" Allendria asked.

"The city is in about the same condition as when you left. We lost a few guards but nothing major. I contacted the criminal underworld and have a working agreement with them. I promised them immunity from petty crime as long as it's nothing overly heinous or dangerous to the city security. That relationship has already resulted in one beneficial tip," Rayne summarized.

"How did we lose guards?" Vana asked.

"Uh, well, I killed them," Rayne admitted.

"You did what?" Arthur asked in disbelief.

"Remember that beneficial tip I mentioned? The thieves' group told me a group of guards was planning a coup in the city. I acted on the info and investigated. After observing them for a while, I confirmed the report and confronted them. A handful attacked me, and I killed them. Their remaining friends quickly decided surrender was a better option. They are in the city dungeon waiting on your judgment."

Arthur let out a breath he didn't realize he'd been holding. "Thanks for handling that issue. I would've been pissed if someone held the city against us when we returned."

"They didn't have as much support as they thought. At best, they could have captured a manor until we drove them out. Either way, I wanted to take this out before it grew into a bigger problem."

"Good work," Samson said. "Arthur, would you mind turning over their punishment to me? They are under my command, after all."

"Feel free." He agreed.

"You mentioned some hunters. Did they find some more volunteers after we left?" Vana asked.

"Yep. About a dozen have shown up since you left. Many of them wandered in from the wilderness and found out about the change of leadership. Seems some of them have been camping out in the woods instead of taking their chances in town."

"I'd like to meet with them. If they can survive out there on their own, they must be good at what they do." Vana told him.

"The leader of the group should be here for the city meeting. You can talk to him about that. His name is Kenneth." Rayne said.

"Speaking of, we should probably get to the meeting hall. I'd imagine our guest should arrive before long." Arthur reminded.

Everyone nodded their heads, and they all left the room and headed for the meeting. It was only a few doors away in the hallway outside of their room, and they made it without issue. They entered through the back door and walked into a room with people already arranged around the table.

Arthur recognized those from the previous meeting. Lords Trip and Ealin sat on one side while Lady Gemmalin sat opposite of them. Theo and Clinton were present in the room, but there were more unfamiliar faces in the crowd.

"Welcome, everyone," Rayne began as the group filed in and took seats. "It looks like you all expected this and were ready to go."

A few chuckles echoed through the room before Rayne turned to Arthur.

"Your Majesty, I believe you know Lords Ealin and Trip as well as Lady Gemmalin. Masters Weer and Loore were also present during that meeting. I'd like to introduce Master Kenneth Wilde, the Head of the Hunt, Mistress Holly Tann, Master of Holds, Mistress Abby Quinn, Priestess of Lianna, and Lieutenant Pete Gruu, Nominal Captain of the Guard."

Arthur looked at each new arrival. Kenneth looked as Arthur expected. A rugged man with a thick, bushy beard, stiff tanned leather armor, and a wooden bow slung over a shoulder. White peppered through his dark black hair, showing some of his age.

Holly wore a simple gown but of fair quality. Neatly brushed light brown hair hung perfectly straight down the sides of her face. Green eyes bore into Arthur as he examined her.

Abby was a bit of a surprise. Arthur had run into a lot of different people during his time in Dravincia, but she was the first he'd seen with black skin. Naturally, the Dark Elves all had darker shades of purple, but this woman was a person of color similar to those on Earth. Her jet-black hair hung to the middle of her back, and she wore a long, flowing gown. Arthur idly wondered if there were more like her in the town and where she originated from.

The last person, Pete, Arthur recognized instantly. He was a guard that came with them from Alurian and an original member of their military force.

"Nominal Captain of the Guard?" Samson asked with a quirked eyebrow.

"We should make it official now that His Majesty is back," Rayne said with a nod.

"Not exactly what I was referring to…" Samson drawled.

"What's the confusion?" Rayne asked.

"I'm the Captain of the Guard," Samson said as his eyes bore into Rayne. To his credit, Rayne didn't even flinch.

"No offense meant Paladin Samson," Rayne assured him. It surprised Arthur how well Rayne navigated this situation. The young man was becoming quite the bureaucrat and putting on a fantastic show. "You hold the title of Captain of the Guard for Alurian and arguably Captain of the Guard for His Majesty's Royal Guard. I only intend to name Lieutenant Pete as the Captain of the Guard for Seora. I imagine you won't be staying here in a permanent position?" Rayne asked Samson.

"Of course. My apologies for the confusion. I wholeheartedly support the Lieutenant's bid as the Captain of the Guard for Seora. I left him in command while we were gone because he is a fine soldier." Samson said.

"So, what say you? Everyone in favor, raise their hand." Rayne said.

All the hands in the room went up except for Lieutenant Pete's. He looked like he wanted to hide in a hole somewhere and forget all of this mess.

Arthur smiled and walked to the soldier. He reached out and shook his hand. "Congratulations Lieutenant Pete Gruu. I name you the Captain of the Guard for Seora."

Pete Gruu has been named the Captain of the Guard. (Seora). While he is in the city, defending soldiers' morale is increased by 20%, Training time for defense skills is reduced by 10%, and archers can fire 10% faster if defending the city.

"Thank you, Your Majesty," Pete said as he finished shaking his hand, and Arthur walked back to the head of the table.

"Now to the matters at hand. Our mission was successful. While on our trip, we secured a sizable amount of supplies and established five fully functional farming homesteads. One of which is dedicated to textiles, primarily cotton and flax. Each of these homesteads has a fully defensible wall and gatehouse, well-provisioned and comfortable housing, a moderate guard force, and a mage dedicated to maintaining the place and assisting in the growth of the plants."

Looks of amazement filled the room, and the shock on each person's face resulted in deathly silence.

"Furthermore, we have brought back a large stockpile of herbs, wild vegetables, and wild game. When we have concluded our meeting, we will need work crews to unload and process these items. The wild vegetables and herbs will remain in the manor storage room to give us a chance to collect all the seeds and plant those that we can grow in the local gardens. We will distribute the rest for food. Are there any butcher shops in the city?" Arthur asked.

Lord Ealin nodded, "Yes, Your Majesty. There are three of them, but they aren't operational. There hasn't been enough game to process."

"Fix that for me, will you, Lord Ealin? Promise portions of food for service to any who can work the facilities. We have a very large surplus to work on. Try and recruit people who are higher level in skinning to skin the carcasses. I want as much of their hide intact as possible for Lady Gemmalin."

"I'll make it happen." Ealin agreed.

"Lord Trip, please work with Lord Ealin to set up distribution of these goods to the appropriate facilities. I know it isn't exactly mercantile, but this is a good start in returning some sense of commerce."

Lord Trip nodded.

"How will the people afford this food, Your Majesty?" Kenneth asked.

"Right now, they won't. I want to make something abundantly clear. This stockpile we brought back is not to be used for personal material gain. It is to be distributed and stockpiled as needed to help this city get back on its feet. Make sure each family gets a decent share, and we can pay any laborer in rations of food for the time being. When things have settled out, we will introduce commerce back into the city. Head of the Hunt, we will work to bolster your team so you can keep these supplies flowing into the city." Arthur said.

Kenneth stood straight and saluted. "Thank you, Your Majesty."

"No, thank you for asking. We are trying to pick this city back up, not squeeze it more."

"How will this work with the textile creation?" Lady Gemmalin asked.

"The same at first. We can pay all of your workers in rations. You can secure these from Lord Ealin upon reporting your total workforce numbers. I want you to prioritize warm clothing. I've noticed the weather getting more chill, so I assume winter is approaching?" Arthur asked.

"Yes, Your Majesty." Lady Gemmalin agreed.

"Then get people in warm clothing. I don't want them freezing and wearing the rags I've seen around. Our construction crews will work to address some of that with the housing, but the people need clothes, badly. Each citizen is to be given one set of clothing in leather for free. Anything past that, you can sell."

A sparkle lit her eye, and Arthur swore he saw a single tear escape and run down her cheek. It disappeared so fast he thought he might have imagined it.

"Mistress Holly, to clarify, your title, Master of Holds, does that refer to the city manors or our new freeholds?" Arthur asked.

"The new freeholds, Your Majesty," Holly said.

"Perfect. Organize some courier crews to haul the supplies from the freeholds to the city. The first ones should head out in three weeks. From there, we could probably run a courier once every week. If that isn't enough time for the freeholds to build up a stockpile to send back, then increase it to a courier every two weeks. The magical aspect of the freeholds should drastically increase yield and decrease growing time."

"Are there carts or anything we can use to haul these supplies? Some of those freeholds are almost a week from the city. It would require a large labor force to haul everything." Holly said with concern in her voice.

"It'll only take one person. I'd recommend they have traveling partners, maybe even a trained fighter or two with them. I'm going to make bags of holding specifically for the couriers. I will bond them to Mistress Holly, so if anything happens to those carrying them, the bags will return to her. Any person found in possession of a specially marked bag of holding without direct permission will face strict punishments. Anyone found to have harmed a courier to gain such a bag will face the death penalty. I will not tolerate theft of the supplies needed to run this city."

Looks of shock met Arthur's revelation. Bags of Holding were almost mythical. Only a few had been seen in the past few hundred years. So casually mentioning handing them out to couriers in mass must've sounded absurd.

"Do you have Bags of Holding, Your Majesty?" Lord Ealin asked.

"Not yet, but I plan on making some with a portion of the leather brought in. That reminds me," Arthur said as he turned his attention back to Lady Gemmalin. "Can you have a couple dozen bags made for me to prepare for this work?"

"Oh… uh sure." She said, shaken from her surprise.

"Does anyone have questions about anything?" Arthur asked.

"The supplies you gathered. Where are they?" Lord Trip asked. "We haven't seen any wagons with you."

"Just gather me a bunch of workers outside. We will get this all sorted and arranged. Lords Trip and Ealin and Lady Gemmalin, ensure you have storage locations prepared. I'll need access to some of your food storage facilities tomorrow. I have to install cold cellars to keep the food from spoiling. If anyone needs tools, let me know. I can create a handful quickly if need be," Arthur said.

Lady Gemmalin perked up at that. "Your Majesty, we have a very limited supply of cutlery for butchering and skinning animals. We also don't have many round knives or punches for our leather working. I also wouldn't turn down some decent quality needles."

Arthur smiled at her shopping list. *Give an inch and she'll try and take a mile.*

"I have a limited supply of metal with me to use, but I'll see what I can do. If you have any old or broken tools I can melt down, it'd help me produce more." Arthur said.

"I'll have the city searched," Lady Gemmalin agreed.

"If there is nothing else, let's head outside and get to work unloading supplies."

No one said anything, so Arthur walked over to Allendria and held out his hand. She rose from her chair and took his hand with a smile before they walked out at the head of the group. In the courtyard outside, he stopped and turned to the small crowd.

"Let's find space for this and get it unloaded," Arthur said, gesturing toward the empty courtyard.

Looks of confusion mixed with looks of anger. Apparently, some of them thought he was making fun of them or that he failed to find anything and led them on.

Instead of dragging out the situation, he started dual casting. Portals popped open all over the courtyard. A few of the storage spaces were packed so tight that boars fell from the doorway as soon as they snapped open. The crowd now looked properly surprised. Some onlookers fell to their knees and cried at the sight of so much food on hand.

You have gained 1,800 total experience in Dimensional Magic.
You have gained 400 total experience in Dual Casting.

Arthur walked over to the first of the three dozen storage spaces and reached in. He couldn't see the back because of the animal carcasses crushed together like a gory Jenga puzzle. Each of these spaces was roughly the size of a small U-Haul truck from back home.

His hand wrapped around the leg of a particularly husky boar and pulled. It popped free and spilled a few other carcasses across the courtyard.

"Lady Gemmalin, where do the animals need
to go for processing?" Arthur asked.

"Your Majesty," she said in shock, "What
are you doing? Such a task is beneath you."

"Nonsense. No task is beneath a king. A
king who isn't willing to do the jobs it takes
to run a kingdom has no business ordering
others to do those same tasks. Now, where to?"

Lady Gemmalin looked like she would protest
further, but she must've seen the serious set
of his jaw and let it go. Instead, she ushered
him out of the courtyard and down a street.
They turned into a sturdy-looking building.
The bottom portion of the wall was neatly
stacked with stone, and the top two-thirds of
the wall was close-fitted wood. Inside were
large wooden tables and countertops, all
cleaned to a glistening polish.

Arthur dropped his animal on the first
counter and turned to head back. He saw the
line of people carrying more animals trailing
behind him. Men and women hefted deer and boar
carcasses. Arthur's smile grew wider when he
saw a handful of children carrying smaller
game. Squirrels and rabbits made wonderful
stew, and the soft pelts could make warm
clothing.

His mind wandered while he went about the
monotonous task of hauling dead animals,
plants, vegetables, herbs, and a plethora of
other supplies around. He remembered the
talents for his combat skills he forgot to
spend. The knowledge of them approaching the
city distracted him, and he forgot to assign
those points. With that in mind, he started by
pulling up his Throwing Knives tree.

You have 6 unspent Talent Points.

Talent	Description
Tier 1	
True Sight (0/5)	*Increases your accuracy with Throwing Knives by 5% per point.*
Chain Reaction (0/10)	*Each point allows you to palm an extra knife without affecting your throws. You can hold up to 11 knives at once and throw in rapid succession if you invest all 10 points.*
Enhanced Reflexes (0/1)	*Increases your perception speed and allows you to better chose the target for your throw. Consumes Stamina during the increased speed.* *Stamina Use: 15/second*

The options were interesting, but there was no way he was passing up Enhanced Reflexes. That sounded like slow-motion aiming from some of the crazy action games. The five remaining points all went into Chain Reaction. His accuracy wasn't terrible, but being able to throw more knives faster would be a big win.

His next set of talents to review was Small Blades. He realized he never spent his last two points.

You have 2 unused Talent Points.

Talent	Description
Tier 1	

Bleeding Strikes (0/5)	Wounds caused by Small Blades will deal 4% additional bleed damage per point.
Blurring Speed (0/5)	Attack speed with Small Blades increase by 3% per point.
Riposte (1/1)	If any of your attacks are parried, you are able to activate this skill for a guaranteed hit with your Small Blade. Cooldown: 45 seconds
Tier 2	
Twist (0/10)	Each point causes wounds inflicted by Small Blades to deal 3% additional damage.
Blade Weaver (7/10)	Increases your chance to parry blows with Small Blades by 2% per point.

Might as well stick with the defense build and put the two points into Blade Weaver. Finally, he looked into Dual Wield.

You have 2 unused Talent Points.

Talent	Description
Tier 1	
Off-Hand Power (0/5)	Increases damage of your off-hand weapon by 5% per point.

Deflection (5/5)	Increases your chance to successfully parry by 5% per point.
Arm Strength (0/5)	Increases damage of your main hand weapon by 5% per point.
Tier 2	
Off-Hand Coordination (0/1)	Allows you to use a full-size weapon (IE sword) without additional penalties to off-hand speed or accuracy.
Main-Hand Dexterity (1/10)	Increases swing speed with main hand weapon by 3% per point.

Think I'll drop those two into Main Hand Dexterity.

With the skills sorted out, he let the work drown his thoughts into the evening.

Chapter 10

Enchanting in the City

Arthur started his morning fulfilling promises. He sought Lady Gemmalin, and she led him to the storage rooms. The large warehouses were cylindrical and reminded Arthur of farm silos driving through the small cities back in Texas.

Shelves lined the walls from top to bottom, and a single ladder stood propped up, reaching all the way to the top. Instead of worrying about the room itself, he activated his Earth Magic and delved his power into the ground. In quick fashion, he carved a spiral staircase below ground and then leveled the floor out. The dirt melted in front of him as it peeled back and created stone. The walls and ceiling formed, and a few pillars of stone helped hold the ceiling's weight.

When all was said and done, a new underground cellar spread out in front of him. The space encompassed nearly a thousand square feet. It took a few of his enchanted temperature controls to keep the entire space cold enough. He designed this room to get gradually colder as you reached the back. When first walking in, it felt more like standing in a refrigerator, and by the time you reached the back, it was the chill of a deep freezer.

"This should suffice," Arthur told Lady Gemmalin as she walked down the stairs to observe his work.

"I'd say so. Bit of a surprise you finished so soon. I was only gone for a little over an hour."

"I've done this enough to move quickly. Try and keep your root vegetables closer to the stairs and meats farther toward the back. It is colder back there and will preserve it better."

"I'll keep that in mind. I have to find some shelving for this space to make it easier to organize, and I'll hire some staff to keep track of the supplies here." Lady Gemmalin said.

"Just make sure they know not to stay down here for prolonged periods of time. It can seriously harm and possibly kill them."

"I'd imagine so. I'm pretty sure they've been through enough winters to understand that." Gemmalin smiled.

Of course, they understand cold. Arthur scolded himself.

"How many more storage buildings are there?" Arthur asked.

"Four more like this and two that are smaller. Do you plan on doing this for them all?"

"Might as well. All it costs is some mana for those maintaining it and working here. It could help keep lots of food from spoiling and causing even more of a shortage."

Lady Gemmalin agreed, and they moved on to the next building. They continued that pattern for the rest of the morning, and around midday, Arthur finally breathed a sigh of relief as he finished the last storage space.

"I can't thank you enough, Your Majesty. Others may not understand the importance of this, but it isn't lost on me. We should have the first shipments of processed meat come in today. They've been working on it most of the night. Those few cooling devices you left with them have kept the carcasses fresh so far, but we can't let it linger."

"It would suck to get all that meat only for it to spoil."

"I'll have everything ready for the feast tonight." Lady Gemmalin said.

"Thank you, My Lady," Arthur said with a curt bow. "I planned to do it last night, but everyone worked late into the evening, and there wasn't time."

"It's fine. The people were thrilled seeing all the supplies. Individual portions were handed out last night for the citizens, so they should be well-fed for today's work. The feast tonight should help raise their spirits higher."

"Then I look forward to the feast. I'm going to run and check in with Samson to make sure nothing needs my attention, and then I'll get to work on those tools you requested."

"I still can't thank you enough. I had a load of scrap metal dumped near the city manor for you to work with. Good luck." She said as she reached up and patted his cheek.

Arthur smiled and headed back to the city hall. The people he passed appeared in higher spirits. Smiles decorated their faces, and some children scurried around. They laughed and played without a care in the world. Arthur stopped in the center of one of the major intersections and just soaked in his surroundings. Just a few weeks ago, this was nothing but a pit of despair. Now joy and laughter riddled the street.

You look like an idiot standing there with your head looking up and eyes closed. Balair huffed.

Arthur cracked an eye and spotted the small drake circling overhead.

It's barely noon. Isn't it far too early for you to be awake? Arthur asked.

Ain't that the truth? I was sleeping near the city hall, and all the noise woke me up. Decided on a quick flight to stretch out. Thought I might go hunting while I'm at it.

Hmph. That sorry excuse for a dragon couldn't hunt anything larger than a house cat. He's too fat and lazy. Calfuray butted in.

Good to see you too, Cal. Arthur sent as he watched the purple streak on the horizon glitter in the sunlight.

That's rude as hell. What did I do to you? Balair said.

You tarnish the reputation of dragons everywhere with your mere presence. Nothing but low-class filth.

Alright, you two. That's enough of this same old argument. Either of you doing anything productive today?

Some hunting and some scouting, I suppose. Cal said.

I guess I can as well. Balair said in what almost sounded like a whine.

Then get to work. I've got some smithing to do. Arthur said.

Anything is better than what you were doing before. Cal agreed.

Really, you too?

We can't all stand around basking in the sunlight. Cal told him.

Arthur didn't even bother responding and just continued his trek toward the city center. As soon as he arrived, he searched for Samson. The large Paladin was nowhere to be found, but he did find Rayne.

"You know where Samson is?" Arthur asked.

"He is at the city dungeon taking care of the guards who were plotting the coup. Passing judgment, I suppose." Rayne said.

"Definitely not going to bother him while he's doing that. Do you know of anything going on that might need my attention before I go hide and do some crafting?" Arthur asked.

"Sure don't. Have fun. I'll keep whoever I can from bothering you unless it is urgent." Rayne said.

"Thanks. You're a lifesaver." Arthur told him.

They shook hands, and Arthur scurried around the building. He found the pile of scrap metal in the back of the building and set to work. Without a proper forge in operational condition, it forced him to use pure magic to work the metal, so it drained him faster than normal. The feeling of accomplishment when the pile of rusty and battered metal was arranged in a neat stack of fresh ingots left him refreshed.

When the metal was prepped, he started with
the leather working tools. While the regular
butcher knives were important, he knew the
city had a bunch of usable knives for that.
Almost everyone carried at least some kind of
small personal blade. Many of them were pitted
and old, but they were still functional. He
also planned on making the butcher blades as
well, anyway.

His Arcane Smithing gave him the
opportunity to make these tools as intricate
as he wanted. It took marginally little extra
effort, and the mana cost was nearly the same.
Still, he went with plain tools. No special
ornamentation or design work. Handing out
fancy equipment usually only led to jealousy
and expectations of more. It could also
stagnate the local economy when it finally
restarted.

Smiths and leather workers would return as
the supplies came in, and he didn't want them
to feel that they needed to compete with his
fancy tools. It could create destabilization.

The problem Arthur had was the handle.
Finding wood wouldn't be a big deal, but
finding people who had the knowledge and tools
to shape it fast enough for his purposes was
almost impossible. It would also take special
resins and glue to connect it all.

Instead of dwelling on that problem, he determined to fix it with a design. Typically, he'd create a long, tapered tang that would slide into the handle, and then you could heat and peen the end over on it. Since that took too long, he cheated with modern technology, similar to how he had done before. He threaded the end of the tang into a rod and created small nuts with a rounded end on them. This would allow him to slide on a handle and just screw it tight instead of having to do the extra steps. It also made it easier to replace damaged handles in the future.

The round knives for Leatherworking came first, and the dozen of them were quick to make. The blades themselves looked rather large, but it was because they were very thin. It didn't require a lot of material in metal for those. He made a dozen punches to go with them and then created a small box full of needles.

Butcher utensils were next. His magic took hold, and the metal melted and formed into shape as the wave of power passed through. A hefty cleaver dropped into the dirt with a muffled thump. A few minutes later, a neat stack of them joined the first. Small paring knives and regular-sized kitchen-style knives joined them. Arthur even took the time to create a hunter's skinning knife, like back home, complete with a gut hook. Since he had a surplus of extra metal, he made three dozen of those to give out to the hunters in the city.

When all the metal was finally in its proper shape, he moved on to the wood. A stack of old firewood lined the back wall of the manor, and while not the best option, it would work for what he needed. He picked each piece up, and any that were thick enough, he cast a spell on. The heat surrounded them and sucked the moisture from the wood.

The neat stack of dried wood quickly transformed into a stack of wooden rods that he created using his Arcane Woodworking skill. Cone of Sanding and the Sanding Wheel spells quickly transformed the rods into a smooth shape and allowed him to set the exact size for each type of knife.

Some controlled Fire Magic let him bore the center hole out to slide them onto their respective tangs, and a few twists of the nuts locked them in place. When he completed the first of the hunting knives, he received an unexpected notification.

Congratulations, you have completed a Blacksmithing project that features a unique design element not before seen in Dravincia. Do you wish to name this element? Yes/No.

Arthur selected *Yes* and named it Gut Hook since that was what it was called where he was from.

This new feature, Gut Hook, has been evaluated and will give the following benefits to items it is on.
- *10% increased skinning speed.*
- *5% decrease in leather wasted or ruined while skinning.*

That was a nice benefit. Who would've thought something as simple as a gut hook on a knife was never thought of here?

A wave of his hand opened a small Dimensional Storage space, and he stuffed it with the new tools. Presenting them at the feast would be a good show of faith in his confidence for the future of the city. Work finally done, Arthur took a moment to check the progress he'd made in his skills.

You have gained 500 total experience in Dimensional Magic.

You have gained 18,420 total experience in Earth Magic.

You have gained 24,110 total experience in Fire Magic.

You have gained 11,720 total experience in Blacksmithing and Arcane Smithing.

Congratulations, you have reached level 18 in Arcane Smithing. Increases the stats on items created using this ability by 34%. That was a lot of junk you transformed.

You have gained 1,400 total experience in Dual Casting.

Congratulations, you have reached level 10 in Dual Casting. Decreases the mana draw of dual-cast spells by 18%. Can you do anything without needing to multitask?

You have gained 2,300 total experience in Enchanting.

You have gained 2,890 total experience in Woodworking and Arcane Woodworking.

Congratulations, you have reached levels 2, 3, and 4 in Woodworking. Decreases the material waste when crafting by 6%. Just had to play with your wood?

Congratulations, you have reached levels 2, 3, and 4 in Arcane Woodworking. Decreases the mana cost of Arcane Woodworking spells by 9%. Can you do anything that doesn't require sand?

The level gain in Arcane Smithing was welcome, and he looked at the full talent tree.

You have 2 unused Talent Points.

Talent	Description
Tier 1	
Eye for Quality (5/5)	Each point increases the chance of the quality of the items you create increasing by one by 5%.
Unlock Steel (1/1)	Teaches you the secrets of forging steel with magic.
Granular Structure (5/5)	Each point increases the amount of armor on items you create by 4%.
Tier 2	
Material Savings (0/10)	Each point decreases the material needed to make items by 3%.
Will of the Many (5/5)	Each point increases the amount of items made when forging multiple items at once by 10%.
Tier 3	

Embellishments (0/10)	Allows the smith to embellish items created using different materials. Different materials will grant additional bonuses to the pieces made. Each point invested in this skill increases the bonus granted by embellishing by 5%.
Mana Saturated (9/20)	Teaches you how to infuse mana into your work to increase latent magical ability and increase set bonus attributes. When you have invested all 20 talent points, you will unlock the talent to make Magesteel.
(Hidden Talent) Soul Bond (1/1) Requirements: • Blacksmithing > 10 • Arcane Smithing > 10 • A Familiar Bond	Allows a smith the ability to soul bond a suit of armor with a wearer. This soul bond enhances natural skills of the wearer to further enhance the armor. Soul bound armor can only be worn by the one bound. A smith with this talent may remove the bond from a wielder.

Looking over the options, Arthur really wanted to get Magesteel unlocked, so he dumped his two points in Mana Saturated.

Dual Casting now had two more points available, so Arthur glanced at the Tier 2 options.

Tier 2	
Arcane Control (0/10)	*Every 5 points invested in this talent expands your control of mana and allows you to cast an additional spell at the same time.*
Pain Threshold (0/5)	*Decreases the likelihood of backlash from interrupted spells by 10% per point.*
Overload (0/1)	*Overload your magical system to allow you to cast two spells at 300% power together.* *Warning: Use of this ability will damage your mana channels, leaving you unable to use magic for 24 hours.*

Overload was a straightforward decision. It was one of those telltale save your ass in an emergency spells. The idea of casting three or four spells at the same time also sounded great, so Arthur dropped the second point in Arcane Control.

  With his talents sorted, Arthur changed his focus and walked back into the manor. Servants scurried around, cleaning and hauling goods and food. Looking out one of the front windows revealed a large crowd of people, all working hard at their tasks. Some hauled buckets of water, others carried chunks of meat or herbs. No one was idle, and everyone was at their task.

  "You finally done playing around?" Rayne asked as Arthur entered the main hall.

  "Someone has to make the tools around here. What've you been doing? Sneaking around with a purpose?" Arthur asked with a smirk.

  "I wish. Slinking around alleys is preferable to dealing with the hustle and bustle of city management." Rayne grumbled.

  "I truly appreciate the work you've done. You seem to be a natural for this type of work."

  "Thanks, Arthur. It is satisfying in its own way. I was stuck here in this unfortunate situation with some of these people at one time, and it's truly rewarding being the person helping them. Before, I felt helpless and was merely trying to survive."

  Arthur clapped the young man on the shoulder and squeezed at his statement. Rayne nodded in appreciation before they both stood straight and returned to business.

  "Everything ready for the feast tonight?" Arthur asked.

"Lady Gemmalin and Lord Ealin have worked hard to get everything ready. It looks like the occasion will be grand tonight. The mages walked through the courtyard and raised stone benches and tables, since most of the wooden ones are damaged or too cumbersome to move. They can use magic to push the seating back into the ground afterward." Rayne said.

"You ready for the feast, Arthur?" Samson asked as he walked up to the two men.

"We were just discussing the preparations," Arthur agreed. "Looks like everything is set, and it shouldn't be long until it kicks off."

"Don't let Rayne fool you. I've seen him scurrying all over and talking to Lady Gemmalin and Lord Ealin, constantly making sure everything was in place and ready. He likes to try and deflect the attention to others." Samson said with a laugh.

"Oh, I'm well aware of our young thief's tactics. I think misdirection is his game, after all. Has anyone seen Vana or Allendria?" Arthur asked.

"Both are in the courtyard of the nearby manor. The place is abandoned right now, and Vana wanted to get some training in. She asked Allendria to help her. Each is trying to work through some weaknesses. Allendria wants to learn how to better fight ranged fighters with her magic, and Vana wants to practice fighting mages. Was a bit of a win for both." Samson said.

"Well, gentlemen, care to go watch a fight?" Arthur asked.

"Sounds like a plan, but not sure gentleman actually applies to me," Rayne joked.

"Would be a pleasant break. Think I'll join you." Samson said.

The three exited the manor and walked through the courtyard. They had to weave around the newly raised benches and dodge the occasional servant hauling food. Arthur knew he didn't have to move for them, but felt it was the right thing to do.

They turned the corner once outside the small wall, and Samson led them toward another large manor. The gate on this one hung from a single hinge and was propped open. The wooden shingles on the roof had signs of dry rotting on them, and he assumed it leaked. It was no wonder this place was abandoned if it wasn't protected against the weather.

Flashes of light lit the air as they approached, but they couldn't see the action on the other side of the wall. When they finally reached the decrepit gate, Arthur saw the battlefield beyond. Small burn marks littered the entire area where Allendria's fire magic hit, and training arrows dotted the landscape. Vana took the time to remove the arrowhead and put small stones on them. They would still sting, but less likely to puncture and kill.

Allendria was also pulling her punches, so to speak. Instead of her normal beams of fire and large AOE spells, she was limiting herself to quick bursts of tiny flame darts. It probably made it more difficult on Vana, since Allendria could pump the small projectiles out so much faster than her more powerful forms. When one of them met with an exposed piece of skin on Vana's arm, the skin sizzled and turned a bright red. The grimace on Vana's face showed they still hurt.

Both continued to dance around the courtyard, Vana launching arrows and Allendria blasting out with small fire darts. The speed the two women moved was incredible. Allendria stumbled on one of her turns and was rewarded with a stone arrow to the shoulder. She rolled with the hit and came up with hands spread. Five of the small fire arrows shot forward and sizzled through the air. Vana's eyes widened before she dove toward the ground and landed on her stomach.

Allendria raced for the ranger, but Vana leaped back to her feet and launched an arrow at her. The dark elf sidestepped the shot and closed in the distance. She withdrew a small dagger from her waist and stopped when the blade was an inch from Vana's throat.

"Looks like this round is mine," Allendria said with a smile around her heavy breathing.

"Are you so sure?" Vana asked with a quirked eyebrow. Her eyes traveled down, and Allendria followed her gaze. Vana had her dagger resting right against Allendria's chest, directly in front of her heart.

"I think we'll call it a draw." Allendria agreed.

The two ladies laughed and turned to see they had an audience.

"Enjoy the show, boys?" Vana asked.

"It was impressive." Samson agreed.

"Oh, you hear that, Allendria? The Paladin thinks we are impressive. That's high praise from him." Vana joked.

Samson's face turned red at the comment, causing Allendria to smile at his discomfort.

"We wanted to come see your training. That and I was killing time until the feast. Rayne was trying to duck away from some admin duties, and I'm sure Samson is dodging work as well." Arthur told them.

"Really? Everyone is skirting work except you, our mighty king." Vana quipped.

"Nope. I'm definitely ducking work myself, but I finished up the cold cellars and a bunch of the tools. I plan on presenting them during the feast. We should probably head back and get cleaned up before we eat. Not to be indelicate, but you too look a little… grimy would probably be the best word." Arthur said.

"I'm glad you said it," Rayne whispered. "I wasn't about to step into that trap."

Arthur grimaced as he noticed the two ladies lock their gazes on him. Their expressions turned cold as ice, and Arthur had to avert his eyes.

"I guess us dirty ladies can entertain our king's request and clean up." Vana quipped.

"I didn't mean it like that." Arthur huffed.

Everyone's face morphed into a smile before turning into laughter. The group left the old manor and headed off to prepare for the feast.

Chapter 11

A Feast

Arthur emerged from the archway and immediately hopped backward. He barely missed the young boy, who zipped past carrying a large tray of food. People rushed down the hall from the kitchen area to the front door, carrying large wooden trays piled full of roasted meats and vegetables.

Inserting himself in a gap between people, Arthur followed the crowd out of the front door and into the courtyard. He stepped off to the side to get out of the way and give him a chance to watch over the crowd.

Everyone sat on stone benches, arranged in neat lines and placed throughout the entire courtyard. Every table seemed to be packed full except for one near one wall. That one was larger, and it sat on a slightly elevated platform. Samson sat in one chair. The Paladin looked happy as he talked to Vana, seated right next to him. Rayne and Zoe were close to the other end of the table in their own conversation.

The meal itself was primarily meat, since that was their major stockpile from the hunting. The crops would take a month to start arriving in decent quantities. None of that deterred the people. They were all stuffing their faces with as much food as they could shovel down.

Arthur walked through the crowd, headed toward the large table on the wall, and watched with fascination. Some people were eating so fast that their cheeks bulged out, and they never finished chewing before the next piece followed. A few of the children looked at the food in disbelief and stared with glossy eyes forward as they slowly savored each bite. Tears were not an uncommon sight as people closed their eyes, and the small puddles of water slid down their cheeks with their slow chewing.

The view brought Arthur a sense of joy while also a huge weight of depression. The thought of what these people suffered to have this kind of reaction was heartbreaking. It didn't matter that he wasn't the cause of their trouble. It was the fact they had to suffer it.

When he was halfway to the table, a voice called out to him.

"Is this cleaned up enough for you?"

Arthur smiled at Allendria's voice and turned to face the direction it originated. His smile faltered, and he almost tripped when he laid eyes on her. Someone neatly braided her long hair in a French-style braid down her back. She wore a deep red dress that hugged her hips, and the neckline plunged down to show a fair amount of cleavage on her dark skin. The bottom of the dress was cut to look like flames licking up from the ground, and the colors faded from red to orange and then to a light blue as his eyes traveled down.

"Well, don't you look hot?" Arthur said.

She rolled her eyes at the poor joke but went along, anyway. "Naturally. I have to represent my people here. It helps to make an impression."

"I'm sure no one will forget that dress. You think it looks as good on the floor?" Arthur asked as he turned toward her with a wicked grin.

"I swear we can't go anywhere nice with you," she said with a light slap on his shoulder. "But I'm happy to test that."

The two laughed and continued toward the table. They walked up a short set of stairs to the small platform. When Samson and Vana turned to acknowledge them, they stopped.

"You two having a good night?" Allendria asked.

"Pleasant enough. It's nice to be off duty for once," Vana said.

"Well, I think we are going to head home soon. This place is currently on the right track, and we have pressing matters to tend to. I'm worried about the dark elves striking toward Alurian and want to return. After tonight, make preparations to leave. We need to have the command structure intact before we go." Arthur said.

"It'll be good to go home. I'm not afraid to admit I'll be excited to see the place. This city has changed so much in the weeks we've been here, and it doesn't have half the resources or skilled people as Alurian. I'll be surprised if we recognize the place." Samson said.

"Hadn't thought it of that way. Now I'm excited to get back. Let's plan for departure in three days. That should be enough time to solidify positions in the city and prepare to leave." Arthur said.

"Shouldn't be a problem," Samson agreed.

"Now, we're off to eat. You two behave and don't do anything I wouldn't do." Arthur told them with a smile.

"I doubt that's a long list," Allendria muttered, and Samson and Vana laughed.

Arthur and Allendria took their seats and enjoyed the food. The seared meats were plump and juicy. *Whoever cooked them must have a decent cooking level.* The small platter that a young man sat on the table for him pleased him even more. A few potatoes were on the small tray, roasted and sprinkled with some kind of herb. He bit into the first chunk, and it practically melted in his mouth. A few pieces later and a message popped up.

You have gained the Well Fed buff. You regenerate 5 Stamina every 20 seconds for the next 4 hours from eating Herb-Roasted Potatoes.

Looks like I need to find the cook and try to convince them to travel with us if they can make some buffing food.

"This food is great," Arthur said to Allendria.

"It is the best I've had in a long time. I wonder which cook made it?"

The two continued eating until they finished and watched the crowd. Many people looked full and content. Arthur went to lean back to relax, only to remember these benches had no backs. In a flash of magic, he poured in power and extended stone from the back of the seat to make a backrest. He wrapped his arm around Allendria, and they leaned back into the rest.

Rayne and Zoe approached them from the end of the long bench.

"Did you enjoy your dinner?" Zoe asked.

"It was fantastic," Arthur said.

"Best I've had in a while," Allendria agreed.

"I'm glad you think so. I wanted to cook for you before now, but we've been too busy. The chef agreed to let me cook your dishes since we had to skip our dinner together." Zoe said shyly.

"You made this?" Arthur asked in astonishment.

"Sure did. I've been practicing a lot while you were gone. Cooking for the work crews helped me increase my cooking skill. It's all the way up to fourteen now. It's hard to get much higher because of our limited ingredients. Most things are too simple to give me much experience."

"Well, that might be remedied soon. Care to sit for a minute?" Arthur asked as he gestured to the empty bench across from them.

Rayne and Zoe took a seat, and Arthur continued by bringing them into a mental chat together. *We are leaving Seora in three days and heading back to Alurian.*

That's fantastic. I can't wait to see my sister again. It feels like it's been a lifetime. Rayne said with a smile.

Zoe looked somewhat conflicted as Arthur watched her expression slowly shift.

I want you to know that you don't have to go with us. Arthur told her. *We will be happy to have you, but if you decide you want to stay here, we will set you up in a permanent position at the manor. Lady Dalia will take over the day-to-day management of this city when we send her from Alurian.*

The expression shifted a few more times before a look of resolve settled over her features. *I'd like to go with you. I think it'll be better for my long-term growth.*

Then consider yourself warned. Make sure you have any personal business taken care of and be ready to leave in three days. Arthur told her.

Arthur broke out of his focus on their mental speech and noticed Rayne and Allendria carrying on a separate conversation and talking about Alurian. He let them continue and scanned the gathering. The good mood settled into the crowd, and he even noticed Lady Gemmalin wandering through the people and talking to everyone. Her pleasant demeanor blended in well and made her popular.

The time felt right, so Arthur stood from his place and walked to the front of the raised platform. He lifted his arms and called over the crowd. "Good evening, ladies and gentlemen."

The crowd all turned to face him, and their expressions were a mixture of contentment and interest.

"I want to thank all of you for your hard work in making this happen. We had a great trip out of the city and set up numerous villages that will be key to this city's prosperity. Many of your fellow citizens went out and proved themselves during our expedition. They will be instrumental in the continued success of this place."

Some of those very people sat straighter as he mentioned their dedication. Eyes shone with pride as others looked around with expressions of gratitude for their sacrifice.

"I will depart Seora in three days' time and head back to Alurian. Any who wish to travel with us are welcome, but you must be willing and able to contribute to the town's prosperity and its defense. I don't want any of you to worry about Seora. We will ensure things are properly arranged before we leave so this city can rise from the ashes. With that in mind, Lady Gemmalin, will you approach?" Arthur asked, seeing the woman standing near the edge of the crowd.

She looked surprised at his request, but she walked over to stand in front of him.

"To show my confidence in this city and its people, I would like to present Lady Gemmalin with some gifts to distribute," Arthur said as he waved his hand and made one of his storage spaces appear. He took his time and removed one of the round knives, a punch, and a butcher knife and handed them to her.

"I have a dozen of each of these for you that I will deliver tomorrow. For now, I present you with these examples of the tools you will receive."

The older lady took them in her hands and bowed slightly. She was no stranger to official presentations and knew her role.

"I pledge to do my best to use these items in a manner befitting the prosperity of the city." Lady Gemmalin intoned.

"I thank you for your hard work, and I name you Mistress of Textiles," Arthur said as he smiled at her and bowed slightly back to her. *He was just happy the system acknowledged his statement, even though he didn't know her first name.*

Gabriella Gemmelin has been named the Mistress of Textiles. (Seora). While she is in the city, you produce textile crafts 10% faster with 10% less waste.

The gesture wasn't lost on her, and she winked at him before walking back toward the edge of the crowd.

"Master Wilde, please approach," Arthur called.

The Master of the Hunt seemed more shocked than Lady Gemmalin and slowly rose from his table. He walked over and stood in front of Arthur, but his stance made him look far more like a wild animal, ready to bolt at a moment's notice.

"I appreciate your dedication to helping feed the city and want to present you with these," Arthur started as he reached into the storage space and produced the dozen hunting knives. The woodsman's eyes grew wide as he took in the fine blades.

"Use them well to fulfill your duty. In addition, I hereby name you as the Master of the Hunt for Seora." Arthur said.

Kenneth Wilde has been named the Master of the Hunt. (Seora). While he is in the city, your hunters move 10% faster through wooded areas and have a 5% increased chance of finding game animals. When he leads the hunt, this rises to 15% and 10%, respectively.

Kenneth looked shocked at the pronouncement but immediately dropped to a knee and bowed his head.

"I won't fail you, Your Majesty."

"It's not me you would fail. Don't fail your fellow citizens." Arthur said.

Kenneth's eyes shone with tears as he nodded, and Arthur dismissed him. The crowd looked excited with all the announcements, and Arthur soaked up the feeling. He considered naming Lords Ealin and Tripp to their positions, but decided to wait and ensure they would make good use of their authority first. They hadn't really been tested yet. Rayne vouched for Kenneth and the food he'd found while he'd seen Lady Gemmalin work harder than anyone since he'd returned to get things back to normal.

"Everyone, enjoy the rest of your night! I have one more special surprise to go along with it." Arthur closed his first dimensional space and opened another larger one. He walked in and rolled out two of the barrels of ale.

"Some ale will warm the soul tonight. Drink in moderation, but have fun." Arthur announced.

The word of ale lit a fire through the crowd. People lined up and filled up whatever wooden dish they had with some ale before settling back at their benches and enjoying the evening. Arthur grabbed Allendria's hand and guided her away from the courtyard.

"Not going to stay for a drink?" Allendria asked.

"I had something better in mind," Arthur said with a grin. Her eyes caught his, and she leaned in to kiss him.

"That'll work."

The two rushed through the manor to their room and enjoyed the comfort of each other for the night.

***

Arthur had tons of minor tasks to accomplish before he left, but most pressing of all were the Bags of Holding for the couriers. Because of this, he started his morning by going to Lady Gemmalin's workshop. He delivered the rest of the tools to her, and she handed over fifteen thick leather bags the size of a backpack on Earth.

He found a quiet space in the corner of her workshop and sat the bags on an empty table. His mind was filled with the knowledge of how to make an item such as this from his talent in Dimensional Magic, but he hadn't attempted one yet. The trick was sorting through his knowledge to figure out the steps.

It didn't take long for him to get the gist of it, and he started his work. Creating a dimensional space was the first step. The limit seemed to be on his skill in Dimensional Magic to determine how large the storage space for the bag could be. The process was identical to him creating a Dimensional Storage space. It changed when he needed to assign a unique identifier for the space.

His talent showed him that most people used intricate symbols to label them. The key was to make it something difficult for people to copy. After trying to figure out some intricate design, he decided he was over-thinking this. The easiest way was just to number it '1' and move on from there. While that might seem foolish, he planned on using the English number '1' and not the '1' from his current language. To anyone else, it would look like a strange symbol, but they'd never see it, anyway.

The space he created stretched a full fifty yards square and was ten feet tall. While it sounded excessively large, he hoped the amount of food these people needed to haul would eventually fill this space. They wouldn't need anywhere near this amount of space in the near future, but as the city grew, and the farms increased production, they should.

For the enchantment, he took out a thin metal rod and used his Arcane Smithing to form the end into a tip. He settled on the option to put the enchanting matrix on the inside of the bag. This would prevent anyone from seeing it since the bag would anchor the space, and you'd only see the empty void inside once they were linked. It also prevented the matrix from being damaged without someone destroying the bag itself.

He used his Fire Magic to heat the metal rod and started by burning a symbol of a foot with wings on the side into a round piece of leather. A little thread and a needle allowed him to sew it onto the side of the bag and identify it as a courier bag. From there, he burned the matrix inside of the bag. The design was a five-symbol pattern he could never have guessed. There was one symbol Arthur couldn't even read with his translation ability. That was almost alarming, but he chalked it up as representing a concept and not a true word. Embedded into the pattern was the identifier for the dimensional space. He also included the symbols for Soul Binding the item. That was reverse-engineered from his knowledge of it in Blacksmithing. With the last piece of the matrix burned into the leather, Arthur sat back and looked it over. He spent a good five minutes examining the symbols and making sure everything was in order. If anything wasn't, he risked the chance of destroying the bag when he activated the magic.

Arthur took a deep breath and completed the pattern. A rush of air whistled through the room and pulled into the mouth of the bag. Swirling dark energy now filled the opening, and he received a notification.

You have gained 2,400 experience in Enchanting for creating Bag of Holding. (Large)
You have gained 1000 experience in Dimensional Magic for creating Bag of Holding. (Large)

The experience amounts surprised Arthur, and he nearly jumped out of his seat. *There is no way that can be right. Is that spell really so rare that it awards such high experience?*

That kind of experience made him realize he needed to focus some time creating a lot of bags. This would be a great way to level up his Enchanting and Dimensional Magic. He still wanted to hit that elusive level twenty in Dimensional Magic.

The high experience excited him and lit a fire in him to churn out more of these. He plowed through them as fast as he could while still taking the time to double-check all his work. A dozen of the bags lay stacked in front of him, ready for use. It was on the thirteenth bag that something strange happened.

Your Dimensional Space has failed. You did not choose a unique identifier to associate.

The message confused him at first until he realized the problem and grew excited. *Someone must have already used that symbol. Can I use that number and tie one of these bags to that space?*

Anticipation pushed him forward, and he raced through the thirteenth bag. When the '13' symbol was placed, he collected himself before finalizing the enchantment. The air rustled again and sucked toward the bag. This time, the leather glowed red, and Arthur felt heat emanate from the item. It grew brighter and brighter until the light faded, and only a pile of ash remained on the now-blackened work table.

You have failed to create Bag of Holding. Leather Backpack was destroyed.

I wish I knew what caused it to fail. I did everything the same as before. The symbols were perfect.
Dwelling on the failure wouldn't do him any good, so he filed that info away for later. Instead, he finished the last two bags and took stock of his experience gains.

You have gained 31,200 total experience in Enchanting.
Congratulations, you have reached level 17 in Enchanting. Your enchantments have a 39% decreased mana cost. Not very original on your numbering, are you?
You have gained 13,000 total experience in Dimensional Magic.

Arthur was thrilled with the level gain and walked around, picking up his trash around the workstation. Gathering up the bags, he left the workshop and walked back toward the City Manor. Arthur waved at people as he passed, and bright smiles greeted him on his trip. The children were out in full force as well, playing some game with sticks that he couldn't begin to comprehend the rules of. He assumed they were just making it up as they went as well.

The courtyard at the manor was busy with people preparing hides on the stone benches from the feast. People sat in the cool air and sunshine as they made neat cuts and trimmed off excess fat from the skins. Arthur didn't want to interrupt anyone, so he walked around the outside edge until he reached the manor. Inside, he searched through the rooms until he found the person he was looking for.

"Mistress Holly, I take it you are staying busy?" Arthur asked.

"Of course, Your Majesty. I've been pitching in with the preparation as much as possible, but I've also recruited people as the couriers and guards like we discussed at the meeting." The Master of Holds answered.

"Even better. I'm actually here to deliver these," Arthur said as he motioned toward the Bags of Holding bundled under his arms. He walked to a nearby table and sat them all down.

"These are the Bags of Holding for your couriers. I'd like you to go through them now and make sure you bind each. If anything happens to the couriers when you lend them, they should return to you." Arthur explained.

Holly looked nervous with the veritable mountain of wealth Arthur just sat in front of her. These items were legendary and could buy small kingdoms. After a few moments, she slowly nodded and began digging through the pile and touching each. Arthur would see a brief flash of purple light when she touched one, and then it would go back to normal.

"You'll do fine," Arthur assured her, trying to ease some of the fear he saw in her eyes.

"I'm not sure I can be responsible for this kind of wealth." She told him.

"No worries. To me, they are quick and easy to make. Just don't tell anyone, okay?"

Her expression told Arthur she wasn't sure if what he said was true or not. "Just remember to stress to the couriers that possession of the bags without proper permission is subject to the death penalty. Also, make sure they know that anyone assaulting a courier has the same rules. That should keep them honest and give them a bargaining chip to talk their way out of trouble if someone is foolish enough to try."

"Uh, alright." She agreed. "Is the schedule still the same?"

"Sure is. Get your groups together and send out the teams. Each of the villages should have two teams that stagger on their trips. The extra bags you can use to haul goods around the town. If you run into issues, contact any guard for assistance." Arthur said.

She agreed with his assessment, and Arthur left to handle his preparations. He only had a couple of days and needed to get everything together before they left.

Chapter 12

Return to Alurian

Arthur lifted his hand, and a swirling portal appeared in front of him. The small ball of power that was headed for him disappeared into the rift. With a wave, the opening snapped close with a soft pop, and he looked at the flying creature in front of him.

The harpy looked back with anger on its face and screeched at him. Its companions echoed the call, and all of them charged for the small group of fighters. Arthur sat in place, with Zoe by his side. She insisted on coming and watching the fight. Arthur wanted to get away from the column of travelers and do a little experience grinding, so he took a handful of people and ran through the nearby forest. The harpies were one of many enemies they'd found.

Arthur's hand twitched on the hilt of his sword, but he was worried about leaving Zoe alone with enemies so nimble. Arrows filled the birdlike creatures and turned them into pincushions as Arthur watched Vana dance around the trees. Bursts of shadow filled the spaces as Rayne jumped from enemy to enemy and plunged daggers into every soft spot he found. Concentrated beams of fire sizzled through the harpies as Allendria let out some of her power.

These enemies were a joke for their power, so they let their fellow guardsmen with them handle most of the fighting. A few employed shields and bashed the frail creatures to the ground, while others employed bows and picked off targets as they became vulnerable. Arthur lost himself watching everyone else and was startled when he felt a tug at his waist.

Before he could register what happened, a screech sounded right by his ear, and his head swung to investigate. A harpy crumpled to the ground with his dagger buried in its chest. Beside it stood a panting Zoe, blood spattered on her hand and chest.

You okay? Arthur asked.

I'm fine. None of it is my blood. You really should pay attention to your surroundings. It dropped from above us.

How'd you sense it? Arthur asked, curious how she noticed something above her head without sound.

I felt the wind on my skin and noticed it was blowing in the wrong direction. I had no weapon when I felt it, so I needed to borrow yours.

Good call. Thank you.

Arthur? She sent with a timid feel to it.

What's up, Zoe?

Do you think I could train to be a fighter and adventurer like you?

The question caught Arthur off guard. He took Zoe as more of the quiet type who wanted a comfortable life and to live in a city. Asking to become a trained fighter wasn't something he considered.

You're free to do whatever you want with your life. I'll be happy to assist in any way I can.

Thanks so much! Can you show me how to use a sword? She asked eagerly.

Don't do that, girl. Calfuray sent through their chat. *He barely knows how to use his own, and most of that isn't proper.*

I'd argue, but she's right. I am not trained in the sword and just kind of flail around with it. A sword probably won't be your best option for a weapon, no matter how cool they look. Arthur said.

A stream of fire burned across Arthur's vision, and he snapped back to himself.

"What are you two doing? Save the chats and daydreaming for when we are not actively in a fight." Allendria told them.

It embarrassed Arthur that he'd let himself get distracted yet again and could've been injured. Worse, he pulled Zoe into it and left herself defenseless as well.

She has a point. We should pay attention to the fight. Afterward, we can discuss your training. Arthur said.

Zoe nodded in agreement, and Arthur turned his focus back to the fight. To prevent himself from getting distracted, he fished out some throwing knives and started randomly picking off targets. It wasn't long until the last of the harpies succumbed to the damage and stilled.

"Great work, everyone," Arthur said as he opened a Dimensional Storage space. "Now, the not-so-fun part."

Everyone groaned good-naturedly and set to work. The corpses piled up in the space, and Arthur snapped it shut. They were still a couple of days away from Alurian, and his experience gains weren't terrible. It was hard to work on his crafting on the move, so he focused on constantly casting magic. A quick summary of the non-stop spell-casting over the last couple of weeks made him smile.

You have gained 106,245 total experience in Dimensional Magic.

Congratulations, you have reached levels 17, 18, and 19 in Dimensional Magic. Decreases the mana draw of Dimensional spells by 45%. Making big empty holes? I'd make a mom joke, but that would be cruel under the circumstances.

You have gained 38,745 total experience in Dual Casting.

Congratulations, you have reached levels 11, 12, 13, and 14 in Dual Casting. Decreases the mana draw of dual-cast spells by 30%. Can you play with yourself with both hands as well?

You have gained 23,210 total experience in Light Magic.

Congratulations, you have reached levels 2, 3, 4, 5, 6, 7, 8, 9, and 10 in Light Magic. Decreases the mana draw of Light spells by 18%. Let there be light!

You have gained 12,150 total experience in Air Magic.

Congratulations, you have reached levels 11 and 12 in Air Magic. Air Magic spells now have a 24% increased effect. You're not The Flash.

With Arthur's Dual Casting, he focused on
his Dimensional Magic since it was his unique
magic ability. He also took the time to work
on some of his lower-level magic skills. Each
of them had leveled up well, but he hadn't
stopped to look over the talent trees. He
started with his Dual Casting Talents. He had
8 points to spend, so he spent all of them on
Arcane Control, bringing it up to 9.

Arcane Control (9/10)	*Every 5 points invested in this talent expands your control of mana and allows you to cast an additional spell at the same time.*

Between dual casting and this adding one
spell, he could cast three spells at once. One
more point, and he could manage four. The
biggest benefit he saw to this talent was that
the additional spell didn't increase in cost
again like his second spell in Dual Casting
did.

Light Magic was his newest form of magic,
so it came with a fresh talent tree.

You have 12 unspent Talent Points.

Tier 1	
Radiance (0/10)	*Increases the illumination of your spells by 5% per point. The final point will increase the overall bonus to 100%.*

Light Enchantment (0/5)	*Spending all 5 points in this talent grants you the knowledge to incorporate Light Magic into your enchantment matrix.*
Purity (0/10)	*Each point in this talent decreases the casting speed of Light Magic spells by 5%.*

The initial options were pretty standard from most of what he'd seen before, but Arthur unlocked the Enchantment option. With those five points spent, he examined the Tier 2 options.

You have 7 unspent Talent Points

Tier 2	
Sustainability (0/10)	*Investing all 10 points in this skill grants you the knowledge to create self-sustaining light effects with your spells.*
Flashbang (0/1) *Requirements: Air Magic Level 10*	*This teaches you the Flashbang spell. It combines a bright flash of light with a loud noise to distract and disorient enemies.*

Holy Light (0/10)	*Your connection with divinity allows you to channel some of that power through your magic. Investing 5 points in this skill will imbue your Light Magic spells with holy power and damage undead creatures. Investing all 10 points will cause minor damage to all enemies and extreme damage to undead and those of evil alignment.*

He picked flashbang without hesitation. Another distraction ability was welcome. The second was a little trickier. While being able to harm evil and undead creatures with some cheap Light Magic sounded great, he hadn't really seen many of either.

On the other hand, making self-sustaining lights was something his entire kingdom could benefit from. The last 6 points all went into Sustainability.

Arthur pulled up the Air Magic talents next. He felt like a fool as he quickly realized he'd never checked them. It was the last magic he gained for his Soul Bond quest, and he raced to level 10. Since then, he'd never checked because he rarely used it for anything but Weak Haste.

You have 16 unspent Talent Points

Tier 1	
Hasty (0/10)	*Boosts speed enhancement effects by 3% per point.*
Air Sense (0/5)	*Spending all 5 points in this talent allows you to feel disturbances in the nearby air.*
As a Leaf (0/10)	*Increases your spell power while lifting things with Air Magic by 4% per point.*

Both Hasty and Air Sense piqued his interest. Hasty tied in directly with his primary use of Air Magic and could be a great boon if it further increased his speed while under the effects of the Haste spell.

Air Sense was something he would've dismissed in the past until he met Zoe. Her sensitivity, which allowed her to feel the disturbance in the air, prevented Arthur from a few nasty gouges of a harpy claw. He could technically max out both with his points, but Tier 2 might have better options. He decided to put the 5 points into Air Sense because it might save his life and was a passive ability that cost no mana. From there, he looked at the Tier 2 options.

Tier 2	
Hover (0/10)	*Investing all 10 points in this skill grants you the spell Hover. This Air Magic spell allows you to float a few feet off of the ground and move around on a cushion of air. Requires mana to sustain.* *Mana Cost: 3 mana/second*
Quickness (0/10)	*Decreases casting speed of movement increasing spells by 5%. Once 10 points are invested, these spells can be cast instantly and by reflex.*
Practice Makes Perfect (0/10)	*Teaches you the theory of using magic to keep things in the air. Decreases casting cost of channeled abilities with Air Magic by 5% per point.*

    The options caused a dilemma. Each of them had very specific things that would be useful. Being able to use Hover would surely lead to him unlocking some form of flying later. It was also great for hovering across short gaps or above traps.

Being able to cast spells like Haste
instinctively could very well save his life in
an emergency. While Practice Makes Perfect
helped with levitating, flying and hovering.

In the end, Arthur went with survivability
and spent 10 points on Quickness and the last
point in Hasty. With that out of the way, he
checked on his final set of talents with
Dimensional Magic. The 6 points he had there
went into Unlock Portals, bringing it to 7/8.

Unlock Portals (7/8)	*Portals are complex things that require a lot of knowledge. This skill will teach you how to summon small portals within 100 feet of yourself that connect to each other upon investing all 8 skill points.*

With all the talents finally sorted out,
Arthur turned his focus back to their task. It
was still a long trek until they reached home.

***

Lady Dalia walked through the streets of
Alurian. The fading sun's rays were barely
visible on the horizon. Work was completed for
the day, and everyone was busy with dinner
preparations or relaxing. Loud conversation
and laughing spilled out of the doors of the
inn, and she continued past without stopping.

Her leisurely walk took her toward the
outskirts of the town. Light thumps punctuated
her steps as she walked along the cobblestone
streets.

"Good evening, Lady." A woman called.

"Good evening to you. May the Goddess bless you this evening." She said out of habit.

I shouldn't even have to talk to the lowly citizens. They are here just to serve.

Her temper almost flared to the surface, but she pushed it down and continued forward. The buildings thinned out as she got farther from the center of town, and she eventually came upon a small village of tents. The old refugee camp was primarily abandoned as they'd moved most people to individual homes already.

She ducked into one of the nondescript tents and looked around. Her eyes quickly adjusted to the low light, and she spotted two men sitting in a corner. Both were thin and covered in leather armor. Small daggers adorned their hips, and she noticed the hint of small blades embedded in straps around their midsections.

"So, what do you two have for me now?" Dalia asked.

"The mistress isn't happy with how badly things were handled on the assassination. Not a single one of the true targets was killed, only a few bystanders." One man said. He was the taller of the two, standing nearly six feet tall, and had a thick black mustache to go with his wavy hair.

"The people sent were fools and low class. None of them had a chance against our strongest, even caught off guard." Dalia said with a dismissive wave.

"She didn't ask for excuses and only cares about results. You should consider yourself lucky you are as highly placed as you are with this new upstart king. Otherwise, your life would be forfeit for that failure."

"I doubt she sent you all the way out here to berate me. What's the task?" Dalia asked, her patience running thin.

"You are to make yourself governess of Seora. Our mistress has it on good authority that Arthur plans to place you in control of the city anyway, but you must ensure it happens and that you don't screw it up. Once there, begin recruiting faithful to the cause." The man said.

"Fine. About time I get a little respect. Placing me in charge of the city is an acceptable step for now."

The second man, who had been quiet and unmoving to this point, stood from his spot and dusted off his pants. His brown eyes bore into her, and it felt like he peered into her soul. "Last chance. Fail here and no amount of friendship will save your ass."

With that warning, the two walked past her and left the tent.

Who the hell do they think they are talking to me like that? Now the messengers won't even show me respect? I'm a damn noble!

Her fist clenched so tightly it cramped, and she shook it out. Her ragged breathing slowly came under control as she focused on steadying herself to return to the city.

I'll make them all pay in the end.

* * *

"You know, that's really distracting," Allendria grumbled as she walked beside Arthur.

"I'm sure it is, but it's the only way to get better. You should do it too." Arthur told her.

"But do you really have to do it in front
of everyone?" She asked.

Arthur looked around at the group as they
trekked across the countryside. Most looked
happy to be nearly home, and very few were
even paying attention to anything he did.

"Pretty sure everyone else is preoccupied.
Have any plans for when we arrive?" Arthur
asked.

"I look forward to a dip in the bathhouse.
I know we have our own house, but there is
something calming about it. Care to join me?"

"I wouldn't miss it. It's a date." Arthur
told her and then froze mid-step.

*You have gained 14,020 total experience in
Dimensional Magic.*

*Congratulations, you have reached level 20
in Dimensional Magic. Decreases the mana draw
of dimensional spells by 48%. The moment of
truth. Will your dreams be answered?*

Regardless of the smart-ass remarks from
the system, Arthur couldn't wait to check his
special skill selection. Since he discovered
Dimensional Magic, there had been one thing
he'd wanted to do with it. The details were
too complex for him to figure out alone, so he
banked on the hope that the level twenty
special skill would grant it. It wasn't long
before the expected message greeted him.

*Congratulations, you have reached level 20
in Dimensional Magic and have been promoted to
Journeyman in the skill. Please choose one of
the following as a bonus for this achievement:*

Ability: Rapid Fire	
Requirements: Dimensional Magic Type: Passive Ability	Description: Improves your rift speed and accuracy. Allows faster, more precise timing on your rift ability in combat.
Mastery Level: 1	

Spell: Transport Portals	
Requirements: Dimensional Magic Mana Cost: 1000 MP Cast Time: 15 seconds	Description: Opens a portal 10 feet tall and twenty feet wide between two previously visited locations. There is no limit to the number of people that can traverse the portal, but it will only last for 4 hours.
Mastery Level: 1	

Spell: Wizard's Den	
Requirements: Dimensional Magic Mana Cost: 250 MP Cast Time: 4 seconds	Description: Grants you a personal Wizard's Den. Use your Dimensional Magic to summon a portal to this space at any time. Living entities can survive in this space, even when the owner isn't present.
Mastery Level: 1	

Arthur's breath caught for a moment before he hollered a cheer. Everyone nearby turned toward him with curious expressions, but he ignored their looks and kept focused on the message.

The Wizard's Den is here. The spell I've hoped for the entire time.

Something stood out about all the options, though. The first option was the first passive ability he'd seen from a spell before. He didn't even know that was possible until now.

The second was a portal power that he dearly dreamed about. Arthur seriously considered it before remembering he was close to unlocking portals using his normal talent tree and was sure he'd figure out the method behind large-scale portals.

The last option was the big ticket. Carving out a dimensional space was a simple task with his magic. Making said space livable was the challenge he hadn't been able to solve, nor did he believe he would. Wizard's Den was his selection.

Allendria stood a few paces ahead of him. With all of his menus dismissed, he waved at her to come back to him.

"Guess you finally reached level twenty?" She asked.

"Sure did," Arthur said.

"Was your dream spell there?"

"Sure was. Watch this," he told her.

    With a thought and a flashy wave, the
outline of a doorway appeared in front of
them. The magic looked almost identical to his
Dimensional Storage spell, but when the door
opened, that comparison faded. Instead of the
empty black void, a bright room greeted them.
It was roughly ten feet on each side and
sported smooth stone floors that looked like
polished marble. The walls were white stone,
placed together so perfectly they could see no
hint of mortar. Arthur and Allendria both
entered the room.

    *You have gained 500 experience in
Dimensional Magic for casting Wizard's Den.*
    *You have entered your Wizard's Den. This
location is currently Level 1.*

    "This is beautiful, but what's the
purpose?" Allendria asked.
    "It is nice, isn't it? This place is
special, though. I can shut it with us in here
without harm. This is a personal retreat and
solves camping on long trips. I can open the
space, we can all pile in to sleep in perfect
safety until I open it in the morning. No more
worrying about setting watches or late-night
ambushes. The only caveat is it opens in the
same place we entered it if I am inside."
Arthur explained.
    "So, if someone sees us enter it, they can
camp outside and wait to ambush us when we
exit…" Allendria said.
    "That is the potential downfall. Thus,
trying to conceal it. Its benefits far
outweigh the risks." Arthur said as he looked
around the space. "Now, to add some
furniture."

"This bright light might make sleeping a problem." She grimaced.

Arthur thought about the lighting and mentally suggested it dim. It pleased him when the room gradually grew darker until he told it to stop.

"Easy solution." He told her with a grin.

"Well, no more lonely nights and worrying about waking up our fellow campers." She told him with a seductive smile.

Arthur laughed. "True, as long as they aren't camping inside with us. Now to find out what this Level 1 thing means."

Arthur mentally checked the level of the Wizard's Den.

Level 1 Wizard's Den.
Mana until next level: 0/1000.

Hmm. Pretty Straight forward. The question is, what does it do when it advances level?

"Something bad?" Allendria asked. "Your face looks like you tasted something sour."

Arthur shook himself out of his concentration. "No, just thinking. Was curious to see what happens when it levels up."

"Is the cost bad?" She asked.

"Not really. I'm sure it gets worse."

"Then give it a shot?" She suggested.

Arthur sighed. "Might as well."

Arthur selected the option and willed his mana to flow into the portal. It started as a gradual trickle while the light in the room grew and slowly pulsed. After a few seconds, the stream of mana flowed faster. When his mana pool was almost empty, he refilled it with mana from his sword and continued. When he hit the 1,000-mana mark, he abruptly cut the flow and received a message.

Your Wizard's Den has the required mana to advance to Level 2. Do you wish to proceed? Yes/No.

Arthur selected *Yes.*

The stone walls around them rippled and distorted. They slowly inched outward. It reminded Arthur of the old school movies where the trash compactors closed in to kill those inside, only in reverse. As the walls expanded, more stone joined to fill in the gaps. Half a minute later, the walls stopped, and another message appeared.

Your Wizard's Den is now Level 2. Maximum space has been increased to 18' x 18' x 10'.

"Looks like it upgrades the size," Arthur said.

"I can see that much," she told him with a light slap on the shoulder. "Anything else?"

"Not with that upgrade. Higher levels may offer other bonuses." Arthur said, but then checked on the mana to the next level.

Mana until next level: 0/2000.

"I guess, if nothing else, it gives me something to sink mana into. As if I didn't have enough magic spells that needed my focus." Arthur grumbled.

Allendria laughed, and they exited the space. Arthur waved it shut, and they continued their trek to Alurian. The city wall came into sight as they crested the final rise.

"Home." Arthur breathed.

Chapter 13

Home Sweet Home

"Form up ranks," Samson commanded as they walked down the road.

Arthur watched as the entire column shifted, their fighters and civilians alike. The trip from Seora turned even the crafters and non-combatants into seasoned campaigners, and their discipline with the simple commands showed.

In the distance, Alurian's wall rose like a shield. Even from this distance, Arthur could make out the soldiers standing guard atop the fortification. Sunlight reflected off of polished helmets and spear tips.

Their group approached at a quick march. Even Samson moved a little faster than he normally would. Arthur assumed it was because of excitement about returning home. While their marching was in step, the non-combatants still murmured a lot. Arthur overheard many talking in hushed tones about the impressive wall and the soldiers they could see.

When Arthur looked at the faces of the guards originally from here, it all hit home. Tears welled in some of their eyes, and they stood proudly as they marched forward. He watched them fight the urge to break formation and run forward into the embrace of the city where most of them had spent their lives.

A hand slipped into his, and Arthur turned to see Allendria in step with him, her fingers interlocked with his.

"Does it feel like home?" She asked, staring at the wall.

Arthur reflected on her question for a moment. *Was this home?* Emotions swirled within him. Part of him almost answered yes on instinct.

"Partially. I feel a bond with this place, but I also still have lingering feelings from my old life. One of these days, those might fade enough for me to answer that better."

"I think you answered it just right," she said as she squeezed his hand. "It can be difficult changing what you consider home. It's still in that in-between state for me as well. As long as you're here with me, I can at least call it home."

Arthur leaned over and kissed her on the cheek before standing up straight and falling back into step with the group. He didn't release her hand, though.

When they drew close to the wall, the massive gates swung open. It surprised Arthur at how quietly they moved. A small group of people stood in the doorway and walked out to greet them. Arthur pulled Allendria to the front of the formation and stood near Samson. Less than fifty yards from the approaching group of people, Samson held up his fist, and the formation halted. Arthur, Allendria, Vana, Samson, and Rayne all continued from the main formation to greet the delegation from the city.

Dalia stood front and center in a regal purple dress. Her red hair curled lightly down the side of her face, accenting her freckles. A smile shone from her as she approached. Right behind her walked Daranth. He wore a vest of dark green that somehow blended well with his deep purple skin. Small wooden accessories dotted his hair and clothing.

Beside Daranth came Daniel. Stoic looking and wearing the apron from his inn. Katherine, the city administrator, and Libby, Rayne's sister, walked beside him. On the other side of Dalia was Toren, in a full set of city guard armor.

The two groups approached each other and came to a halt when they were only a dozen paces away.

"Welcome back, Your Majesty," Dalia said with a bow.

"It is good to be home, Lady Dalia. How is Alurian doing?" Arthur asked.

"The city is growing well. I'm not sure how much you will recognize when you enter. Everyone has wo…," she said before Arthur heard the rustle of footsteps and turned to watch Libby cross the gap in a few long strides and leap into Rayne's arms.

A huff from Dalia drew his attention back to her, and she had a slightly sour look on her face. It appeared as though she would rebuke Libby, but as her mouth opened, Arthur raised a hand.

"It's no problem, Dalia. Let them have their moment." Arthur said as he turned back to watch the two embrace with a smile. Tears ran down Libby's face as Rayne squeezed her tight.

"It's good to see some things remain the same," Allendria said as she walked over and laid an arm on Rayne's shoulder. He looked at her with red eyes and nodded his agreement.

"I'm sure we have much to discuss, but I think we should head back to the city first. We can catch up on the way… wait. Did you say city?" Arthur asked.

Katherine beamed brightly and nodded enthusiastically. "We raised it all the way to the base city level since you left. You should have some surprise notifications when you enter."

"Thank you, Katherine." Dalia cut her off. "It looks like we have more people to tend to, though."

The group looked behind Arthur at the crowd of people. Arthur only nodded and turned to address everyone.

"Ladies and Gentlemen, we have arrived. Welcome to Alurian. Take a day or two to get acquainted with the place. We will have people find you accommodations and eventually get you settled in with jobs." Arthur told them.

The crowd began murmuring in excitement, and Samson stepped forward. His commanding voice thundered through the space, "Everyone, dismissed."

Arthur and his crew joined the party from the city, and all walked through the gates. They followed the perfectly laid road toward the city, but Arthur was bombarded with messages as soon as they entered the gatehouse.

Alurian has successfully advanced to Town Level 1. As the Mayor and owner of this settlement, you receive a 15,000 experience bonus for this feat.

Alurian has successfully advanced to City Level 1. As Mayor and owner of this settlement, you receive a 50,000 experience bonus for this feat.

Congratulations, you have reached level 23! You now have 5 available skill points. Kinda feels like cheating since everyone else did most of the work, but it is what it is.

"That's sweet. Bonus experience when the settlement tiers up is nice. I got experience when it reached Town level one and City level one." Arthur told Allendria.

"I've heard of this but have never seen it. Once a settlement reaches City status, it rarely ever advances past that." She told him.

"I'll take what I can get. It was enough experience to gain a level. Now, to assign some points."

It had been a while since he gained a level, so he carefully studied his stats.

You have 5 unspent Stat Points.

Name: Arthur Firebrand	
Level: 23	
Age: 26	
Race: Human	
Class: Spell Blade	
HP: 550/550	
MP: 1080/1080	
Stamina: 530/530	
Strength: 20	**Experience:** 21080/63000 (5 stat points available)
Agility: 32	
Intellect: 34	
Wisdom: 16	**Skills** (225% boost to any skill for level up)
Endurance: 26	
Charisma: 12	**Combat Skills:**
Luck: 11	

Archery: 10 (5170/6000)
  - Aim Shot: 7 (1695/3200)
Block: 3 (810/1000)
Dual Wield: 8 (180/3800)
Identify: 1 (75/500)
Light Armor: 6 (700/2500)
Medium Armor: 5 (1680/1900)
Parry: 4 (670/1000)
Scan: 6 (810/1900)
Small Blades: 9 (510/4600)
Spears: 2 (450/750)
Stealth: 4 (590/1400)
   - Detect Hidden: 1 (50/500)
Swords: 11 (6875/7200)
Throwing Knives: 4 (1155/3200)
Unarmed: 1 (275/500)

Magic:

Air Magic: 12 (1230/8500)
Dimensional Magic: 20 (2975/52000)
Dual Casting: 14 (9485/14000)
Earth Magic: 24 (38610/76000)
Fire Magic: 24 (26245/76000)
Light Magic: 10 (3560/6000)

Water Magic: 11 (550/7200)

Professions:

Barter: 4 (900/1400)
Blacksmithing: 18 (25510/38000)
 - Alternate Heating: 1 (160/500)
 - Arcane Metal Construction: 3 (300/1000)
 - Arcane Smithing: 18 (5785/38000)
 - Metal Construction: 3 (300/1000)
Cooking: 2 (400/750)
Enchanting: 17 (17745/30000)
Farming: 8 (1635/3800)
Firemaking: 2 (700/750)
Herbalism: 6 (10/2500)
Jeweler: 9 (1680/4600)
Leatherworking: 7 (195/3200)
Mining: 6 (2400/2500)
 - Magical Mining 6 (2025/2500)
Skinning: 4 (175/1400)
Woodworking: 4 (1035/1400)
 - Arcane Woodworking: 4 (995/1400)

Most of his combat style still relied heavily on magic, so he put two of the points into Intellect, bringing it to 36. Since speed was his next biggest concern, he put the other three into Agility, bringing it to 35. The Intellect brought his mana pool up to a respectable 1,120, not including his gear.

An elbow in his rib broke him out of his concentration, and he looked to his side at Allendria. She nodded her head in their direction, and Arthur turned toward the city. His jaw almost hit the floor.

The rundown and ramshackle mess they left behind no longer existed. From this distance, Arthur could make out a fully sprawling city. The southern side, near the forest, showcased greenery of all kinds. Vegetable plants, vines, and even small bushes littered the landscape. He couldn't determine everything there from this far away, but it was obviously far more than they started with.

In the southwest corner of the landscape, an orchard dotted the fields near the wall. A few specs in their leaves shone with a red hue, so Arthur guessed someone may have cultivated some apple trees.

"It's hard to believe they did all of this in a couple of months." Allendria praised.

Vana bounded up to them. "I guess you can see it now. I wanted to tell you guys about all the changes when our scouts first spotted the city, but figured it'd be better to let you experience it."

Fields were the least of the surprises. The city itself expanded out nearly three-quarters of the distance to the wall. What used to be a small collection of buildings morphed into a sprawling city complex. The original inn and the Temple of Lianna stood out near the center, and the roads spread out in a spoked wheel pattern from there.

"Dalia, where did all the people come from?" Arthur asked.

She turned toward him and smiled. "They actually found their way here. No one is entirely sure how they discovered this place, but we believe it was partially from rumors of Rayne's expedition here and a mixture of a little divine influence."

The last statement was punctuated by her glancing skyward briefly.

"We had multiple large groups of refugees arrive and then randomly have small groups show up at the gates. There were a few skirmishes in the nearby countryside. With the population increase, we recruited more guards and even began sending out patrols. Patrols stumbled across more lost people and escorted them back to us. The city now boasts more than a thousand people." Dalia explained.

"A thousand?" Arthur asked in disbelief. "Seriously?"

"Around a hundred of that are Dark Elves. We randomly find some in the forest who are trying to escape their home city."

"It must be getting worse," Allendria grumbled.

"You should probably check in with them later today, Princess. The tales I have heard are not good," Dalia told her.

"Thank you for informing me, Lady Dalia. I think I'll go with Daranth back to their portion of the city when we get closer." Allendria said.

"Go check on your people," Arthur encouraged her with a squeeze on her hand. She looked distracted, but nodded and walked toward Daranth. They entered a hushed conversation shortly after.

Their trip through town showed off more than just fresh stone buildings. Wooden furniture was on display everywhere. Benches lined many of the streets and fronts of the buildings. A few shops had wooden signs above their doorways, welcoming customers.

"Dalia, who thought up the fountains?" Arthur asked as they walked by one in a large intersection. The circular stone piece was in the dead center of the intersection and was three levels tall. Each cascaded down a steady stream of water, and Arthur noticed people sitting along the edge and enjoying the attraction.

"The construction crews," she answered. "I think it was honestly out of boredom. They've become so good with their spells that they run out of work to do from time to time. When they get bored, they find random stuff to do. A few of them banded together to create fountains. With the water pipes already running underground, it was easy for them to tap in for the features. A few of them even began competitions. They band together and see who can create the best artistic feature and pool their money for the bet. The last team to win created a breathtaking mural wall, showing a scene from the battle with the goblins and orcs."

"This is truly amazing," Samson agreed as he clomped along in his armor.

The bland buildings were now covered in different decorations. Small planter boxes filled with herbs and flowers decorated windows. The city as a whole felt more like a nice place to live instead of an abandoned nightmare.

When they reached the intersection before the inn, Dalia and Daranth turned and headed for the Dark Elf quarter of the city. Everyone else continued until they reached the inn. Daniel rushed from the group and went behind the counter. Trisha and Paula, his two assistants, immediately spilled out of the back and brought cool mugs of water for everyone. Arthur took a seat with Katherine, Dalia, and Samson to discuss the business of the city.

"Looks like you two have been busy in our absence," Arthur observed.

"The entire city has been busy. I've just tried to keep things running," Katherine quipped. "On the bright side, I have done some more work on my paper-making skill."

"Hopefully, it's working out for you. Do you enjoy doing it?" Arthur asked.

"It helps calm me down and unwind, so yeah. That's not important at the moment. We currently have a large group of people that arrived with you. Care to fill us in?" Katherine asked.

"I was hoping for that explanation as well." Dalia agreed.

So, he told them the whole story. Arthur talked about traveling to Seora. Getting ready for battle. When he mentioned proposing to Allendria, Dalia's face grimaced but brushed it off as her aversion to the nonhuman side. The battle was briefly discussed, and then the eventual surrender of the city. Finally, he told them about their trip around the local area, establishing freeholds to grow food. Katherine looked immensely pleased. Dalia was much harder to read.

"Who is in charge there now?" Dalia asked.

"There was something of a council when I left. Mainly people I named to positions in the city. I actually want to ask you to go to Seora and take control of the city on my behalf. I believe someone with a true title might inspire a little more loyalty from some nobles already there." Arthur said.

Dalia smiled at that and bowed her head to him. "I appreciate the confidence in me."

"You've worked hard in this town to keep things in line. I know you can keep control of the few squabbles among the nobles in Seora." Arthur said with a dismissive wave.

"Kat, we need to figure out what to do with our new arrivals. Is there anywhere they can stay for housing?" Samson asked.

The question surprised Arthur, mainly because Samson called her Kat and not Katherine.

"It is good to see you, Paladin Samson. We should be able to accommodate all you brought. They may have to share with a few more people than normal while we make additional housing, but it shouldn't take long. We built a dozen new houses that have no tenets to prepare for any new arrivals. With our patrols finding new people, we like to keep open space. We didn't want to go overboard and build way too many at once, though."

"That's a great plan," Arthur praised. "How long do you need to get this situation sorted out?"

"A couple of days should do it."

"Wow. That's a lot faster than expected." Samson said.

"Our crews have perfected their work. Once we unlocked the quest system, it dramatically helped." Kat said.

I totally forgot about that.

"Now our workers get experience and rewards for their tasks. It has allowed many of the crew the chance to level up with their bonus experience and gain more stats. A lot of them have invested heavily into Intellect and Wisdom to make better use of their mana." Kat said.

"It helped a lot back in Seora," Samson agreed.

"Wait, what?" Arthur asked.

"You didn't realize it then? When you assigned tasks and asked for things to be done, it was handing out quests automatically. The coins rewarded were based on the poor quality of that city, but we had some in reserve in the treasury before we left. It allowed many of our people and the craftsmen in the city to make progress. That, more than anything, was where a lot of the morale was coming from." Allendria said with a chuckle.

"Well, I'll be damned. I guess I never realized it because I received no notifications about it."

"It usually doesn't as long as it can meet the base criteria. The system is really flexible when it comes to rewards. It can often fill in gaps of one kind or another." Kat said.

"So, I was just handing out quests like crazy then. Good to know. There isn't a limit, right?" Arthur asked.

"Not exactly. The only way we cannot create a quest is if there isn't a sufficient offer for rewards. As I said, the system can be pretty forgiving and open to its interpretation of rewards," Kat said.

The group all sat in silence for a little while and finished their food. When Arthur sat back and sighed in contentment, Kat cleared her throat.

"I don't know any other way to bring this up," she said while glancing nervously at Allendria. "What are we going to do about the declaration of war by the Dark Elves?"

Allendria laughed at her question. "No need to be nervous, Kat. It is an unpleasant situation but must be addressed. Most of our military are firm supporters of my traitorous uncle. There are a handful of loyalists to my father, but not enough to sway the tide in any engagement. I'd suggest we build up and prepare for now. It isn't uncommon for my people to wait long stretches after declaring hostilities to actually do something."

As if on cue, a muffled thump sounded outside the building. Everyone inside froze for a few seconds. Another sound followed close behind, and the crowd began looking around in confusion.

"That can't be good," Arthur groaned as he stood up.

Samson jumped up as well and dashed outside, presumably to find a guard. Arthur and Allendria followed. Arthur called back over his shoulder as they exited the inn, "Dalia and Kat, get everyone safely indoors."

When they reached the middle of the street, they turned toward the sound. Flashes of red punctuated the sky near the outer wall. Small explosions peppered the stone fortifications in the distance. A young man in city guard armor ran up to them.

"Your Majesty, the Dark Elves are attacking."

Chapter 14

Rally

Arthur and Allendria looked at each other.

"You just had to jinx it," Arthur told her with a wry smile.

"Oh, shut up, and let's get to the walls."

Arthur felt a mental link form and opened himself to the communication.

There are about fifty of them. Half appear to be casters. The rest are standing in front to guard them with tall tower shields. Balair said.

Should we go in and fight? Calfuray asked.

No! Allendria projected into their shared mental communication. Apparently, Cal added her in the loop. *Their magic is probably strong enough to hurt you.*

That's the point of a fight. Cal added.

If you insist on fighting, be careful. Arthur pleaded.

Nope, I'm good. Balair said. *I'll take Allendria's advice.*

Arthur expected nothing less from the little beast and chuckled at his response. A streak of purple fell toward the section of the wall under siege. Arthur and Allendria ran down the road toward the assault.

Cal dipped lower than the wall, and more flashes of bright red and orange lit the sky. They couldn't see the fight from this far away, especially not behind the wall itself.

Calfuray lifted off again and gained altitude. She moved in lazy circles as she rose higher.

You were right. She told Allendria. *A hint of a grimace in her communication. That one little bastard's lightning spell stung a little. Good thing I bit his head off.*

Arthur and Allendria continued running toward the fighting while Calfuray and Balair kept them apprised of the situation.

They appear to be testing the defenses. They are primarily aiming large siege-type spells at the crenelations. Judging by their expressions, they don't like how well they hold up against the onslaught. Calfuray said.

One of the construction crew mages is here on the wall with me. I'm traveling with her to make sure no stray spells get her. She is quietly repairing what little damage they do as they cast their spells. Balair told them.

I don't know who that is, but I can guarantee I'm giving them a bonus when this is over. Arthur thought.

They finally got within range of the wall and saw Samson on the battlements, shouting orders. Archers fired arrows, but they couldn't see if it had any effect. Arthur and Allendria looked at each other, dashed up the stairs to the walkway, and observed the scene.

The large shields the elves carried easily brushed the arrows from their forces off. They shone bright silver in the midday sun.

"Samson, have them hold the arrow fire," Arthur yelled to the paladin. He could have given the order himself, but he didn't like to command people he placed under someone else. It could be demeaning to the person in charge.

Samson relayed his message, and the arrows stopped. The elves with the shields visibly relaxed ever so slightly. The casters didn't stop their assault. A small fireball exploded near their position, and Arthur felt the heat wash over him. It wasn't close enough to actually cause any harm, but it was noticeable.

Arthur gathered power in both of his hands and Dual Cast Searing Beam at one caster. The two beams of power jolted forward and sizzled through the air. Waving frantically in the air, the dark elf caster caused a slightly opaque shield to spring into existence around him. The two beams struck the shield, and sparks flew from the impact.

Looking more confident, Arthur saw a grin on the dark elf's face. It vanished in a flash as he saw his shield melt like candle wax, and the beams burned into his chest. Smoke curled out of his mouth, still open from his attempted scream.

You receive 315 experience in Fire Magic for Dual Casting Searing Beam.
You dealt 390 damage to Dark Elf Magician (Level 12) (Critical Hit).
Dark Elf Magician (Level 12) has died.
You receive 180 experience.

Man, my spell bonuses and that crit hits hard.

Another Searing Beam crossed the space and hit a different elf. Their shield held, and Allendria grimaced.

"Not fair. Yours made it through, but not mine."

"I Dual Cast mine. Want to give it a shot?" Arthur asked.

"Are you sure it will wo…" she started, but then they both ducked when they saw a flash. A line of red fire blasted over their heads. Both were currently working Fire Magic, so their elemental protections against fire were high enough that it didn't hurt them.

"Screw it. Show me." She said.

She placed a hand on him and sent pure Fire Magic mana into him. He appreciated the refined mana and activated his Dual Casting, while gathering power in each hand for Searing Beam. This spell kicked off and dashed across the gap. The mages seemed to have a better grasp of their power, and multiple shields popped into existence in front of his target. The spell burned through three of the shields before finally scorching the face of the fourth a deep black.

Looks of fear flashed across the dark elf casters, and they began yelling at each other. Arthur couldn't make out what they said from this distance, but it sounded heated.

"That worked!"

Arthur turned to see Allendria building up her Fire Magic in both hands.

"I wasn't sure if that would also pass on Abilities as well, but good to know. Have some fun with it." Arthur suggested, pointing toward the gathered warriors.

Allendria lifted her hands and blasted both of her spells off at one warrior holding a shield. Arthur watched the man's shield visibly shake as he prepared for the impact. The fire seared into the metal, and the waxy polish burned to a crisp and floated away like ashes in the wind. The point of impact glowed red hot, and the man screamed from his position on the field.

The spell dissipated, and the entire shield was a beacon of red. The screams continued as everyone around backed away from the item. It shook a few times before it collapsed backward onto the ground. A deep, sizzling noise came from underneath, and black smoke curled out of the edges.

One guard near Arthur made a gagging noise at the sight.

"That's pretty rough. Hopefully, he was dead when he hit the ground." Arthur said.

The fire in Allendria's eyes died as she realized what she had done. A look of grief took over, and she sighed. "It is gruesome. I'm sure the heat scorched his lungs, and he was dead before it collapsed. I hope that will get them to see reason, and they will stop attacking. Killing them isn't my first option. Half of them probably don't even want to be here."

Both of them turned their focus to the attacking force. They were slowly regrouping after their earlier scattering from the molten hot shield. All the fighters reformed into their existing formation, a little farther to the side of the scorched fighter.

A large purple streak swooped by, and a jet of flame sprayed over the force. All the remaining mages lifted their arms, and another opaque shield sprung up over their heads. The combined effort shielded the tightly knit group, and the flames dissipated to the sides.

Hey Cal, how about you and Balair stand down? I'm going to see if we can get them to talk and withdraw. Arthur told them.

Arthur built up power with his Air Magic and projected his voice. "I am King Arthur Firebrand. I would like to meet to discuss terms with the officers of your force."

The dark elf mages clustered up in conversation. A few minutes later, one raised a stick with a ripped white cloth on it, which Arthur took as a temporary peace banner.

"Let's go talk to them." He told Allendria.

The two of them walked to the base of the wall and he motioned for Samson to join them.

"Come with us during our discussion, will you?" Arthur asked the paladin.

"Of course." He agreed. After a couple of seconds of scanning the wall, he pointed. "Noah, you have command until I return."

The guardsman saluted, and the three companions walked to the nearest gate. They exited in quick succession and shut the large doors behind them. Loud *thumps* punctuated the beams locking in place.

Arthur watched three members of the attacking force peel away and continue toward them, holding the makeshift white flag aloft. They trekked across the grass and finally met halfway.

Arthur lifted a hand. "I'm King Arthur Firebrand. This is Paladin Samson, the Captain of the Guard," he continued, pointing toward the man. "I'm pretty sure you all know Princess Allendria."

The eyes of the elf that Arthur assumed was in charge smoldered at that statement.

"Of course. Good to see you, Princess," he said with a slight bow of his head.

Allendria sighed, "Come now, Tirithan, just leave. You're outmatched, and you know it. Arthur was even kind enough to hold back Lady Calfuray. Please don't waste our peoples' lives."

"I obey the order of my King and not you. He wants that man dead," he punctuated with a jab of a finger at Arthur.

"So, you want all your men to die for nothing?" She asked.

"I want to do my duty to my people."

"Your duty is to protect our people. Waging this useless war protects no one. As you can see, I'm not under any duress. I'm here by my choice. Stop falling into the lies of that traitor." She spat.

His eyes softened for a few moments, and the rigid lines in his forehead relaxed. "I wish it was that simple, Princess. I have my orders. It's time we get back to the fight."

"Good luck, Tirithan. Please retreat." She said.

"I have to fulfill my oath." He said while waving the others to return to the main force. When they were a few steps away, he leaned in and whispered something to Allendria. Arthur couldn't hear what he said, but she smiled at him and nodded with tears in her eyes as he backed away. With a last nod to her, he turned and walked back to his forces.

Arthur, Samson, and Allendria all did the same and headed for the wall.

"Did he say something we need to know, or was it personal?" Arthur asked her.

"He told me another force with around two hundred and fifty more fighters is roughly two days behind him. He also told me to stay strong, and my father would be proud of me." She finished with a sniffle.

Arthur reached over and grabbed her hand as they entered the gates.

They gathered together, and Vana came down to join them. The four held a makeshift meeting out of earshot of the rest of their guards.

"So, what's our play?" Samson asked.

"Allendria," Arthur started as he turned to look at her, "they are your people. I'll let you make the call."

"Let's just hold them off for now. Nothing overly lethal. They are probably close to running out of mana and will retreat for the time being. Keep guards on alert around the entire perimeter of the wall to see if they try a sneak attack anywhere else. I have a feeling we will end up having to kill them, but I want to avoid that." She said with obvious pain in her voice.

Arthur reached over and gave her shoulder a light squeeze. "Then that is what we'll do. Samson, fight back. Try not to kill any of them. If it happens, there is nothing we can do about it. Let's just force them to retreat for now and monitor them."

"Allendria, are any of them rangers?" Vana asked.

"None that I saw wore regalia denoting that. They may have one or two in the woods watching their back, though."

"I'm going to send some of my best to keep an eye on them when they enter the forest, so they can't sneak up on us as easily," Vana told them.

"Great thinking. Standard flare signals for a threat?" Arthur asked.

"Yep, the ones I have picked all have Fire Magic."

They agreed to the plan, and Samson climbed the walls and started shouting orders. Arthur turned to walk to the battlement.

"I'm going to throw a few more spells to chase them off and make them waste mana blocking with their shields. I won't Dual Cast for now. Why don't you go visit with Daranth?" He suggested.

Allendria nodded, and he kept to his word. A few Searing Beams flew from the wall, but he deliberately aimed for places no lethal damage would happen even if it punched through their shields. A few of his targets received some burns, obvious as they flinched from the fire, but nothing threatening. After half an hour, the Dark Elves appeared to run out of mana and formed up to leave. The group slowly filtered into the trees, and one lone figure remained. Arthur was fairly certain it was Tirithan. The soldier saluted with his fist across his chest before following his forces.

It's a shame when men of honor are used in such dishonorable ways.

Arthur left the wall and yelled over to Samson. "I'm headed back to the inn. Set up a full watch rotation. May want to double the numbers if we have the people."

"Already done. I'll manage this," Samson said.

Arthur continued toward the inn and contacted Balair and Calfuray on the way.

Thank you both for your help. If you see them return, just try and deter them for now. Keep them on their toes and make them waste their mana.

Yeah, we can do that. Balair agreed.

Is she going to be okay? Calfuray asked. The soft tone and concern in her voice honestly surprised Arthur. She always seemed so aloof.

Probably not, but this world is cruel like that.

His return to the city prompted the citizens to emerge from their hiding. He smiled and put on a friendly face for everyone as he walked back into the inn. There was a large crowd when he entered.

"It's safe for the time being. You can all return to normal business. No one is to leave the walls until further notice." Arthur said over the crowd. They all slowly filtered past, and Arthur motioned Dalia and Kat back toward the table in the corner. The three sat down to continue their conversation.

"Want to tell us what happened?" Dalia prompted.

"Just a small force to harass us from the Dark Elves. There is another group a couple of days behind them. Nothing serious right now." He brushed off with a wave.

"Back to the status of the city. How are our smiths doing?" Arthur asked.

"Production is great. Samson has two apprentices now in the realm of Arcane Smithing. They have a full operation of assistants over there. We were lucky and uncovered a few metal deposits that supplied a lot of resources. We also uncovered a pretty hefty amount of copper, silver, and gold. This helped us greatly expand the treasury and really get the economy running on pure coinage instead of just promises." Kat told him.

"I'm proud of the work both of you have done. Dalia, I want you to arrange your transfer to Seora. The city needs help, and I know you can handle it. Take a small guard force with you. Include at least one mage. The city already has the beginning stages of construction crews, so there is magic there. Take any of your personal items you need with you. Any luxuries you need also take. It's still a pretty slim market there. You may also take some of our excess goods and basic items. Old furniture, kitchen utensils, scrap cloth, cast-off clothes, etc. Anything that this town could've used when I arrived, they still need in Seora. Try and leave in a few days, if possible."

"I'd be honored," she said. "Can I start now?"

Arthur waved his agreement, and Dalia hurried from the inn.

"There's something odd about her," Kat said in a low voice.

"She is a little spoiled and thinks way too highly of her position sometimes. It is what we would normally consider 'stuck up.'" Arthur said with a nod.

"There is that," Kat agreed. "But it also feels like something else. I don't fully trust her."

"Nothing wrong with staying on your toes. She's given me no reason to mistrust her yet, so we will just have to play the cards we are dealt. We set most of Seora up to recover before we left, and a couple of those left in charge should be able to keep things running. The leadership's hands have been untied, and we gave them access to resources previously denied."

Kat just sighed in agreement. "I'll admit most of the success around here has been because of a handful of people. Rowan has been a force of nature. He ramped up production and got our guard forces equipped and still stayed on top of making all the everyday items. I'm truly grateful you taught him that Arcane Smithing skill because without it, I'm pretty sure he would've murdered someone with all the requests for nails."

"Ha, making nails sucks without it, for sure." Arthur laughed.

"Daniel has been a stalwart force in the wellbeing of the people. The inn is a huge attraction, and his meals are nigh on legendary. Finally, Daranth has been a massive driving force. He has single-handedly whipped the Dark Elves into a frenzy with their woodworking. I'm sure you noticed all the new decorations on your way into the city?" She asked.

"I did indeed. They had the look of elven work."

"That's not even half of it. They strove to make sure each household had the bare essential furniture before worrying about decorations. Each house has a seating bench and a bed at a minimum. They make sure that families have a bed for the parents and then one for each child as well. They have made many other pieces but sell those, and they keep the prices very fair."

"Sounds like I need to go thank him as well."

"You probably should. Honestly, the city runs itself fairly well."

"That's some of the best news I could have got today. Sadly, I have to prepare for war, and the last thing I need to worry about while on a campaign is if the city is going to collapse on itself while I'm gone." Arthur sighed.

"You set the right policies early and put the correct people in charge. It also helps that those in charge are passionate about what they do. We can take care of this city. You go win the war."

"Wars." Arthur corrected with a soft smile. "Thanks, Kat. I'm going to go see Daranth. Need anything from me?"

"No, Your Majesty."

"We are way past that nonsense. Still just Arthur to you. Can you make sure Vana, Samson, Dalia, and Daranth are here for a meeting in the morning? We need to discuss our upcoming fighting."

"I'll take care of it. What about Lady Allendria?"

"I'll tell her tonight. Oh, I forgot to mention, I proposed to Allendria, and she said yes. She will be the future queen of the kingdom."

"That's great news." Kat blurted. "Congratulations."

"Thanks, Kat. Off to see an elf about some wood." He said as he stood and walked out of the inn.

The cool breeze outside swirled around him, and he realized just how warm he'd been in the inn. His armor wasn't nearly as thick or padded as Samson's, but it still held a decent weight to it. Airflow was a sincere concern.

The trip to the Dark Elf quarter of the city didn't take long. Daranth stood in front of the main building in the square with Allendria. This was their version of city hall, from what Arthur recalled.

"I hear you've been a tremendous help around here," Arthur began as he walked up to Daranth and firmly shook his hand.

"I've tried to keep things in order. We've had a great time getting back to our roots and enjoying the craft. Back home is far too depressing with all the restrictions and mandates."

"It's apparent they are fools to limit your craft. The few decorations coming into town drew the eye with their artistry, and Kat tells me that furniture has been rolling out in quick fashion." Arthur praised.

"It really is fantastic." Allendria agreed.

"Thanks, Arthur. You gave us a place to call home for now, and we want to repay the favor. Your lumberjacks have helped to supply us with the wood we need. We even have custom work for sale now instead of the city labor we provide for base furniture. All that said, I'm sure that's not the main reason you came by," Daranth prodded.

Arthur nodded along and frowned as he finished. "It was the main reason I came over, but I wouldn't say it is the only reason. I want your opinion on the attack against us. I really don't want to alienate your people by fighting against people they may consider friends."

"I won't say we like it," Daranth said, "but we understand the necessity. Tirithan is truly an honorable man, so I wish there was another way. I'd hate to see him as a casualty of this nonsense."

"Can you think of any options?" Allendria pleaded.

Daranth shook his head. "No, Princess. He will follow orders to a fault. I fear it will take a show of force to make them retreat. That is sure to come with a nasty butcher's bill."

Chapter 15

War Council

Arthur and Allendria walked down the street and into the inn and found a group of familiar faces staring back at them. The city leaders were seated at a large table in the corner, and Kat was standing near the table with an expectant look in his direction. Arthur waved at the people, and they walked over to join them.

"Everyone is here and waiting," Kat told him as he approached.

"Thanks, Kat," Arthur said.

Allendria walked to the table and sat in an empty seat.

"Foremost, thank you all for your hard work. I left a budding village and returned to a full-on city. Every one of you worked hard to make this happen. If you need anything from me, please let me know after the meeting. That being said, this meeting is a touchy subject. I assume you all saw the message about the declaration of war from the Dark Elves?" Arthur asked.

Heads nodded around the table, and he continued.

"It is a difficult position we are in. Like any other war in history, many of the people fighting us are doing so because they have to or are honor bound. While not the best argument to make, it still leaves it to us to win this war without destroying an entire people. I'd like to open up a discussion of possibilities in this war." Arthur said.

Daniel cleared his throat and raised an eyebrow. "Not to be indelicate, but should Lady Allendria and Daranth be here for this?"

"Daniel, I assure you I understand the necessity of this action. I have to remove my uncle from his stolen throne one way or another. This is as good of a reason as any," Allendria said.

Daranth immediately followed. "I am with my Princess in this. The corruption is getting worse with my people. They are worshipping evil, and I wish for us to root out this corruption now before our race becomes a footnote in history."

"Also, I know it is a little impromptu of an announcement, but I proposed to Lady Allendria, and she has accepted. She will be the future queen of the Kingdom of Fire."

Looks of shock greeted them for a moment before clapping and cheering took over. Everyone said their congratulations, and Arthur calmed the crowd back down.

"Now, back to our original topic. I am considering a quick attack with any volunteers we can muster. We would wait for the reserve forces to arrive outside for the siege, push back their fighters, and immediately march on the capital. Our assault on Seora showed our magical superiority." Arthur said.

"I wouldn't recommend that." Both Allendria and Daranth said in unison. They looked at each other and smiled before Daranth waved for Allendria to continue.

"Our people aren't as numerous as yours. We have roughly five hundred soldiers in our main military. They could probably call upon another two hundred and fifty to supplement those numbers in an emergency. The major difference is magic. Our people are all trained in at least basic magic. Even those outside of the gates with shields have minimal magic to use. They usually focus more on augmentation spells instead of projectile style."

"Are there any true masters of magic? So far, I haven't been impressed with what I've seen from them." Samson said as he crossed his arms.

"They don't look that impressive compared to Arthur or me, but we have special skills that put us ahead. They can easily go toe to toe with any of the standard mages in our force." Allendria said.

"What about equipment? Could we outmatch them in that department?" Samson asked.

Allendria looked thoughtful. "Our armor and weapons are all quality pieces and well made. They aren't overly flashy and, if enchanted, are only lightly so. The city guard armor that is used here is better than almost all the standard gear back at home. Only the true elite warriors would have something equivalent or better."

"How are the exterior defenses? Do they keep scouts out or have frequent patrols? Any traps or magical wards?" Vana asked.

"There are some wards, but they are usually not dangerous. They are used to alert them of intruders." Daranth said.

"That sounds dangerous to me," Arthur chuckled.

"I meant dangerous as in inherently deadly." Daranth clarified. "There are occasional patrols, but I don't know the rotations."

"Let's plan to march on the capital in two weeks' time. That gives us time to mass manufacture some armor and weapons with real enchantments on them. During that time, we need to have our battle mages rotating out on the wall and burning mana for experience every chance they get. The day before we will leave, we will organize an assault on the siege force around us. Hopefully, by then, we have convinced them to turn and leave." Arthur proposed.

"I don't know, Arthur. I think you may be underestimating their capabilities." Allendria told him.

"Not sure what else we could do. It's going to be a nasty fight, no matter how it happens." Arthur said.

"I find myself siding more with Allendria here," Samson told him. "She has far better knowledge of our enemies' capabilities."

"I think we proceed with this plan. If we can think of a better one before then, I'm all ears." Arthur said.

"We have a good surplus of metal since you left. Any idea what you want to create?" Rowan asked.

"We need a few regiments of fighters. I'd say we create a heavy armor unit that is outfitted similarly to our guard forces. We can create shields for them. I'll find an enchantment that can help against spell damage. We will use another with a set of lighter chain armor. That one will focus on speed and strength. We'll give them spears to be our primary damage dealers in formation. That leads us to the rangers," Arthur said as he shifted focus to Corianne. "How are our leather stores?"

"We should have more than enough for anything you need. The hunters have been working overtime, and we have focused hard on stockpiling resources."

"Good," Arthur agreed and turned to Vana. "Can you get me a head count of volunteers for this fight? I want to know how many sets of armor I need to make. If you need anything special on them, let me know."

"Can you create enchantments to help conceal their movement? Something with shadows or the like?" She asked.

"Not sure. I bet we can try it out." Arthur said. "Do we have any cloth produced here yet?"

All eyes turned to Kat. "We have some, but not enough to use as armor. I figure you were planning to ask about the mages?"

Arthur nodded in agreement.

"I'd suggest you focus on lighter leather for them and the good accessories. We found a large deposit of copper and silver while you were gone. Samson used it to supplement our coinage, but there is plenty left for some more necklaces. The finer metal should hold better enchantments." Kat said as she made a few notes on her sheaf of paper.

"Sound advice. I'll use thinner leather and some furs to make them something. Any questions related specifically to the war?" Arthur asked.

Everyone shook their head in the negative. "Thanks for your input. You're all free to resume your normal business. Keep anyone from going outside the walls for now."

Everyone stood from their spots and dispersed. Arthur noticed a couple of faces lingering around. Dalia was the first to approach him.

"You need anything from me?" She asked.

"Not currently. Just focus on preparing for your trip. I don't want to delay you, so we will send you North from the city and then have you turn toward Seora. I'll also ask Calfuray to shadow you for the first couple of days of your trip to ensure no one tries to attack you."

"Thanks, Arthur. Is there any chance I could commandeer one of those carts you used for the army? I need something to pack my stuff into."

"Go for it. Hauling it could be a pain since we don't have the livestock for that. I won't be there for my golem spell to do the work. I'll think of something in the meantime and ensure it's ready by the time you leave."

She thanked him again and left the inn. Zeke was the next to approach.

"Mind collaborating on a couple of bows with me? Our lumber guys have found a few fine specimens, and I'd like to do them justice with some enchantments."

"Sounds like fun. I'll stop by when I can," Arthur agreed.

Zeke left, and Daniel and Kat approached.

"I guess it's up to us two to make sure you stay supplied?" Daniel asked with a laugh.

Arthur winced at that. Feeding an army was never an easy prospect. They should be able to forage a lot of food from the forest, but probably not enough to feed everyone. They would have to ensure they had enough rations to travel with them, just in case.

"I'd appreciate that. Start setting aside what we can. We will know in a week about how many volunteers we can expect to feed."

"Fine, fine. As if I don't already have a mountain of things to do," Kat said with a good-natured sigh.

"Find an assistant?" Arthur suggested.

"I have two of them already. You think I could do this all by myself?" She scoffed. "That's far too much credit.

"While I trust your judgment. If you think of anything you need to make your job any easier, make it happen."

Kat left, and Allendria took her place.

"Care to take a walk?" She asked.

"I'd love that."

Arthur reached over and grabbed her hand, and they both walked out of the inn together. As soon as they were outside, Allendria turned and pulled him along behind her as they headed west, away from a majority of the buildings. She didn't say much but just kept moving forward and pulling him with her. Not knowing what was going on, Arthur walked along behind in silence. When they reached the outskirts of the city, she stopped and turned to look him in the eyes.

"Arthur, you can't do this. It's going to cause a lot of unnecessary death."

"I don't see any alternative, and you
didn't have anything else to expand upon
during the meeting. I don't like the idea of
fighting in this war either, but we both know
that your uncle will never give up and has to
be removed. I can't think of any other way
other than just directly assaulting the
capital and taking them out."

"Surely there is something that we can do
to lure him out. Bait him with something.
There's got to be something he wants that we
can entice him to come and get." She said.

"Even if we could find what that was, we
just don't have the time for that. I don't
believe for one second that King Wailyn is
standing by doing nothing while Gliran is
waging war against us. If I were a betting
man, I would assume that he's going to be not
far behind on this assault."

"So maybe we should bide our time and use
our military force when Wailyn arrives and
take him out first. That part of the human
kingdom seems to be weak short of his few
lackeys." Allendria said.

"Another valid point that I'm sure is
actually correct, but if your people are as
formidable as you believe, there's no way we
can go toe to toe with both of them at the
same time. Not even long enough to fend off
and kill Wailyn first."

Allendria huffed in frustration. Her fist
quickly clenched and unclenched repeatedly as
her jaw worked back and forth. A small tear
formed in the corner of her eye and ran down
the side of her cheek. Arthur reached over and
brushed it away with his thumb cupping the
side of her face.

"I promise we'll do everything we can to minimize casualties during this fight, but it's a fight that has to happen no matter what."

"I know. I just fear the price we pay will be worse than we expect."

"I can only hope that you're wrong," Arthur said as he brought her closer to him and wrapped her up in a hug. They stayed that way in each other's arms for a few moments before Arthur leaned down and kissed her on the forehead.

"We have a lot of stuff to do and not enough time to do it. I need to get to work on some outstanding tasks. You gonna be okay?"

She took a step back, sucked in a deep breath, and then slowly exhaled. "I think I'll be okay."

"Good. If you need anything, just come find me."

She nodded at him, and they both walked back toward the city. When they reached the edge, they split and went separate ways. Allendria headed toward the Dark Elf quarter of town, while Arthur turned and went toward the blacksmith.

As he neared, Arthur could hear the rhythmic pounding of hammers on metal. The once sizable shop had now grown drastically. What had once been two small workstations and a tiny apartment, now was a sprawling multi-building complex.

The original building was still made of lumber, but there was a stone extension to it that expanded its size. Two other large stone buildings were recent additions. When Arthur approached, he saw one of the new buildings and noticed that it only had three sides to the building with a roof. Inside were three fully stocked workstations with their own anvil and furnace. Sturdy racks of stone lined the walls, while ingots of metal were stacked in neat rows throughout the shelves. Rowan's two apprentices each manned an anvil. Arthur noticed three other people running throughout the work area, grabbing tools, hauling metal, and carrying unfinished items.

In the other vacant building, Arthur saw Rowan hammering away on an oversized anvil. This building was similarly arranged, but everything looked more ornate. Scrollwork stood out on the racks, and a large steel box sat in one corner of the building. The box itself was nearly ten feet tall and twice as long, with a solid door on the front.

"Hey, Rowan," Arthur called as he approached.

The smith looked up from his work and smiled. He set his piece of metal on a nearby rack and waited until Arthur reached him.

"Sounds like you had a hell of a trip."

"It was a lot of work, for sure. The fight was a little dicey at one point." Arthur agreed.

"I heard about the nastiness with Lord Preston. Make sure you stop trying to fight alone. Next time, have everyone with you."

"Circumstances don't always work out how we want them to, but I'll try," Arthur said as he looked around the shop and settled on the partially worked piece Samson had laid down. "Why do it the old-fashioned way? Why not Arcane Smithing?"

"Sometimes you just need to feel the rhythmic pounding of the hammer on steel. I learned how to do a bit of both. I use the hammer to move the metal but also feed in some magic with it to smooth out the strikes. When in a rush, I go straight with Arcane Forging, but we haven't been in a rush lately. With the war on the horizon, I wanted to make one last piece in relative peace before going all out."

"Can't really say that I blame you. Figured I'd stop by and flex some of my smithing skills. It's been a while since I did anything other than basic tools and equipment. Tackling a new design for our medium armor infantry seemed like the perfect task. It will save you guys some time and allow you to reproduce faster with a model to work from." Arthur said.

"It definitely helps. Will also need you for the new enchantments. I've picked up the Enchanting skill myself, but that was just from reproducing copies of your guard armor with the runes intact via Arcane Forging and feeding them mana. I still don't grasp the concept of how they fit together and don't know other runes to make different effects."

"Another valid point. Do me a favor. Have one of your apprentices put together a list of enchantments you think might be needed around here. I'll put together a book that details each of those effects and the pattern to use. You can keep it in a secure space to be passed down by village smiths as needed."

"Oh, I like that idea. I'll get one of them started on it today."

Arthur looked toward the two apprentices and watched as they also pounded on the steel with hammers.

"Rowan, not judging or anything, but have you not taught them Arcane Smithing as well?"

"They have the skill for it. They also use it when necessary, but I put a foot down and make them do a lot of work by hand. It helps hone their craft and also makes them focus on the minor details better than doing it all visually. Those two aren't far from being full-fledged smiths of their own. The three new workers I have running errands are going to be my next set of apprentices."

"I don't envy their position," Arthur said. His gaze really took in the expanded smithy and all the little details. A closer look at the metals surprised him. "You learned Magesteel?"

"Ha," Rowan bellowed, "thought you'd never notice. When you explained the process you used, it took a while to figure out, but I've had nothing but time lately. I turn most of the ingots refined by the apprentices into Magesteel. It only costs mana and is superior to normal steel."

"That's awesome work to figure it out on your own. There also seems to be a large metal box in your part of the shop."

"Oh, that," Rowan dismissed with a wave. "It's just a vault where I keep the best pieces of equipment and any precious materials. Figured we needed somewhere better than a wooden chest in my bedroom."

"Good thinking. I'm not going to keep you
from your work any longer. Mind if I use the
original workstation to start my work?" Arthur
asked, gesturing toward the small forge
attached to Rowan's home.

"Not a problem. I can make an apprentice
use it instead, and you can take their place
in the larger shop," Rowan suggested.

"Don't worry about it. Let them keep their
spots. They worked hard for them. I think the
familiarity of the old workshop would suit me
better, anyway."

"If you need anything, just wave down one
of the new helpers. I'll make sure they supply
you with what you need," Rowan said.

"Appreciate it."

Arthur walked across the adjoining space
and into the original workshop. *It may be
smaller and not as well furnished, but Rowan
sure keeps a tidy shop.*

Arthur's mind went over the different items
he needed to worry about. The priority was
loosely locked in his mind, and he began work.
First item of business was the chain style of
armor for the melee fighters.

Functionality was key, but Arthur always
believed that armor should be stylish and not
just functional. Since he was no longer
struggling to keep his head above water, he
wanted to plan out a design that would be
easily repeatable and make a statement.

With that in mind, he waved one assistant
over. The young lady ran up to him and quickly
bowed her head before returning her eyes to
his. "Can I help you, Your Majesty?"

"Yes. Can you get me five ingots of
Magesteel and three square yards of whatever
leather is the current standard?"

The young woman began to turn and follow his instructions, but she froze. "Uh, what's a square yard, Your Majesty?"

It took Arthur a moment to register the question. He didn't understand how she didn't know what a yard was. It was on many of his descriptions for spells and abilities.

"The unit of measurement. You know, roughly three feet per yard, so a square yard would be a piece that was three feet by three feet."

"Who would use feet as a standard of measurement? Everyone has different size feet. Is it your feet or my feet?" she asked, obviously confused.

"Wait a minute. What units of measurement are you familiar with?" Arthur asked.

"I know meters and imperial standard units." She told him with a smile.

"Which one shows on your item descriptions when you look at them?" Arthur asked.

"Whichever one I choose…"

Arthur covered his face with his palm and mumbled to himself. "Have I been forcing it to my measurement criteria all along?"

With a quick thought, he called up his Fireblast skill but willed it to use metric units of measurement.

Spell: Fireblast	
Requirements: Fire Magic and Air Magic Mana Cost: 250 MP Cast Time: 5 seconds Distance: 92 Meters	Description: Condenses a ball of flame and pressurizes it with air. The resultant orb of fire explodes on contact with its target for the following effects: • Targets within 4.5

	meters of the blast take 300 fire damage and are knocked backward 9 meters. • Targets between 4.5 and 9 meters of the blast take 180 fire damage and are knocked back 1 meter. • Targets between 9 and 13 meters take 80 fire damage and stumble, causing interrupt to any casting.
Mastery Level: 2	

Son of a bitch. Sabotaging myself this whole time. Not only that, using my style of measurement creates spells with odd sizes for the metric system. Looks like it tries to round out some numbers by itself, but that explains why others have a hard time copying the dimensions of my spells. They don't understand the units of measurement I base things on. Must be odd for them trying to figure out why I pick such random numbers.

"Thank you for helping me understand that. In that case, just bring me three square meters of leather."

She only nodded to him and ran to fetch his items.

Now I have to try and consciously break myself from using standard measurements and embrace the metric system. If it is common enough for an apprentice to know it, it must be pretty widespread. Should help a lot with standardizing buildings and roads.

The matter of measurements settled, he returned to his task. He took a charcoal pencil and sketched out rough designs of the breastplate. It wasn't long before the assistant returned with his items.

Arthur picked up the first ingot and examined it with his magic. Tendrils of power seeped into the block of metal, searching for impurities or imperfections. He found none, not that he expected to with Rowan's workmanship, and began heating the block.

Deciding to take a page out of Rowan's book, he heated the metal to temperature and then used his power to hold it steady on the anvil in the room. Selecting a heavier hammer from the rack, he walked over and began pounding it into a rough shape. Before he realized it, he was panting, and sweat was dripping from his forehead. The occasional splash sizzled on the hot metal and pushed him forward.

He worked until the bar was roughly teardrop shape and flat. A slight curve remained so it would fit the torso of a person correctly. With the rough shape complete, Arthur sat down and wiped his forehead with a small rag he found in the shop. His shoulders rose and fell in rhythm with his heavy breathing. The chunk of partially formed Magesteel sat on the anvil, slowly cooling.

Doing that by hand sure felt great. Feels like the high you get after a good workout at the gym.

Feeling a little more centered and relaxed, Arthur focused on his desired outcome for the piece. The crude metal form on the table hovered in the air, and Arthur focused his Arcane Smithing on it. Power filled the area as the line of magic crawled its way across the metal and shaped it into his desired form. The rounded edges sharpened and became more pronounced. A ridge formed down the middle of the piece, and four points became prominent.

When it fell in his hands, he ran his fingers over the details. It now looked like a traditional fantasy-style dragon scale with a raised ridge and sharp edges.

He set that piece to the side and grabbed a fresh ingot of Magesteel. The thought of using a hammer to get the base form in shape crossed his mind, but he dismissed it. There were so many things he needed to do and not enough time to do them already. For now, he needed to get this taken care of.

His Fire Magic enveloped the ingot and quickly pumped the temperature to the necessary level. From there, the power took over and formed the piece to his wishes. The metal flattened and formed into a piece of tightly woven chain mail that made up one side of the chestpiece. To give it some extra flair, he made the chain pattern look like small scales of their own, interlocked with tiny wires. It consisted of a full-length sleeve and the complete back and side panel. He quickly repeated the process with a mirror image of the same piece.

Arthur laid all three pieces on the table in the shop. With careful precision, he worked to heat and forge weld the pieces together. The edges of the chain blended into the edges of the main scale in the chest. On the back, he added metal clasps to make them easier to get on and off. The traditional method of tying it by hand was annoying.

This new piece was impressive. The thick scale to protect the chest looked intimidating, while the tightly woven chain would block most glancing strikes and projectiles.

Before he completed the piece, it was time to add enchantments. With the item being Magesteel, it could hold a large amount of power. Arthur wanted to maximize the potential. The question was, how to enchant it?

They need to be strong but also quick. Being able to move and avoid strikes would be beneficial. The armor could handle glancing blows easily…

His thoughts trailed off as he realized his train of thought was all wrong. The design needed to be focused on fighting as a team and not as an individual. A shield wall would support these people in conjunction with ranged support. They needed to strike quickly and get back into formation. They also needed protection.

    With the new idea in mind, he began his
work. The Expert Matrix was a complicated
pattern, so he pulled out a scrap strip of
leather and began drawing it out using a coal
pencil. The design moved in the rotating
staircase pattern as he sketched it out. When
he was sure the elements he needed were all
present, he picked up a chisel. Turning it
over in his hand, he frowned.

    Surely, I don't need this anymore.

    He set the chisel back on the workbench and
grabbed a small scrap of metal. Calling his
Fire Magic to him, he built up a thin beam of
fire on his fingertip. Using the knowledge and
basic spell form from his Searing Beam spell,
he pushed the power out. The thin lance of
flame slid across the metal and cut it
smoothly in half, also burning through part of
the workbench underneath.

    *Shit. Too much power. Also, need to avoid
the wood.*

    It took him five more tries to get it
right, but he felt a breath of relief as the
spell just carved thin lines and didn't cut
through the metal. The depth was almost
perfect as he looked over the basic cuts he
had practiced.

Pulling the metal back to him, he planned out the pattern in his mind and used his magic to cut the design on the inside of the center scale. It took a large amount of concentration, but he finally finished and looked over the finished product. One symbol was slightly off, so he used a small blast of power to correct it. When he was happy with the inscription, he pumped mana into it to complete the piece. The initial rush of mana left him, and the amount surprised him. 500 mana disappeared in a flash, and then the second half trickled out in a steady flow. He siphoned mana from his necklace and continued the enchantment. When it finished, a sense of calm washed over him, and he examined the armor.

Item: Enchanted Masterful Magesteel Breastplate	Defense: 48 Durability: 350/350 Rarity: Epic Quality: Exquisite Weight: 6.0 kg Mana Capacity: 500/500 Slot: Chest Traits: A specially enchanted Magesteel breastplate. Will absorb damage based on the available mana capacity.

	Enchantments: Absorbs damage at a rate of 1 HP of damage per 1 Mana. This armor grants +4 Agility to the wearer.

   The piece was incredible. Arthur gently ran his fingers over the scaled design and noticed a slight reflective gleam to the shine on the outside. It was a sight better than most people could ever expect to get, and he would hand out as many as he could make.
   People are going to be thrilled about thi…

   Your trade agreement with the Flintforge Clan has been accepted. All trade between the two kingdoms is now permitted freely. Any acts of war from one nation to the other will nullify this agreement.

   I'll be damned. Wesley made it happen.

Chapter 16

The March Begins

The trade agreement was a great start, and he was sure people would pester him about it by the end of the day. Only a select few people would even see that notification, though.

His attention went back to the armor. The insane stats on it made it a must-have for anyone. He expected the absorption enchantment to reduce some of the damage as it came in, but instead, it effectively added 500 HP to the wearer's health pool. That alone was almost equal to his current health total. Thoughts of arming his forces and them becoming unstoppable filled his mind until he realized there was a downfall to it.

I bet it only absorbs damage to the piece itself. So, if someone gets hit in the head, it won't negate any damage...

Not letting despair settle in, he absolved
to make the whole set the same way. The only
difference would be the base stat. He picked
up his trusty coal pencil and sketched out
rough ideas for the rest of the pieces. He
made a helm that wrapped around the cheeks but
left the eyes open in the barbute style. A
stout pair of chain leggings were next to and
then matching boots and gloves. All of them
used the same dragon-scale-looking pattern of
the chest piece. The pants had larger scale
plates around the waist and the finer chain
down the legs. The gloves and boots were
designed around standard leather that was
merely layered with the fine chain, making
them standalone pieces that would be easy to
remove and store but still maintain their
flexibility and durability.

When all the designs were finished, he set
to work making each. He sent an assistant to
fetch him a standard set of guard boots and
leather gloves to work with for modifying
those pieces and used his Arcane Forging skill
to churn out the chain. The absorption
enchantment was the same for each piece, but
he changed the secondary stat. He used
Strength for the pants. Endurance for the
boots and the Grip enchantment to prevent
being disarmed on the gloves. The final one
was the sight enhancement he used before on
the helmet.

Piece by piece, he churned out the designs
and completed each one with their respective
enchantments. The results were fantastic when
he looked them over.

Item:	Defense: 22
Enchanted Masterful Magesteel Barbute	Durability: 250/250

	Rarity: Epic
	Quality: Exquisite
	Weight: 5.0 kg
	Mana Capacity: 200/200
	Slot: Head
	Traits: A specially enchanted Magesteel helmet. Will absorb damage based on the available mana capacity.
	Enchantments: • Absorbs damage at a rate of 1 HP of damage per 1 Mana. • 10% decreased chance to be blinded.

Item: Enchanted Masterful Magesteel Chausses	**Defense: 34**
	Durability: 300/300
	Rarity: Epic
	Quality: Exquisite
	Weight: 4.0 kg
	Mana Capacity: 400/400
	Slot: Legs

	Traits: Specially enchanted Magesteel leggings. Will absorb damage based on the available mana capacity. **Enchantments:** Absorbs damage at a rate of 1 HP of damage per 1 Mana. This armor grants +4 Strength to the wearer.

Item: Enchanted Masterful Magesteel Demi-Gauntlet	**Defense:** 48 **Durability:** 350/350 **Rarity:** Epic **Quality:** Exquisite **Weight:** 2.0 kg **Mana Capacity:** 500/500 **Slot:** Chest **Traits:** Specially enchanted Magesteel gauntlets. Will absorb damage based on the available mana capacity. **Enchantments:** Absorbs damage at

	a rate of 1 HP of damage per 1 Mana. Reduces chance to be disarmed by 20%.

Item: Enchanted Masterful Magesteel Chain Boots	**Defense: 24** **Durability**: 200/200 **Rarity**: Epic **Quality**: Exquisite **Weight**: 3.0 kg **Mana Capacity**: 500/500 **Slot**: Chest **Traits**: A specially enchanted Magesteel breastplate. Will absorb damage based on the available mana capacity. **Enchantments:** Absorbs damage at a rate of 1 HP of damage per 1 Mana. This armor grants +3 Endurance to the wearer.

Luckily, the other notification he hoped for also appeared.

Congratulations, you have successfully crafted a full set of high-quality gear. Due to the Rarity and the Quality of the set, it has been granted Set Bonuses. Your Masterful Magesteel Armor Set has the following bonuses:

2 pieces - Increase base Defense of all pieces by 6.
4 pieces - Increase Endurance of the wearer by 5.
5 pieces - Unlock Passive Ability - Damage Reduction - This ability enables the set to drain mana from other pieces to protect the current piece taking damage. It will not reduce any piece to less than 2% of its own mana by redistributing the points.

That is amazing!
The last ability was the best part of it all. The stats were great, but having it automatically adjust mana capacity in each piece to protect vulnerable areas was awesome. Deep down he hoped it would just make it one big mana pool, but this way could honestly be better. There may be a time when you want to sacrifice that damage to a leg or an arm and save the absorption for a fatal blow to the head or chest.

As if on cue, Samson approached his work area.

"What is this beautiful thing?" he asked as he picked up the new breastplate. His eyes widened in surprise when he saw the stats.

"An epic! And those stats, by the Goddess, man."

"I know, right? It is outstanding. Plan on making a lot more where that came from."

Samson continued to marvel at it as he moved to look at each piece laid out on the table.

"This set of armor would buy an entire kingdom by itself." He whispered.

"I plan for it to buy a life. People are what make a kingdom. The more that I can keep alive in our inevitable fights, the better."

"Uh, not ungrateful or anything, but do you think I could get an upgrade?" Samson asked as he looked over his armor.

Arthur chuckled at the sheepish-looking paladin. "Of course. That's what friends do. Now, with access to Magesteel, I'll recreate your armor in its current form with new enchantments."

"Thank you. It's more than I should ask for, but I feel it is necessary. Could I request you keep the enchantments the same and just add the absorption effect to the pieces?"

"Absolutely. Makes it much easier that way, to be honest. I can quickly recreate each of your armor pieces with Arcane Smithing. Modifying the existing enchantments shouldn't be hard. I assume Divine Fury is still fine. Need a new sword?" Arthur asked.

"I'm definitely keeping Divine Fury, but a new sword would be welcome."

"Let me crank out a few more of these armor sets, and I'll work on the new enchantment layout in between them. When I have it all planned, I'll make your new set. Might have to wait until tomorrow, but we'll see."

"No rush. Tomorrow is fine. I actually came to find you to report that our Dark Elf siege party has been relatively quiet. They pop up from time to time and send a few attacks before retreating. I honestly believe this commander is trying to avoid the fight and just doing the bare minimum to say he is following orders as his honor dictates."

"Good. I want him on our side. Allendria likes him, and you can't ask for better men. Well, Guess I could ask for him not to blindly follow orders from a traitor, but loyalty is loyalty."

Samson snorted at that but didn't add anything.

"Can you do me a favor?" Arthur asked.

"I'm sure I can. Especially after you just agreed to upgrade my armor."

"Can you check with the other party members and see if they need anything? Armor or weapons? Any special requests on their function would be welcome. If Vana or Rayne need leather armor enchanted, I can do that as well."

"I'll ask them. Need to do rounds around the city, anyway. Think I'll head out now and quit bugging you so you can get back to work." Samson said.

"Thanks. I'll catch up with you later. Meet for dinner at the inn?"

"It's a plan," Samson said and waved goodbye as he walked off.

Arthur had an assistant bring him a small stack of Magesteel and went to work. He wanted to focus on ten breastplates to start. Making the pieces in batches felt like the right approach to him.

Each of the sections of the armor was as intricately as detailed as before. Any time he saw a slight flaw in the design, he carefully smoothed it out. Some edges were occasionally rough or not at an ideal angle. It wasn't long before the components for all ten chest pieces were scattered on the table.

Assembling them went by fast since he had included the enchanting matrix on each as part of the Arcane Forging process. Five completed pieces of armor were on the desk when that all changed.

The sixth one he assembled started just like the rest. When he melded the last seam together and officially completed the armor, the air shifted. Power swirled in the area, and sparks of electricity sizzled in the air. The chestpiece floated a dozen feet in the air and began to spin. A smile grew on Arthur's face as he realized what was happening.

Looks like I have a new chestpiece for myself.

The air stilled, and the loud *gong* noise filled the space.

Hark and Rejoice, a named weapon has been created! Essence of Lifeblood joins the fray!

Congratulations, you have successfully created Essence of Lifeblood. This is a unique, named chestpiece. You have gained 1,000 experience in Arcane Smithing and Blacksmithing for this feat.

Item:	Defense: 60
Essence of Lifeblood	Durability: 405/405
	Rarity: Unique

	Quality: Masterful **Weight:** 5.0 kg **Slot:** Chest **Mana Storage:** 0/2,500 **Traits:** A named chestpiece created by an Arcane Artificer. This armor is unique and another like it has never existed on this world. **Enchantments:** • This chestpiece draws in 10 mana per minute and fills its internal mana storage. • Absorbs damage at a rate of 1 HP of damage per 1 Mana. • This armor grants +5 Strength to the wearer. • This armor grants +5 Endurance to the wearer. • The mana in this item cannot be used for anything other than its ability, but the absorption effect covers the entire body of the

	wearer.

"Holy Shit!" Arthur yelled as he cradled the new chestpiece. "I'm damn near invincible in that thing.

The large mana storage alone equaled 3,500 HP of damage. While he couldn't siphon that mana away to cast spells, he could add mana to it from his other items if he somehow took way too much damage. This felt like some kind of power armor on steroids. It also meant his mana pool became even more important to maintain. The fact that it worked for his whole body was just icing on top.

Not only did it have insane stats, the design slightly changed. All the dragon's scales gained even more detail. The entire suit of armor now shimmered a deep red, and between all, the scales glowed a reddish-orange color. It almost looked like molten magma flowing in the grooves. The colors never stopped moving, and it felt like the piece was alive.

Arthur looked up to see multiple faces staring at him. Rowan and his apprentices all watched as he gathered up the armor and walked toward the head blacksmith. He extended the piece out to the man and waited for him to examine it. Rowan's hands nervously gripped it before he held it up in front of his face. Tears rolled down his eyes.

"It's beautiful." He whispered as he looked over every seam. "The stats on this armor are godlike."

"They are indeed. It is going to become my new chestpiece."

"As well, it should be. With your high mana and those abilities, you should be almost impossible to kill."

A near-breathless Samson ran up to the crowd and stared at the piece as well. Arthur swore he saw a tear in the corner of the man's eye as he reached out and asked Rowan if he could examine it.

The smith nodded and handed the chestpiece to him. Samson almost looked scared to touch it when he gently grabbed the glowing metal.

"If something kills you now, it's your own damn fault for being an idiot." He told Arthur.

"Can't say I disagree with that."

Arthur slipped off his current chestpiece and took the new one from Samson. It slid over his head and felt like a perfect fit. The colors didn't really match the rest of his armor, but he wouldn't complain about the massive upgrade it gave him.

He looked up from admiring his armor to see everyone still standing and staring at him.

"You guys gonna get back to work or what?" He asked.

They all shook out of their stupor and grumbled before slowly trudging back to their workstations. Arthur smiled at the display and returned to his own. He was determined to get as much of this armor made as he could by the end of the day.

Arthur considered passing the design out to Rowan and his apprentices so they could begin mass-producing them with their Arcane Smithing, but he wasn't sure they could replicate the runes correctly with their level of control. If he still had to burn the runes in and power it, there really wouldn't be much time saved. He figured they were better off working on the pieces they specialized in for now.

Many hours and a fairly depleted mana
reserve later, he stood in front of a pile of
fifteen full sets of enchanted armor. There
was still daylight left, but his mana reserves
had drastically dwindled with all the
enchanting and smithing. His sword was
completely empty, and his necklace was pretty
close as well. Instead of chancing it, he
called it a day and walked over to Rowan.

"Hey, I'm wrapping up here for the day.
I'll head back to the inn and see what's
popped up for me to attend to since I've been
gone. You need anything before I leave?"
Arthur asked.

Rowan looked around the shop and toward his
apprentices. "Don't think so. Should we shift
focus to make those armor sets for you to
enchant?"

"Don't worry about those. I'll make more
tomorrow. Easier to do the enchantment at the
same time as the forging."

Rowan nodded in agreement. "I think I'm
getting closer to being able to do it myself.
My visualization is getting better. I can
recreate the simple rune patterns and some of
the advanced ones."

"You'll get there. Keep practicing, and
it'll eventually come to you. You guys keep up
with the need of the city for now. I'll handle
much of the war preparation." Arthur said.

Rowan agreed, and Arthur headed for the
inn. No one bothered him on the way there, but
he got a few waves that he returned with a
smile. Once inside, he found Kat and sat down
with her at a table.

"Anything urgent that needs my attention?"

She looked over the stack of paper she held and scanned down the page. "Nothing urgent. I assume you were working on armor. That's a pretty new glowing piece of armor you're wearing, by the way."

Arthur looked down. He'd already forgotten about the new armor. *That explains some of the strange looks when I came here.*

"Yep. Figured I needed an upgrade."

She only nodded and continued. "Food production is running smoothly. With the farms inside the walls, the current raids against us aren't affecting that."

"Do we still have mages working the fields on rotation?" Arthur asked.

"Sure do."

"Make sure they are extra vigilant about fire watch. Don't want a stray fireball coming over the wall and destroying our food supply."

Kat scribbled the note on her paper and then tucked a stray strand of hair behind her ear as she returned to meet his eyes.

"Are there any plans to do anything about that force yet?" Kat asked.

"Not yet. They seem to be holding back and not trying to get into a full engagement from what Samson has briefed me on. We will continue war preparations as normal until their relief force shows up. May have to change that strategy then."

"Then I don't have any need of your time. Maybe try to relax for a while? Visit the bathhouse, maybe?" Kat suggested.

Arthur began to argue and then stopped himself. "I think I will. I could use a brief break. I'll catch you later."

The time he spent soaking in the bathhouse was relaxing. He sank down low in the water so only his nose and higher were exposed. When he finally dragged himself out and put his clothes back on, he wandered to the market. The vendors carried a decent selection of goods, so Arthur found a few nice steaks and some fresh vegetables. A handful of potatoes followed, and he headed home.

It took him a few minutes to get the stove ready and find a couple of pans, but he wanted to surprise Allendria. She walked in an hour later. Arthur had the lights down low and a few candles burning at their table. Plates and utensils already sat waiting, and Arthur came out from the kitchen to see a look of astonishment on her face.

"Welcome home, Hun. Wanted to do something special for you. Go have a seat. I'll bring the food right out."

Back in the kitchen, he laid out a perfectly roasted stack of potatoes and some sauteed vegetables. The seared steak followed, and he took the dish out to present to his future wife. A quick kiss on the cheek was all she got before he hurried back to the kitchen and returned carrying his own plate.

They sat in comfortable silence. Both enjoying the food and obeying the 'no work during dinner' rule.

When they were done, Arthur took the dishes back to the kitchen and left them on the counter near the sink. The look on Allendria's face was full of mischief when he returned.

"You're in so much trouble tonight," she said with a sardonic grin before kissing him deeply and pulling him toward their room.

***

Dalia traveled along the shadows of the buildings, headed toward the outskirts of the city. Her destination was an old portion of the refugee camp that was largely abandoned now. They kept the temporary housing there in case of an emergency, but almost no one, other than the occasional teen love affair, ever visited the area.

The door slid open quietly, and she entered a room with a dozen people holding knives.

"At ease. Just me." She said, pulling her hood back to reveal her face.

"Do we have a new mission now that Arthur has returned?" One lady in the group asked.

"Kind of." Dalia agreed. "I'm being sent to Seora to take over the governing body there. My mission is to subvert the leadership of the city to my control. I'd like to take two of you with me."

Everyone fidgeted, and she could see they all fought back the urge to bombard her with requests to take them.

She had worked hard to cultivate this group of people. Each one of them was hand selected by her to become members of her shadow organization. *Was damnably hard with the zealotry toward Arthur and Lianna here, not to mention that damnable blessing at the church.* She still hated having to sneak into the building from alternate entrances.

"What about the rest of us who remain behind?" Asked one man.

"Your goals are to learn everything you can about the habits of the leadership in the city. Try to bribe as many people as you can to our side. I'm hoping Arthur makes this easy and gets himself killed fighting the Dark Elves. If that happens, your orders are to seize control of the city using any means necessary. Assassinations, bribes, brute force, I don't care. I'll be doing the same thing in Seora."

Her gaze searched the crowd before she pointed at two different people. "Gallant and Jennie. Both of you have been to Seora, correct?"

"Yes," they answered in unison.

"Good. You'll accompany me. I want you both ready to leave in a day." Dalia said.

She laid out the details for a few of her contingency plans before everyone discreetly left,

Getting closer to my goals.

Chapter 17

A Change in Tactics

"I don't like this," Samson grumbled.

Arthur scanned the force arrayed along the tree line. They stood in their standard formation with their large kite shields out front. Their archers remained still, with arrows on their bows in a relaxed position. Sparks of electricity and flickers of flame danced around the mages.

"I'm not fond of it either, but don't know what else to do. They left us alone for a week now. Their reinforcements were here days ago, and they did nothing. They finally form up to attack. Maybe it's time to push back and drive them off?" Arthur mused.

Samson looked up and down the walls at the arrayed defenders. Freshly made armor and weapons glinted in the midday sun. The entire guard force was now decked out in the best Magesteel armor available. The combined power and wealth represented on the wall alone was more than the entire kingdom had at its disposal. Arthur didn't doubt the Dark Elves had a large contingent of enchanted weaponry, though.

The one benefit of the full force showing up had been the event trigger.

Attack on the City	
Requirements: Participate in actions to directly or indirectly influence the outcome of the raid. Rewards: 17,000 experience, 2 Talent Points	Description: A new r started near Alurian either side in the f the side you assist the raid, you receiv rewards.

"I assume they have some kind of plan. Can't think of any other reason they would wait so long to attack."

"Unless they are just trying to pin us in and buy time?" Samson suggested.

Arthur thought about that before shaking his head. "I don't think so. They have been largely unmolested. I don't believe they weren't prepared for this attack before they declared war. It also would be foolish for them to pin us in. Most of the countryside is still evacuated following the orc and goblin raids. If they tried to march on Seora, they are literately putting their back to us and making themselves susceptible to being flanked."

"I guess we just wait and see," Samson agreed before rolling his shoulders and twisting his neck from side to side in a light stretch.

Arthur spent time during the last week upgrading all of their weaponry and armor to Magesteel. Samson now wore a full set of plate Magesteel that was visibly identical to his last set. He even kept most of the enchantments from his previous set the same while adding in the shared damage absorption from the mail armor sets. Samson now had nearly forty percent more defense and a ton of extra effective health.

They arrayed their entire force in that line. I don't see any hints of movement in the trees and nothing in the surrounding area. Calfuray sent to him.

Thanks Cal. Can you keep over-watch for me? I don't plan on you engaging them unless necessary.

Sure. The little rat can come back down to assist in the fight.

Little rat! I swear one of these days I'm going to pay you back for these insults. Balair grumbled through their connection.

What are you going to do? Get drunk and pee on me too? Cal chuckled.

Balair, come down here and join me on the walls. Might need your help depending on what they decide.

Fine. Balair sent before his figure grew larger in the clear sky. The orange and red of his scales glittered in the daylight as he came to a smooth landing behind the wall. The scratching of claws on stone was audible as the drake climbed the staircase to take his place near them.

Arthur's attention snapped back to the elves outside the city. Magic built in the air as he felt mana condensing near the enemy lines.

"Get ready. They are preparing something." Arthur told Samson.

The paladin immediately passed the warning down the line and the soldiers all stood straighter, nervously squeezing the shafts of their spears or the hilts of their swords. Archers nocked arrows and laid them along their bows, ready to lift and loose.

The building power made Arthur nervous, and he began gathering his own mana. He wasn't sure the goal of their spell, but if the amount of mana they used was this big, he wouldn't have time to counter or negate any of the damage if he didn't start gathering power early.

To his shock, the other casters on the wall mimicked his actions and built up their own power. The ambient mana energy that the forces emitted shimmered in the air like heat in a desert. It gave him hope to see them responding as they should. The heat pouring out of Allendria washed over him and warmed his skin as she gathered her energy.

The buildup of power abruptly ceased and Arthur watched with his breath held in anticipation.

Will it be a fireball? Do they plan on blasting the wall with lightning? Earth siege power? The many possibilities sped through his mind during that moment.

All at once, multiple spells zipped forward from the Dark Elven line.

"What the…" he breathed out as the action registered. Arthur felt the power in each spell and had to make a snap decision on which ones to fight against. His mind jumped from spell to spell.

Fireball, Ice Lance, Earthen Spikes, Shatter Stone, Magic Arrow, Crumble to Dust, and a host of others sped toward them. Arthur quickly picked out those that would deal the most damage to his people or his walls and launched his mana in return. He wrestled control of half a dozen of the spells. The conflict of his mana smothering them lasted only moments before each fizzled. Dozens more continued forward.

Arthur felt the other casters extend their mana and smother some of the other spells as well. *Hopefully, they picked the best options to mitigate damage.*

Chunks of ice splashed across the wall and the crenelations, sending shards ricocheting in every direction. An odd groan came from the gate and Arthur ran down part of the stairs to see what happened. The hinges holding the doors in place were now rusted and looked like a stiff breeze might break them loose.

Shaking his head, he ran back to the top of the wall as fire splashed and lightning sizzled along the walkway. Looking through the crenelations, he saw the Dark Elves approaching in their solid formation.

"Fine, two can play at that game," Arthur said as he activated Dual Casting and built the power for Searing Beam in each hand. In true anime style, he placed both hands together and shot out a concentrated beam of power that would make Goku proud. It rushed across the open field and battered headfirst into one of the shield wielding defenders. The power barely slowed as the shield turned molten hot and the beam blasted a hole through the chest of the person behind it.

You dealt 450 HP damage to Dark Elven Defender with Concentrated Searing Beam.
Dark Elven Defender has died.
You gain 150 experience.

Hmm, it even recognized it as a concentrated spell instead of just two separate Searing Beams.

Arthur shook off the thought and started lobbing spells. Balls of ice and fire splashed into the attacking force that had now transitioned to a run. They were charging for the gatehouse and its damaged doors.

He kept pouring out spells as fast as he could conjure them. Shards of earth pelted into the enemies while he used his magic to make spikes appear from the ground and spear into their army. Their casters worked against him and tried to negate most of his attacks, but they didn't have enough power to fight back.

His effectiveness waned as most of his spells went on cooldown. An arrow flashed through the space in front of him and splintered against his shoulder. The force of the projectile caused him to take a step back.

Dark Elf Ranger dealt 0 HP damage to you with Steel Arrow. (40 HP damage negated)

Arthur looked at his shoulder and saw the armor was completely unblemished. He smiled at the notification and made sure his visor was down and shut tight.

My armor can protect me from lots of damage, but not sure it will work if I get shot in the face.

He kept launching spells the minute they came off of cooldown, but it was inconsistent. Once again, he resolved to expand his selection of magic spells he could use to avoid this kind of scenario. Most of his normal spells ruptured armor and dealt small amounts of damage but weren't lethal. The shields the Dark Elves carried were all battered and dented now from the onslaught but still serving their purpose.

The Dark Elves approached the gate, ready to bust through, when it surprised them and opened. Arthur heard the creak of the door and rushed down the stairs to see Samson standing in the doorway. Arthur sighed, jumped off the side of the stairs, and rolled to a standing position. He raced to the Paladin's side and drew Ember while bringing a new Magesteel dagger into his offhand. Shadows danced along the wall, and Rayne emerged to stand with them. Arthur glanced backward to see Allendria and Vana both behind them and on the edge of the stairs covering their backs.

Arthur turned back to the attacking force and stepped forward.

"Tirithan. Call off this attack. You can't beat us. I'd hate for your death to be a waste." Arthur yelled over the battle.

"Tirithan no longer commands this force. I'm Indatha and I'll be the end of you. Remember my name well for what little time you have left, human." Someone in the back of the force called.

The elf commander called for a charge and Arthur stepped back into their line. The shields led the way, but Arthur didn't care. He lobbed out a dual cast Fire Blast and both of the spells crossed the distance and exploded with an enormous boom, rattling the stone and causing bits of dust and debris to rain down.

"Arthur, we are in here too!" Rayne said.

No further conversation happened as the
remaining fighters closed the distance. Arthur
placed his dagger back in its sheath and
reached forward with his empty hand. Latching
onto the top edge of the shield in front of
him, he pulled it forward, knocking the
wielder off balance and causing them to
stumble. He angled Ember around their side and
slid the sword through their ribs under their
arm. Warm blood ran down the blade and dripped
from the guard as he pulled it free and pushed
the fighter out of his way.

*You dealt 250 HP Damage to Dark Elf
Defender with Ember. (Critical Strike) (Fatal
Blow)*
Dark Elf Defender has died.

A sword slashed at his head and he ducked
to the side before bringing his own weapon
around in a backhanded slash. It clanged
against the defender's armor, but cut a deep
rent through the breastplate. He parried the
next attack from the random elf and used his
strength to knock the fighter off balance. A
blast of ice shattered against his chest,
interrupting his follow up attack, and causing
him to step backward.

*Dark Elf Mage dealt 0 HP damage to you with
Ice Shards. (58 HP damage negated)*

The defender regained their stance and
slashed forward again. This time, Arthur
caught the blade on his own and held it while
conjuring Searing Flame and blasting a beam of
power through the unsuspecting mage.

*You dealt 300 HP damage to Dark Elf Mage
with Searing Beam. (Critical Hit) (Fatal Blow)
Dark Elf Mage has died.*

The defender used his moment of distraction
against him and disengaged from his blade,
causing Arthur to stumble with the loss of
force. The blade came back around, and Arthur
lifted his arm to block his head. Metal met
metal, and his arm smashed into the side of
his helmet with the force of the attack.
Arthur tried to shake his head clear as
ringing dominated his senses. Another impact
hit him in the side and he winced.

*Dark Elf Defender dealt 0 HP damage to you
with Steel Broadsword. (35 HP damage negated)
Dark Elf Defender dealt 0 HP damage to you
with Steel Broadsword. (62 HP damage negated)*

The ringing subsided and his vision cleared
just in time to see the next attack coming for
his head. He bent backward, and the blade
passed in front of his face. Lunging forward,
he tried to run the elf through with Ember.
The fighter was formidable and pulled his
shield over. The screech of metal sent a
shiver down his spine as his blade skated
across the shield. He continued forward to get
inside the elf's guard, drew his dagger, and
stabbed. It sank into the soldier's gut and
the man doubled over.

*You dealt 135 HP damage to Dark Elf
Defender with Enchanted Magesteel Dagger.
(Critical Hit)*

    With the elf out of the fight, Arthur swept
a glance across the area. Rayne darted among
the fighters in his shadow form. Wherever he
went, Arthur saw deep puncture wounds leaking
blood.
    Samson stood toe to toe with a group of
defenders. Each tried to push back at him with
their shields, but his strength was more than
they could handle. He used some enchantments
in his armor to push back and turn the tide.
Arthur averted his eyes when he saw the face
on his shield burn with fire. Heat washed over
his side as Divine Fury bathed the area with
flame.
    Elves writhed on the ground as the heat
consumed their clothes and flesh. Their steel
armor glowed red and continued to cook them
after the fire ability completed. Arrows sunk
into many of the unfortunate souls and stilled
their thrashing.
    Arthur spotted the grim look of finality on
Vana's face as she placed arrow after arrow to
end the undue suffering. Allendria did her
part and sent in Searing Beams and Flame
Arrows to finish those she could.
    *Almost seems cruel with them already
burning to death.* Arthur mused.
    "Dammit, Samson! Warn people if you plan on
setting the whole place on fire. You're almost
as bad as Arthur." Rayne yelled as he patted
out a small flame on his cloak. The shadows of
his ability retreated into himself and he
looked slightly weaker. His ability taking its
toll on him.
    Arthur saw a line of fighters forming up
just outside the gatehouse, presumably waiting
for the heat to subside. Not wanting to get
into another prolonged skirmish, he turned to
Allendria.

"Go all out?" he asked.

She looked at the elves arrayed in formation and nodded in agreement. Fire swirled around her hands and Arthur shifted focus back to the attackers. He pulled on his own mana and began dual casting everything he could think of. Explosions from Fire Blast pushed the fighters out of ranks while he used the Fireball and Searing Beam spells to pick off some of their mages and ranged fighters. Spears of Earth launched forward, impaling rangers, and he sent spikes up through the ground, killing even more.

Allendria's assault was no less impressive as she built her power into one large spell. Arthur felt the energy rolling off of her and turned to see everyone standing far behind her as fire swirled around her body. The flames grew hotter and even Arthur had to step away despite his fire protection being active. The power changed from a light orange to a deep red and slowly shifted into blue as the heat intensified. With a cry, Allendria pushed the power forward and a ten-foot-tall wall of blue fire rushed forward. When it cleared the gatehouse, it expanded to cover an area nearly eighty feet wide. The elves turned and ran, but most weren't fast enough. The flames ate the distance until it passed over each person. Once touched by the flame, their skin and armor blackened and they fell to the ground, unmoving.

Allendria looked at him and grinned. "I think I win."

Her knees wobbled, and Arthur dashed forward. He arrived just in time to catch her as she collapsed.

"You're not supposed to burn yourself to the point of collapse. Still a battle happening." Arthur whispered as he brushed the hair back from her face.

"After that spell, I doubt any of them are still interested in fighting today." She mumbled.

Arthur turned and watched the raiding party retreat into the trees. A few of them dragged some of their wounded with them as they went. He looked back at Allendria and made sure she was seated and resting before standing up.

"Samson, order a force of rangers and shield bearing fighters to pursue and harass." Arthur said.

"Are you certain?" Samson asked, glancing at Allendria.

"We don't have any other option. We need them to retreat to their own capital. I don't want them lingering in the area anymore. Make sure our fighters know they are not to engage in a full skirmish. Only hit-and-run tactics to keep them moving."

Samson paused and didn't say anything for a few moments.

"As much as is pains me, it must be done." Allendria said.

Samson nodded in agreement and left the gatehouse. Arthur heard the man's voice echo around the area as he issued orders. Reaching down, Arthur grabbed Allendria's arms and helped her stand.

"Thanks. Ran out of Stamina with that last spell."

"Everyone else alright? Any injuries?" Arthur asked.

"Few minor cuts." Rayne waved off.

"All well." Vana confirmed.

Arthur spent a few minutes casting healing magic on Rayne and sealing up the minor cuts. The young man protested, but Arthur wasn't taking any chances.

"I'm heading back to the inn. It's time to plan the next phase of this," Arthur told them.

They all agreed and walked back with him. Daniel ushered them to the back so they could wash up and then led them to their customary table in the corner. Without a word, he rushed to the back and returned with drinks. Food followed immediately after and everyone fell into a comfortable silence as they ate.

When the last person finished and everyone sat back in their chairs, Paula came and cleared off the table. Katherine and Daranth approached and took a seat with them. The door swung open as if on cue and Samson clomped into the building. He saw them all and joined them.

"Looks like most of us are here. Guess we can start." Arthur said as he clasped his hands together on the table in front of him. "I think it's time to prepare for our attack."

Looks of somber agreement were all that met him. Everyone remained silent for a handful of seconds before Daranth spoke up. "I still believe it reckless to attack all at once with minimal preparation, but I'll stand by your decision. The longer we drag this out, the more unnecessary deaths there will be."

"Any objections? If so, now is the time." Arthur said.

"I'm not sure we have enough fighters." Samson admitted.

"Did we lose a lot during the skirmish?" Arthur asked.

"Our death total from the fight was six. Our mages shielding the walls from their spells made all the difference. We overwhelmed their magical defenses and wreaked havoc with our magic. I just feel we need a much larger force based on the caution recommended by Lady Allendria and Master Daranth."

"How many do you think we need to keep here to protect the city?" Arthur asked.

"I'd say no less than two hundred. With our superior equipment, that many should be able to hold it with sufficient magical support. I'd request five mages stay behind, preferably armed with some of your mana capacity enchantments."

"Done," Arthur agreed. "I'll create some more accessory pieces to store mana for them to use and make sure they are properly outfitted. How many does that leave us with for the fight itself?"

"Four hundred. Maybe. We could probably recruit more from the people we brought with us from Seora and maybe even some from Alurian itself."

"Let's put out a call for fighters and set a marching date for a week from now. That should give me time to make more armor and weapons to outfit the assault force." Arthur said.

"Do we have enough metal left for that?" Daniel asked. He stood near the table, polishing an ale mug with a rag.

"Not sure. I know there is a decent pile of it still left at the blacksmith, and Rowan's helpers are churning out more as we speak. If push comes to shove, I can assist in the smelting process as well. Either way, I'll make everything I can."

"Wish I could wear mail," Rayne rumbled.

"You're much more nimble in leather. Why would you want mail?" Arthur asked.

"That damn damage absorption enchantment you put on the mail armor makes those people almost unkillable. All six of our losses from the fight were people wearing leather or cloth. Hell, one man in mail fell backward over the wall during a Fireball blast, landed on his head, and got up and walked away like nothing happened. The damage absorption even worked for his falling damage."

"Good to know. I hope to adapt something similar for leather but we need to find a higher quality source of it. The basic stuff we use now can't hold enough power for that enchantment. Even basic steel couldn't do it. Only Magesteel can right now."

"I guess I just have to suffer with the damage for now. We should keep our eyes open for higher quality leather, though." Rayne said.

"Add it to the list, Kat. Maybe someday we can get some trade rolling through and purchase exotic hides." Arthur said.

"Rayne. I need you to take a trip to Seora. I have a feeling there will be some turmoil with Dalia showing up and taking control. Our absence may have emboldened some to make foolish choices. Do me a favor and work your contacts to prevent any issues. Don't stay for more than a month." Arthur said.

"Are you sure? I don't like leaving when you are planning an attack."

"I am. You work better in the shadows and in cities. Your skill set isn't meant for open warfare. I'll miss you by my side, but your assignment is just as important."

"I'll take care of it. Am I making the trip solo?" Rayne asked.

"You can take people if you need to. Only volunteers, though."

"See you in a couple of months." Rayne agreed.

"Sounds like we have a week to prepare. Everyone do everything you can to help in that time." Arthur concluded.

Everyone went their own way while Arthur and Allendria left and headed for home. Arthur took the chance to look over the mountain of advancements in his experience. He had everything from the crafting spree for a week, on top of the experience from the battle itself.

You have gained 140,280 total experience in Fire Magic.

Congratulations, you have reached levels 25 and 26 in Fire Magic. Fire Magic spells now have a 75% increased effect. Nothing like the smell of roasting flesh in the morning.

You have gained 36,205 total experience in Dual Casting.

Congratulations, you have reached levels 15 and 16 in Dual Casting. Decreases the mana draw of dual-cast spells by 45%. Need to vary up your combos some more.

You have gained 109,990 total experience in Earth Magic.

Congratulations, you have reached level 25 in Earth Magic. Increases the effect of your earth magic spells by 72%. More stabby things?

You have gained 8,100 total experience in Air Magic.

Congratulations, you have reached level 13 in Air Magic. Air Magic spells now have a 27% increased effect. You need a better imagination.

*You have gained 3,880 total experience in
Water Magic.*

*You have gained 1,005 total experience in
Swords.*

*Congratulations, you have reached level 12
in Swords. Swing speed with swords increased
by 33%. You seriously need training.*

*You have gained 1,005 total experience in
Small Blades.*

*Congratulations, you have reached level 9
in Small Blades. Swing speed with Small Blades
increased by 24%. Magesteel is a nice touch.*

*You have gained 880 total experience in
Dual Wield.*

*You have gained 2,750 total experience in
Medium Armor.*

*Congratulations, you have reached levels 6
and 7 in Medium Armor. You now have 18%
increased defense on pieces of Medium Armor
you wear. Damn cheat armor. Take a hit like a
man!*

*You have gained 980 total experience in
Parry.*

*Congratulations, you have reached level 5
in Parry. Increased success chance with parry
by 12%. Didn't know you even knew how to parry
anymore.*

*You have gained 98,180 total experience in
Arcane Smithing.*

*Congratulations, you have reached levels 19
and 20 in Arcane Smithing. Increases the stats
on items created using this ability by 38%.
Wonder what sweet goodness you'll get.*

*You have gained 98,180 total experience in
Blacksmithing.*

*Congratulations, you have reached levels 19
and 20 in Blacksmithing. You are granted a 57%
bonus to forging speed. Time for an upgrade.*

You have gained 54,340 total experience in Enchanting.
Congratulations, you have reached levels 18 and 19 in Enchanting. Your enchantments have a 54% decreased mana cost. Oh, so close to the unlock.

You have gained 5,670 total experience in Leatherworking.

Congratulations, you have reached level 8 in Leatherworking. You are granted a 21% bonus to crafting speed. Thought you forgot this skill.

You have gained 13,210 total experience.

You have completed the Raid Quest Attack on the City. You gain 17,000 experience and 2 Talent Points.

Chapter 18

Preparation

Rayne studied the crowd as he approached the city gates. It had only been a few weeks since he departed Alurian, and he'd made great time getting back to Seora. The quicker he could check on things and ensure everything was in order, the faster he could return.

People crowded through the entrance one by one. The main gate wasn't open, so they were forced to enter through the small wicket door. Nothing seemed out of the ordinary as he waited his turn and slipped through. The guards didn't seem very attentive as people shuffled by with barely a glance. *That could cause a security issue in the future.*

Once inside, Rayne took in the city roads. The main thoroughfare was now clean and fully repaired. The stylized cobblestones a stark contrast to some of the slightly rundown buildings dotting the street.

People smiled and joked as they walked. The first major intersection held a performer juggling small objects that Rayne couldn't determine. He considered getting a closer look, but focused on his mission. His primary goal was to get back to the city manor and talk to Dalia.

He was never overly fond of the woman. She seemed like an entitled snob the few times he met her, but he figured Arthur had a good reason to put her in charge. The fact she had a true title of nobility definitely helped.

Two blocks from the manor, Rayne's senses kicked in. Something felt off, and he focused on his surroundings as he moved. The errant wind, thudding footsteps, a slip of a hand… He twisted around with almost inhuman speed and snatched a young boy's hand in mid-air.

"Ahh!" the boy yelped in surprise.

Rayne looked down to see a small piece of parchment in his hand.

"What's the deal?" Rayne asked.

"Uhm. Sorry, mister. Someone paid me a copper to slip this into your pocket before you reached the manor. Said if I could do it without you catching me, they'd give me five instead."

Rayne examined the kid. Dark hair hung down into eyes of green. His thin frame suggested he was still recovering from the famine that had plagued Seora for so long. He reached down and plucked the paper with his other hand, and tucked it into his coat pocket. At the same time, he fished around and came back with a silver coin. He turned the boy's arm over and slipped the coin into his palm before closing his fingers over it.

"Thank you. Consider this payment for your deed and go eat," Rayne said.

The boy's wide eyes nearly popped out of his head. His mouth moved to speak, but nothing came out and he just nodded before staring down at his hand. Rayne released him, and the boy stumbled backward before turning and running off.

A few people around him looked at him with curious expressions. Making a scene in the middle of a busy street wasn't ideal. Rayne walked toward the manor, but turned into the closest shadow near the corner of a shop and fished out the note.

We need to meet before you go to the city manor. Find me in the last alley we met at sundown. Do not go to the manor yet.

S

Odd. I wonder what's going on here?
He felt obliged to trust in Scarlett, so he wandered around town to check out the sights. Some stalls held vegetables and raw meat from various game. A few people set up small cooking stands on the street and served grilled meat and vegetables on sticks.

Everything he saw told him the city was returning to life. He passed leather-working shops and watched customers exit carrying bundles with goods. There were even two active blacksmiths. Their hammer blows rang through the streets for blocks.

All of his sightseeing didn't kill enough time, so he went into an inn and enjoyed a good meal. The fare was the standard wild animal with a scattering of vegetables he'd seen everywhere else in town, but it was hearty and filling. *If nothing else, Arthur's homestead plan seems to be paying off.*

He sipped on a pitcher of water with some sliced cucumbers in it. It gave a slight hint of flavor to the otherwise bland drink and provided a fresh take on something so mundane. His seat near a window gave him an unobstructed view of the people passing by, and he spent his time watching.

As the sun sank toward the horizon, he left the inn and walked toward the designated meeting place. When he was close, he activated One With the Ground and let his Earth Magic extend from him. He felt the footsteps of a few people behind him, but they faded away as he turned into the alley. Halfway through, he froze.

He felt two sets of footsteps behind him. They were moving slowly and making no noise, but his spell sensed their pressure as they stepped. Instead of turning to face them, he made a show of looking at a pile of discarded items and kicking through them piece by piece. He shrugged to himself and kept walked. The two figures were still in pursuit, but creeping slowly.

Metal shod boots clattered down the alley in front of him, heading his way. Two figures in heavy chain mail rushed toward him, swords out and ready to strike. At the same time, Rayne felt the two behind him charge forward.

His mind sped through his possibilities, and he didn't like his options. He needed to get to the other side of one group and not get surrounded. His mind led him to a foolish idea, but he went for it.

Running forward, he fished both his daggers out of his belt and ran toward the enemy on his right. When he was a dozen yards away, he jumped at the wall and used some of his wall running skill to bounce twice. The final step hit and he jumped as if to sail over the attackers' heads, only to look over and see one of them swinging their sword right at him.

Unable to change directions in midair, an idea came to him. With a force of will, he pushed out Air Magic into a thick cushion right below his right foot. His leg came down and he felt a slight resistance. He kicked off to his left while still traveling forward. His foot slipped through his pocket of air, but the light pressure pushed him off course enough for the sword to pass near him.

You have discovered the Air Magic Spell Air Step. You have gained 250 experience for discovering a known spell.

I'll be damned. That's neat.
The glee at his new spell faded as he landed on his feet and turned to meet the attackers. Both of the chain wearers faced him shoulder to shoulder while he finally got a look at the two that approached from behind. They wore dark clothes with leather hoods obscuring their faces. Each held a pair of daggers in their hands.

"Hmm. So, Scarlett turned her back on our deal. Fair enough. Looks like I need to clean house." Rayne said as he readied his blades.

"She was too weak. We own this town and the boss wants everyone to know. He will ensure her cooperation. He is awfully persuasive." One of the cloaked figures said.

*She's still alive. Looks like this turned
into a rescue mission. We had a deal. I can't
just abandon an ally.*

Rayne dashed forward and activated Weak
Haste. His mana was badly depleted from his
hail Mary with the mid-air step, but he had
enough to maintain the Weak Haste ability. The
momentum carried him forward in a quick burst
until he came face to face with the first
attacker. Shock registered on the man's face
right before Rayne smiled and slashed his
throat.

*You dealt 180 HP damage to Bandit with
Enchanted Magesteel Swordbreaker. (Critical
Hit) (Mortal Blow)*

The bandit dropped his weapon and clasped
both hands over his throat as he sunk to his
knees. Rayne never slowed his attack and moved
to the next bandit. He sidestepped a sword
swing and expertly plunged his dagger into the
bandit's armpit, eliciting a gush of blood.

*You dealt 200 HP damage to Bandit with
Enchanted Magesteel Stiletto Dagger. (Critical
Hit) (Mortal Blow)*
Bandit has died.
You gained 200 experience.
*You have absorbed 80 Spiritual Power from
Bandit.*

His spirit inside pushed him forward and
urged him to kill more of them to absorb their
energy. He saw no reason to deny that feeling,
so he embraced it and let the ability pull
spiritual energy as he attacked.

One of the assassin style figures jumped toward him, leading with a dagger. To show his superiority, Rayne whipped his stiletto dagger around and drove it straight through the wrist of the approaching weapon. The blade buried in a nearby crate in the alley, leaving the man trapped and in agony.

He wasted no time in dispatching the other assassin with a quick dash to their side and a puncture through their neck. The initial Bandit he attacked also died from their bleeding.

You dealt 160 HP damage to Assassin with Enchanted Magesteel Swordbreaker. (Critical Hit) (Mortal Blow)
Assassin has died.
Bandit has died.
You gained 400 total experience.
You have absorbed 160 total Spiritual Power.

Rayne let his Weak Haste ability fade as he walked to the trapped assassin. They had dropped their weapons and were using their free hand to pry the dagger free of the wood. Each jerk of the blade made them whimper at the pain. Slowly, they were working the dagger free.

Rayne stepped up beside them and placed his swordbreaker along their neck. The assassin froze mid pull and turned to look at Rayne with terror in his eyes.

"You're not human…"

Rayne looked down at himself and then to his empty hand, turning it over and looking at each side.

"Pretty sure I am. Just the wrong human to fuck with. Where is Scarlett?"

"Her? Why do you want to know about her?"

"I have an agreement with her and I hold up my deals. If you tell me where she is and agree to leave this city and never return, I'll let you go. If not, you die," Rayne said as he slowly pushed his swordbreaker. A thin line of red appeared along the assassin's neck and a trail of blood ran down.

"They have her at warehouse four in the east quarter. Please let me go."

"Describe it for me."

"Near the city wall. Large building. The wooden panels on the outside are painted light blue and the paint is flaking off. Three large windows line the wall touching the road and one giant door for wagons."

Rayne considered his words and nodded. Before the man could do anything else, he reached forward and pulled his dagger free in one motion. The assassin collapsed to the floor before grabbing their wrist and frantically trying to reach their feet. It took a few seconds, but Rayne watched as they managed the feat and took off running.

Five steps away, Rayne grabbed a throwing knife and launched it. It sunk into the base of their skull and caused them to collapse face first into the alley. Rayne walked over, retrieved his knife, and cleaned it off on the man's clothes.

"I'm not dumb enough to let an enemy leave." He muttered as he surveyed the scene. He took the few coins he found on each person but didn't bother with their gear. Without a storage ability like Arthur, he had no way to hold them.

Leaving the alley, he scraped the blood off the sole of his boots and entered the street. He kept a quick pace as he headed directly for the warehouse the assassin had mentioned. It took him nearly half an hour since he was on the other side of town, but he finally spotted the place. Two guards stood near the wagon door on the road. No one else was near the building. On a whim, Rayne walked around the side and peeked around back.

Three people stood near a small doorway on the back. Two looked like the mail wearing bandits he fought earlier. The last he wasn't sure of. The man was lithe and skinny. Almost too skinny. A hawkish nose stood out in their side profile and his shoulder length dark hair blended into the shadows.

Rayne leaned on his shadow power and activated Shroud of Shadow. His power would make everyone want to look away from him unless they had shadow abilities of their own. It would only last two minutes, or until he inflicted combat damage on someone.

He walked toward the group and tried to angle himself between one bandit and the unknown man. He didn't want to Scan him and set off his senses.

"Don't let anyone in this door before I return." The unknown man said.

"Does that also apply to Mister Shadow?" One asked.

"Even to him. Tell him to come find me first."

Rayne reached striking distance and brought both blades into his hands. With a quick thrust, he sent one toward a bandit and the other toward the unknown man. His strike on the bandit sunk deep into his side while the attack against the other man caught flesh, but he turned in time to prevent it from doing lasting damage.

You dealt 170 damage to Bandit with Enchanted Magesteel Stiletto Dagger. (Critical Hit) (Mortal Blow)
You dealt 30 damage to Bandit Lord with Enchanted Magesteel Swordbreaker. (Glancing Hit)

His ability faded and the Bandit Lord locked eyes with him.

"You! You're not supposed to be here anymore!"

"I'm not that easy to kill," Rayne said with a smile and activated Weak Haste. To his surprise, the Bandit Lord did something similar. Rayne wasn't sure if it was the Haste spell or some kind of special ability, but they boosted their speed at the same time.

Rayne's daggers clanged against the lords as he deflected the blows away from his body. He had half a step on the lord in terms of speed, but the man held his own. Ducking a sword strike overhead, Rayne disengaged from the fight with the Bandit Lord and instead focused on the other Bandit. He stabbed into the bandit's arm as they swung for him again, and then thrust his second blade into their throat.

His senses screamed at him, so he leaped to the side. Coming back to his feet out of a roll, he saw the Bandit Lord charging for him. Mixing it up, Rayne dropped low and swept his leg out. The Bandit Lord grinned as he hopped over the leg and then raised his foot to stomp on Rayne's stationary foot.

Rayne did something unexpected and instead of dodging, he thrust his stiletto dagger upward as the foot came down. The blade sunk into the heel and the lord fell backward. A scream of pain exited his mouth as he grasped his foot.

"Looks like it's time for you to die as well."

"It's not like that. We were planning on bringing you in when you returned to the city." The man pleaded as he pushed himself backward along the ground.

"Having me murdered in an alley is an awfully nice way to bring me in on some kind of deal."

"That was just a test to ensure you were worthy. I swear."

"I don't like tests. I also don't like liars. Don't mind thieves too much, but can't stand liars. Already have a deal with Scarlett anyway, and I hear you have her captive here."

"Of course. You can have her. I didn't know she was spoken for or we would've left her alone."

"Yeah, no you wouldn't. Had we been together, she would've been killed first. Not the point, though. Your organization now belongs to me. I tried to let you be, but you had to do something stupid. Now I'm going to kill you and go get Scarlett. Then I'm going to kill everyone who was in on this with you. When you get to hell, pick out a spot for your fellow conspirators. They'll join you shortly."

Rayne hopped forward and stepped on the injured foot, causing the lord to cry out in pain again. The act was short-lived as Rayne used the distraction of the pain to reach forward and slit his throat.

A click came from the door and Rayne turned to see a man emerge. "What's going on out here?"

With no words, he threw a knife, and it sank into the bandit's eye before he, too, collapsed to the ground.

You dealt 20 damage to Bandit with Enchanted Magesteel Stiletto Dagger.

You dealt 180 damage to Bandit with Enchanted Magesteel Stiletto Dagger. (Critical Hit) (Fatal Blow)

Bandit has died.

You dealt 30 damage to Bandit Lord with Enchanted Magesteel Swordbreaker. (Glancing Hit)

You dealt 40 damage to Bandit Lord with Enchanted Magesteel Stiletto Dagger.

You dealt 160 damage to Bandit Lord with Enchanted Magesteel Stiletto Dagger. (Critical Hit) (Fatal Blow)

Bandit Lord has died.

You have gained 390 total experience.

You have absorbed 1050 total Spiritual Power.

Not a bad haul. Must have been worth a lot of Spiritual Power since he was a lord.

Inside, the building smelled musty. Scattered remains of old and dried grain spotted the floor in multiple areas. He could see someone hanging from chains in one corner and rushed over. Scarlett hung by her wrists from metal manacles. Bruises covered her face and torso. Her lips were split in two different places, but the blood had already crusted over. Her outfit was slashed in multiple places and milky white skin showed through.

Rayne's eyes followed the chain through the rafters and traced it to a nearby wooden post. He ran over and removed the ring from the post and slowly lowered Scarlett to the ground. Walking up to her, he reached down and removed the manacles. Her eyes popped open and looked around in bewilderment. When they landed on his face, they locked on.

"Rayne? This must be a dream. You're not even in the city. How desperate things must be for me to dream of you." She mumbled.

"I'm here. Came back to check on things and see you got yourself into a mess. I've got you now. You're safe with me. I'm getting you out of here and once I get some answers, I have a lot of people to kill."

Chapter 19

Through the Forest

Arthur crept around a tree and crouched low to the ground. Over his head, he heard a bird call and looked up. Vana stood on a branch above him and motioned forward before showing four fingers. He nodded in understanding and withdrew Ember.

Silently cursing himself for sending Rayne back to Seora, he stepped through the underbrush, doing his best to remain quiet.

This is the type of work for Rayne. His powers are much better suited for hunting down scouting parties.

Arthur heard a twig snap and froze. In front of him and to the left, he saw fabric moving through the leaves of the bush. Knowing Vana had his back, he got as close as he could before leaping from the foliage and attacking. There were no battle cries or warning calls. Just Ember flying forward and skewering the man through the chest. Correction, woman.

You have dealt 240 damage to Dark Elf Scout with Ember. (Critical Hit) (Fatal Blow)
Dark Elf Scout has died.
You have gained 310 experience in Swords.
You have gained 475 experience.

The woman's body slumped to the dirt, and the sound caused two others in front of her to turn. Time wasn't on his side, so he took three steps and swung for the next fighter. Their look of confusion morphed to a snarl of range and they brought their bow around in time to deflect much of the attack. The weapon snapped, and the bowstring sprang loose, slapping the elf in the face.

Arthur saw an attack coming from the other elf but ignored it to finish the now stunned one. He lunged forward, point extended, and the tip slid directly into their chest. A screeching noise followed, and it felt like someone punched him in his ribs.

You have dealt 230 damage to Dark Elf Scout with Ember. (Critical Hit) (Fatal Blow)
Dark Elf Scout has died.
You have gained 300 experience in Swords.
You have gained 460 experience.
Dark Elf Scout has dealt 0 damage to you with Steel Dagger. (46 damage negated)

Damn, I love this armor.
Turning to face the elf who struck him, it was too late. An arrow shaft protruded from the man's throat and his hands clutched at the offending projectile, trying to pull it free while blood leaked down the front of his armor.

Looking around, Arthur spotted the fourth scout on the ground with an arrow in their chest.

"Little reckless, don't you think?" Vana asked as she jumped from a low branch and landed next to him.

"I have the utmost faith in my armor. It was faster to kill him and be done with it. There was no way he could have done enough damage to me in that short of time."

"Curious here. The armor protects from damage, right?" Vana asked.

"Yep," Arthur agreed with a smile.

"Does it stop status effects? Curses, paralysis and the like?"

"Uh… not sure." Arthur stammered.

"Thought so. Then what happens if you get hit by a paralysis effect when you give them a free attack? You think they can inflict enough damage in that time to break through?" Vana asked.

"Now that you put it that way, I see your point. Thanks for looking out."

"Always happy to point out when you're being foolish. Sometimes I swear you are as pig-headed as Samson." She said as she searched the pockets of one scout.

Arthur leaned forward and did the same, looking for anything of value. The man's belt had a small compartment that he flipped open and found a vial with a red liquid. Arthur held it up to look at it.

Item: Minor Vial of Healing	Durability: 30/30
	Rarity: Uncommon
	Quality: Good
	Weight: 0.02 kg
	Slot: Consumable

	Traits: A healing potion that restores 110 hp over 5 seconds.

He dropped the vial into his bag before checking the belt. It was a common item, so he ignored it. Picking up the elf's legs, he pulled the body into a clump of bushes and out of sight. They continued that pattern and he found nothing other than some coins for his trouble. "This was the last scouting party, right?" Arthur asked.

"Sure was. Now we have a clear shot for the city." Vana confirmed.

The two worked their way back through the trees. They maintained their stealth as much as possible in case a new patrol showed up that they weren't expecting. One of the camp lookouts spotted them as they approached and they delivered the password, Scooby, to them for access.

Arthur thought it was a delightfully fitting password. They found Samson in a central tent, planning their attack.

"Perfect timing. We just finished the last of the scouts." Arthur told him.

"So, the way is clear?" the paladin asked.

"Unless a new patrol deploys, it will be. I have my rangers keeping eyes on our path still." Vana said.

"Well, Arthur. Game plan?" Samson asked. "You haven't shared much of your strategy and make this sound like a normal frontal assault."

"I don't see any reason for much more. We should have the advantage in power. After equipping so many with the damage absorbing armor and their mana storage necklaces, this should be a pretty standard fight."

"That's really your plan?" Allendria asked.

"Yeah. What more do we need? Am I missing something?"

"I told you our people have skill in magic. Their gear isn't as good as ours, but it is much better than a normal person or a goblin raiding party." Allendria reiterated.

"What do you suggest?" Arthur asked.

"Go home and come up with a proper plan that has some strategy to it." She murmured.

"Little too late for that. I'm still not sure what we could accomplish with more planning time. We have some of the best weapons and armor possible and our force is well versed in magic." Arthur said.

The faces around the group were stoic, but no one said anything further.

"Fine. When do we march?" Samson asked.

"As soon as you can get everyone ready." Arthur said.

The group left the tent and Samson bellowed orders. The camp around became a beehive of activity as everyone formed up and stripped down their small camping areas. Less than half an hour later and they were on the march.

They ran into no resistance on the way and formed up directly inside the tree line. Beyond the last branch was a long stretch of clear ground. Arthur estimated it to be a couple hundred yards. At the end of the clearing stood the city wall of the Calzas. Arthur expected to see an imposing stone wall, but was surprised to find a thick wall of interwoven tree branches.

Raiding the Capital	
Requirements: Participate in actions to directly or indirectly influence the outcome of the raid. Rewards: 34,000 experience, 5 Talent Points	Description: A new r started near Calzas. either side in the f the side you assist the raid, you receiv rewards.

    He could see the sun reflecting off of helmets on the wall. As one, Arthur's army emerged from the trees and stood in defiance of the Dark Elves. After their call for volunteers, nearly eight hundred people answered the request on their side.

    I sure hope this works out.

    Calfuray, you in range?

    On approach now. Me and the rat should both be there shortly.

    I heard that! Balair screeched.

    I know you did, idiot. Cal said.

    Not now, you two. We have a job to do. Close in and give me a strafing run along the wall when we engage with magic.

    I'll give it a shot. Cal said.

    "Men and women of the Kingdom of Fire. Today, we put an end to a tyrant and a murderer. Let's restore Princess Allendria to her rightful place." Arthur said, using Air Magic to amplify his voice.

A cheer rose from the assembled army, and they all marched forward. Arthur didn't want them too close, but everyone had limited range on their spells. One hundred yards out, and they called the line to a halt. Arthur reached behind him and someone placed one of their new bows in his hand. The strap to a loaded quiver followed, and he slung it over his shoulder. It was time for him to put his Archery skill to use once more. Throwing knives were great in close to mid-range combat but would never hold up at this distance.

"Archers ready!" Samson called.

Arrow nocked an arrow to the bow and examined the finish. It was a standard-looking bow of ash, but if you looked closely, you could see faint lines of power reflecting in the grain. Almost like wet sap shining through the cracks. They enchanted each of these bows with Air Magic to make their projectiles fly farther and faster.

Lifting his bow to the ready position, he steadied his breathing.

"Loose!"

Arthur used his Aim Shot ability to zoom in on a defender and let the arrow fly. The bow bucked with the power of the release, and Arthur felt the Air Magic engage as a small cocoon of power engulfed the flying projectile. It arced over the field and hit the soldier in the chest. The impact caused the elf to stumble backward a few steps.

You dealt 38 damage to Dark Elf Guard with Steel Arrow.

Arthur put another arrow on the string and activated Aim shot to zoom in on the damage. The shaft stuck out from the guard's chest and only the arrowhead itself had made it past the armor.

A volley of arrows flew from the city walls and Arthur lowered his bow and deactivated Aim Shot. He drew on his magic and caused a heavy down burst of Air Magic in the direct path of the arrows. The draw on his mana was heavy, but he only had to maintain it for a few seconds. As each arrow hit the invisible wall of air, they plummeted straight down and lodged into the dirt point first. With a sigh, Arthur released the power.

This triggered a notification as he learned a new spell.

Congratulations, you have discovered the Air Magic Spell: Downburst. You have gained 250 experience in Air Magic for discovering a known spell.

You have gained 110 experience in Air Magic for casting Downburst.

Spell: Downburst	
Requirements: Air Magic Mana Cost: 80 MP/second channeled Cast Time: 1 seconds Distance: 100 yards	Description: Forces air downward at great pressure. Can hold items in place or deflect projectiles.
Mastery Level: 1	

A cheer echoed from his soldiers, and they released more arrows with pinpoint accuracy. Arthur joined in and began firing with abandon. He cycled through targets with Aim Shot until his Stamina got low and then put the bow away. It was time for some more magic.

His most powerful spell was his Fireblast spell, but it didn't fly far enough on his own. He contemplated options as he built a Fireblast in his left hand. A flash of insight gave him an idea, and he lifted his left hand up in front of him, palm up. The spiraling ball of dense air and fire magic swirled in his palm as though a tiny star was ready to burst.

Placing his right hand even with his left, palm facing the orb, he aimed in the general vicinity of the wall. Air Magic created a vortex of power in his right palm and he pushed the power out. The cylinder of Air Magic encased the Fireblast spell and launched it forward at incredible speed. The ball hit the rampart and exploded, sending splinters of wood in all directions.

Congratulations, you have discovered the Air Magic spell Air Launch. You have gained 250 experience for discovering a known spell.
Congratulations, you have discovered the Magic sub skill Combination. You have gained 250 bonus experience.

Spell: Magical Launch	
Requirements: Air Magic Mana Cost: 40 MP Cast Time: 1 seconds Distance: Double Original Spell Distance	Description: Builds a vortex of Air Magic that can launch numerous magical spells. The distance is determined by the base distance of the spell launched multiplied by a factor of 2. Note: Only works on projectile spells.
Mastery Level: 1	

Combination is a sub skill that unlocks the ability to combine multiple spells together to form a new outcome. This is a passive ability and does not level.

Interesting. A passive ability is a bit of a change. Better yet, my Fireblast spell has a base distance of one-hundred yards, meaning it can now launch up to two-hundred yards.

Armed with this new knowledge, Arthur practiced this new ability and worked on aiming. It was four more shots before he finally hit near a guard on the wall. The previous three shots all impacted the wall itself. Two created large scorch marks on the exterior, and the third blew up one of the wooden crenelations on the wall.

He'd pulled excess mana from his necklace to refill himself from the current use. Each of the Fireblast and Magical Launch combos used 300 mana. Needing to take a break, he surveyed the battle. Elves still held their positions on the wall. Scanning the top of Arthur didn't find nearly as many defenders as he expected.

Did we kill that many already? Are they holding back a reserve force inside?

Two more arrows flew for him and he knocked them out of the air with his magic. Footsteps crunched through the grass behind him and he turned to see Vana running toward him.

"Vana? What's g…"

"We have to retreat now!" She yelled as she skidded to a halt.

"What do you mean? We've barely even taken damage." Arthur pointed out.

"They almost have us surrounded. This was a trap from the start. There is a large army approaching from each side, hiding in the forest. My scouts spotted them and barely made it back in time to warn us. If they get behind us, we are as good as dead."

"Fuck." Arthur said as he looked around. The fight was going too smoothly, and now he knew why. They'd been outplayed.

"Form into marching blocks and retreat in an orderly fashion." Arthur yelled down the line, slightly amplifying his voice. Samson heard the call and turned to face him in confusion. The paladin rushed over.

"They are surrounding us. We have to get away." Vana told him.

Samson's face went pale, and he looked back toward the trees. He nodded and ran down the line, repeating Arthur's order and pushing everyone into formation to leave.

Arthur watched as Calfuray appeared in the sky and dove for the wall. The small form of Balair followed on her flank, but he turned and aimed toward Arthur.

Calfuray. We are retreating. Arthur sent.

Already? Fine, I'll light this wall on fire and join you.

A powerful aura of magic drew Arthur's attention, and he turned to face the wall. A figure in robes stood on top of the main gatehouse and held some kind of artifact high overhead. Power radiated from the item. It looked like a prism of silver, but Arthur couldn't see many details from his distance. Arthur's magical senses screamed out a warning. Calfuray must have sensed it as well, because she flared out her wings and adjusted her course.

Her current speed drastically impeded her maneuverability, and she barely veered to the side of the wall. The effort was in vain as a beam of silver energy speared forward from the artifact and pierced her in the chest. Arthur yelled and dashed toward Calfuray. No blood came from the impact and he received no damage notifications. Only one unnerving message came through.

Your companion Calfuray is affected by Curse of the Suppressed Dragon.

The beam of power dissipated, and Calfuray continued her downward path toward the ground. Her body shifted as she fell and slowly shrunk. Arthur picked up speed, watching her falling trajectory and estimating where she might land outside of the wall. A quick glance over his shoulder showed Balair chasing after him, with Vana next to him. Samson and the rest of the army were retreating, as ordered.

Calfuray was on the ground ahead of him and he couldn't believe the sight. Her body was still shrinking. Her scales transformed into a smoother form. Long purple hair cascaded from the top of her head as her horns slowly retreated into her scalp.

Thirty yards from reaching her, Arthur realized they had a problem. The elves hadn't stopped their attack, and a volley of arrows filled the sky. With an angry yell, he exploded with uncontrolled Air Magic. The power saturated the area and gusts of wind blew in all directions. Arrows flew in odd patterns as the breeze clipped their feathers and knocked them off course.

Arthur skidded to a halt near Calfuray and couldn't believe his eyes. A tall and slim woman now lay in the field in front of him. Metallic purple hair spread out like a blanket under her and she looked at him with equally bright purple eyes.

"Arthur… help me."

He fought past the fact that she was completely naked and bent down to pick her up.

"Incoming!" Vana yelled.

Arthur looked up in time to see a dozen arrows flying directly for them. Instead of using Air Magic, he focused on a place on the wall and ripped a rift open in front of them. He set the exit near the wall. Arrows flowed into the hole and burst from the other portal on the wall, impaling startled elves.

You have dealt 1,855 total damage.
You have gained 160 experience in Dimensional Magic from casting Dimensional Rift.
Dark Elf Defender has died. (x8)

Letting the rift snap close, Arthur turned back to Cal.

"We've got to go. Come on."

He pulled her to her feet and tried to take off running while keeping hold of her arm. Barely half a step later, he was pulled to a halt as she collapsed to a knee.

"Cal, I don't know what happened, but we can't stay here. We're about to be trapped inside an entire army of elves."

"I'm not used to this body. It is difficult to maintain balance, much less walk." Calfuray grumbled.

"Damn. Vana, can you help?" Arthur asked.

The ranger nodded and slung her bow over her shoulder. She reached down and wedged her body under one arm while Arthur lifted her by the other. It was awkward since they were different heights, but they made it work. In a quick shuffle, they pulled her from the field and hobbled toward the trees.

Balair, cover us!

I've got you.

Arthur felt Fire Magic flare out behind him
and he turned his head to see Balair roasting
an incoming wave of arrows.

They continued forward, but two elves
emerged from the trees when they were only a
dozen yards away.

Uh, Balair? Can you get them?

A blur of orange swept around them and
plowed into the first figure. Balair clamped
his jaws over the elf's head, and a sickening
crunch sounded through the area. The second
elf backpedaled and pulled out a sword. Balair
pounced at him, but he fared a little better.

The elf stepped to the side and brought the
blade down on Balair's hind leg. The drake
roared in surprise when the blade dug into
scales and produced a thin line of blood.

Hang in there. Arthur encouraged.

Balair whipped his tail out and it smashed
into the elf's face, sending him to the
ground. A few steps and Balair stomped on his
chest, digging claws in and killing him.

The three of them stumbled into the trees
and ducked behind a larger trunk. A bird call
caught their attention, and they turned to see
one of Vana's scouts.

"We have to hurry. They've almost closed
the trap. The two you killed were the advanced
group to deter escape." The scout reported.

"Damn, we'll never make it dragging her."
Vana said.

"Cal, any luck with walking and running
yet?" Arthur asked.

"I'm sorry, Arthur. I can't." She began
before her eyes welled with tears. "Please
don't leave me."

"Silly dragon. I'd never leave you, but we
need to move faster. Only one option."

He turned and popped open his Wizard's Den. During his prep for war, he'd placed a couple of generic beds in the space and one chest for belongings.

"You'll have to ride in here." He told her.

Calfuray looked skeptical as she stared into the magical room.

"There's no other way. I'll let you out as soon as we regroup with our main force and are in relative safety. I promise."

Cal still didn't look happy, but she wiped the tears from her face and hobbled in before sitting on a bed.

"Don't leave me in here or my ghost will haunt you forever."

"Noted. See you shortly." Arthur said before snapping the entrance closed. "Alright, let's go."

Their dash through the forest became more stressful as shouts came from all around them. They weaved a slight zigzag path, attempting to take the path of least resistance for the foliage. An arrow clunked into Arthur's shoulder and knocked him off balance. He clipped a tree with his other shoulder and it slowed down his movement.

Dark Elf Ranger dealt 0 damage to you with Steel Arrow. (28 damage negated)

You suffered 0 damage from your impact with Tree. (20 damage negated)

Arthur got his feet back on track and picked up speed. Two arrows crashed into Balair, but he shrugged them off without issue. His scales provided plenty of protection against normal arrows.

In the canopy, Arthur watched Vana and her scout running through tree branches. The scout stopped for a moment and pointed ahead of them.

"The army isn't far ahead. We're almost there."

"Bekka, look out!" Vana yelled as she slammed into the woman and Bekka fell from the branches.

Balair, catch her! Arthur sent.

The drake darted forward, and Arthur looked up to see a scene of pure terror. Vana stood on the branch where Bekka just stood. She looked at him with a shaft sticking out of her chest. Her eyes bore into his soul as she tried to speak. Another arrow hit her in the throat and she tumbled from the tree limb.

"No!" Arthur yelled as he ran forward. He leaped into the air and caught the ranger as she fell.

He couldn't see any sign of life, so he broke each shaft off even with her body and cast his healing spell.

You have gained 220 experience in Water Magic for casting Minor Heal.

Minor Heal has no effect on this target.

Dammit. What can I do? Do I know anything else? Are there any other spells that might work?

Unwilling to give up, he used his Water Magic to delve into her body and poured in as much mana as he could muster. The energy circulated and he could feel it repair damage to the tissue on the edge of the wounds. The spell ended, but the notification filled him with dread.

Congratulations, you have discovered the Water Magic spell Major Heal Wounds. You have gained 250 experience for discovering a known spell.

Spell: Major Heal Wounds	
Requirements: Water Magic Mana Cost: 120 MP Cast Time: 2 seconds Cooldown: 20 seconds	Description: Use the power of Water Magic to speed up the recovery process of the body. Heals target of 400 HP and closes minor and some major wounds.
Mastery Level: 1	

He glanced at her face and saw the blank stare of her eyes and the truth sunk in.

She's gone…

"Oh, no." Bekka said. Arthur looked up and her hand covered her mouth. Tears flowed down her face. Balair stood nearby, and his head hung low. Arthur noticed an unmistakable shimmer in his eyes as well.

I shouldn't have let her follow me. I should have forced her to retreat with the army. Arthur admonished himself.

His vision grew blurry as he clutched onto her body, wishing she would return.

It's not your fault. She chose to save Bekka. We can't let her sacrifice be for nothing. We have to get to safety. Balair said.

Arthur shook himself out of his grief and
looked around to realize they were indeed
still standing in the forest and in danger. He
couldn't bring himself to leave Vana's body
behind, so he slung her over his shoulder.
There wasn't enough time to open his Wizard's
Den again to place her inside.

"You're right, Balair. Live now and we
shall mourn tomorrow."

The three continued their mad race for
their army. The extra weight slowed Arthur, so
he activated his Weak Haste spell. This added
weight also inhibited his maximum speed. Using
Earth Magic, he infused his body with power
and somewhat mimicked the motions he used to
create the Haste spell. Earth Magic flowed
through his system, pushing his muscles
further and strengthening them. His speed
picked up, and he traveled faster. Before
long, he was back to running his normal speed
with Weak Haste active.

*Congratulations, you have discovered the
Earth Magic spell Fortification. You have
gained 250 experience for discovering a known
spell.*

*You have gained 220 experience in Earth
Magic for casting Fortification.*

Spell: Fortification	
Requirements: Earth Magic Mana Cost: 2 MP/ sec Cast Time: Channeled Distance: Self	Description: Circulates Earth Magic in your body, strengthening your bones and muscles. Effects: • Increases your Endurance by 10 while active.

	• Increases your carrying capacity by 25%. • Removes the speed penalty from carrying objects as long as they are within your weight capacity.
Mastery Level: 1	

Arthur wanted to be excited about the new spell, but he couldn't muster anything but sorrow and regret.

Up ahead, he saw fighting. They had caught up to their main army, and they were engaged in a fighting retreat. Arthur drew Ember as he ran and stabbed it into the back of the nearest assailant. A slash caught the second one in the back of the neck. He bounced from one enemy to the next, slashing exposed skin or stabbing through leather armor. No one expected an attack from behind.

You have dealt 1,455 total damage.
Dark Elf Ranger has died. (x7)

With the bulk of elves out of the way, he signaled one of his fighters and they opened a space for him to pass in the line. Arthur worked his way through their ranks until he saw a bright set of glowing wings sprout from a figure ahead of him.

Samson is using his Paladin ability to heal our fighters. If only he was with us earlier.

The group approached the Paladin and a look
of relief briefly crossed his face before
morphing into a look of confusion as his eyes
fell on the figure draped over Arthur's
shoulder.
"I'm sorry, Samson. I couldn't save her."

Chapter 20

Retreat

"What do you mean, you couldn't save her?" Samson asked. "You pull off magical miracles every day."

Arthur couldn't answer and merely hung his head in shame.

"It wasn't his fault," Bekka said from beside him. "I was scouting in a tree and not paying enough attention. Vana pushed me out of the way to save me and took the arrows intended for me. Arthur tried, but it was too late."

The young woman began to cry and Arthur heard the heavy sniffles as she tried to hold it back. Two rangers approached and Arthur handed over her body for them to carry.

"I'm truly sorry, Samson. I promise to tell you everything, but we need to get out of here. It's not safe and we have a lot of people we are responsible for." Arthur said. Regret lacing his voice.

Arthur looked up and the Paladin's eyes were covered in a sheen of tears. His mouth moved, but nothing came out. He looked down at his hands, and they flexed and loosened, seemingly on their own.

"Samson?" Arthur asked carefully.

"We were going to get married… We hadn't told anyone yet, but we were planning for it. Neither of us had any family, so there was no formal request needed."

"I can't imagine. I don't know what I would do in your shoes. Need me to take command here and get everyone moving?" Arthur asked.

The question shook Samson out of his thoughts, and his eyes blazed with fire. "I've got this. I will keep my people alive."

The statement stung and felt like a personal attack, but Arthur shrugged it off as grief. Samson issued orders, and the column resumed their retreat. Arthur considered letting Calfuray out, but didn't feel it safe for her in this scenario. One stray arrow could be the end of her.

Arthur didn't feel right hiding in the back of the column as they ran away, so he moved into the rear guard. The men around him stood straighter as he joined them and even gave a cheer. All of his grief and anger bubbled to the surface, and he mustered every bit of mana he had left to launch spells with wild abandon.

Spears of ice pinned elves to trees while balls of fire melted skin and leather armor just as easily. Large portions of the forest went up in flames with his spells, and he used that as a chance to screen their retreat. Rushing through a wall of smoke with no visibility was a surefire way to die.

Arthur's mana became critical and his reserve in his items was nearly empty. Instead of fall back, he grabbed a bow and arrows from a nearby soldier and started picking off elves one by one. He lined up shot after shot with his Aim Shot until his Stamina reached critical levels and then continued to fire normal shots as it slowly refilled. One quiver of arrows emptied, and another magically appeared in his hands. The entire experience couldn't have lasted more than an hour, but it felt like days.

His arms burned and his head pounded from the exertion, both physical and mental. A feeling flashed over him, and he couldn't determine if it was relief or anger. He couldn't find any targets. They continued their backward march, but the weapons all fell still. No elves came.

Another hour of marching with a few soldiers watching their backs, and then Samson called a halt. He ordered everyone to rest and eat. They wouldn't stop for long, but he knew everyone was running on pure adrenaline.

His footsteps faltered as he walked near Arthur. With barely a glance, he continued his trek. Arthur took the chance to open up his Wizard's Den. When the portal opened in mid-air, Calfuray popped up off the bed and walked toward the entrance.

"So glad to see you. Was worried I'd never get out of there."

"Sorry about that. I found the army, but it was still under attack. Wanted to wait until the fight was over before letting you out." Arthur said.

Are you going to be okay, Cal? Balair asked into their minds.

"I'll be fine, I hope. Glad to see you made it out alive," Cal told him.

"Where have you been?" Arthur asked the drake.

What the hell do you mean? I know it has been a traumatic experience, but I've literally been by your side fighting this whole time. You seriously don't remember?

Arthur almost snapped back out of reflex. His mind reeled at the thought and he examined the last bit of time. His anger clouded almost all reason and he could only remember bits and pieces of the fighting. He vaguely recalled seeing streaks of red and orange, but that was all.

Sorry Balair. Thanks for the help. I guess I am a little out of it.

"What happened, Arthur?" Calfuray asked. Concern marring her features.

"Vana didn't make it. They shot her after she saved the life of one of her rangers."

Cal's hands shot to her mouth, and she cried. "I'm sorry, Arthur. It's all my fault. If you didn't have to come rescue me, she wouldn't have died."

"None of that." Arthur told her as he reached forward and placed a hand on her shoulder. "Vana was always a caring soul. She put on the tough act, but she had a soft heart. She went out to save you, and that was her decision. Don't tarnish her memory by taking away from her heroism."

Calfuray wiped at her face. "Why do you humans leak so much? This ungainly body is bad enough."

"And who is this?" Allendria asked as she approached. "I mean, honestly, how did you find a pretty damsel to rescue in the middle of a battlefield? Is it some unknown ability you have? How high is your Damsel in Distress skill?"

"Ah, come on now. You know I only have eyes for you. Is that a real skill, though?" Arthur asked.

"Hell if I know. I'm sure if it was, you'd already have it. Now, back to my original question. Not trying to be rude, but who are you?" Allendria asked as she walked up to Calfuray.

"The hair doesn't give it away," Calfuray said as she brushed her hair to the side. "Come on now Allendria. I'm Calfuray."

"Uh… Cal, you shrunk… and lost your scales…" Allendria looked confused before she turned and whispered to Arthur. "Are her boobs bigger than mine as well?"

He only smiled and ignored the question.

"I admit I'm curious. What is going on with your new form? We haven't had time to stop and discuss it."

"That might be a bit of a story. The short version is the Dark Elves possessed an old artifact that allows them to trap a being in their alternate form. Dragons can transform into humans when they wish, but only after learning the ability. The item transformed me into my human form. The curse itself has worn off, though." Calfuray explained.

"Then why haven't you changed back?" Allendria asked.

"I don't know how. I largely ignored humans for my whole life, so I never learned the ability. Since I didn't learn the transformation, I'm locked in this form until I do."

"Then how do you learn the transformation?" Arthur asked.

"I have to venture to a dragon temple and learn it from my spiritual ancestors."

"I suppose it's not as simple as it sounds?" Arthur asked.

"Naturally. Dangerous creatures usually surround dragon temples and they require effort to reach. Once there, it requires me to overcome a trial on my own. On the bright side, the closest temple is only around a week away from Alurian."

"Another thing to add to the list. Are you going to be okay in the meantime?" Allendria said.

"Hey, only I get to add things to the list." Arthur grumbled.

"Quiet now. Soon we'll be married and it'll be my list of things for you to do, anyway. May as well accept it now."

"I'll be fine. I haven't quite managed running yet, but I was able to adjust to walking in the Wizard's Den. Given time, I'll be able to move and even fight in this form."

Good. I can't carry you to the dragon temple alone and you'd be a sitting duck otherwise. Balair shared to the group.

Everyone laughed until Samson gave the order to move out. They all gathered together and trekked through the forest, returning home in defeat.

***

Rayne peered out of the windows of the abandoned building. He moved to each side and scanned the perimeter, looking for any signs of movement. After he was sure he wasn't followed, he returned to the figure seated against an interior wall.

The building was abandoned and much of the wood on the walls was deteriorated. Old finish flaked off the wood.

Scarlett was still in terrible shape, but her eyes had some fire of life to them instead of the empty hollowness he'd first seen when he found her.

"Pretty sure we're in the clear. Can you tell me what happened?" Rayne asked.

"Not completely sure. Things were proceeding as planned once you left. It stayed steady and became the normal day-to-day for a while. Then everything changed. A couple of the leaders in the thieves group questioned the deal. Eventually, they started disobeying the guidelines. Those of us who were happy with the arrangement pushed back. It wasn't long before it was a shadow war between factions. Capturing me was their hope to stop the fighting and have me concede victory to them. I was close to it before you arrived."

"Is there anything specific you can think of that may have triggered the change?" Rayne prodded.

Scarlett considered the question before she finally said, "I'm not sure if it is related or not, but the stirrings happened about a week after the new noble lady took over the city. I can't stand her myself and I barely know her."

"You and me both." Rayne agreed.

"Then how did she end up in charge?" Scarlett asked.

"She has helped Arthur and proved her worth. I'm not entirely sure he really likes her either, but she has a legitimate noble title, so he hoped it would help calm some of the upper class in the city."

"At least he had a true diplomatic reason to send that woman here. Still don't think I could ever put someone like her in a place of power." Scarlett said.

"Do you think she had something to do with it?" Rayne asked.

"I don't know, but I definitely wouldn't put it past her."

Rayne stood up and paced around the room. His mind moved through different scenarios and possibilities, but in the end, did nothing to help the situation.

"Think my only choice is to go to the city manor and check on things in person. Will you be okay if I leave you here for now?" Rayne asked.

Scarlett looked at her surroundings.

"I can manage. I've definitely seen worse. Do you at least have some food?"

"Crap. I'm sorry." Rayne untied a bag on his hip and opened the flap. The small pouch looked like a deflated cantaloupe, but he reached in until his shoulder was flush with the opening of the bag. Scarlet stared at him wide-eyed before he realized what this looked like.

"Dimensional bag," he said, as if that simple statement explained the odd scenario. A few moments later, he pulled his arm back out, and a plate covered in food emerged. Rayne carefully wiggled it side to side so it would fit through the mouth of the bag and not spill its contents. He extended the still steaming venison steak with vegetables over to Scarlett.

"That should settle your craving. I shouldn't be gone very long."

She looked at the plate as though it were a predator, ready to pounce. Her hands didn't attempt to take it from him, and she looked questioningly into his eyes.

"It's perfectly fine. These bags let us store lots of stuff in them and everything inside stays perfectly preserved. This meal was cooked and placed here weeks ago and it will taste like it was cooked an hour ago. They are so much better than field rations. I have some fruit and cheese in here, if you prefer that?"

"Uh, no. I'll take the real food. It looks delicious but was a little odd seeing it emerge from such a strange bag. I guess those bags must cost a pretty copper?"

"I don't know. I'm not sure what they would actually cost. Perks of being friends with the King. He makes them. Don't know if anyone else even can."

"Guess you really are the right hand of the King, after all." She mumbled.

"Me? Nah. That's probably Samson, if we are being honest. I'm more of the unseen left hand. The tricky one that no one watches until it's around their throat." Rayne said with a glimmer of humor. "Either way, I'll come back and get you before long. I'll find us somewhere more comfortable and more secure to hide you until we sort this mess out."

Rayne exited the building and used stealth to vacate the area. Wouldn't do for someone to see him in this neighborhood and start searching buildings.

After he reached a central area of the city, he followed the main thoroughfare and headed to the city manor. Two guards posted at the gate of the short wall challenged him as he approached.

"Can't enter here without permission." A guard said.

"I assure you I have permission. Tell whoever is in charge that Rayne is here."

The second guard's eyes grew wide. "Death's Shadow? You are *the* Rayne?"

"Haven't heard that nickname yet but I think I like it," Rayne said.

"Not trying to be difficult," the first guard began, "but do you have proof?"

Rayne fished out a metal disk embossed with the kingdom's seal. Arthur began using these things for just such proof, and Rayne hoped Dalia at least instituted that when she arrived.

"Oh, perfect. A seal plate works nicely." He used Scan on it and confirmed it was real before allowing Rayne to pass.

The interior courtyard wasn't nearly as busy as before. Most of the makeshift tables and seating areas were missing and very few people milled about. Rayne made straight for the manor and entered.

It didn't take him long to locate Dalia in one of the larger reception halls. Lady Gemmalin and Lord Ealin were talking with her.

"… but the bandit problem is only getting worse. We are working toward keeping the food distribution running, but with it constantly being attacked, it is difficult." Lord Ealin complained.

"They have also stolen more supplies and pieces of finished leather than I care to admit." Lady Gemmalin added.

"Can neither of you do your job and protect your interests? Thieves exist in every major city. Hire guards if you " Dalia said with a dismissive wave.

Rayne cleared his throat as he walked closer to the group. "The safety of the city is one of your primary duties, Lady Dalia. I'd say protecting its industry and especially its food would classify as part of that duty. What I want to know is, who stirred up the criminal element? I was pretty sure it was under control when I left."

"Rayne? What are you doing here?" Dalia asked.

"Arthur sent me to check in on things and make sure you didn't need any help. Looks like his caution is warranted. Now, can anyone answer my question?"

"We don't really know," Lord Ealin said. "It started off with petty thefts here and there. Nothing major and nothing out of the ordinary. More recently, it has escalated into more serious thefts and even back into the realm of major injury and murder."

"What's been done so far to correct this?" Rayne asked.

Gemmalin and Ealin both looked at Dalia before turning back to him. Lady Gemmalin answered.

"We haven't had any official assistance from the city itself. Both of us have tried hiring guards to mixed success. Once, I'm pretty sure a person I hired was a part of the thieves' group or on their payroll since he disappeared along with the products. City guards are also stretched thin as it is, so we can't really hire those."

Rayne's anger rose at the lack of response from Dalia on the matter. These were serious issues, especially for a city on the brink of recovery.

"I'll look into the matter personally. I'm already pissed that they tried to kill me when I arrived," Rayne told them.

Dalia's face morphed into anger, but Lady Gemmalin and Lord Ealin beamed with happiness.

"Who do you think you are barging into city business? I'm in charge here, not you."

"I'm the guy who is saving your ass because of your mismanagement. You should've dealt with this before it got to this point, but failed to do so. Don't worry. I have no intention of taking your job and plan to sort this out and head back to Alurian." Rayne said.

She still looked furious at the situation, but kept her mouth shut and nodded.

"I'll start digging around for answers. Other than this issue with bandits, is there anything else causing you problems, Lady Gemmalin or Lord Ealin?" Rayne asked.

"None on my side," Ealin confirmed.

"Stop the supply thieves and everything else should sort itself out." Gemmalin agreed.

"I'll get to it. Lady Gemmalin, can I speak to you in private for a moment?" Rayne asked, only to notice the others send interested glances his way. "It's a matter of crafting."

The eyes on him slowly faded at the subject, and their interest waned. Gemmalin seemed to catch on to what he was doing and winked at him. "We can meet in the courtyard. I feel the need for some fresh air with this stuffy manor."

Rayne and the older woman walked back through the manor house and found a secluded portion of the inner courtyard.

"What do you need? I know it isn't anything crafting related, so don't bother." Gemmalin waved off.

Rayne smiled at her sharp wit. "I need some help and you're the only person here I feel I could trust. When I arrived, I was indeed assaulted, but I also discovered they'd taken one of my associates captive. I rescued her, but I fear they will hunt for her while I hunt them. I need somewhere to keep her safe and hidden and thought you might know of a place."

"An associate, huh? That's a lot of trouble for a contact." Gemmalin said with a raised eyebrow. "I haven't known you long, but don't think you'd stick your neck out for a random associate. You sure there aren't some other feelings there?"

Rayne paused at the question before answering. "I honor my deals and she has kept faith. It was only fair to return the favor. I can't lie, though. The second part of that might be one reason as well. I don't know her well, but feel I would like to get to know her better."

"I'm not one to judge, young man. Just want to make sure you keep all the reasons in your mind and don't try and fool yourself. That only causes problems. I can help you, though. Come with me and I'll lead you to a place."

Rayne followed the older noblewoman out of the wall surrounding the manor and into the city proper. She led him on meandering paths through the streets before finally circling around and stopped at a modest-looking house. She looked up and down the road in each direction before slipping in a metal key and opening the door. Once inside, she handed him the key.

"I'll leave you here. Just bring the key back when you're done. No one lives here anymore and I own the place. You'll be safe here."

"Thanks, Lady Gemmalin. I owe you." Rayne told her.

"Take care of our infestation and I'll consider us even. Good luck." She told him before she left.

Rayne checked the house and found it had everything that Scarlett would need. He'd need to bring food in as necessary, but it was fully furnished otherwise.

Not wanting to waste any more time, he located an old cloak in one cabinet and headed to Scarlett. He entered the building he'd left her in and was welcomed with a knife along his neck.

"Come on now, Rayne. You know you can't just walk in when someone is hiding." Scarlett huffed as she put the knife away.

"Good to see you, too. Where the hell did you find a knife?"

"I'm resourceful." Was the only response he got, so he dropped it.

"I have a place for you to lay low in comfort. Throw this on and we will get moving." Rayne said as he tossed her the cloak.

They stuck to the shadows and avoided as many people as possible until they reached the house. Inside, Scarlett whistled.

"Definitely seen nicer places, but this one is toward the top of the list for a home this size. Won't even ask how you got access to it." She said.

"Good, because I wouldn't tell you." Rayne told her with a grin.

"I'm off to hunt for bad guys. Any suggestions on where to start?"

"Pretty much any alley in the southeastern corner. That was where everything went quiet first before it spiraled out of control." Scarlett said.

"Got it. I'll come check on you from time to time. If more than a day passes and you don't hear from me, you can find Lady Gemmalin. I assume you know of her, since she is a noble. She's a friend and should be able to help get you out of town if necessary."

Scarlett nodded at that, and he turned to go.

"Rayne?" Scarlett asked.

He turned back toward her. "Yeah?"

"Thanks for this. I truly appreciate it."

"You're welcome." He told her before leaving the building and heading southeast.

Chapter 21

The Belly of the Beast

Rayne spent the next two days watching over the city's southeastern corner. During daylight hours, he spent time with Scarlett and slept, while during the night, he hunted. His quarry wasn't very good at hiding their activities. They didn't need to be, since no one in the city would stand up to them. The few who would didn't have the numbers to do anything about it.

His conversations with Scarlett were refreshing, even though they primarily centered on his work. She provided a lot of insight into what he saw on the streets. Many small and seemingly inconsequential things meant a lot more than he realized and helped them narrow down their area to search.

They identified their primary target as a small house in a back alley. Scarlett wasn't familiar with it, but she also acknowledged that the crime lords knew next to nothing about each other's hiding places and bases of operation.

Once identified, the plan was simple. Rayne would sneak in and kill anyone who resisted to root out the problem. Not the most elegant of designs, but one he could work with.

"Anything I should look out for?" Rayne asked Scarlett.

"Not that I can think of. If things get terrible, they might try poison. Catch them off guard, and you should be safe."

Rayne nodded and checked his weapons. Each was in good shape and sharp. The latest iteration of Arthur's work was well balanced and held an edge better than anything before. Reaching down to his waist, he checked the vial holders on his belt and verified that his few potions were still intact. He was smart enough to keep two vials of Cure Poison and two more of Lesser Healing at all times.

"Alright. I'm out. I'll see you when it is done." Rayne said before turning to leave. A touch on his shoulder stopped him.

"I know I told you this before, but please come back. I nee… this city needs you. Whether you know it or not."

Rayne placed his hand over hers. "I'll come back. I have far too much to do to die now."

Smiling, he let go and walked to the door. In a flash, he was through and out into the street. He made a beeline for the nearest building and used Wall Run to gain the height he needed to grab the roof's edge. With a quick pull, he vaulted up top and ran for his destination, leaping from roof to roof.

The house itself was nothing remarkable. Peeling paint and banged-up shutters were the most exciting features of the place. The small yard was just dirt and a few dead patches of grass.

A group of two men and a woman stood in the street near the building. They casually leaned against the wall as they spoke in what appeared to be a harmless conversation. His distance was too far to hear their exact words. The facade fell away when Rayne spotted the glimmer of weaponry tucked in their cloaks and belts. The amateurs weren't smart enough to conceal their metal from the moonlight.

Instead of just rushing the three of them, Rayne looked around for another approach. Down the road was an area along the rooftops where he could feasibly leap across the street and land in the house's backyard. Any decent crime lord would have guards back there, but judging from his observations over the last few days, he doubted that would be an issue.

Slowly moving from rooftop to rooftop, he got into position. With a deep breath, he took off in a dead sprint across the roof's wooden shingles and leaped forward. His jump was timed perfectly, clearing the space, and tucking into a roll as he hit the packed dirt in the back of the house.

He scanned the area as he rested in a kneeling position. A few old crates sat out back, but nothing else caught his attention.

In a quick dash, he scurried behind the broken crates. The pile of debris covered much of his form now, and he wasn't worried about being spotted from behind. Movement drew his attention, and he immediately twisted his body.

A blade appeared where he'd been standing with a cowled figure holding onto it. Rayne threw his hand down with as much force as possible and connected with the attacker's wrist. A small yelp of pain punctuated the action, and he dropped the blade.

You dealt 8 damage to Assassin with Unarmed. (Disarm)

Rayne reached for his weapon but had to duck when the attacker's other hand came around in a slash toward his head. The second weapon passed harmlessly over him. He ripped his stiletto dagger free and stabbed it into the exposed underarm of the attacker.

You dealt 105 damage to Assassin with Enchanted Magesteel Stiletto Dagger. (Critical Hit) (Fatal Blow)

The assassin slumped to the ground, holding the wound as best as they could. Not wanting to wait for the person to bleed out, Rayne lashed out with a quick stab to the side of their neck.

You dealt 60 damage to Assassin with Enchanted Magesteel Stiletto Dagger. (Critical Hit) (Fatal Blow)
Assassin has died.
You received 325 experience.
You received 280 experience in Small Blades.

With a sigh, Rayne reached down, grabbed the body under the arms, and pulled it out of sight and behind the pile of crates. He didn't plan on leaving anyone here alive, but didn't need extra trouble while clearing the place out.

A quick swipe across the dead man's shirt cleaned the blade. He approached the door and, in a slow motion, eased it open. A faint glimmer of light spilled from the doorway. A quick peek from side to side confirmed the room was empty, so he slid inside and closed the door behind him with a soft click.

Not wanting to draw this out any longer, he activated Shroud of Shadow. Without the fear of being spotted, he could search the place at full speed. The effect only lasted for two minutes, so he couldn't delay.

Searching the rooms on the first floor, he found no one. The situation seemed odd. A thief hideout usually had plenty of people around, even at night. The only remaining place was the basement. A small set of stairs took him down, and he walked through a stone corridor before finding a single door. Taking a deep breath, he grasped the handle and walked in.

Two men stood in front of him on the opposite side of the room. Both held swords and appeared to be waiting for him. The distance was less than thirty feet, so Rayne walked across the opening. One man spoke when he was close to the midway point.

"Care to show yourself, Rayne? We both know you will lose your stealth as soon as you attack. Might as well face us."

With a small sigh, Rayne let the spell fade. It only had a handful of seconds left, but he hoped to use those to surprise his enemy. *I suppose a door opening all on its own gave that away.*

"Good to finally see you in person. Sadly, it'll be for the last time."

"You're right," Rayne said as he spun his stiletto dagger in his hand. "I'm taking out the trash, and none of you will leave here alive. I don't play nice with people who break agreements."

"Awfully sure of yourself for a man who is surrounded." The man said.

Rayne looked around him in confusion. Nothing but solid stone walls were visible. Before he could respond, the man clapped twice. Low grinding noises echoed through the room, and Rayne watched as small panels opened in the surrounding walls. All of them were nearly head height, and the tip of an arrow was visible in each.

"Well, shit," Rayne muttered.

He dropped straight to the floor and landed on his chest. The twangs of bowstrings followed, and arrows clattered against the stone around the room. Fortunately for Rayne, his quickness saved him.

I need speed, Rayne thought.

I'll help you out. Open up to me, and we can have some fun. His inner voice told him.

Giving into the power, he activated his Shadow Form.

Darkness engulfed him and flowed through the room, obscuring his body. He jumped to his feet and grabbed a couple of throwing knives from his harness. Working on memory and reflex, he launched them at two different slits in the wall.

Cries of pain echoed from both sides of him, and he repeated the action for two more of the openings. This pattern continued until he sent a knife at every crevice.

Lost in his trance, he failed to notice
he'd been hit. Blood leaked from a deep gash
on his left arm. Glancing at his
notifications, he found it.

*You have dealt 120 damage to Bandit with
Enchanted Magesteel Throwing Knife. (Critical)
(Mortal Blow) (x10)*
*Bandit dealt 25 damage to you with Iron
Arrow.*

Searching the space, he found the two
original men in question. One stood near the
back of the room and cowered in fear. The
other had a snarl plastered on his face as he
ripped a sword free and charged with a roar.
The thrill of a fight in command, Rayne
pulled out his stiletto dagger and
swordbreaker before charging. The distance was
short, and he feinted a forward thrust. As
soon as his opponent reacted, Rayne pivoted
his foot and dashed to the side. He took
another quick turn and closed the last couple
of feet toward the man's side. Both daggers
dug deep, and blood splashed from the entry
wounds.
A soft gasp escaped the bandit's lips. "You
are as good as they said."
"I agree," Rayne replied, as he grinned at
the man. Fear blossomed over the bandit's face
before Rayne jerked the stiletto dagger free
and plunged it into his neck.

*You dealt 160 damage to Bandit Leader with
Double Stab. (Critical Hit) (Mortal Blow)*
*You dealt 80 damage to Bandit Leader with
Enchanted Magesteel Stiletto Dagger. (Critical
Hit) (Fatal Blow)*
Bandit Leader has died.

Rayne reveled in the feeling of the man's spirit energy flowing into him and feeding the soul power inside. An unexpected notification popped into his view.

You have fed the Soul of Shadows the souls of your enemies, and it has now advanced to Level 3. You have unlocked the ability Shadow Decoy.

Ability: Shadow Decoy	
Requirements: Soul Ability Mana Cost: 40 MP Cast Time: 1 second	Description: Create a shadow copy of yourself that you can direct to any action with your mind. This clone cannot affect the physical realm.
Mastery Level: 1	

The bandit's body collapsed to the floor, and Rayne looked at the lone figure remaining.
"Care to try your luck?"
The man looked around. Unsure he'd seen what had happened.
"Uh… Well… No?"
"First smart decision you've made all day. Care to tell me where this foolish idea came from?" Rayne asked.
The Thief hung his head in resignation. "We were approached by a man a while back. He told us we had the perfect window to flip this city and take over the criminal portion of it. He even knew of our agreement with you. They promised us we could take over the underground, and he would start interjecting us into higher positions. He planned to infiltrate…."

His words cut off as a knife slammed into his right eye socket and rocked his head backward. Rayne spun in the direction the knife came from and launched a throwing knife into the opening in the wall.

A clatter of his blade on stone was the only sound he heard, so he knew the killer fled as soon as he released the knife.

"Why do the bad guys always have such good timing? He couldn't wait another minute to tie up the loose end." Rayne mumbled to himself.

Not taking any chances, Rayne crept along the entire room before finding the access point for the hidden murder holes. A narrow hallway wrapped the entire room and exited through a hatch on the first floor. Verifying no one else was around, he finally released his Soul of Shadows.

Exhaustion flooded his body, and he fought to steady himself. He kept a slow pace to allow himself to recover while investigating the room and the bodies. He retrieved all his throwing knives, even though two were damaged and needed repair. More weapons were liberated from the assassins and stuffed into his bag of holding.

That thing is fantastic.

Some of the better leather armor in the group joined the weaponry. Rayne considered leaving some valuables in place for Scarlet to use when they took this place back over, but changed his mind. To do this right, he needed to send an unmistakable message.

    With that thought in place, he stripped the
area of anything valuable and stuffed it into
his bag. Bags of coins disappeared into the
bag, and even a set of fine dinnerware. A
storage room worth of food supplies also
joined the bag's contents. Rayne wasn't
entirely sure how much this thing could hold,
but stashing away an entire storage room was a
delightful marvel. Confident that nothing
usable remained, he walked through the house
and dumped lamp oil everywhere. He stopped at
the front door to examine his work.

    *This should send the correct message. Mess
with me or those I protect, and I will destroy
you and everyone allied with you.*

    He poured a small ball of Fire Magic into
his hand before lobbing it into the room and
walking out the door. Flames consumed the
building in mere moments. Rayne could feel the
heat pounding on his back as he sauntered away
from the scene. He was sure people were
watching, so he wanted to put on a good show.

***

    Dalia turned as the door to her private
study swung open.

    Who dares enter here unannounced?

    Her anger cooled when she recognized
Gallant.

    "Did you tie up our loose end?" Dalia
asked.

    "I did. Rayne is far better than I
imagined. I watched him dismantle the entire
group in one fell swoop while trapped and
surrounded. He almost hit me after I launched
the last strike."

"Damn him. He has ruined our plan here. Move to our backup plan. Start getting leverage on every guard member you can. Those you can't get enough dirt on, threaten their families. I want as many on your payroll as possible. Don't expose yourself, though. You're not as useless as most that our goddess keeps around." Dalia commanded.

"I'll take care of it. What do we do about Rayne?" Gallant asked.

"Nothing. We will play his game and let him return to Alurian and out of our way. Wait to make your moves until he leaves. I also recommend steering clear of the thieves. He will task them with hunting you down."

"As you wish," Gallant said with a bow before turning and leaving her room.

Dalia tapped her fingers on the desk and pressed her lips tight. *That meddling kid drives me crazy. If only I'd gotten to him before Arthur. I'm sure I could have turned him to my side.*

Chapter 22

Picking up the Pieces

Arthur walked to the front of the army as the city gates came into view. Allendria walked along beside him, hand in his own. She spotted the gate and then looked at him, gently squeezing his hand.

"It will be all right. Just remember the type of leader you want to be." She told him.

He nodded and took a deep breath, trying to calm his nerves. The entire precession behind them walked at a slow and steady pace. The group looked demoralized and lacked cohesion.

Arthur realized no one was keeping them in line and yelling orders. A scan of the crowd left him unable to find Samson. The soldier was usually the first to keep people in line, especially during tough times.

Except he's going through a tough time of his own. Arthur thought as he hung his head in defeat.

His life seemed like a cycle of wins, followed by a massive overwhelming failure. The process just continued. Every time he was helpless to prevent it. *I have to get stronger so I can save those I care about.*

As before, the city's leaders waited for them at the gates. Instead of the smiling faces, he remembered from their last return. They greeted him with a wall of somber expressions. A runner had been sent ahead to inform the city of their arrival. They must have conveyed the news.

Arthur held up a hand and called out, "Halt!"

The meandering force behind him shuffled to a stop, and he walked forward to see his friends and city leaders. Daniel was the first to approach him.

"I'm sorry for your loss," the innkeeper said, as he put an arm on his shoulder in comfort.

"Thank you, Daniel. She will be missed by all," Arthur said, trying to stop the tear from rolling down his cheek.

"Part of being a leader is accepting other people's right to make their own choices. Don't beat yourself up over her choice." Rowan told him.

"I'll try to remember that," Arthur told him with a forced smile.

Katherine and Daranth approached and offered their condolences before everyone settled around him. Arthur stood with his head low in shame in front of the people who trusted him most.

A hand wrapped around his arm, and Allendria stopped next to him.

"There will be time for that. There are other pressing matters you must attend to." Allendria said.

He looked at her face, and she motioned to the army behind him with her eyes. He picked his head up with another sigh and addressed those in charge as the King, not their friend.

"We must arrange a memorial service tonight for those who fell during the attack. The army needs to rest and recuperate. Any objections?" Arthur asked.

Everyone shook their head no, so he turned to face the army.

"Warriors of the Kingdom of Fire. Words cannot express my gratitude as you fought by my side. We may have failed this time, but we won't make the same mistake twice. Tonight, we will hold a memorial and mourn those we lost. Tomorrow, we make preparations and begin planning. Dismissed!"

Arthur returned his attention to his friends and waved them back toward the city. Everyone turned and headed inside. They walked the long road, and headed straight for the inn.

They already loaded the table in the back with a meal, and Paula and Trisha stood nearby, waiting to help.

"Thanks for this, Daniel," Arthur said.

"It's the least I could do. Let's all sit and eat," Daniel said.

The group took their seats, and each person slowly filled their plate from the large serving trays. Arthur looked up as he put the first piece of food in his mouth and finally noticed the empty seat. Everyone's gaze seemed to drift to the chair as well.

"We will leave him be. He is taking Vana's death harder than most. I knew they were getting close, but did not know how close. He told me they were planning a wedding. We will give him all the time he needs to grieve." Arthur told them.

Everyone nodded in silent agreement and returned to their food. A heavy silence drifted through the room and settled on everyone there. Light clanks of silverware on dishes punctuated the quiet.

Arthur pushed his plate away as he finished and sat up straight. Most of those gathered had already finished and waited for him patiently.

"I guess we can get started. Continue eating if you haven't finished…." Arthur trailed off as the door opened. Calfuray walked through the doors and waved at him when she found him in the crowd. He forgot she'd never really been in here. A quick wave of his hand motioned her to come to him. The gathered people all looked at the newcomer in confusion.

"Uh, Arthur. Did you pick up a new companion?" Daniel asked.

"Not a new one," Arthur said with a smile. "That is Lady Calfuray."

"But isn't she a dragon?" Katherine asked.

"That is true. She was cursed by an artifact the Dark Elves had and forced into human form. The curse is now lifted, but she never learned the magic to shift forms that others of her kind know. For now, she is trapped as a human woman. I plan on fixing that shortly." Arthur explained.

Confusion and disbelief still plastered a few faces, but they seemed to accept the situation. Calfuray sat near him, and Trisha brought her a plate of food.

"Thank you," Calfuray said.

Trisha only smiled and headed back to the bar. Arthur watched for a moment as Calfuray poked at the food with her fingers before handing her a fork and gesturing at the meal. Calfuray took it carefully and began working through the motions of learning to use a fork and eat like a human.

"Back to our discussion. As most of you are aware, our attack was a failure. It wasn't a total loss, although it feels like it. We successfully attacked their wall and did a decent amount of damage, but not nearly enough. They almost caught us in a trap, but thanks to the terrific work of our scouting teams, they warned us in time to escape. I take full responsibility for this loss. Allendria and Daranth, I'm sorry for not fully heeding your words. I knew them to be true, but felt we could power through the obstacles on the fly. I didn't plan for tricks or ambushes.

"All that said, we still have to face them and defeat them. I don't foresee them giving up anytime soon, and I expect it won't be long before they start another attack here. Our people need time to recover and process our losses. We will have a remembrance of the fallen this evening and celebrate the lives they lived. The army can have a three-day break from all training and activities. After that, they can return to drilling and practice. Questions so far?" Arthur asked.

"Who should I talk to for details about the fallen?" Katherine asked. "I don't want to bother Samson."

"I'll take you to the captains after the meeting so we can gather that information." Allendria offered.

"Thank you."

"I have to take a trip. As mentioned before, I plan on fixing Calfuray. We have to go to a Dragon Temple roughly a week away. When we succeed, we can fly back, so the return trip will be much quicker. I'd guess a week and a half total. Before we leave, I want to ensure everything is prepared for defense here in case of attack. Rowan, how is the smithing and enchanting coming along?"

"We are making good progress. Five of us are proficient in Enchanting with the basic patterns. None of us can complete the latest iteration of damage absorption armor that you can, but I don't think it will take much longer to gain the skill levels needed." Rowan said.

"That is good. Katherine, how do we fare with our magic forces?" Arthur asked.

"I assume you're referring to those under my purview with the civil service. We have nearly sixty fully trained mages at an advanced level, and can sustain stone magic and repairs for extended durations. As instructed, they are not well versed in attack magic but are very good at repair and fortification." She summarized.

"That should work nicely. Allendria, is it possible to create a shield that surrounds an entire city? I've been going over this in my head for some time now, trying to find a solution for a large-scale defense. I think it's possible, but I want to run the idea by you." Arthur said.

"Possible, sure. Whether we have the resources to pull it off, I don't know. We had some of our older cities protected by similar constructs before the Great War that reduced the Dark Elf population to its current size. I've seen the drawings in our library so know it is possible. What do you have in mind?" She asked.

"I'd let to set focus areas around the entire perimeter of the wall and have them all tie to one central power source that can activate and deactivate the shield at need," Arthur said.

"It's a good idea, but I see a few flaws," Daranth said. "Connecting power at those distances would require a highly conductive substance to create the pathway, or all the mana would dissipate before it reached its target. You would also need a rather large focus to concentrate the power into to fuel that spell."

Arthur only shrugged and said, "Crystal."

Daranth's eyes widened before he leaned forward in his chair. "How do you expect to source that much crystal in such a short time?"

"Magic," Arthur said again while waving his fingers. A few in the crowd chuckled while others groaned. "I have a spell that lets me convert ordinary materials, silica, dirt, et cetera, into crystal. I propose I use this ability to create large focus crystals and implant them into the wall around the perimeter. I will then convert material below the surface into crystal pathways that connect them all. I'll use the same power to craft a large focus crystal for a centralized command center."

"That might just work," Daranth agreed.

"Is there anything pressing supply or administration-wise I need to address?" Arthur asked Katherine.

She flipped through her bundle of parchment and scanned the entries. After a few seconds, she looked back at him. "Nothing urgent. Primarily status reports on recruiting, food levels, raw materials and the like."

"Good. I trust you guys to address those issues. My focus is on this new barrier for the next few days. As soon as that is complete, or if I have to give up on it because I can't make it work, I plan to head for the dragon temple." Arthur said.

"I hate to bring this up, but with all the fighting, what do we do if something happens to you?" Daniel asked in a whisper.

"That's a good question. I expect everything to revert to Allendria's control unless specified otherwise." Arthur said.

He considered the question for a little while, in quiet contemplation. *I really need something a little longer term for a plan. At least for the city.*

"To help prevent issues, I make this declaration. Henceforth, the capital city of Alurian is now governed by a council. This council will consist of nine members. At least one of each major race within the city must be included to represent their people. I leave it to the council members to decide the additional rules of the council and how new members are voted on and inducted into office. The initial council members include Katherine, Daniel, Rowan, Daranth, Samson, Zeke, Corianne, the captain of the guard, and a representative of the king. I reserve emergency override power to the King or Queen of the Kingdom of Fire."

"Well, that's unexpected." Daniel breathed.

"I don't want this city to fall apart because it loses a leader. It needs to be a beacon long after I'm dead and gone from this world. I trust you to continue the work we started, no matter what happens. This city already stands on its own without me. Now it can truly shine." Arthur said.

Rowan held up his mug. "To King Arthur and the Kingdom of Fire!"

A chorus of cheers echoed around the room, and everyone took a drink.

"This would be so much better with some alcohol," grouched Rowan as he eyed the water in his cup with disdain.

"Well, if spirits are what you're looking for, I might be able to help," Came a voice from the door.

Arthur looked over and smiled as he recognized the figure in his dashing three-piece suit. He stood and walked to greet the Dwarf.

"Wesley, it's good to see you. I'm surprised you made it back here so soon."

"I presented the agreement and immediately left with the first shipment. I expected it would take them some time to declare it officially, but I knew they would in the end, so I didn't delay. Can't stand being around those stuffy buggers, anyway." The dwarven bard explained.

"Two questions," Rowan said. "Who are you, and what do you mean about alcohol?"

"Oh, where are my manners?" Wesley said with a curt bow. "I am the bard Wesley from the Blackrock Clan. We now have a trade agreement with your kingdom, and I have arrived with the first shipment of ale."

Rowan rushed up to the dwarf, and the shorter man took a few steps backward.

"You better not be messing with me. Where is it?" Rowan said in a low and menacing tone.

"On the wagon outside," Wesley said as he gestured toward the door.

Rowan took off in a dead sprint and hurdled a table on his way to the entrance. Arthur could only shake his head in disbelief. He hadn't realized anyone here was that passionate about ale.

"It's good to see you," Arthur told the dwarf and clapped him on the shoulder. "I wish it were during happier times."

"I noticed a gloomy feel to the place," Wesley whispered to Arthur. "What's up?"

"We have returned from a recent battle and lost some of our people. There will be a celebration of their life this evening in their honor." Arthur said.

"I'm sorry to hear that," Wesley told him. "I know we don't know each other well, but would you allow me to play a song for them at the ceremony?"

"We'd appreciate that," Arthur agreed and looked back to see the rest of the council nodding at him.

"I shall prepare at once. Who do I need to talk to about this trade stuff and overall accommodation? New to this diplomat thing." Wesley said with a chuckle.

"No problem. Daniel, over there, will handle your room, and you can stay at the inn. You will be housed at the city's expense as a trade ambassador. The terms of the trade and your return shipment of goods can be negotiated with Katherine." Arthur finished as he pointed to the young woman.

"That works. Need anything from me?" Wesley asked.

"I don't think so…" Arthur began before the door crashed open and Rowan appeared in the frame, tears rolling down his cheeks.

"Rowan, are you okay?" Daniel asked.

"This ale is amazing," Rowan sniffled, and everyone laughed. The mood settled in the room for a few moments before Arthur looked back at Wesley.

"How about you hang out with the council here and get to know everyone?" Arthur said.

"I think I will wait until the ceremony." He agreed.

"Arthur said farewell to everyone and then left the inn with Allendria and Calfuray in tow. The three walked a direct path back to their home and entered. The temperature was a little chillier than he expected, but he remembered no one had recharged their temperature regulator recently. He dumped a supply of mana into the device, and the temperature shifted momentarily. Not knowing what else to do, he dropped to sit on the wooden couch.

Allendria sat near and cuddled up to him, laying her head on his shoulder. Calfuray sat on his other side and remained motionless. Arthur looked at her face, and she seemed lost. *All the unfamiliar sights and sounds of being a human must also be taking a toll on her.*

Arthur wrapped an arm around each of them and pulled them to him. The group sat there in silence, taking solace in each other's presence.

"Do you want to talk about it?" Allendria asked.

"I don't know. I can't help but keep blaming myself for her death. I know it was her choice, but the whole thing was my decision. I am rethinking my position on war." Arthur sighed.

"Vana wouldn't want you feeling that way, and you know it. I worry about your resolve, though. We can't give up the fight. This will never end so long as our enemies are alive. We can never have peace."

"You misunderstand me," Arthur said. "I don't plan on giving up the fight, but I've been hesitant about waging war. My world may not have magic, but the technology we use to wage war would easily decimate the factions we stand against. I've seen the destruction it can cause and am hesitant to bring that same power to this world. Now I wonder if I should use all of my knowledge to bring down our enemies. Maybe if we employed some weapons from my world, we could have defeated the Dark Elves with no losses. It's hard to know."

"War is inevitable in humans. You have always been known for your creative ways of killing each other. That was part of what kept dragons from interacting with your kind for so long," Calfuray said.

"You're not wrong. Even then, it may be time to take the kid gloves off and fight for real." Arthur lamented.

"How about we focus on defense for now and get Calfuray back to normal? After that, we can revisit this," Allendria suggested.

Arthur nodded at that. At the same time, mental communication came through.

I'm all for killing people however you need to. Balair chimed in.

Arthur laughed. *Thanks, Balair. Going to need you to keep an eye out in the sky for us. Now we all rely on you.*

Yeah, yeah. You need the all-powerful Balair to hold down the fortress. I got you.

Well, damn. We're screwed. Calfuray said.

Everyone laughed at that comment and settled into a comfortable silence.

***

Arthur stood in front of the population of Alurian. He erected a small stage on the edge of the space to address those who lined the streets.

"Citizens of Alurian. I come before you to confess that I failed you. We went forth to assault the Dark Elven capital and failed. I take full responsibility for this action, and the burden of those we lost is on my shoulders. I'd like to promise you we won't let anyone else die for us, but I can't lie to you. We are in a war for our freedom and independence. I will promise you to do better and fight smarter."

Arthur walked back and forth across the stage, pacing as he talked.

"We are not here to mourn the dead. We are here to celebrate their life. Your loved ones don't want you to feel bad for them. They want you to remember the good times and cherish those memories. Every person we lost was important, but I lost a friend and companion. Someone who has been a pillar of this kingdom since before its inception. Ranger Vana fell in battle, saving one of her fellow rangers. She trained the ranger squads that warned us of the incoming ambush and allowed us enough time to escape before we met a gruesome fate. This city and its people owe her more than can ever be paid. We will start with this," Arthur said as he walked to a small hill next to his platform.

He stood and eyed the location briefly before building up power. Red and yellow mana with hints of orange light flicker down his arms as he drew in the magic to weave his spell. He pictured Vana in extreme detail, down to her crooked smile.

With a slight tremor, he let out the breath he was holding and directed the power into the ground. Dirt shifted and slowly rose in a swirling pillar. The soil solidified, starting at the bottom, and moving upward. He maintained his concentration as dirt packed tight, and Fire Magic flared to life to zap it into stone.

Leather boots began the sculpture before continuing into a standard set of leather breeches. Her hips and belt formed next, moving into her torso and arms. Her head was the last piece to finish and flare with Fire Magic. Vana stood with her trusty bow in hand, and an arrow nocked and ready to fire.

Before he completed the spell, Arthur shifted the power and drew heavily on his Mineral Compression spell with his dual casting ability. The entire statue began to shimmer and glow while Arthur dumped massive amounts of mana into both spells. The Mineral Compression spell tried to consume the stone and transform it into gemstones, but it would've destroyed the statue. It forced Arthur to keep feeding more rock into the spell, to transform it into a gemstone without losing the sculpture itself. Sweat poured down his forehead as he shifted mana from his sword and amulet to continue to feed the spells.

With one last flash, both spells stopped. A low rumble of oohs and awes filled the space as everyone looked at the new feature. A beautiful emerald statue stood and depicted Vana in all her glory. Every detail was carved with the precision of a master sculptor and the waning light of day shimmered across the stone.

Arthur walked up to the eight-foot statue and laid his hand on its thigh. "We will never forget you, Vana."

City Notice!
A new monument is complete. The Vigil of the Ranger now watches over Alurian. The city receives the following bonuses.

- *All ranged defenders gain a 10% increase in range and damage.*
- *Enemies are unable to stealth within fifty meters of the city walls.*

Note: This statue is considered a minor wonder. Due to this, it could have religious repercussions.

"To Ranger Vana!" the crowd called out across the clearing. Wesley picked that time as the perfect moment to begin his song. The hum of his instrument filled the air as he spun the wheel. His clear and powerful voice filled the area.

Enemies quivered in fear at her gaze.
The fine lady ranger with weapons ablaze.
None dare trespassed on the woman's home ground.
Fore, she just as quickly put them down.
She held a strong love for her home and her friends.
The brave archer died saving a friend.
We all strive to be worthy of her love.
As the Ranger of Alurian watches over us from above.

You are in the influence of Song of Remembrance. Consuming food has a calming effect on the user for the next 24 hours.

Chapter 23

A Matter of Defense

Arthur started his morning reviewing all the notifications he'd ignored since their failed battle. He collapsed all the experience gains into comprehensive summaries instead of displaying them separately.

You have gained 11,300 total experience in Fire Magic

You have gained 7,230 total experience in Earth Magic.

You have gained 3,455 total experience in Dimensional Magic.

You have gained 5,890 total experience in Water Magic.

Congratulations, you have reached level 12 in Water Magic. Increases the effect of your Water Magic spells by 24%. A little wetness always helps.

You have gained 2,435 total experience in Air Magic.

You have gained 4,255 total experience in Medium Armor.

Congratulations, you have reached level 8 in Medium Armor. Armor bonuses granted by Medium Armor increased by 21%. About time you get some real armor.

You have gained 5,345 total experience in Small Blades.

Congratulations, you have reached level 10 in Small Blades. Swing speed with Small Blades increased by 27%. Still a wimp with that puny dagger.

You have gained 6,005 total experience in Swords.

You have gained 585 total experience in Parry.

You have gained 675 total experience in Stealth.

You have gained 810 total experience in Archery.

You have gained 485 total experience in Aim Shot.

You have gained 4,765 total experience in Dual Wield.

Congratulations, you have reached level 9 in Dual Wield. Accuracy penalty with off-hand weapons decreased by 24%. Excellent fit of rage you pulled there.

You have gained 6,245 total experience in Dual Casting.

Congratulations, you have reached level 17 in Dual Casting. Decreases the mana draw of dual-cast spells by 48%. Need to vary up your combos some more.

You have gained 8,945 total experience.

You have crafted a Monument in the city of Alurian. For this feat, you are granted the following experience bonuses:
- *10,000 experience in Jeweler.*
- *10,000 experience in Earth Magic.*
- *10,000 experience in Fire Magic.*
- *10,000 experience in Enchanting.*

Congratulations, you have reached levels 10 and 11 in Jeweler. Increases the stats on Jewelry you make by 14%. That was a work of art.

Congratulations, you have reached level 26 in Earth Magic. Increases the effect of your earth magic spells by 75%. I've got nothing…

The flood of information was much easier to condense now that he practiced it. His primary goal for the day was to develop a focus crystal for his defense idea. That thought brought him to another problem. Where would it be held? It needed to be in a somewhat secure location and preferably centrally located to the perimeter walls.

Those thoughts in mind, he left his house and headed through the city. Not knowing exactly where he needed to be, he reached out to Balair.

Hey Balair, you up in the sky?

Sure am. What's up?

Can you tell me roughly where the center of our ringed wall is in relation to the city?

You mean like where the center point of the entire defensive perimeter would be? Balair asked.

Yep.

Arthur looked up and spotted the small blob of reddish orange as the drake flew around the area. He continued on his flight path, circling a few more times to see his surroundings before settling in a spot and hovering in the air.

I'm at the point that is roughly centralized. Balair told him.

Great. Anything below you?

Not directly. I'm pretty close to the edge of the initial housing development we built.

That's perfect. I'm headed your way. Mind sticking there for a bit?

I guess so. Hurry it along. I need to go find some food. Been flying most of the morning.

Fine. Fine. I'll be there soon. Arthur said as he picked up his pace and began a steady jog.

It was early in the morning, so the streets weren't very crowded. His enhanced speed and strength combined with his large Stamina pool allowed him to sustain a quick pace and he arrived under Balair within a couple of minutes.

Thanks for the assist. Arthur told him. *Go get you some food.*

Meh, whatever. The drake grumped before flying toward the inn.

Arthur examined the space and found it was clear for a distance. It was nearly a hundred yards to the south of him for the initial housing project they started. All of those houses were now full, but they continued with the additional housing to the south and east and didn't move north toward the main road.

He currently stood on the edge of the original village and close to the main road. It was a perfect space to begin.

But what size should it be? Should I make a true fortress for defense and a place to retreat? Maybe a reinforced building that is like a guardhouse to only house the orb? Hmm. It needs to be both easily accessible and difficult to access. What a stupid conundrum.

    While keeping it safe from enemies was obviously focus number one, his other challenge was charging it. The orb would need to be powered by the citizens of the city. That meant they'd need to begin some kind of charging ritual to help keep the device full of energy for emergencies. It would also need to be constantly fed if it was ever employed.

    His mind churned over the implications and challenges of the project before a stray thought snapped him out of the issue. *The orb itself doesn't have to be accessible to recharge.*

    That thought resonated with him. He was already planning to create crystal pathways to crystals all along the wall to distribute power. *Why not create similar pathways and place charging crystals throughout the city?* This would also keep the place from becoming overcrowded while they tried to fill it with power during sieges. If everyone could just dump mana into a local focus and it all was directed here, the process would be far faster and much more efficient.

    That brought him back to the size. Now that the need for access was moot, he could create a large fortress that could house their guard force as a military headquarters. He'd reinforce a centralized room, so there was only one entrance and exit while making the walls extra thick. They would keep the orb there under guard.

    Keeping these thoughts in mind, he walked through the space and cast his Flatten Earth spell, ensuring everything was prepped. Wanting to make the structure large enough, he decided on a base level that was one-hundred yards square. He began to cast the spell before stopping himself.

I'm doing it again. Yards are an odd measurement for everyone else. It will throw off their normal designs.

He instead went with one-hundred square meters. They were close enough in measurement that he wasn't worried about the difference. Starting with the stone foundation, he used his variable size spell Stone Slab and created pieces of the foundation that were twenty meters square and stacking them side by side to reach his final shape.

With all the large tiles in place, he walked between each one and fused them all together. None of it was new, so the work sped along quickly.

Standing on a one-hundred-meter square stone slab felt kind of surreal, and he looked around in amazement at what he created in such a short time. Walking to the edge, he cast the spell for the first wall. Power weaved through his body and the glow appeared before he stopped the spell abruptly.

No point in all this if the gem doesn't work. This is a proof of concept. I'll make the pedestal and the gemstone itself. I'll test it out to make sure it works and then come back to finish the defense. Or better yet, send one of our construction crews to handle it.

With a smile, he walked to the center of
the platform. Examining the area, he used raw
Earth and Fire Magic to weave an intricate
swirling spire from the ground. When the
pedestal was nearly waist high, he smiled and
adjusted the design. The top flattened into a
smooth space and six dragon wings formed along
the edge. The wings started where the limb
would attach to the dragon and connected to
the top of the pedestal. They were extended
upward with the first joint on each, nearly
touching the center while the final portion of
the wing stretch out to the side. It left a
perfect spot for the orb to rest. That, and it
looked cool.

Happy with his handiwork, he checked his
mana supply. The level was at about 20% but he
hadn't drawn any from his sword or necklace
yet. Taking a deep breath, He pulled in power
and repeated his process from the night
before. This time, he funneled more stones
from the ground, through the pedestal, and
made it coalesce into an orb shape resting on
top of the wings. He kept the power going as
he activated Mineral Compression. The stone
broke down and turned into smaller quantities,
so he kept feeding it power from his Earth and
Fire Magic, feeding it more material as it
kept burning through what was there.

His goal was to make it as large as
possible, so he kept pouring power in as he
siphoned all the mana from his sword and
necklace. The power hummed, and the air
vibrated from the magic being employed and
when the last speck of mana he wished to use
trickled out, he ended both spells.

In front of him, resting on the dragon pedestal, was the largest ruby Arthur had even seen. The object was nearly three meters in diameter and the object dwarfed the small pedestal.

Yikes. I'll need to beef up that pedestal when I recover some mana.

Arthur examined the item itself.

Item: Manufactured Ruby Focus Crystal (Giant)	**Durability:** 3,000/3,000 **Rarity:** Epic **Quality:** Exquisite **Weight:** 150 kg **Slot:** Magical Item **Traits:** A man-made ruby created using magical means.

That's an impressive stone.

Arthur walked around it and admired the smooth and utterly flawless appearance of the gem. Most of that was due to him having nothing he could do without mana.

Figuring now was as good a time as any, he examined his experience for the morning.

You have gained 6,890 total experience in Earth Magic.

You have gained 5,160 total experience in Fire Magic

Not too bad. Guess I should deal with my talents as well.

Arthur browsed through his Water Magic talents first. He had two points to spend for his most recent level. He dropped both into Soothing, bringing it to 4/10 and increasing his health and mana regeneration.

Soothing(4/10)	Water Magic suffuses your body and constantly improves it. Every point grants 0.5 HP and 0.5 MP regeneration per second. Every 5 points increases all your stats by 1.

The next skill was his Medium Armor Skill. To his chagrin, he realized he'd never even looked at it before. He looked at the first tier of options.

You have 8 unused Talent Points.

Talent	Description
Tier 1	
Reinforced Medium Armor (0/5)	While wearing at least 4 pieces of Medium Armor, increases the base armor of all pieces of Medium Armor worn by 3% per piece.
Mighty Resist (0/5)	While wearing at least 4 pieces of Medium Armor, reduces damage dealt to you by spells by 3% per point.

Proper Durability (0/5)	*While wearing at least 4 pieces of Medium Armor, increases the durability by 3% per point.*

All three had their merits. The first and last were almost identical to the options he had during Light Armor talents. His attention was drawn by Mighty Resist. His armor naturally absorbed damage thanks to its special ability. The Defense on each piece already contributed to physical damage reduction but nothing reduced the damage dealt to him by spells. Making up his mind, he put five available points into Mighty Resist.

From there, he checked the Tier 2 options.

Tier 2	
Articulating Plates (0/10)	*While wearing at least 4 pieces of Medium Armor, decreases speed loss due to the weight of armor by 10% per point.*
Slick Plating (0/5)	*While wearing at least 4 pieces of Medium Armor, raises the chance that hits on you will be Glancing Blows by 3% per point.*
Regenerative Bounceback (0/5)	*While wearing at least 4 pieces of Medium Armor, increases the speed you respond to attacks by 3% per point.*

The final three points he settled on Slick Plating.

Happy with his decision, he moved to Small Blades. The first thing he noticed was he forgot to assign his points for level nine. Hitting level ten with it also opened up access to the third tier of talents, so he looked at them.

You have 4 unused Talent Points.

Tier 3	
Dagger Master (0/5)	*Increases your damage done with daggers by 5% per point but doesn't work if you Dual Wield any weapon not a dagger.*
Damage Bonus (0/10)	*Every 2 points invested in this talent increases your base and maximum damage with your Small Blades by 1.*
Flash (0/1)	*Learn the ability: Flash. This makes the blade of your Small Bladed weapon emit a bright flash of light that disorients your opponents for a brief span of time.* *Cost: 40 mana* *Cooldown: 30 seconds* *Effect Duration: 3 seconds*

The options were nice, and he immediately spent the point for Flash. He had a small list of abilities already, many of which he forgot to use, but a crowd control or disorient ability was too good to pass up.

He considered investing in Damage Bonus, but he already had decent weapons. His combat style relied on his Small Blade to do more parrying anyway, so he dropped the remaining three points into his tier two talent, Blade Weaver, bringing it to 10/10.

Blade Weaver (10/10)	Increases your chance to parry blows with Small Blades by 2% per point.

Finally, he looked into his Dual Wield Talents. There were no new options, with it only being level nine, so he dropped the two points into Main Hand Dexterity, bringing it to 5/10.

Main Hand Dexterity (5/10)	Increases swing speed with main hand weapon by 3% per point.

With his talents sorted out, he returned his attention to his surroundings. To his surprise, Calfuray stood next to him. Her purple hair shimmered in the morning light.

"There anything I can do to help?" She asked.

"Not sure. I'm currently out of mana. Just giving my regeneration some time to kick in."

"That's easy," she said as she put her hand on his chest. He felt a rush of heat and his mana shot back up to 600.

"Oh. Thanks. Wasn't sure you'd be able to
share mana as easily in your human form."
Arthur said.

"It's actually easier in this form. In
dragon form, I have to convert the power from
Dragon Magic to normal human mana. It's
partially instinctive to our kind but still
requires effort. In my human form, I natively
store it as human mana."

"Interesting. Is that part of why you can't
shift back? You're unfamiliar with how to use
magic in a human style?" Arthur asked.

"I can use magic without issue in human
form," she said as a ball or orange flame
popped into existence over her palm before she
brushed it away.

"I already know all the spells from our
bond, anyway. I just don't know the special
trick required to shift. I appreciate you
agreeing to help me get it, though."

"No problem. We are a team. Bonded together
for our common interest and pledged to one
another. Your problems are my problems. As
soon as I can ensure the city has bolstered
its defenses, we will head out."

"Thanks." She mumbled. Her gaze drifted to
the large ruby near them before pointing at
the pedestal.

"You may want to hurry and beef that thing
up. I can see small hairline fractures already
spreading across the surface of the stand."
Calfuray told him.

"Oh, crap." Arthur exclaimed before
channeling some of his new mana from Calfuray
and expanding the size of the stone while
repairing the defects and heavily reinforcing
it. To ensure there was enough mass, he
expanded the base until the original base was
nearly head height where the wings began.

Both of them examined the new base before Calfuray spoke up.

"Why did you start with this? Shouldn't you have done a much smaller scale test for this before you tried to go the full route?"

"I plan on starting with a smaller scale proof-of-concept right here. This building will have its own personal shield as a test. It's another reason I don't want the walls on it yet. I plan to make only the outside perimeter and attached smaller crystals to each. A crystal pathway will run underground to connect all the points. I need the top off, so it simulates the city itself."

"Isn't this a waste if this doesn't work?" She asked.

"Not really. We can still use this large focus crystal as a mana battery. I plan on building a full garrison here to house the local guard and military forces. If they are ever under siege, they can keep the orb filled with mana and draw on the reserves in an emergency. I'm curious to know how much it will hold when I enchant it." Arthur said, while looking at the large orb.

"Looks like you have some waiting to do. Care to take a break?" Calfuray asked.

"You know what? Let's do that. Have you eaten this morning?" Arthur asked.

"Not yet."

"Perfect. We can go to the inn and have some breakfast."

＊＊＊

Rayne walked into the city manor and looked at the occupants. No one looked out of place, so he continued through the building and headed for the room that Dalia usually frequented. Upon arrival, he found the usual suspects. Lord Ealin, Lady Gemmalin, and Lord Trip stood in the room while Dalia remained seated in the central throne-like chair.

"…heard any progress on the cleanup." Was the snippet Rayne heard from Lord Trip as he entered.

"I took care of it." Rayne told them. "Someone was inciting part of the criminal underground and actively turning them against the city. I took care of the problem. Things should slowly return to normal as everything settles down. My contact is working to get the thieves back in line. I have eliminated those who were part of the plan."

"Oh, thank you, Rayne. It was making people worry that we were falling back to the old ways. Hopefully, this will lift people's spirits." Lady Gemmalin said.

"I agree. Thank you." Lord Ealin echoed.

"Just my job. I've been here far too long, though. Things were moving at a quick pace when I left and I have a strange feeling I need to hurry back. I expect things to keep moving smoothly from here. If I return to another mess like this, I'm going to be pissed." Rayne said with a pointed look at Dalia.

Her face reddened before she responded. "I have everything under control. You're free to leave."

Rayne gave a mock bow to Dalia before turning once more to Lady Gemmalin. "Thank you for your assistance, lady."

"Any time, young man. Hurry on back. They probably need your help," Gemmalin said.

Rayne turned and left the room without another word. He had no time to deal with the politics of running the city. He solved their immediate problem, so there was no reason to stay. Scarlett confirmed she'd keep an eye out for anyone trying to stir up trouble while he was gone. Now that it'd happened once, she knew what to watch for.

Rayne had to admit to himself he felt compelled to stay and spend more time with her, but knew he had other duties to attend to.

Maybe in the future we can find some time together.

He walked through town without issue and stepped out of the city gates and into the open countryside. The trip here was made in near record time, so he was hoping to make good time on the way back. He took one long breath before trucking forward toward Alurian. A feeling of dread settling within himself as he felt something very wrong.

Chapter 24

A Magical Barrier

Arthur and Calfuray emerged from the inn, and he squinted into the midday sunlight.

"Didn't think we were in there that long," He reflected.

"You kept insisting I try all that different human food. I'll admit, most of it was really tasty."

"Have to keep you on your toes somehow." Arthur said with a chuckle.

"I really appreciate this, Arthur. I know you're trying to distract me and keep me from dwelling on my problem. We'll solve it, but…" she trailed off as she looked toward the sky. "I miss flying. I miss being up there and looking over everything. The wind breaking on my scales and the rush of the speed are hard to replace."

"I really can't imagine. We will get you back up there, though."

The long downtime had allowed Arthur to fill up a substantial amount of his mana storage, both personally and in his items. With his goal in mind, they walked back to the base of the new garrison building.

Arthur saw a few guards walking over the space as he arrived. One of them he recognized.

"Hey, Noah. How are you?"

To Noah's credit, he only slightly flinched before turning and smiling.

"Doing great, Your Majesty. Just watching over that exceptionally large gem," he said with a wave toward the focus crystal.

"Yeah, I kinda put that there earlier. This is to be the location for the new city garrison and a small defensive fortress."

"Makes sense." Noah agreed.

"You guys mind vacating the space while I get back to work?" Arthur asked.

"Not at all," Noah said before whistling and signaling the other guards to move out.

Arthur examined the space and started by casting his Raise Stone Wall around the perimeter. He left one small doorway in one wall but kept the rest solid. It was easy and relatively cheap to add in windows and additional doorways in the future. He raised the wall to a height of twelve feet. That much clearance on the floor would allow plenty of space to carry around materials and weapons without fear of running into things. Full sized spears could be very tall and difficult to maneuver. Since the armory would likely end up here, it was important they could access it easily.

He wanted to start small, so he placed an individual gem on each of the four walls, directly in the center. The gems in question were roughly the size of his thumb. Using his Mineral Compression with his Raise Stone Wall, he focused the power and forced the Mineral Compression to create a thin line of crystal, starting at the gem and slowly running down the wall. He shifted his magic when he reached the ground and ran the crystal path under the stone slab, using his magic to feel its pathway.

The magic continued until he reached the base of the focus crystal pedestal. Realizing what he needed to do, He focused his magic back on the pedestal and made a solid crystal cylinder inside the pillar itself. Now he had a three feet wide crystal cylinder that touched the bottom of the focus crystal, ran down the pedestal and tied into a small line of crystal, roughly the size of a crochet needle.

Arthur checked his mana and noticed it didn't take nearly as much as he feared, so he continued. Repeating the process, he placed the gem and created a small line of power for each of the four walls.

"What's your plan now?" Calfuray asked.

"Now the tedious job of drawing on all the enchantments and empowering them. It also doesn't help. I don't know how to do this. I know the enchantment for the storage principles and channeling of power. The shield itself will be tricky since I don't know how to do that yet. It's going to be some trial and error."

"Yep, sounds boring. I'm going to go find Allendria and bother her for a little while so you can play with rocks."

Arthur laughed. "I don't blame you. Have fun."

He gave her one last wave as she left to go have fun somewhere else. A bit of envy crept into him as he watched her leave, but he knew this was important work.

Digging in his bag, Arthur found the jar of mixed water and charcoal he kept for his enchantments. The runes for the central focus crystal were simple. He created them similar to the storage necklaces he'd done in the past, only he used the most advanced matrix he knew. Weaving the symbols back and forth, he painted the design over the entire orb and watched as it spiraled around the entire surface.

He put a hand on the orb and began feeding it mana. The initial chunk burst out and nearly caught him off guard as he quickly pulled some of what he had stored in his necklace to cover the second half. The enchantment finished and Arthur marveled at the complete gem.

Item: Enchanted Manufactured Ruby Focus Crystal (Giant)	Durability: 3,000/3,000 Rarity: Unique Quality: Exquisite Weight: 150 kg Mana Capacity: 0/100,000,000 Traits: A large focus crystal that can be used to store extreme amounts of mana.

That mana pool is mind-boggling. If nothing else, it should provide a long-lasting defense.

Now that he knew his limitation on mana, he focused on the first crystal in the southern wall. He sat on the stone floor and went through the list of possibilities he could try. His mind originally went to Shield, so he painted that on the gemstone and infused it with mana. The result was worthless and merely gave the gemstone and the wall additional durability. With a sigh, he plucked the gemstone from the wall with his magic and created a new one in its place.

He went through multiple variations as he tried to find something that worked. Barrier was close as it prevented a small amount of damage to the wall, but it only extended a short distance from the gem itself.

Multiple iterations came and went as Arthur continued to pull off failed gems and replace them. His frustrations peaked, and he smashed the last crystal to the ground as he pulled it free.

It doesn't make sense. These enchantments are so limited based on how I enchant the material. I have them channeling power and projecting that into the ability itself. There are only so many things I can do here. The stupid thing doesn't even have to channel itself since the power comes from…

He stopped his train of thought as the possible solution hit him. Reworking the enchantment was possible if he removed some parts that make an active spell necessary. This only needs to be a focus to project the result. All the channeled power would come from the main power source, as well as the spell activation itself.

Giddy at the idea, he began work. Wanting a larger space to work with, he made the gemstone a square plate, so he had more room to write on it. The design here incorporated the Barrier word, but he also added in Force and Extend. The three words were tied together with a Bind symbol.

The Bind portion tied down into the crystal channel and would be the focal point for mana to enter. With a brief hesitation, he touched the crystal pathway and fed mana into it, pushing it toward the small focus crystal. He watched the power with his magical vision as it entered the gem, only to gather in its core and do nothing.

Damn it. I really thought that would work. The power just sits there, though.

His thoughts swirled over the problem. He tapped his hand against his leg as he paced back and forth, searching for answers in his own head.

A wand!

The thought hit him and froze him in his tracks. Maybe that's the problem. He said he was removing the active portion of the enchantment, but he was still using the rune words for pieces of the spell. If he just made the final crystal an amplifier that directed any spell fed to it, similar to wands, he could enchant the originating stone with the actual spell.

Pattern in mind, he created a new gem and used Bind, Amplify, and Enhance as the runes in the pattern. The enchantment settled in without a problem and he received an actual notification from this one.

You have gained 280 experience in Jeweler for creating Enchanted Manufactured Sapphire Crystal of Amplification.

You have gained 650 experience in Enchanting for creating Enchanted Manufactured Sapphire Crystal of Amplification.

Item: Enchanted Manufactured Sapphire Crystal of Amplification	**Durability:** 1,000/1,000 **Rarity:** Epic **Quality:** Exquisite **Weight:** 8 kg **Mana Capacity:** 0/10,000 **Traits:** A crystal that amplifies any spell sent to it and directs it outward in a space proportional to its size and power.

That should work!

Arthur placed the new gemstone on his test wall and went back to the focus crystal. Using one more manufactured gemstone, he engraved the active style spell on it as he normally would for an enchanted item.

Item: Enchanted Manufactured Jade Crystal of Shielding	**Durability:** 500/500 **Rarity:** Rare **Quality:** Exquisite

	Weight: 3 kg **Mana Capacity:** 0/5,000 **Traits:** A crystal that projects the Shielding spell to the nearby area. Effects: • Projects a field that is impenetrable to physical and magical attacks in a line that extends 4 feet wide and 6 feet tall.

Taking a breath, he fed the crystal a small amount of mana. A shield popped into existence and he watched as the mana drained from the crystal. The shield was exactly as described and stretched a sizable distance for such a small crystal. It was an opaque-looking field of power and was hard to see unless he used his magesight.

Before it ran out of power, he pressed it against the large focus crystal and fed it some more power. A jolt of magical energy surged in his fingertips as the two crystals touched and he looked toward the mock wall in time to see an even larger version of the same spell spring to life.

Fuck yeah!

His excitement was difficult to contain, and he jumped up, breaking contact with the crystal and halting the larger spell. The last of the mana drained from the smaller crystal, and the shield faded completely.

Reflecting on the situation, he realized the mana drain was significantly slower when the focus crystal powered the ability. With the mana capacity of the larger crystal, he could run that spell nonstop for a month. He knew that would change when he connected an entire network of these crystals for it to power, but he would cross that bridge later.

Holding a spellstone to the gem to power it wasn't feasible. He also needed a quick way to activate the spell, preferably where anyone could do it, regardless of magical aptitude. Turning the flat gemstone tablets over in his hand, he looked back at the pedestal.

With a grin, he approached the pedestal and channeled his magic into it. At the top of the pedestal and directly below where the focus crystal rested, he created a small gap. This would allow them to keep spell plates in this room, and all someone had to do was to slide a plate into this space. That would automatically activate the plate and project it outward from the walls. This also made it versatile since they could use multiple spells, not just shields. If he wanted his walls to breathe fire, they could.

Flexing more of his power, he created a shelving unit inside the crystal's room and placed his current shielding tablet in it. He would create a large stockpile of them and other spell tablets they could use. They would also keep spares in other major buildings in town in case of theft or sabotage.

Some more power trickled from him and he recharged the stone a small amount before placing it into the crevice. He stepped back and admired the work as his mock wall flared to life again.

Now is the time to get to work. Arthur thought as he cracked his knuckles.

***

It took Arthur three days, a lot of walking, and a fair handful of cursing to complete the gemstones, enchantments, and crystal pathways. The worst part was mana. The sheer scope of the project meant he had to use loads of mana. He ended up conscripting everyone from the city he could that wasn't actively working, so they could feed him mana as he worked.

When one of his mana batteries dried up, another would step up to take their place while the original went back to work at their normal job. The process was time-consuming, but if he had to do it by himself, it would have taken him weeks.

During this time, he'd tasked Allendria with coordinating with the city building crews. They met with the members of the city council and guard forces to plan out the central fortress design. While Arthur worked on the perimeter, they continued building the defensive structure in the center of the city.

The ground floor housed the armory and mess hall. They made it with taller ceilings than normal to accommodate, moving around with weaponry. There were three additional floors above. Each of these contained numerous living quarters. The top floor was primarily open barracks space, designed to be lined with military style cot beds and a storage trunk. The floor below featured a similar layout, but there were dividing walls between each bed.

Down on the second floor went another step farther. Designed for the commanders and higher ranked guards, this floor was a long hallway that was lined with private rooms. Each room had a modest space for a bed and dresser with an attached bathroom. The bathroom was small, but each featured one of the newer style disposal toilets and a small shower. It was a life of pure luxury as far as most military men were concerned.

This design was very purposeful. Higher rank people didn't want to have to climb all the way to the top of the fortress to sleep every night. It also had the added benefit of any lower rank soldiers having to walk past the commanders' floor to sneak out in the middle of the night.

Arthur reflected that the basic square structure of the building reminded him of Norwich castle in England. He walked up to the building, and the crowd cleared the way for him. Inside, he found the city council. They stood in a line in front of the crystal room while guards lined the entire space.

Regular city residents filled the hall itself and the excess spilled out into the hall. This event would mark the official opening of the building and coincidently the unveiling of their new defense system. Something that had, so far, been kept relatively secret.

"Hello citizens of Alurian." Rowan began. Arthur discovered the council had named him to lead many of their announcements. He thought it was a good idea. Rowan had a very lovable charm to him and his loud, booming voice played in well to the effect.

"We have gathered here today to open our new defensive fortress. This building will be used by our city guard as a place to store their armaments, eat their meals, and have a safe place to live. They spend their days keeping us safe, so we owe it to them to return the favor."

The crowd cheered at his words. It took a few moments for them to get the crowd under control and for the noise to die down, but when they did, Rowan continued.

"I'm sure you've seen this building going up at a rapid pace and might have some confusion over it. Arguably, there are many other buildings that might be more beneficial to the city. I also know many of you have been drawn into helping King Arthur with his magic. We didn't want to reveal the true purpose of this work until it was complete. King Arthur Firebrand, do you wish to address the city?" Rowan asked.

Arthur gave Rowan a quick bow before walking to the front of the council members.

"I thank you, Councilman Rowan," Arthur began and turned to face the crowd. "Ladies and Gentlemen of Alurian. I know we have faced a lot of challenges in such a short time. With war looming over us on two fronts, I felt it was time to protect the city. I appreciate everyone that helped provide me the mana I needed to complete my work, even though most of you didn't know what I was using it for. That wait is now at an end. The reason for that work and indeed for this fortress is right there." Arthur said as he turned and pointed to the crystal room. The council members moved to the side so the crowd could get a glimpse of the massive ruby on its stone pedestal. A quick hum of awe filled the space.

"That is far more than a pretty stone. That is the core of the new defensive enchantment for this city. I have worked to connect multiple points on our walls to this centralized crystal. The guard forces can now activate a barrier that projects from our city walls and blocks all physical and magical damage and intrusion into the city during conflict. This allows the city the ultimate protection."

Quiet muttering filled the room before a few slow claps took its place. It wasn't long before the room was full of cheering and clapping. Arthur held up his hands to calm the crowd. When the celebration finally ended, he continued his speech.

"Tomorrow, I will erect small pillars throughout the city that tie into this network. I encourage every citizen to dump excess mana they have at all times into the network. The more power that is stored here, the longer this barrier will last in an emergency. If you do your part to provide this mana, the city council and guard forces can ensure you stay safe within these walls. I'll leave it to the council to dictate the exact guidelines around this defensive enchantment. Until then, take care of our fine city. For Alurian!" Arthur ended his speech.

The crowd, all pumped up by the announcement, echoed him in a thunderous and unexpected response. "For the Kingdom of Fire!"

The city of Alurian now has a City Level Fortification. All defenders of the city receive a 10% boost to Health, Mana, and Defense while in the city.

The city of Alurian now has a Master Level Defensive Enchantment. This city has a permanent boost to citizens morale by 35%. Mana use of defensive enchantments is decreased by 65%.

Arthur left the front of the crowd and found Allendria along the edge of the room. He grabbed onto her hand and they walked with the crowd out of the building as the council members dismissed everyone.

They walked hand in hand through the streets and toward the inn. They were due to have a city council meeting in just a few minutes.

Inside the inn, everyone took their normal seats. Allendria sat to his left and Calfuray showed up and took the chair to his right. Trisha and Paula passed out food and everyone enjoyed their customary meal before the group discussed the business of the city.

When the last plate was removed from the table, Daniel spoke up.

"I wasn't sure you could actually do it. Good thing you tend to prove us wrong."

"I wasn't entirely sure I could either, but a little trial and error worked in my favor. I felt bad having to run off and leave you guys without some protection during a siege. Our guards and mages are great, but it's a lot better just being able to erect a shield and not worry about a stray spell or arrow hurting someone." Arthur said.

"True enough," Daranth agreed. "I assume you plan on leaving soon?"

Arthur looked to Calfuray. "I do. We will leave the day after tomorrow for our journey."

"Any idea who is going with you?" Rowan asked.

"Calfuray and Allendria will go with me. I'm not sure if we will take anyone else. While I enjoy having a full group, I also want us to fly back once Calfuray is in her dragon form. I'm not sure she can carry more than Allendria and I without drastically slowing down."

"I don't like it, but I agree with your logic. I'm tempted to ask you to take more time and a bigger party, but I also know the Dark Elves could attack at any moment." Daniel grumbled.

"We will hold back any attackers that we must." Samson said with a cold and dispassionate response. Arthur was still worried about him and had tried to talk to him on multiple occasions, but hadn't had any luck. At least he was present for the meeting. Any progress was better than nothing.

"Are there any other agenda items of concern?" Arthur asked.

"Do you have any specific guidelines for us regarding the city function or growth?" Rowan asked.

"Consider that all at your discretion. I don't have much interest in running the city. Ensure that the defensive enchantment remains safe. When you have free members of the construction team, have them encase the crystal pathways underground with stone for added protection. Unless there is an emergency or an issue that needs my attention, I turn everything over to the council. Make this the best city it can be." Arthur said.

The council adjourned, and Arthur approached Daranth.

"Daranth, can I have a moment?" He asked.

"Of course, Arthur. What can I do for you?"

"Are you able to help me acquire some furniture?" Arthur asked.

"Is your home not furnished? If you need replacements, I'm sure I can get them." Daranth said.

"Nothing like that. My home is in great shape. I need to furnish my traveling arrangements."

Daranth looked at him in confusion for a few moments. "I don't know if we ever made any folding cots or portable furniture."

"No worries. I need full size furniture. Probably four beds and the same number of trunks for gear."

"You plan on dragging that bulky furniture around with you?" Daranth asked.

"Kind of. I have a couple crappy beds right now, but want to replace them with quality furniture. I have a magical space, similar to my dimensional storage spaces, that allows people into it. We can sleep in these spaces and close ourselves from the outside world. It's the safest form of camping you can get. I just need some better furniture in it."

"Oh, that's good to know. I'll have it brought to your house tomorrow."

"Thanks for the help."

Arthur grabbed Allendria and Calfuray by the hand and led them out of the inn. When he neared the bathhouse, he slowed down and released them. With a sly grin, he turned to Allendria.

"Want to take a dip for old time's sake?" She returned his grin and agreed.

"We'll see you back at home." Arthur told Calfuray.

"Humans," Calfuray mumbled in a tone so low Arthur barely caught it before she walked off toward their house.

Arthur took a quick glance at his experience gains over the last few days while he happily bounced along toward the bathhouse with Allendria.

You have gained 12,800 total experience in Fire Magic

You have gained 89,110 total experience in Earth Magic.

Congratulations, you have reached level 27 in Earth Magic. Increases the effect of your earth magic spells by 78%. You could be rich with all those gemstones.

You have gained 18,860 total experience in Dual Casting.

You have gained 68,120 total experience in Enchanting.

Congratulations, you have reached level 20 in Enchanting. Your enchantments have a 57% decreased mana cost. That was some truly impressive work.

You have gained 52,080 total experience in Jeweler.

Congratulations, you have reached levels 12, 13, 14, 15 and 16 in Jeweler. Increases the stats on Jewelry you make by 30%. That network is a true marvel.

Excited about the skill ups, he looked over his Earth Magic Talents. To his surprise, there was a new tier.

You have 12 unspent Talent Points.

Tier 5	
(Hidden Ability) Instant Bulwark (0/1) This ability will only become available if you have the following prerequisites: • Fire Magic > Level 15 • Have learned at least one stone	Teaches you the spell Earth Magic: Summon Instant Bulwark. This creates a stone wall border around you that is twelve feet on each side and four feet tall. Mana Cost: 220MP Cooldown: 6 Hours

spell	
Mineral Artist (0/10)	*You have increased knowledge of the composition of gemstones. Each point reduces the amount of raw material needed for your mineral compression and the mana cost by 5%.*
Fortification Master (0/10)	*Any defensive structures of dirt or stone you create have the following benefits per point:* • *5% additional Durability* • *4% increased Physical Defense* • *3% increased Magical Defense*

Arthur nearly kicked himself for forgetting his talent points yet again. Most of the earlier talents weren't much use to him anymore, so he took Instant Bulwark, put all ten points into Mineral Artist, and the last point into Fortification Master.

Fortification Master looked great, but he had already built the walls and didn't think the boosts would be retroactive.

Dual Casting was next to review, and it also had a new tier.

You have 6 unspent Talent Points.

Tier 3	
Mana Weaving (0/10)	*Decrease the cost of combination spells by 3% per point.*
Magical Supremacy (0/10)	*Every 2 points in this skill grants you a native 3 defense. Every 5 points grants you 1 Intellect and 1 Endurance.*
Auto Dual Cast (0/1)	*Allows the user to auto cast Dual Cast spells without failure and removes the auto cast penalty on effectiveness.*

He put one point into Arcane Control, bringing it to 10/10 and allowing him to cast an additional two spells simultaneously.

Arcane Control (10/10)	*Every 5 points invested in this talent expands your control of mana and allows you to cast an additional spell at the same time.*

The Arcane Control ability was one he wanted to max out first and then he eyed the other options. He put the last five points into Magical Supremacy.

His excitement built as he checked his Enchanting for his special ability.

Congratulations, you have reached level 20 in Enchanting and have been promoted to Journeyman in the skill. Please choose one of the following as a bonus for this achievement:

Schematic: Magical Engineering Press	
Requirements: Enchanting	Description: Provides you with the knowledge and designs necessary to build a full-scale magical printing press. This machine is capable of mass-producing enchantment plates.
Mastery Level: 1	

Ability: Master Enchantrix	
Requirements: Enchanting Type: Passive Ability	Description: This passive ability decreases the mana cost to activate enchantments by 40% and increases all of your enchantment's power and effectiveness by 15%.
Mastery Level: 1	

Spell: Mechanical Familiar	
Requirements: Enchanting Mana Cost: 800 MP Cast Time: 10 seconds	Description: Summons and binds a mechanical familiar that will assist you in any way possible. This being lasts until killed or dismissed.
Mastery Level: 1	

The first two possibilities intrigued him. Mechanical Familiar, while interesting, wasn't as useful since he already had Balair and Calfuray in addition to the other magical creations he could summon. His initial instinct drew him toward Master Enchantrix. That much of a boost to his enchanting ability would be tremendous.

Magical Engineering Press kept drawing his attention, though. Something like that would be a benefit for the entire kingdom and not just for him. If he could put some of the power back in the hands of the people and ensure there would be a more secure future, it would be worth it. The key point was that he would never have enough time to do everything on his own. With one last longing look, he made his choice and selected Magical Engineering Press.

The knowledge flooded into him and he knew what he needed to make it. Even better, the design melded with his current knowledge level of enchanting and the different magic skills to enhance the design and provide him with an updated list of materials for the improved version. The materials needed weren't even very rare for him to gain. He could see the challenge with most since it required Magesteel, but he had that problem solved already.

Building one of these would have to take precedence tomorrow. He had enough time to complete the machine and build the pedestals for recharging throughout the city.

The last skill to check on was Jeweler.

You have 24 unspent Talent Points.

Talent	Description
Tier 1	
A Rare Gem (0/10)	Each point increases the chance of the quality of the gems you create increasing by one by 5%.
Selective Manufacturing (0/1)	Allows you to select the type of gem produced while using your Mineral Compression skill.
Pretty Baubles (0/5)	Each point increases one stat on jewelry you create by 1.
Tier 2	
Reduced Stress (0/10)	Each point decreases the material needed to make gemstones by 4%.
A Special Treat (0/5)	Each point adds a 2% chance to create an additional gemstone of equal type, size, and rarity when manufacturing a gemstone.
Tier 3	
Fine Carving (0/10)	Each point boosts your craftsmanship ability and increases the maximum magical capacity of jewelry you create by 5%.
A Leg Up (0/15) Requirements: • Arcane Smithing • Enchanting	Each point reduces the mana needed to empower jewelry by 5%.

<table>
<tr><td></td><td>At 15 points, this ability grants you the skill, Quick Scribe. This allows you to instantly engrave jewelry with the patterns for enchanting.</td></tr>
</table>

Arthur yet again felt like an idiot for finding another skill he'd never looked into the talents. While he felt like chastising himself, he knew it would do no good. The sad reality was he had too many skills to keep up with and the lesser used ones only became important in the sparse times he used them. The options lined up pretty well with his other talent trees, though. He immediately dumped the fifteen points into A Leg Up to max out that skill and allow him to instantly scribe the runes needed for enchanting onto his jewelry. With some practice, he was sure he could figure out how to do it on other materials as well.

Selective Manufacturing wasn't very useful since he never truly cared what type of gem it created. They all seemed to be identical in function, regardless of type. He spent the five points to max out A Special Treat because the thought of free gemstones was nice. Finally, he went over the other options. Pretty Baubles, he dismissed because he didn't make a lot of jewelry. The mana necklaces were the key items he created, and he hadn't made many of those recently. In the end, he put his remaining four points into Fine Carving. The increased magical capacity would make all of his jewelry far more powerful when he made it.

    With all the talents sorted out, he turned
his attention back to Allendria, who had been
half pulling him into the bathhouse pool with
her. Arthur even noticed she undressed most of
him on her own while he was zoned out. They
sunk into the relaxing warmth and washed away
their cares.

Chapter 25

Back on the Road

Arthur spent the first part of the next day working on the charging pedestals throughout the city. Each of these consisted of a stylized stand that contained a smaller version of the dragon wings holding a scaled down gem. It looked almost identical to the large focus crystal pedestal, but he also had a dragon's claw reached up from the pedestal to grasp it over the top, preventing anyone from 'accidentally' removing the gemstone. There were open spaces between the stone that the users could touch to deposit their mana.

Another concern was someone stealing mana or overriding the enchantment. Because of this, Arthur was careful to make the pathway only one way from each pedestal. He placed them near areas where he ran the main mana lines out to the wall enchantments and tied them into the major crystal flow.

He tested each one with a small dump of mana and confirmed that it registered in the focus crystal. When he was satisfied that enough of the stations were available, he returned home to find Daranth and a small load of furniture. Thanking the Dark Elf, he opened up his Wizard's Den. He'd slowly been feeding excess mana to it every chance he got, so the space was roomy.

The second room was a great addition when the den reached level ten. He knew the skill said it could gain new properties as he leveled up, but the massive increase the second room brought was great. Arthur also discovered he could change the style of the walls, floor, and ceiling. To make things interesting, he made the walls and floor look like a gray slate stone while the ceiling was a soft white rock that glowed with light.

Arthur spent a couple of minutes moving the two old beds out of the space and stacking them outside. Daranth watched him with an expression that Arthur took to be awe.

"Do you mind disposing of these old beds?" Arthur asked. "I don't care if you give them to someone needs them or break them down for parts. Up to you."

Arthur's words brought Daranth back from his stupor and the Dark Elf nodded. "Of course. We always have people in need of furniture. I'll give them to someone who truly needs them."

"Thanks. Want to come in and see the place?" Arthur asked.

"Not sure. It's still difficult to trust these spaces. The magic in them is just strange."

"I thought elves loved magic? I figured you'd be more comfortable with this than most."

"We do, but Dimensional Magic is a beast of its own. We've never had someone from our race with that power. It has always been closely tied to your bloodline."

"Well, I won't force you to do anything you're not comfortable with. Sure you can't help me carry this new furniture in? My Strength allows me to do it by myself but it's awkward trying to maneuver that way."

Daranth sighed. "No, I'm fine. I can help you move the furniture."

The two of them spent half an hour carrying beds and trunks into the space. They lined them up, so it looked like a barracks with the head of the bed against the wall and the trunk at the foot.

"Not very private, is it?" Daranth asked.

"What? Oh, not a problem," Arthur said as he waved a hand. A stone wall appeared between each set of beds, dividing the space. The right side of the room was completely open still and led back to the kitchen space.

"I left the walls out for now, so it would be easier to move the furniture. I gained the ability to place the walls at level six. When people stay here, I'll include a wall along the front and a door for privacy."

"That's amazing. This ability is truly powerful. What's in the back?" Daranth asked.

"Nothing right now. It is labeled as a Kitchen Space but I haven't done anything with it since it was added at level ten. Now that the furniture is complete, I'll at least put together an oven in here to cook. I think I'm going to segregate the pieces of this room from the back. I'm going to make one of them into a freezer space and the other into a temperature regulated pantry. I'll need to create shelves for each. Unless you can help? I need two shelving units and a table for the kitchen, if possible?"

Daranth scratched his head. "Guess I can. It'd be much easier if we were back at the woodworking quarter so I could build it directly into the space."

"Well, I need to build the oven in there and secure some of the temperature regulators so I can just open it at the shop and leave it there for you to work in. I also need to go to the blacksmith for another project before I leave."

"That should work. Want to move it there now so I can get started?"

"Sure."

Arthur closed the space and the two of them walked back to the Dark Elf quarter and into the assorted woodworking shops. Daranth led him to his personal workspace. All of his tools hung neatly along an ornate wooden bench. Nearby sat a stack of lumber, ready to use.

Arthur opened his Wizard's Den again, and the doorway opened in the center of the workspace.

"Do you have something to haul dirt with? A lot of dirt?" Arthur asked.

Daranth nodded and jogged outside. He returned, pushing a wheelbarrow.

"You made one?" Arthur asked, surprised.

"Oh yeah. After you described it, they sounded useful. We made a couple to test them out, and they have become popular. So many of the farmers use them now."

"They are useful but will probably become obsolete when I'm able to work up more dimensional bags."

"Possibly, but those have a size limit for the opening. Either way, you can use this to haul dirt."

Arthur grabbed the handles and wheeled it outside. A small amount of his Earth Magic dug into the ground and created a spout of soil that slowly filled up the wheelbarrow. Using this thin stream of magic was much easier than trying to dig it up by hand. When the weight of the wheelbarrow became precarious, he cut off the magic and wheeled it back inside.

Taking it to the Kitchen area, he dumped the pile into the corner. He repeated this process three more times until he had a substantial stack of dirt. Weaving his magic, he slowly shaped the dirt until it resembled the oven he needed and then began infusing the Fire Magic to form it into stone. This was becoming so routine he could almost do it without concentrating on the work itself.

Instead of designing this one similar to the one at his house, he incorporated Enchantment and gemstones into this. Not only that, but he made it so the burners on top and the heating gems on the inside were designed similar to his Amplification Crystal, only smaller. He also added slots in each so he could insert small spell plates to activate them. The main power supply gem was embedded into the back portion of the stove and covered a large area of the back panel.

    The design would need to be incorporated
into future projects. With the new Magical
Engineering Press, he wanted to include his
spell plates into all of their normal
applications. He wished more people had his
Mineral Compression skill, though. His lucky
break was that enchantments could be placed on
other materials with the press. They could go
into metals, hides, wood, essentially anything
he could normally enchant. Their power wasn't
as high or as efficient, but it would work.
    Arthur left the den and waved to Daranth.
"I'm off to see Rowan at the Blacksmith. I'll
leave this open for you here. If you need
anything, send someone for me, otherwise I'll
come back by when I'm done."
    "Sounds good." Daranth said.
    Arthur took a straight path down the road
for the blacksmith. He had every intention of
taking no detours, but a delicious smell
wafted into his nose and his stomach grumbled
in protest. It was at that point that Arthur
realized he hadn't eaten all day and it was
nearly noon. He told himself to keep on track
with the plan, but his feet betrayed him and
took him to the inn. A quick meal and he was
headed to Rowan's place.
    The familiar ringing of hammers on metal
greeted him as he neared, and he watched
people hurry back and forth to take care of
their jobs. People hustled by with ingots of
metal and an assortment of tools and half-
finished weapons and armor. Arthur continued
past, trying to not interrupt anyone in their
duties. Rowan stood in front of an anvil with
his hands in front of him. Arthur could see
the magic flowing from the big man and shaping
the metal. He stepped up next to the smith and
watched his progress.

The line of power crawled across the metal and the edges took shape. Runes flowed through the piece, and Arthur recognized the pattern as one of his own. To his surprise, it was one of the advanced designs and not the basic.

He must be working hard to have picked up the advanced pattern well enough to use it in Arcane Forging.

Arthur walked to Rowan's side and watched as he completed the pieces. Rowan's eyes popped open as the metal reached its final shape.

"Another successful one! That makes five I've done with the Advanced Matrix." Rowan cheered.

"That's great. Every time I come back, you're making progress."

"I have to try and keep up with you somehow. I thought you'd be on the road by now?"

"Have one last project to take care of. I hit level twenty on my Enchanting and gained my special skill. It taught me how to make a magical press for Enchanting. It'll allow us to mass produce Enchantment plates to use for the entire kingdom."

"That sounds great, but plates?"

"Oh, removable pieces that activate enchantments built into items. It's based on the work I did with the city's shield. You can build up generic enchantments on items or buildings and then activate any ability by inserting a plate with predefined spells on them. The plates activate the enchantment itself and can be changed quickly. You can also build in mana sources to the items, or the enchantment can run based on the latent mana that the plates themselves can store."

"I think I understand. That would be useful for sure. We don't need to go on some grand adventure to get the items for it, right? No strand of hair of a golden newt, or the tear of a naga's firstborn?"

Arthur chuckled at Rowan's suggestions, but couldn't fault him for being skeptical.

"Sadly no. The only thing that is difficult is Magesteel. Well, difficult for normal people. We have that down now. Depending on our stock, I think I'll make three of the machines to keep up with demand."

"Do we need that many? You're the only one that can make the gemstones, anyway."

"It works on any material that can take enchantments. I'm trying to look toward the future. Right now, I doubt we'll use them all, but as the city grows and we distribute our luxuries to other places, we will need to have higher production capabilities."

"Can't fault that logic. You need anything from me?" Rowan asked.

"Not really. Just permission to use your facilities."

"Have at it. No one should give you any trouble, so if you need anything, just yell at one of the assistants."

"Will do."

Arthur found an empty workspace among the different buildings and settled in. Running through the design in his head, he pulled it apart to see what he needed to do. The contraption looked similar to a large press that dry cleaners used. A simple base provided the support and the panel that closed down wasn't overly complicated. It was rather lackluster, all things considered.

Arthur considered changing the design, so
it was more of a slot fed creation but decided
against it. It would be great for the tablet
style enchantments but if he needed to enchant
metal bars, wood, or cloth, this style would
work better.

The trick to this machine was the
enchantment itself. The script was extremely
complex and weaved multiple patterns through
the design. Arthur wasn't aware that was
possible until he saw it now. He wondered how
people combined functionalities that didn't
seem to match. He'd done it by enchanting the
different components and then placing them
together. This showed he could do it to
finished products and all at once.

Arthur wasted no time sourcing all the
Magesteel he needed and two different
assistants delivered the materials to him. It
took them a couple of trips, but it gave
Arthur the time he needed to go over the
design and become familiar enough to do it
with his Arcane Forging.

He quickly decided against trying to
incorporate the runes into the process, so
when all the materials were present, he
created three separate bases. From that point,
he created the three tops, and all the
associated hinges and pins he needed to
connect it all.

Recruiting the assistants again, he had
them help him lift and attach each of the tops
to the pieces. Well, more accurately, they
lifted, and he just attached. Benefits of rank
and all.

The contraptions had no stops or safety mechanisms to prevent the top from swinging too far backward or slamming closed too fast, so Arthur created some springs and stops to add to the devices. After everything was mechanically sound, he began work on the enchantments. To prevent errors, he started with his small brush and charcoal ink. There were a few times he needed to clean the charcoal substance and redo small portions, but he worked diligently. Every few inches' worth of runes, he'd channel magic in and sear them in permanently. He didn't need the charcoal rubbing off and him having to repeat a lot of his work.

Two grueling hours later, and the runes were all burned into place on the three devices. He was able to power the enchantments on two of them before running out of mana. Chatting with Rowan helped him pass the time as he waited for enough mana to regenerate to finish the last device.

Arthur brought Rowan with him to charge the last one and then explained how the machines worked and showed him how to use them. The top of the press had an insert area where you could place a metal plate with your predetermined pattern on it that would be transferred to the material in question. Arthur had made a few of them while experimenting with the contraption and handed them to Rowan.

"Keep guard over those for now. Use them as needed and try to make plates for all the major enchantments we currently use. You can store them in one of your secure locations here."

"I will. I'll be honest that I didn't see the point of these before, but I'll also admit I overlooked one major fact. These can be used by anyone, especially how you designed it. I didn't realize that even people without the Enchanting skill could use it."

"Indeed, they can. They can't charge the rune at the same time. It is imprinted on the material but, with the runes burned in, they can hand it off to someone who can. It will also make training Enchanting a lot faster. If you make a lot of basic patterns, have them press them in, and then empower them with their mana. It will teach them the skill and keep bumping up their experience."

"Thank you. This will help us a lot."

"I'm trying to make sure you have the tools you need, whether I'm here or not."

"We really appreciate that. Some of us were skeptical when you first came around and declared yourself the king. Don't get me wrong, we were behind your decision. Just kings have an annoying habit of becoming tyrants and feeling the need to lord over everyone."

Arthur laughed. "I don't know if you noticed, but I'm trying everything I can to do the opposite. Do you think I turned this city over to a council for my power? Please, I want you guys to take care of all the administration duties. I just want to have fun, spend time with friends, and occasionally go on a cool adventure. I'll leave the business matters to those best suited to them."

"And that's why we support you all the time. Speaking of, good luck on your fun little adventure." Rowan said.

Arthur looked to the sky and realized it was mid-afternoon already.

"You're right. I think it's time for me to go. Keep an eye on the place while I'm gone."

"I always do." Rowan agreed as Arthur kept a brisk pace on his way back to Daranth's shop.

Arthur thanked the Dark Elf for his work as he saw his two storage rooms now had all the shelving he needed. He stopped by the inn and stocked his room with some basic food items, and then told Daniel he was leaving soon. Everyone wished him good luck and bade him to hurry back.

Back at home, Calfuray and Allendria both waited in their living area. Each had a bag of traveling items with them and both looked eager to go.

"Sorry. I thought I'd be done quicker than I was."

"No problem. It's almost guaranteed you would underestimate the work you had to do, so we expected this. Did you still want to leave today or just wait until the morning?" Allendria asked.

"Let's leave now. Every bit of distance we can eat up today will help. You can pack your things away in here." Arthur said as he opened the Wizard's Den.

The two ladies walked in and looked around. "You've done some work." Calfuray said.

"Yep. Wanted to make it cozier, especially since we will sleep here for the next couple of weeks. I look forward to restful sleep without the need to post guards at night."

Arthur noticed Allendria carried two bags
with her and was relieved to see she'd packed
some of his stuff as well. Grateful that she
took care of it, he gave her a kiss on the
cheek as she passed. The group exited the den,
left the house, and headed for the wall. Their
quest would lead them northwest and into the
nearby mountains.

They each checked their weapons and
equipment as they left the city. Most of it
was just nerves setting in before the trip.
Arthur looked over his shoulder one last time
to get a glimpse of the city. It'd changed so
much since he first arrived. He felt a swell
of pride for what they'd accomplished so far.

A streak of orange through the sky caught
his eye and Balair dropped near him.

Time to go? Balair asked.

"I guess so. I wasn't sure if it would be
better for you to stay here or to go, if I'm
honest. The city can probably use your help
scouting from the air." Arthur said.

*They could, but you probably need it more.
Someone needs to help watch Calfuray. I know
you've helped her with her magic and done some
work with her to help defend herself, but
let's be honest. She's not a very good human.*

"Usually, I'd chase you down and beat you
for that comment, but I can't disagree with
it." Calfuray huffed.

"Well, one more sure won't hurt. I prefer
you with us, anyway. Also, don't want to test
how far your familiar bond will actually
work." Arthur said.

The group continued through the open field
and off towards the looming mountains in the
distance. He looked over his experience for
the day as they trekked into the distance.

You have gained 34,780 total experience in Enchanting.

Congratulations, you have reached level 21 in Enchanting. Your enchantments have a 60% decreased mana cost. So now you're too lazy to even do the Enchanting yourself?

You have gained 4,240 total experience in Earth Magic.

You have gained 3,935 total experience in Fire Magic.

You have gained 3,125 total experience in Dimensional Magic.

You have gained 2,340 total experience in Jeweler.

You have gained 1,910 total experience in Metal Construction.

Congratulations, you have reached level 4 in Metal Construction. Decreases the time it takes to assemble metal constructions by 9%. Going to start a book empire next?

You have gained 1,910 total experience in Arcane Metal Construction.

Congratulations, you have reached level 4 in Arcane Metal Construction. Increases the effectiveness of metal constructions created with magic by 9%. At least charge royalties or something.

You have gained 4,110 total experience in Blacksmithing.

You have gained 4,110 total experience in Arcane Smithing.

Arthur checked his Enchanting Talent tree and sighed again, kicking himself for being stupid.

This is becoming a bad habit.

You have 18 unspent Talent Points.

Talent	Description
Tier 1	
Mana Conservation (0/10)	Each point decreases the mana needed to complete an enchantment by 3%.
Powered Enchantments (1/1)	Teaches you how to use gems to latently power enchantments.
Power of Symbols (5/5)	Each point teaches you how to use an additional rune in your enchanting symbol structures.
Tier 2	
Charge Up (10/10)	Each point increases the base amount of charges on enchanted items by 20
Secrets of Mana Cycling (0/5)	After investing all 5 points, this will teach you the secret of naturally recharging your enchantments using latent mana.
Tier 3	
Blessing of the Ancients (0/10)	This talent increases the chance any item you create will be Blessed by the Ancients. Each point invested increases this chance by 1%. Blessing of the Ancients:

	Divine inspiration influences the item to change its properties and improve it. The possibilities are endless and unable to be predicted.
Power Overwhelming (0/10)	*Each point invested in this talent increases the base charges on an item by 10%.*
Enchantment Mend (0/1)	*Allows you to repair damaged items with enchantments on them without damaging the enchantment itself.*
Tier 4	
Font of Power (0/10)	*Draw on the magical knowledge of your Enchanting to increase your raw power. Every 2 points invested in this skill grants you 1 Intellect and 1 Wisdom.*
Efficiency (0/10)	*Improves the speed that you can carve, draw, and/or forge runes into desired materials by 5% per point.*
Enchantment Weaving (0/1)	*This ability teaches you how to weave multiple rune patterns together to create a more powerful and varied effect.*

The tier four options were all new, but he had a lot of extra points he'd neglected to assign, as usual. It was almost a blessing considering his new options, though. Keeping with tradition, he immediately invested the ten points into Font of Power. Raw base stats always trumped other things. That brought his raw mana pool up to 990. With his item bonuses, he had 1,290.

Enchantment Mend and Enchantment Weaving both received a point. While he could probably learn to weave from the design of the press, it was much quicker and far more intuitive if he got it from the talent. It would just immediately click with him.

Increasing the charges on his items sounded great, but he already had pretty good capacities on the items he already used and created. He put the last six points into Blessing of the Ancients. Arthur was relatively sure that would allow his Jewelry to also proc Legendary items if done at the highest quality.

With his talents sorted out, he turned his focus back to the trek.

Chapter 26

A Tall Mountain

The small party walked down the road at a steady pace. They were in a bit of a rush, but Calfuray was still getting used to traveling as a human instead of a dragon. Her stamina was perfectly fine since she had the power of a dragon coursing through her. Arthur had also discovered her strength was slightly higher than his own in her human form, making her formidable in battle.

To accentuate that, he'd created a set of mail armor for her that was like his own. It had the damage absorption abilities that all of their standard armor had. Her weapons were unique. He created a small buckler shield for her left arm that was enchanted as a caster weapon and was resistant to magic. Her main hand weapon was a sleek short sword that he'd created a magic channel in to amplify spells.

Item: Enchanted Masterful Magesteel Buckler	Defense: 15
	Magic Defense: 40
	Durability: 400/400
	Rarity: Epic
	Quality: Exquisite

	Weight: 4.0 kg **Mana Capacity:** 500/500 **Slot:** Off-hand **Traits:** A specially enchanted Magesteel shield. Will absorb damage based on the available mana capacity. **Enchantments:** • Absorbs damage at a rate of 1 HP of damage per 1 Mana. • Reduces magic damage taken by 15%.

Item: Enchanted Masterful Magesteel Short Sword	**Attack: 14** **Magic Attack: 32** **Durability:** 300/300 **Rarity:** Epic **Quality:** Exquisite **Weight:** 1.5 kg **Mana Capacity:** 600/600 **Slot:** Main-hand

	Traits: A specially enchanted Magesteel short sword. Will amplify magic damage based on the available mana capacity. **Enchantments:** You can spend mana to boost the base damage of spells cast through this weapon. Increases damage done by your magical spells and abilities by 10%.

Arthur was pretty proud of the equipment he'd made for her. It was a different style of enchantment than he'd normally done. Calfuray had asked him to focus on defense and magic, so he did exactly as instructed. He wanted to go with mail because it offered a high amount of damage absorption without sacrificing a lot of mobility.

The sun was slowly sinking toward the horizon and Arthur was considering finding a stopping point when a heavy thudding noise plodded through the trees behind them.

Calfuray was the first to notice and stopped in her tracks, slowly tilting her head back and forth. Noticing her reaction, Arthur stopped and then heard the noise as well. The party all turned to face the noise and Arthur, Calfuray, and Allendria all drew weapons.

Branches rustled on a nearby bush before a short man tumbled out. He looked at the group and held up his hands in a show of submission before dropping them to his knees and doubling over. Giant, labored breaths were all he could manage for a few moments before he finally regained enough composure to stand.

Arthur put away his weapon, and the rest followed suit. He walked over to examine the figure.

"Wesley, what are you doing out here?" Arthur asked.

"Didn't get… to say bye," he said.

"I appreciate the gesture, but I'm sure we would have seen each other when we returned."

The dwarf shook his head. "I want… to go… with you."

"This trek is dangerous. It's not a diplomatic mission."

Wesley finally stood up straight with one long breath. "I want in on a real quest. I'm tired of running around as an errand boy. The dwarves treat me as an outcast and just look for excuses to get rid of me. I can be of help, I promise."

Arthur looked at the party. Balair just huffed before turning back in the direction they were headed. Allendria and Calfuray both shrugged.

"Will we be able to carry him back?" Arthur asked.

I can do it. Balair sent to him.

"You can?" Arthur asked in surprise.

Sure. He has a much smaller frame than you guys. I can carry him. I won't be able to sustain flight as well as Cal, but it will be fine with brief breaks.

"Looks like you're good to go. Try and keep up with us. Let us know if we need to take a break for you." Arthur told Wesley as he extended a hand to shake.

The dwarf smiled and grasped his hand with a surprising amount of force.

"I appreciate it. You won't regret it."

"Let's continue for a little longer, and then we can stop for the night. Want to cover as much distance as possible." Arthur said.

"I'll help with that," Wesley said. He pulled out his hurdy-gurdy and tested a few of the keys before cranking the wheel and walking along with them. The music picked up a steady rhythm. The bard didn't sing along with the song, but the tempo slowly rose until it hit a quick pace.

To his surprise, Arthur realized his steps were moving in sync with the music, and they were traveling at a fast clip. His notification confirmed it.

You are under the influence of The Travelogue. Your walking speed is increased by 25%, and you gain travel fatigue 20% slower.

That could definitely come in handy.

Their journey continued until the sun sank to the horizon and the sky dimmed. The last rays of the sun were barely visible, so Arthur found a secluded spot and opened his Wizard's Den.

"Welcome to Arthur's Inn. I dare say it's a far deal better than sleeping on the ground."

Arthur was thankful that Daranth included enough beds and trunks to fill what would normally be his entire party. The elf figured he'd need space for Rayne, Allendria, Samson, and Arthur. There was also one spare bed for traveling companions. Arthur and Allendria also slept together anyway, so it left one more open.

Wesley whistled in appreciation as he walked through the doorway.

"Damn. This is fancy. You mean we don't have to sleep in the grass?"

"Sure don't. Nor does anyone have to stand watch. I'll close the opening when we all enter and reopen it in the morning when we are ready to go. Perfectly secure."

"I could sure get used to traveling like this," Wesley muttered.

The dwarf walked around the space before dropping his small bag near the first bed. He continued into the back room to see the kitchen before returning to Arthur.

"Uh, if I have to pee in the middle of the night, do I need to wake you up?" Wesley asked.

"What…," Arthur began before he realized the issue. There was no bathroom in the space.

"Knew I forgot something," Arthur said, before walking back to the dirt outside of the room. He pulled on his Earth Magic and concentrated. In a slow and deliberate pattern, he built up a gradual ball of dirt in the air in front of him. He kept it suspended with magic and then shaped it to be the general size and shape of a toilet from Earth, minus the tank on the back. A flash of Fire Magic turned the entire mass into a single piece of stone.

Continuing to pour mana in, Arthur carried the makeshift toilet to the back corner of the structure and sat it down. In a rush, he raised walls around it to create a private room with a door.

Arthur dug through his Bag of Holding until he found the items he needed and created the enchantment to dispose of the waste with no mess in the toilet bowl. One last burst of magic fused it with the toilet, and it became fully functional.

"There we go. Problem fixed." Arthur said with a smile.

"Yep. Definitely going to like this," Wesley said.

Arthur and Allendria dropped their gear near the bed in the back. The chests in here were enchanted to be dimensional storage compartments as well, so each could hold an incredible number of items. Arthur kept a lot of bulk supplies in their own chest and only carried the essentials in his personal bag.

Calfuray placed her travel bag near the bed by Arthur and Allendria, and then the party walked into the kitchen. With a mental command, Arthur closed the entrance to secure the space and leave them alone. He dug through the pantry and found a large surplus of food stocked in there. They made a quick dinner, and all sat in the bedding space. None of the walls were up, so it was open.

"Mind me playing something for us before bed?" Wesley asked.

"Go ahead." Allendria encouraged.

The bard spun up his hurdy-gurdy and played a low and haunting song. The sound was peculiar, and to Arthur's surprise, it also made him sleepy. When the song finished, Arthur was ready for bed, so he bid everyone goodnight before raising the internal walls and separating their sleeping spaces.

This travel pattern continued for five days before things changed.

* * *

The morning of the sixth day started out completely normal. The group woke up inside the Wizard's Den and ate some breakfast. They'd made impressive time and were already at the foot of the mountain with the shrine. If everything went according to plan, they could reach the shrine early.

"Arthur, what do you plan on doing once all this is over?" Wesley asked.

"Not sure what you mean."

"Well, do you plan on staying king? Are you going to retire away to a life out of the spotlight? I'm curious to know your plan."

"You know. I honestly never thought of it. There are so many…"

"Hey, guys. We are going to go out and look around for a minute. Feeling a little cramped in here. Arthur, can you open the entrance?" Alexandria asked.

"Sure thing." He told her and then activated the entrance. The ladies left the den, and Arthur shifted back to Wesley.

"As I was saying, haven't really thought
about it. I'll probably stay king for a while
until I'm sure things are stable. Once that
happened, I'd try to hand the reins over to
some sort of council or governing body so
Allendria and I could live in peace. I doubt
she'll do the same, so we would probably live
in the Dark Elf capital. If we are lucky, we
may have kids to raise."

"You worried about that? Especially living
with the Dark Elves?" Wesley asked.

"Not particularly. Why?"

"Prejudice. I know many people look down on
those who are mixed race or just different. I
hope that isn't true in this world, but I've
already experienced my fair share of it
myself. I'd hate for that to happen to your
children."

The statement wasn't something Arthur had
dwelled on much, but the thought sank in.

*Will our kids be the target of hate? Are
mixed races looked down on here as well?*

Arthur heard soft scraping on stone and saw
Balair walk through the den and head toward
the entrance. Apparently, he wasn't interested
in the conversation.

"Well, thanks for that small nightmare. Yet
another thing I hadn't fully thought about."
Arthur grumbled.

"Sorry, man. Didn't mean to bum you out."

"It's fine. I actually need people to
remind me of things like this. I'll have to
consider it some more, but luckily, I should
have a long time to consider this before it
becomes relevant. The path ahead has no simple
end in sight."

Arthur! Get out here. Now! Balair sent.

Arthur shot upright immediately and ran for the entrance. He heard Wesley behind him as he rushed out of the opening and into the clearing ahead. A handful of trees dotted the area, but nothing seemed out of the ordinary. The mountain loomed near them.

"What's wrong?" he asked as he spotted the drake up ahead near the main walking trail.

Balair didn't answer and only motioned toward the path with his nose. Unsure of what was happening, Arthur walked over and spotted the concern. The ground was churned up in a few places, and footprints littered the area. The prints weren't human, though. Amongst the prints were burn marks, where it looked like fire was employed. A few strands of rope rested around the area.

Arthur looked around in confusion before he snapped his attention back to Balair.

"Where are Allendria and Cal?"

I'm not sure. Haven't seen them since I left the den.

Arthur's blood ran cold at the sight of the struggle.

"Can you get in the air and start searching? There was some kind of fight, and I want them found."

Balair didn't delay and took a few bounding leaps before launching skyward. Arthur turned to Wesley, who looked ready to go. He waved the Wizard's Den closed, and the two men began following tracks from the site of the scuffle.

Their search took them toward the base of the mountain, and within minutes, Balair sent him a message.

I found them. There are a group of lizardmen that have them captured in a net. Looks like they put them to sleep somehow. They are strung up in the net and tied to a long pole. There is a cave on the side of the mountain that they are headed for.

Okay. We are following the trail in the direction they headed. Can you come back toward us and lead us to the cave? Arthur asked.

On my way.

"Balair found them. Looks like we have a fight on our hands. Are you able to help?" Arthur asked.

"I'm more of a support role, but I can fight. I only have a couple of damage abilities and my dagger," he said while pointing to the hilt on his belt.

"The instrument?"

"I can maintain a buff and cast the occasional damage ability. I'll help however you need, though."

"No worries. They messed with the wrong person. I can take them. You just provide buffs if possible and throw in attacks when you must. We need to get rid of them quickly and save the girls before they decide to kill them." Arthur said.

As if on cue, a notification popped up.

A Rescue Mission	
Requirements: Level 15 Rewards: 35,000 experience and unknown rewards are also possible.	Description: A group of lizardmen have captured two of your companions. Rescue them within the time limit or lose them forever.

Arthur sighed. *That could be a problem.*

"Did you get a quest as well?" Wesley asked.

"Yep. Time to save the girls and earn some experience. Man, I wish Rayne was here. This type of mission was damn near tailor-made for him."

"Who's Rayne?" Wesley asked.

"That's right. You never met him. He's a friend of ours that is a rogue type. When we met the first time, he was in Seora helping sort that out. It's also where he is now."

"We definitely could use a stealth person for this mission." Wesley agreed.

"I have some skill in stealth but am nowhere near as good as he is. We have to get moving, though. Strict time limit on this."

A thud interrupted their conversation as Balair came to a sliding halt.

You two done chatting, or can we get this show on the road?

"Fine, you're right," Arthur said.

You're damn right I am. I'm always right.

"Lead the way, oh mighty Balair."

Balair grumbled at the sarcasm, but the situation made him overlook it and get moving. They darted straight for the base of the mountains, and Balair took them to a small trail winding through a tight canopy of trees.

Scrub brush lined both sides of the road and made it difficult to deviate from the path. When they closed in on the base of the mountain, they ran into their first obstacle.

They rounded a bend, and two lizardmen came into view. The creatures stood out and looked like oversized iguanas that stood on two legs. Their heads contained the same style of frill as the lizards from Earth. Both of them held rudimentary-looking spears, so Arthur drew Ember from its scabbard and rushed the one on the left. A flash of orange near him let him know Balair was after the other.

They both looked surprised and were slow to react as he ran up and leveraged a diagonal chop. The blade whistled through the air until it hit the scaled space between the monster's shoulder and neck. A muted crunch sounded as the blade broke through scales and sliced deep.

The enemy cried on in pain, but Arthur whipped out his dagger and stabbed it in the throat. Its eyes misted over, and it slumped to the ground. A loud crack caused him to look to the side to see the other lizardman's head broken in half inside of Balair's jaws. Blood and brain matter leaked from the head and dribbled off his teeth.

You have dealt 160 damage to Lizardman with Ember. (Critical Hit) (Mortal Blow)
You have dealt 110 damage to Lizardman with Enchanted Magesteel Dagger. (Critical Hit)
Lizardman has died.

"That's disgusting," Wesley said as he made a gagging noise.

Balair dropped the body and shook his head, causing some of the matter to sling around the area.

You're not wrong. Tastes foul.

"Holy crap. I heard him…." Wesley muttered.

"He can project his inner voice to others. Eventually, he will be powerful enough to be a proper dragon and speak like Cal." Arthur explained.

That's assuming this meat bag will live long enough for me to reach that level.

"When do you get to that stage, anyway?" Arthur asked.

Level 30. It's difficult to get to, but I'm getting close.

"Really, how close?" Arthur asked as the three of them continued jogging down the path.

I'm level 27 now. You know you have access to my stats, dumbass. Just look yourself.

"How are you further along than me?" Arthur asked.

Probably because you spend most of your time crafting while I spend my free time killing and hunting. At least when I'm not patrolling.

"He always talk to you like that?" Wesley asked.

"He's usually worse. The situation must have him a little more serious than normal. Time to cut the chatter, though."

The group continued their trip toward the mountain. Trees and greenery thinned as they closed in on the base, and Arthur came to a halt near the last of the trees. The group hid behind one particularly large specimen as they surveyed the scene beyond.

A short clearing stood between them, and an enormous cavern outlined against the mountainside. The clearing held no enemies, but there was a guard posted on each side of the cave entrance. An orange light glowed from deep in the dark recesses of the cave. Arthur assumed it was firelight from their camp deeper in.

"I'll take the one on the left. Can you grab the one on the right?" Arthur asked as he looked at Balair.

I got it. I'll back up, take to the air, and then pounce on him from above. Less chance he can call out an alarm.

"Go for it. I'll watch for your approach and be ready to hit the other with ranged. Wesley, stick near me."

Arthur waited for Balair to backtrack and take to the air. He kept a close eye on the sky, waiting for his sign to start. When the telltale streak of orange was on target for its prey, Arthur spun up his own attack.

Fire Magic burned in his palm as he rushed from the trees and headed directly for the lizardman on the left. The element of surprise worked again as the creature just watched the lone human running at him. Arthur unleashed his Searing Beam right as Balair came into his field of view.

The dense bar of concentrated fire magic launched from his palm and carved a path directly through the creature's chest. A brief squeal escaped from its lips before it looked down at its chest. It dropped its spear and both of its arms came up to the hole in its chest. A moment later and its brain finally caught up as the creature fell face first to the ground.

You dealt 210 damage to Lizardman with Searing Beam. (Critical Hit) (Fatal Blow)
Lizardman has died.

Arthur ignored the experience notifications and looked over in time to see Balair finish the other guard with a quick twist of its neck in his jaws.

"Didn't want to eat brains again?" Arthur asked.

Not this time. We have work to do and that takes time to get out of my mouth.

"Burn it out with a little flame?" Arthur suggested.

Why would I… You know what? That might work. I'll try it next time.

"Not sure I've ever heard of people talking this much during a rescue mission," Wesley said.

"Why not? Who are they going to tell?" Arthur asked, pointing at the dead guards.

"Just seems odd. Aren't you worried about the girls?"

"A little. I'm honestly giving the lizardmen fifty-fifty odds on whether we get there in time or the girls get out on their own and slaughter them all."

Fair warning, little dwarf. If you see a lot of big fire, just run. Allendria can be very scary. Pretty sure all of us except you are damn near immune to fire if we use our magic.

"Good to know." Wesley gulped.

They continued deeper into the cave before they slowed down and used a stealthier approach. The light brightened as they closed in on the bend, and Arthur slowed on the approach.

At the edge, he stuck his head around the corner and took a quick peek before popping it back.

"At least a dozen. Some kind of stone altar in the middle that they have Cal and Allendria on. They still have the net on them, which must be suppressing their magic, because I still can't reach Cal through our mental link."

Can we rush them? Balair asked.

Arthur thought about the situation before answering.

"Possibly. It seems this place is lower level since it should be an earlier stage of dragon maturity. The lower levels make them pretty useless against me or you, but I worry about Wesley."

Arthur and Balair looked at the bard with concern.

"What? I can protect myself." He said indignantly.

"Fine. Looks like a rush. Wesley, remind me to make you some damage absorption armor if you are going to keep traveling with us. Normally I'd just blast the place with my Fireblast spell, but I don't want to take the chance if Cal and Allendria can't access their magic."

Arthur withdrew both blades and channeled his Spellblade powers into each. Mana and elemental energy wreathed each blade as he nodded to Balair. They each rounded the corner and charged for their foes.

Chapter 27

More Than Bargained For

Arthur rounded the corner, and he was immediately surprised by the scene. The first problem was he was horrible at counting. In his defense, the group of ten lizardmen he missed were all wearing robes and in the back of the room.

The other concerning factor was an eerie green glow building from the base of the altar and slowly illuminating the stone as it rose. A glance at his quest timer showed he had five minutes left.

Always have to cut it close. Arthur muttered.

He closed the distance and slashed at the first lizardman in line. They wielded a crude iron sword, and they swung in a pathetic display of power. Arthur batted it away with a quick flick of his wrist, and the ice enchantment on the blade caused crystalline frost to cascade down the lizardman's weapon until his hand was encased in a thin sheet of ice.

The paltry damage from the spell was irrelevant as Arthur's swing with Ember cleanly severed their head.

You have dealt 210 damage to Lizardman with Ember. (Critical Hit) (Mortal Blow) (Decapitating Blow)

Lizardman (Level 16) has died.

Arthur never slowed his pace as he sliced into the next target. A lizardman to his right stumbled into him, while Balair barreled through the group. These creatures were so weak that they couldn't really damage the drake if they wanted. His power difference was much the same, so he pushed through without trying to dodge attacks. The notifications of his carnage made him smile as he watched these creatures' foolishness unfold.

Nonstop damage and notifications scrolled in his view as he cut through scales and eviscerated leather armor. Arms flew as they separated from their bodies, and blood fountained like a scene from a b-slasher movie. The damage he received was practically nonexistent.

Lizardman dealt 0 HP damage to you with Crude Iron Short Sword. (8 HP damage negated)
Lizardman dealt 0 HP damage to you with Crude Iron Spear. (6 HP damage negated)

A pang of guilt flashed over him as he contemplated the action he now took. On one hand, these things were sentient creatures and just trying to survive in their own way. On the other, they kidnapped and tried to sacrifice his wife and friend in one of their twisted rituals. At the end of the day, he'd still choose for them to die every single time.

"Stop them," One of the robed figures hissed as Balair closed in on the altar. He'd given up on much of the fighting and was just pushing through at whatever pace his strength allowed. The iron weapons rebounded off his scales with dull thuds.

When he was only a few steps away, Balair reached out with a claw and snagged the edge of the net covering the altar. A quick tug caused it to tumble free, and Allendria and Calfuray stirred.

One of the robed figures screeched in protest and dove at the girls with a small blade in each hand. It cut Allendria on the left shoulder while Cal took a deep scratch to her forearm. Before anything further could happen, Arthur released a Searing Beam. It burned a hole through the center of its skull, and the two blades clattered to the stone, droplets of blood splashing on the altar.

Cal and Allendria both came to full alertness with the damage from the knives and took stock of the situation. They clambered off the altar toward Balair. Free from the stone, they pressed up against the drake as he used his claws and teeth to push back the crazed lizardmen.

A Rescue Mission	
Requirements: Level 15 Rewards: 35,000 experience and unknown rewards also possible.	Description: A group of lizardmen have captured two of your companions. Rescue them within the time limit or lose them forever. Time Limit: 15 minutes.

Quest Completed!

You have completed the quest: A Rescue Mission. You have gained 35,000 experience. You do not qualify for special rewards.

Congratulations, you have reached level 24. You now have 5 available skill points. Cutting it a little close?

Well, better than nothing.

"They can't escape!" One cultist yelled before they jumped onto the stone altar.

Black energy poured from the monster's hands and engulfed the base of the altar. Balair and the two women headed for Arthur, fighting through the few remaining lizardmen. Most of them were in a panic and running around in confusion at the change of events. A few even watched the spectacle on the altar with what appeared to be fear.

The energy solidified until it looked like a thick black shell coating the stone altar. Dark power coursed through the robed figure, and they drew a dagger from their waist. Arthur didn't know what was happening, but he decided he didn't like it and cast Searing Beam at the creature.

The power sizzled across the gap until it found the energy on the altar. The dark power swallowed the flames as if they had never existed.

Your Searing Beam is Negated.

That's new.

"Any ideas?" Arthur asked the group.

"Where the hell are we?" Allendria asked.

"Lizardmen kidnapped you two. This is their cave. We are here to rescue you." Arthur explained in short order.

"Sounds right, based on what little I remember," Cal grumbled.

"What do we do about that?" Arthur asked and pointed at the altar.

"Can we do anything?" Cal asked.

"I don't know…," Arthur began until a notification hit him.

Summoning a Minor Deity	
Requirements: Level 20 Rewards: 568,000 experience and unknown rewards are also possible.	Description: You've cornered a desperate group of lizardmen and forced them to summon something to defend them. The presence of dragon's blood and the blood of a royal has amplified this process a thousand-fold and instead of a shadow protector, expect a Minor Deity. Defeat the Minor Deity.

"Oh, fuck." Arthur said, just as everyone else mirrored his sentiment.

The party worked backward, keeping themselves faced toward the altar to avoid any surprises while putting distance between them and the ritual.

The foul energy built in the cave until it felt like an oppressive air, weighing them down. Dark power was so thick that it felt like breathing at high altitudes. A foreign language spewed from the creature's mouth, but Arthur had trouble deciphering it with his ability. He assumed it had something to do with the concentration of dark power.

The lizardman's words grew louder as it continued to recite whatever it was saying. It brought its dagger up above its head before it finished with one final yell and slammed the blade into its own chest. Blood pooled around the blade and leaked toward the floor. Arthur watched in fascination as the blood was grabbed by the swirling black power, and thin rivulets were pulled into the air. Ribbons of blood soon filled the space before the lingering blood, and dark power all converged on the creature in a tight ball.

The group collectively held their breath until the power hummed and exploded in a wave of energy. Pain blossomed in Arthur's chest, and he sunk to a knee as the cascading energy swept by him. When the power leveled out, the pain ceased, and he returned to his feet. He could see the rest of the group doing the same. Even Balair was unsteady as he stood back up.

The altar was now split in half, with a sizeable chunk on each side of the room. Each section was lodged in the wall, and it looked like the blast was the cause.

The monstrosity at the center of the room
drew most of the focus. Where once stood a
little lizardman, now stood a ten-foot-tall
hydra with three heads. Each head had a large
frill on the top, and all of them were laser-
focused on his group. With a gulp, Arthur
activated Scan.

Name: Kythiss	
Level: 25	
Type: Minor Deity	
Class: Beastmaster	
HP: 15,580/15,580	
MP: 5,000/5,000	
Stamina: 6,000/6,000	
Strength: 38	Experience: N/A
Agility: 30	Skills
Intellect: 27	Combat Skills:
Wisdom: 23	
Endurance: 55	? (???/???)
Charisma: 3	
Luck: 12	

"Well, fuck that," Arthur said. "We're not
even attempting this. Let's get the hell out
of here."

No one bothered raising an objection, and
everyone turned and fled back around the
corner. Wesley stood near the side of the
tunnel up ahead and wore a look of pure
confusion as the full group came running his
way. Arthur waved for him to turn and run as
they closed in. The dwarf caught on and ran as
well.

Open grassland and fresh air greeted them as they broke free from the cave and headed for the trees. Arthur stopped when they were fifty yards from the cave entrance and turned. He could see the creature rounding the corner in the back of the cave. Luckily, it seemed to be slow.

"Allendria!" he called.

Arthur turned to see the dark elf running back his way.

"Why'd you stop?" She asked.

"We can't let it escape that easy. We'll never be able to avoid it, and it could make it all the way back to Alurian." Arthur explained.

"Have a plan?" Allendria asked.

"That doesn't involve some suicidal charge?" she quickly amended.

Arthur laughed at that, but quickly dismissed it. "I need to collapse the entrance. The only spell I have that might be able to do it is Fireblast, but I don't think it's strong enough."

A roar rattled the cave as a deep and sinister voice reached out from its depths. "I'll find all of you filthy creatures and devour your souls."

Arthur scanned through his list of spells and plucked one to cast. In a flash, he surged with mana, and the ground rose in front of him. A giant chunk of stone lifted from the earth before pieces sliced away from the edges and fell free. When the spell was completed, a solid stone golem stood in its place.

"Go stop that monster," he told it and it trudged forward. The creature itself stood nearly nine feet tall as it marched at a steady gait for the cave.

"That won't work. Can you raise a stone wall to block the entrance?" Allendria asked.

"Not enough time. As powerful as that creature is, I need to collapse part of the cave on it and truly bury it. It'd be able to break through any wall I could make."

"Channel it through me then." She suggested.

"What?"

"My Pyromancer abilities. Cast a Dual Fireblast through me. I can amplify them and send them forward at much greater power."

"Perfect," he said with a kiss on her cheek. Walking behind her, he placed both a hand on each of her shoulders.

Fire Magic swirled around both as Allendria channeled her mana as well. Arthur focused his power into Allendria as he activated a Dual Fireblast. A message appeared in front of him.

Do you wish to channel Dual Fireblast through Pyromancer Allendria? Yes/No.

He selected *Yes*, and the spell burned through his veins. He felt the magic building stronger, and he considered using Overload. That thought was dismissed since he didn't want to cripple his magic for 24 hours when they were out in the wilderness and still had a quest to complete.

Kythiss rounded the corner, and the stone golem slammed into her at full speed. The clash rocked the minor goddess, and she slid backward before gaining her grip. Stone sprayed from the golem as Kythiss slashed it with her claws. The assault didn't seem to bother the golem, but it was being knocked backward with every swipe. It also lost some of its mass as pieces continued to rain off the creature.

Arthur pumped the last of the spell into Allendria, and her entire body lit with fire. Arthur had to pull on more of his Fire Magic to avoid being burned by Allendria's power.

The energy swirled between Allendria's hands as she took the two spells and pushed them together. Her mana a veritable firestorm of power. The sky turned a deep shade of red in Arthur's vision as her energy leaked in all directions.

With both spells combined, she spun the spell at a faster rate than his default speed. The ball shrunk as the energy condensed, only for Allendria to pump extra power into it and have it grow again.

She went through four cycles of condensing and growing the power before the toll looked too much to handle. With a final shout, she pushed forward, and the ball launched at incredible speed for the cave.

Arthur watched fear blossom in Kythiss' eyes as the molten ball of flame flew directly toward her. The golem ignored the entire predicament and battered the minor deity with his stone fists.

Allendria sunk to a knee, and Arthur dropped to catch her as she went down. The two of them remained kneeling as the orb reached Kythiss and exploded.

The explosion flashed a brilliant white, blinding both of them and making them lower their gaze before a monstrous blast spewed flame from the cave. Arthur and Allendria dropped to the ground, trying to avoid any debris as shards of stone rocketed out of the entrance. The ground around them shook as the blast finished, and Arthur looked around.

The field around them was scorched solid black, their Fire Magic the only thing keeping them from being turned into a charred mess. Nothing remained of the cave. The area of the mountain where it once stood looked like a massive landslide covering the entire face of the cliff for over two hundred yards.

Something hit him on the shoulder, and he turned to see Allendria talking to him, but he couldn't hear anything she was saying. He responded with "What?" and she looked at him in confusion.

After a moment, she had an Ah Ha look plaster on her face, and she pointed to her ears. Arthur caught on and guessed that neither of them could hear right now because of the sound of the blast. To remedy that, he cast Major Heal on himself.

It took two casts on each of them before they could finally hear again, and he looked back at her.

"You okay?" She asked.

"Fine now. That was some impressive work," he told her with a nod toward the mountain.

"We make a good team." She agreed.

The two of them looked at the scene for a few more moments before Arthur checked his notifications.

You have dealt 6,475 damage to Kythiss with Pyromancer Enhanced Dual Fireblast.

*Kythiss has suffered 1,895 damage from
Landslide.*

Kythiss is suffering from Severe Burn.

*You have suffered 55 Sonic Damage. You have
been deafened.*

"Damn, that's a lot of damage," Arthur
mused.

"Sure is. Looks like we have our new
massive damage spell. Let's try not to use it
too much because it drains almost all of my
mana and nearly all of my Stamina to do."

"Noted. Let's keep moving. That explosion
is bound to draw the attention of other
things. We shouldn't be here at that time."

They got to their feet and walked back
toward the trees. The ground was scorched all
the way to the barrier of foliage, and the
outermost trees themselves showed signs of
fire damage. A few of them even smoldered and
smoked.

Their boots crunched along the dead and
crispy ground as they headed for their target.
They were near to the trees when an answering
crunching noise sounded ahead of them. They
scanned the area and found their companions
creeping out of the trees and looking in their
direction.

"You two okay?" Wesley asked.

"Perfectly fine. How about all of you?"
Arthur asked.

"I'm good. Sorry we caused all of this
mess," Calfuray said with her eyes downcast.

"Not your fault you were ambushed and
kidnapped," Arthur dismissed with a wave and a
laugh. "Just glad it worked out in the end.
Sure you want to hang around with us, Wesley?
This kind of mess seems to find us all the
time."

"Are you kidding me? This was the most fun I've had since I've been here. Guess I was always a bit of an adrenaline junky."

"Let's get out of here. I'm hoping that minor deity we buried under the mountain stays put or goes back to the realm it came from after time."

I'll scout ahead so we can avoid this mess again. Balair sent them.

The group nodded in agreement, and Balair launched from the ground. They checked their equipment and then started off toward the trail leading up the mountain. It was luck that the lizardmen didn't have their home near the main trail itself, or they would've collapsed their path forward.

They were partially up the cliff when a thought struck Arthur. It nagged at him for some time before he couldn't stand it and had to ask Wesley.

"Wesley, I'm curious. Why don't you have much of an Australian accent?"

"Oh, that? Well, not all Australians talk with that over-exaggerated accent that so many always mimic for them. I don't run around yelling crikey at everything. That said, I wasn't born in Australia. My family was military. My dad was born in the United States, and mom was from Australia. They met while he was deployed and got married. We lived in the United States for a while and bounced from city to city every time he changed duty stations. When he retired, they moved to Australia. I've lived there since I was sixteen."

"Military family, huh? That's nice. I've known lots of previous service members myself." Arthur said as they continued their climb up the mountain. The trail was smooth with few obstructions and while the path itself wasn't cobbled, it was heavily packed down and clearly defined.

"Did your dad teach you how to fight with a sword?" Allendria asked the bard.

"No, Lady Allendria. We don't fight like that in our home world. We have firearms and large explosive weapons. In many ways, our technology of war is far deadlier than what is found here. We have bombs that do more damage than that explosion you and Arthur just set off with magic." Wesley said.

"Is that what you mentioned you were so hesitant about?" Allendria asked Arthur.

"It is," he confirmed.

"But why be worried about being strong enough to live?" Calfuray asked.

"It's about the escalation of power. If I introduce items like ours here in this world, we will be much more powerful. Eventually, that technology will spread to other civilizations here, and then we are back on close to equal footing again. The key difference is both sides of the conflict have weapons that can level entire cities at their disposal. It can cause an exponential growth in destruction and casualties." Arthur explained.

"Do you think you could do that?" Wesley asked him.

"With time, I'm sure I could use magic to accomplish some of the same results as the weapons we had. I'm even confident that I could make a magic version of a firearm if given enough time. Do you have a Scan skill?" Arthur asked.

The dwarf nodded, and Arthur fished through his bag at his waist. His arm disappeared up to the elbow as he dug around in the Dimensional Bag and eventually got close enough to call out the item he needed. When his hand emerged, Feathers came first, followed by a wooden shaft and, finally, a very peculiar-looking arrowhead.

Arthur handed the device to Wesley and told him to Scan it. The dwarf concentrated on the arrow for a few moments before his eyes widened in surprise, and his jaw dropped.

"You created this?" He asked in astonishment.

"Yep. Figured it out in an afternoon. The scary part is that although the item never existed before. Some skills used to make it, such as Metal Construction, already exist." Arthur said.

"Wait, advanced engineering type of skills exist here?" Wesley asked.

"Seems so. I haven't looked into it much deeper. That is where I stopped before I took it too far."

"Are you sure that's the right idea?" Wesley asked. "Not trying to second guess your decision. I just know you recently lost a fight, and having more advanced weaponry sounds like a great way to prevent that from happening again, and it could save more of your own people's lives."

"That is my struggle. I keep telling myself that maybe Vana would be alive if I hadn't held back and just pushed forward. I just worry about how many more will be lost because of my actions now."

"Plan for your people today and do what is best for them now. As long as you understand the long-term risks, you can aim to prevent or mitigate them." Wesley said.

"The short man has a point. Protect yourself and your people above all else," Calfuray agreed.

"I agree with them as well," Allendria added.

"I hoped that by bringing you along, it might help balance things in my favor from the two ladies, but man, was I wrong." Arthur laughed while looking at Wesley.

"Ha, I've seen her throw fire. Not about to cross her," Wesley said.

"Smart man," Allendria said with a smile as she let fire dance around her fingers.

It took them the rest of the day and half of the next, but they finally made it up to the shrine with no further issues. The building itself wasn't even a building. It was a cave built into the side of the mountain, and on each side were intricate carvings of dragons curled up and facing outward.

The details on the carvings were exquisite. Everything was visible down to the scales. Red light shone from the eyes as they approached. When they were a hundred yards away, Arthur froze. He looked around and noticed the others doing the same. An eerie feeling settled over him, and the hairs on the back of his neck stood on end. He felt danger but couldn't figure out where it came from.

"What's wrong?" Calfuray asked as she turned back to see them all standing still.

"You don't feel that?" Allendria asked.

"Feel what?"

"It's like an overwhelming sense of danger," Wesley said.

A thud near them marked Balair's landing, and they turned to watch him stroll over to Calfuray.

What's up with them? He asked.

"This place exudes a sense of danger. It must be to keep anyone not dragonkin away." Arthur decided.

"It has an aura," Calfuray agreed. "I recall asking my mother how they keep these places hidden from others, and she said they didn't. She told me an aura could keep them from entering, and if that didn't work, the guardian could stop them. Didn't know what the aura actually did until now."

"You didn't want to share this information with us?" Arthur asked.

"Sorry. I didn't remember this until you just said that."

"So, should we worry about this guardian?" Allendria asked.

"Possibly. The trial is one of strength. They want to make sure we can handle ourselves as a dragon before granting us the ability to shapeshift. To gain the transformation, I have to beat the guardian. It isn't a fight to the death, only to submission. I'm just concerned because we typically fight it in our dragon form."

"Oh, so you have to beat a guardian designed to fight a full-grown dragon? And you have to do it in human form now?"

"I think so…," she said.

I'll help. Balair said. *I have a feeling these guys can't take part in your challenge, but since I'm dragonkin, I should be able to.*

"Would you really help me?" Calfuray asked.

Sure. We have to stick together.

"Thank you. The rest of you should stay outside of the boundary of the aura. The guardian isn't lethal to me, but they will be to you."

"You sure you don't want our help?" Allendria asked.

"I do, but I'm pretty sure you can't help me here. I have the bravest drake around on my side, anyway. We'll be fine." Calfuray said with a nervous grin.

Arthur stepped forward and unbuckled Ember from his waist. He snapped the belt around Calfuray, and it shrunk to fit her with its enchantments.

"Let Ember keep you safe," Arthur said.

"Thank you. Alright, Balair. Let's do this," Calfuray said, and the two of them marched for the cave entrance.

"I hope they'll be okay." Arthur said to Allendria.

"Those two are too stubborn to lose. They'll be back before long." Wesley assured him. "I know that, and I haven't known them for very long."

Arthur worried about their predicament as they marched on and entered the cave. His nervous anxiety getting to him, he went over his experience gains since they left.

You have gained 6,290 total experience in Earth Magic.

You have gained 7,950 total experience in Fire Magic.

You have gained 1,125 total experience in Dimensional Magic.

You have gained 1,690 total experience in Swords.

You have gained 1,310 total experience in Small Blades.

You have gained 235 total experience in Scan.

You have gained 2,355 total experience.

Chapter 28

An Unexpected Trial

Calfuray walked forward with a confident stride. Far more confident than the nervousness in her chest should even allow. Her thoughts kept intruding on her, and doubts crept to the surface. She couldn't turn to look at Arthur and his friends for fear of losing her courage.

I just have to push forward. I can do this.

Her inner struggle was interrupted as Balair brushed against her, and his warm scales comforted and soothed some of her nerves.

Thanks. She sent to him.

That's what I'm here for. I always knew you needed me around. He said with a slight chuckle to his inner sound.

Normally I'd argue, but what's the point?

She ran her hand along his scales to calm herself while placing the other hand on Ember at her waist. There were many days she questioned whether pairing herself with Arthur was the right idea. Today was one of those days she was absolutely sure she'd made the right choice.

The cave entrance loomed overhead as they approached, but instead of an ominous or dangerous feeling, a sense of welcome greeted her.

That's odd. Feels inviting. Balair remarked.

"It does indeed," Cal mumbled.

Calfuray drew Ember and walked into the cave opening. The inside of the mountain was spacious. A large stone platform lay on her right against the far wall, while an assortment of chairs and comfortable furniture surrounded the area near it. To the left were many odd-looking obstacles. Directly in front of her was a small pedestal with writing in Primal Draconic. The language was taught to her by her parents, so she understood it, but it was too far away yet to read it all.

"Who dares trespass in my cave?" A voice rumbled through the room.

Calfuray looked all around before she noticed movement in the back left portion of the cave. She kept her eyes on the area until she saw a noticeable snout emerge from the darkness and move in her direction.

"Humans are not allowed in here. Leave now or die!"

The voice confused Cal. She was sure it was draconic in nature. Her mother had never mentioned the guardian was another dragon. Why would they have to fight another of their kind?

"Did you not hear me? I said you must leave, human." The voice continued, "Otherwise I'll… wait, you're not human."

A loud sniffing noise filled the room as the dragon fully emerged from the shadows. Her long body and lithe frame told of a dragon built for speed and not for combat. Silver scales covered her body. The creases in the leathery folds of her face, coupled with the yellowing of the horns and teeth, told the tale of an old dragon.

"Another dragon. One of high standing at that. Ha, what's this? You brought a drake with you too? What a cute little guy."

I'm not little. Balair grumped.

The dragon whipped forward and came to a stop in front of them. It reached out a claw and scratched Balair under the chin.

"Of course you're little, fine drake, but you have a chance to evolve. You actually seem really close." She ran a claw along his neck and down to his shoulder.

"Strong and proud. You'll make a fine dragon."

Her attention snapped back to Calfuray. "And what brings you here? In human form, no less."

Calfuray hung her head in shame. "I was hit with a spell during a fight. It forced me into human form and I never learned the transformation spell, so I'm unable to change back."

The dragon chuckled at that. "Ah, dear. Definitely could be a problem. Do you just want me to change you back, or are you hoping to unlock the transformation skill?"

"Can I attempt to unlock it and if I fail, you change me back?" Cal asked.

"Of course. The trial is pretty simple, so I'm sure you'll master it, but if that fails, I'll change you back."

"Simple? How am I supposed to defeat the guardian in human form?" Cal asked, confused.

"Guardian?" The old dragon asked before breaking out into laughter. "It's been so long I forgot about that. My dear child, there is no guardian here. That is the story all who leave the temples agree to tell. It helps keep brash young dragons from attempting to join the outside world too soon."

"Really? I suppose I can see that. Well, my name is Calfuray."

I'm Balair.

"Nice to meet you both. My name is Antima. I'm the so-called guardian of this temple. Now with that out of the way…," she began before stopping and peering at the entrance. "Do you have companions with you? I sense something at the edge of the aura?"

"I have my bond mate and our friends. Please don't hurt them. I asked them to stay outside during my trial."

"That explains the drake. I assume he is the one who summoned you?" she asked Balair.

He nodded in agreement, and she looked back to Cal. "I won't harm them. They are perfectly fine. If they can brave the aura, they are welcome to join us. I have a few human friends who come to visit from time to time. It gets really boring up here all alone. Not enough dragons around to visit."

"Don't you kill intruders? You even threatened me." Cal said.

"That's just to weed out the weaklings. If they stay and don't have an evil presence to them, I invite them in for some tea."

"I just might," Cal agreed. "Can you tell me about the trial?"

"Of course. Are you the only one taking part, or are you as well?" She asked, looking at Balair.

I can participate? He asked.

"The transformation is slightly different since you're still in drake form, but overall, you can learn this now. It will save you time when you earn your dragon form."

Balair became excited and bounced around a little before darting toward the entrance.

I'll be right back. I'm going to grab the others so we can get started.

"Ah, to be young again." Antima mused. "So, the Soul Bond exists again?"

"It does. I kinda went against many other dragons in my decision, but I made a deal with this mortal, and he held up his end of the bargain." Calfuray said.

"Must be a special person for a dragon to invoke that sacred oath again."

"I think he is. I've seen him do marvelous things, and he really tries to help people. He's fighting with the Dark Elves right now, which is how I was transformed."

"The Dark Elves did this?" Antima asked as she examined her form. "I wasn't aware they knew transformation spells."

"Oops, that's my fault. I said spell, but it was actually an effect from an artifact they brought to the fight."

"I always wondered what happened to the Idol of Suppression. I guess the Dark Elves absconded with it." Antima said.

Balair came bounding back into the room, and not far behind him, Calfuray saw Arthur and friends approaching. They each looked nervous, and the aura was clearly bothering them, but they came anyway.

"Oh my. You found a Firebrand. I thought them all gone. No wonder you agreed to the deal. Hmm," Antima said, eyes narrowing at Calfuray. "I recognize your name. You were bound to the last Firebrand child before they died."

"I was, and that is him." Calfuray agreed before pointing at Arthur.

"I sense a deeper story here, but let's get through your trial first before the little one there goes crazy with his bouncing again."

Antima waited a few moments until the whole group assembled.

"Welcome, guests. A little unorthodox, I know. I need you to swear an oath not to reveal the true nature of what you will see during this trial. If you do, I'll permit you to stay and support Calfuray and Balair."

They all agreed, and she led them on the quick ritual oath. With that in place, she waved a claw, and the group calmed down.

"That's much better," Allendria breathed.

"A Dark Elf, too, huh? You sure have some interesting companions, Calfuray." Antima quipped.

"We can discuss that later. Now that the aura isn't in effect for your party, I'll fill you in on the trials. It's pretty straightforward. Balair may struggle a little more. Typically, I cast a spell and transform you into a human. From there, you have to pass three tests. Each test rewards you with a Ritual Orb. Take all three to the pedestal over there, and you can complete the ritual to gain the transformation. Since these are tests in the human form, you will have a slight advantage since you should be acclimated to yours by now." Antima said with a pointed look at Calfuray.

Calfuray nodded in agreement and waited for her to continue.

"The first test is one of agility. You need to complete that obstacle course over there. It's about balance and being able to traverse tricky situations. The second is one of climbing. You will climb to the top of that rock wall over there," she gestured to the face of the wall on the southeastern part of the cave. "And finally, there will be a combat test, but it will be with wooden human weapons. It doesn't require any advanced skills to pass that test. Just proof that you can defend yourself. Any questions?"

Do I get time to get used to the human form? Balair asked.

"Of course. You'll need it. There is a special exception to your form. Since you're still a drake, you don't get transformed into an adult human, but are transformed into a human teenager. Nothing else changes, and you maintain some of your strength benefits the same as Cal. You just look younger."

Another small downgrade. I don't think I can handle puberty.

"Cal, you can begin the obstacle course. Accept this quest, and it will give you directions. Balair. I'll cast the initial transformation on you over there," she said as she pointed toward the corner of the room.

A notification popped up for Calfuray.

Dragon Transformation Trial (Part I)	
Requirements: Level 10 Rewards: 24,000 experience and unlock your permanent Human Form Transformation ability.	Description: Complete all three trials and use the Ritual Stones at the altar to complete the ability.

Calfuray accepted the quest and moved toward the obstacle course.
I'll have this done in no time.

★ ★ ★

Arthur watched Calfuray walk away yet again. This time he felt better about the situation, since she was walking toward an obstacle course and not toward a fight meant for a dragon to complete. He glanced over at the old dragon with an amused grin. She was fussing over Balair and trying to get him to stand still so she could complete her spell.

Arthur watched as the magic built around her, but he couldn't decipher any of it. It didn't have the feel of normal elemental energy. He felt hints of Light and Dark Magic in it, but both were in limited quantities.

Apparently, there are still other magic types I don't know.

The power rose and swirled around Balair until disappearing in a flash of gray smoke. In his place stood a young teenager with deep orange hair and a splash of freckles across his face. Blue eyes glimmered as he turned toward the group and ran for the obstacle course.

"That's definitely unique," Arthur observed.

"Young ones can be hard to wrangle. He has a lot of spirit to him." She said before a flash of magic enveloped her, and she walked from the cloud of smoke as a human.

Her form resembled what Arthur considered a sixty-year-old woman to be. At least a sixty-year-old that took good care of herself. There were small wrinkles around her mouth and eyes, but her green eyes held a deep fire to them, and she walked with firm steps. Her auburn hair was streaked with fine lines of gray.

"He'll be fine. His spirit should allow him to acclimate quickly." Antima said.

Balair ran toward the obstacle course in front of them before promptly stumbling and face-planting into the ground. He hopped back up in a moment. "I'm okay!"

He continued for two more steps before he froze. "Wait, I can talk. That's awesome."

"Hey, Arthur. I can speak like you guys now. Antima. Do I keep this ability in my drake form?" Balair asked.

"No, you don't, little one. You can't speak as a drake because your vocal organs have not developed. The magic is translating your mental speech into words. It's also why you can't use mental communication while in your human form." Antima explained.

"Neat," Balair said before continuing toward the course.

Arthur focused on the action and saw Calfuray climbing along a small rock face. Her expression was pure concentration as she examined all the hand and foot holds around her to plot her path. Their strength in human form allowed them a little more freedom than a normal human, so her path wasn't challenging yet.

"Do you realize just how important she is?" Antima asked Arthur.

"What do you mean? Cal? She is a great friend, and I treasure her."

Antima shook her head. "No, young man. Do you understand how important she is to dragon kind?"

"I can't say that I do. She rarely speaks about her dragon heritage or the ongoing political situation with the dragons."

"I guess that's understandable. Let me fill you in. She is the daughter of Harithra, leader of the Aspect of Enlightenment. The second strongest of the dragon clans. It will be her duty to lead the flight one day."

"Really? So, she is like a princess on her own?" Arthur asked.

"In human terms, yes. There is a lot of strife amongst the dragon clans right now. I've heard rumors of activity within the Aspect of Rage clan. It appears they are involving themselves in matters of other races as well. Might be something to look out for in your travels," Antima said.

"I appreciate the insight. Is there anything I can do to repay the favor?" Arthur asked.

"It gets rather dull up here. Any chance you have something interesting we can play to pass the time?"

Arthur thought about the request and dug through his bag. He shuffled through the contents of the storage, but found nothing.

"Afraid not. Haven't had a lot of time for games recently. Always some conflict or another to work through."

"A dimensional bag? Have you resurrected that branch of magic again?" Antima asked.

"I did. I learned it from a spell book left to me by my father. Cal had it in her safekeeping."

"Intriguing. That takes the fun out of it.
Was hoping we could relax with a nice game,"
Antima complained.

Arthur considered the issue and looked
around. He found a handful of stones on one
side, and an idea struck him.

"Give me a minute. I'll make us a game."

"Make?" she asked, but Arthur waved her
off.

He ran over to the stones and wove his
magic. Earth and Fire poured out of him as he
took multiple small stones and shaped them as
he wanted them. He continued the process until
he held twenty-four stones in a perfect disc
shape. They were polished flat on each side.
Half of them he made of a lighter hue of
stone. Adding in a little extra Fire Magic
allowed him to scorch the second set a little
darker.

That out of the way, he walked back to
Antima and gestured for them to move toward a
set of chairs on the side of the cave. The
older dragon looked intrigued as she watched
him walk past, and it wasn't long before he
heard her footsteps following him.

He dropped the pieces onto one chair and
focused on a space nearby. Pulling on his
magic again, he pulled stone from the ground,
and a column rose. He continued funneling
stone through until a flat, square plate
formed on top. He took the time to form the
grooves for the lines on the top and color the
alternating pieces.

When finished, he admired his work.

*Congratulations, you have created a new
Combination Spell. Do you wish to name this
new spell? Yes/No.*

Congratulations, you have created a new Combination Spell. Do you wish to name this new spell? Yes/No.

Arthur selected *Yes* for both and named the first Create Checker Pieces. The second was named Create Pedestal Checker Board.

For creating the new Combination Spell: Create Checker Pieces, you have been granted a one-time bonus of 250 Earth and Fire Magic Experience, 250 Personal Experience, and 1 Intellect. Have a little fun.
For creating the new Combination Spell: Create Pedestal Checker Board, you have been granted a one-time bonus of 250 Earth and Fire Magic Experience, 250 Personal Experience, and 1 Intellect. A little crossover action?
You have gained 885 total experience in Earth Magic.
You have gained 885 total experience in Fire Magic.

"That's some impressive work with your magic," Antima complimented.
"Thank you."
Arthur took the pieces and laid them amongst the squares on top. He arranged the pieces and then pulled two of the chairs to the playing board. With a wave, he gestured for Antima to take a seat.
The dragon took her seat and looked at the board with a hint of interest in her gaze. Arthur could see the spark of imagination fuel her as she looked over a new game.

He went into the full explanation of the rules of checkers with the old dragon. It was a simple enough game and not uncommon for kids to play. The ancient being had no problem picking it up and quickly caught on.

"It's been a long time since I played checkers," Wesley mused nearby.

Arthur broke out of his reverie to see Wesley and Allendria standing nearby, watching the game.

"I think I understand the rules of it." Allendria agreed. "Looks fun."

"I'd be happy to make more pieces and another board if you two are interested. We can switch off with challenge partners."

The two agreed and found a small pile of stones. Arthur activated his magic and repeated his earlier process. Before long, another board stood a few feet from theirs, and Allendria and Wesley were seated in them, playing their first match.

"This game is fun and, best of all, easy to teach to others," Antima said.

"How about you tell me your story, Arthur?" Antima requested.

So they continued playing, and Arthur laid out his story. He told it in the order he lived it, not mentioning how he ended up on Earth until he learned that fact after arriving here.

They stopped from time to time to watch Calfuray and Balair on their journey. Cal finished the first trial in almost no time. Having used a human body for a while now, she was used to it and navigated well. Balair failed a few more times and suffered some nasty falls, but he was resilient and brushed it off.

The second trial was proving far more difficult for Balair. Climbing the large wall wasn't clicking with him, and he kept misjudging distances. Cal took her time and made it to the top with only a few stops where she had to backtrack to find a clear path up.

"Looks like that's my cue," Antima said as she rose to her feet. "I'll be back shortly."

The ancient dragon walked toward the trials and entered a small stone circle that reminded Arthur of a scaled-down fighting pit. The walls were short, so he could see her grab a wooden weapon and motion for Calfuray to do the same.

Arthur stood to watch the fight unfold. Pride swelled inside him as he watched Calfuray fight back and defend herself well against the wiry old woman. The ancient dragon was no slouch, but Arthur didn't doubt for a moment that she was holding back.

After a few long exchanges between the two, Antima abruptly halted the duel and declared her trial complete. Calfuray looked confused but accepted the win and her Ritual Stone.

Calfuray walked over to the ritual altar and placed her three stones. She pressed her palm to the center of the stone and closed her eyes. Arthur watched power radiate from the ground and spiral around Calfuray.

A torrent of red and green energy swirled around her and slowly increased in speed. After a few seconds, it shrunk inward and smashed into Cal. She barely acknowledged it, but when she opened her eyes, a bright smile lit her face.

Calfuray hurried back over to the party and made it to them at the same time Antima did.

"It worked! I now can shift when needed." She said in excitement.

"That was fine work in the last trial. I assume one of you taught her how to use the sword?" Antima said as she scanned the rest of the group.

"Yeah. We didn't want her undefended while she was trapped in her human form." Allendria agreed.

"Thank you for watching over her. I hope you continue to do so in your travels," Antima said.

"Of course, Cal is family." Allendria agreed.

Cal looked shocked at the statement, but she slowly walked over and hugged Allendria.

"Thank you." She said to Allendria before backing away.

A loud thud sounded from the trial area, and they all turned to see Balair on his back at the base of the second terrace, wheezing for air.

"That might take a while." Arthur mused. "Is there a time limit on this?"

"Not really. Just depends on whether or not he gives up." Antima said.

"Well, shit. Guess we are stuck here for a while. That guy doesn't know how to give up unless it involves a nap. Care to go back to our game?" Arthur asked.

Everyone agreed, and they shuffled partners around. Antima played with Allendria, and Wesley sat down with Calfuray to teach her the game. It took another two hours, countless matches of checkers, and multiple partner changes before Balair finally cleared the obstacle course and had to face off against Antima.

The battle with Antima and their wooden swords didn't go nearly as smoothly as it had with Calfuray. Arthur was mildly surprised that Balair had a bit of skill. He spotted certain moves and stances that he had taught to Cal and realized Balair must've been paying attention to some of their training. Antima took pleasure in whacking Balair a few times with the sword, but after half an hour of randomly striking him, he improved noticeably, and she declared an end to the trial.

"Not as bad as I expected." She told him. "I guess you picked up a few things from your companions."

"I tried to watch them when I could, but swinging this thing around is more difficult than it looks," Balair grumbled as he looked at the wooden weapon.

He took his stones and completed the same ritual at the altar. The magic snapped into place, and Balair immediately activated his ability to change back to a drake.

Much better. He acknowledged.

Cal took that same chance to put some distance between them and activated her transformation. Her form shimmered and slowly expanded in a flash of golden light. It took only a couple of seconds for her body to elongate into shape, and then the last glimmer of light revealed her in her full dragon form. She arched her back and stretched out her wings.

"That feels so much better. I felt like I'd never get to fly again."

"As much as I hate to say goodbye, we really must get going. The city needs us to return as quickly as possible." Arthur told Antima.

"I understand, young one. Do me a favor and come visit once in a while. You and your friends are welcome here anytime. I'll have to teach some of my other friends this intriguing game as well. Can I keep the pieces?" She asked.

"Of course. They are easy for me to make. Consider it a gift of hospitality."

"Until we see each other again, Arthur. Take care of yourself."

The party said their goodbyes to the ancient dragon and then walked to the entrance. A surprise notification caused the entire group to stop in their tracks.

Congratulations, you have successfully completed the quest: Summoning a Minor Deity.

Summoning a Minor Deity	
Requirements: Level 25 Rewards: 568,000 experience and unknown rewards also possible.	Description: You've cornered a desperate group of lizardmen and forced them to summon something to defend them. The presence of dragon's blood and the blood of a royal has amplified this process a thousand-fold and instead of a shadow protector, expect a Minor Deity. Defeat the Minor Deity.

"What the fuck?" Was all Arthur could say before the experience and notifications rolled in.

You have gained 568,000 experience.

Congratulations, you have reached levels 25, 26, 27, 28, 29, and 30! You now have 35 available skill points. Leave it up to you to suffocate and bleed a goddess to death under a mountain.

You have gained 5 Dragon Talent Points for completing the Legendary Quest: Summoning a Minor Deity.

You have gained 2 Dragon Talent Points for unlocking Calfuray's Transformation Ritual.

Chapter 29

Evolved Tactics

"Is something wrong?" Antima asked as she approached the now frozen group.

"Maybe," Arthur said with some hesitation. "We just completed a substantial quest that we all thought was over and failed."

"A quest, huh? Sounds like fun. How substantial?" Antima asked.

Arthur turned to look right into her eyes before he answered.

"A legendary quest."

Antima's face turned white as she stared at him with a slack jaw.

"Now you know how we feel," Allendria quipped.

Uh… guys. I think it's time. Balair sent them.

A look of confusion plastered Antima's face as she turned her gaze to something behind them. It quickly morphed into a look of wonder, and an ominous orange glow filled the area. He spun around to lay eyes on the drake.

Light spilled from the grooves in his scales, and his entire form shimmered with orange and yellow light. The brilliant energy pulsated in a steady rhythm. Arthur imagined it matched Balair's heartbeat.

"What in the world?" Arthur asked.

A hand touched his should as Antima walked up beside him.

"You're about to witness a wonder," Antima told him.

Arthur wanted to respond, but he couldn't take his sight off of the drake. The pulsing light sped up as the drake's scales glowed. Stone rose from the ground and slowly encapsulated Balair until it formed a solid shell over him.

This shell then shimmered with a red light as the stone shifted form and slowly melted. The smooth dome gained rigidity, and details spread from the top to the bottom as though being sculpted with his arcane forging technique.

When the process finished, an exquisitely detailed dragon egg stood in the clearing. It was a large oval and appeared to be covered in countless small scales along the surface. The ground around it churned and spun until molten hot stone filled the space and cradled the egg in its grip.

Allendria walked over to him and grabbed his hand as they watched the scene unfold.

"Is he evolving?" She asked.

The question sparked the memory of their conversation from earlier. Balair was a higher level than he was. When he gained that enormous chunk of experience, his level would remain higher than Arthur's, and Arthur was now level thirty. Balair was finally going to change into a true dragon.

"I think so," Arthur told her.

A light flashed inside the egg every few seconds. Each time it did, Arthur could see the silhouette of the drake as he remained curled into a ball. The flashes resembled that of a strobe light and slowly gained momentum. As they did, Balair's form grew. It was slow at first, but the faster the light flashed, the quicker the growth happened.

The group watched for a solid ten minutes before the flashing ceased. In moments, a large *crack* filled the space, and a claw reach free and latched onto the shell. The solid black nail broke through the surrounding casing and left broken streaks across the face of the egg.

Without warning, the egg exploded in all directions. Arthur turned his head and lifted his arm to protect against any sharp shell flying outside. To his surprise, nothing touched him. He looked back to see particles of dust floating in the air. *The shell must've disintegrated with the ability.*

In the center of the transformation zone stood Balair in all of his glory. The little drake had doubled in size, but now looked like a miniature version of Cal. He still retained his signature reddish-orange coloring, but the form itself closely resembled the Calfuray. His massive wings stretched out to each side.

"Looking good," Arthur told him.

"Feels good." He told them. He blinked and looked down before looking back up and smiling. "I'm a dragon! A real one this time."

"You were always a real dragon to me. Now the outside reflects the inside." Allendria told him.

"I'm going to have to come up with a song for that. That was incredible." Wesley said.

"Welcome to the family, Balair," Antima told him with a quick bow.

"It's an honor, Lady Antima." He said, bowing back.

"Looking a little scrawny there, Mighty Balair," Calfuray said as she walked over and poked at him with one of her claws.

"I'll catch up in no time. You don't worry about me."

"I have to thank you again, Arthur," Antima told him. "I've been around for a long time and have only been blessed to witness that three times in my life. It's truly a wonder to meet someone special enough to raise a dragonling to a dragon with them on their journey. On behalf of my kind, I thank you."

A cloud of smoke engulfed Balair, and a striking man with bright orange hair and a powerful jaw emerged from the flame. Long gone were the freckles that marked his face. His body was no longer spindly and was now filled out with muscle. Arthur was almost a little jealous of his figure, if he was being honest with himself.

"I think I can get used to this," Balair told them.

"Oh, Goddess, there will be no tolerating him now." Allendria moaned.

The group chuckled at her statement, Balair included.

"I guess our transportation issue is definitely sorted out now," Wesley said.

"That appears true. He can definitely carry you as a full-size dragon. Well, partially full size, anyway." Arthur agreed.

Balair grumbled a little at the statement but didn't respond.

A notification flashed into Arthur's sight.

Congratulations, you have completed a hidden legendary quest line: Raise a Dragon.

You have received 85,000 experience.

You have received 1 point to each of your stats.

Notice: Since you also have a Soul Bond with a different dragon, you receive 5 Soul Bond Talent Points.

Damn, another significant boost. And now I'm almost level thirty-one.

It'd been so long since Arthur had even considered his Soul Bond Talent Tree that he pulled it up to check it.

You have 12 unused Talent Points.

Soul Bond	
Tier 1	
Shared Mana Regeneration (1/1)	*Combines the mana regeneration of both parties to create a higher mana regeneration rate for both. Both mana regeneration rates are added together and then multiplied by 0.8 to reach your final mana regeneration rate.*
Dragon Healing (1/5)	*Grants you the ability to heal HP like a dragon does. Each point after the first increases the healing speed by 10%.*

Hard as Iron (0/5)	*Each point increases your base defense rating of all pieces of armor by 15.*
Feed the Flames (0/5)	*Increases the effectiveness of your special dragon bond abilities by 10% per point and reduces their cooldown by 3 hours.*

"Hey, Cal."

The dragon turned to look at him as he spoke to her.

"Do you know how many talent points it takes to unlock the second tier of our Soul Bond Talent Tree?"

She nodded at his question and answered, "five."

So, the question becomes, do I just spend three more in Dragon Healing and see what pops up next or YOLO it and cap that out and check?

Arthur mulled over the question for a bit before he played it safe. He remembered how hard these points were to obtain and wouldn't be surprised if he never got any more again. He added three points to Dragon Healing and checked on the Tier 2 options.

Tier 2	
Partial Transformation (0/1)	*Allows you to partially shift into a draconic form. This new form hardens your skin on your arms, legs, and torso to resemble scales and decreases the damage you take. It also increases your Strength by 10%. This effect lasts for 3 minutes.* *Cooldown: 8 hours*
Protect Your Partner (0/5)	*Each point in this ability grants you and your Soul Bond companion the following:* • *2 Strength* • *1 Intellect* • *3 Endurance*
Form of Ferocity (0/5)	*Each point unlocks a new tier of the ability Form of Ferocity.* *The first tier boosts the speed and combat damage of both partners by 15% for 5 minutes.*

	Subsequent tiers improve these criteria and can even unlock additional effects. *Tier 1 Cooldown: 5 hours.*

A solid selection of abilities.

Arthur looked into Cal's eyes before activating their mental communications.

So, what do you think we should use these points on?

Hard to say. I think you should get Partial Transformation. If nothing else, it could increase your survivability.

I agree in principle, but I worry about adding another powerful ability to my arsenal when I already rarely use the ones I have.

You seem to be bad about that.

I'm only human. It's difficult to remember the laundry list of stuff I can do in the middle of a battle. Arthur grumbled in his mind.

What were you thinking then? Cal asked.

I always like raw stats. They are useful at all times and have no cooldown. I want to use five for Protect Your Partner. I'm sure those stats would be great for you as well.

I can't argue against that, and I agree with that plan.

That leaves four points. Arthur said.

I'd cap off Dragon Healing, get Partial Transformation, and put the last two in Feed the Flames. Cal suggested.

Why? Arthur asked. *Not that I'm complaining,* he quickly amended.

Feed the Flames will increase all current abilities and future ones. Partial Transformation can come in handy in a pinch, and Dragon Healing is easy to determine. I would tell you to save the points, but you have to spend 15 points to unlock Tier 3, so might as well use them now.

Can't really argue with any of that. I'll take care of it now.

From there, Arthur looked over his overall stats. With the large influx of experience and levels, he now had 35 stat points he could assign.

Normally, Arthur favored trying to min and max his build when playing video games, but this world was real life for him now. He couldn't afford to have a crippling weakness because he super-specialized. That in mind, he looked at his lower stats.

Agility, Wisdom, Charisma, and Luck were his only stats below 30 points. His first 10 points went to Agility, bringing it to 36. He put 8 into Wisdom, lifting it to 30. Spreading the love some more, he added 8 points to both Charisma and Luck, bringing them to 21 and 20, respectively. The last point he used for Strength, taking it to 32.

The other thing he forgot was his skill percent boost. The level ups left him with 200% allocation. He took the straightforward route and used all of it for Dimensional Magic.

You have gained 109,000 experience in Dimensional Magic.

Congratulations, you have reached levels 21 and 22 in Dimensional Magic. Decreases the mana draw of dimensional spells by 54%. Might as well be a cheat code.

After assigning the points, he looked at his basic stats to see how well he stacked up.

Name: Arthur Firebrand
Level: 30
Age: 26
Race: Human
Class: Spell Blade
HP: 870/870
MP: 1530/1530
Stamina: 830/830

Strength: 32
Agility: 36
Intellect: 50
Wisdom: 30
Endurance: 43
Charisma: 21
Luck: 20

That's beyond impressive. Arthur mused to himself.

"You done with whatever you're doing over there?" Allendria asked.

"Yep. Everyone ready to go?" Arthur asked.

Everyone nodded in agreement, and Balair shifted back into his dragon form. It took only a few moments for each to mount on their respective dragons and launch from the ground. Arthur flashed one last wave at Antima as they rocketed into the sky.

They ascended quickly, and Calfuray banked
to turn them toward Alurian. Their trip away
had left Arthur nervous, and he was eager to
get back. No feelings of dread were
encroaching on his mood, but he had a sense of
unease about the city. He just hoped his fears
hadn't come to pass. He couldn't shake the
feeling that the Dark Elves would capitalize
on their rout during the battle and assault
Alurian.

* * *

Rayne jogged at a steady pace down the
narrow dirt road, headed for Alurian. He'd
been on the road for a while and was looking
forward to finally being back. He was
accustomed to being on the move and hadn't had
a place in a while that he considered home
until now.

That thought left him wondering why he kept
agreeing to leave it, but his mind quickly
squashed that fear as irrational. He left
Alurian to make sure things stayed stable, and
the city itself was safe for him to return to.
Keeping the kingdom stable would lead to a
better quality of life for all.

His thoughts on the matter were interrupted
when he heard muffled noises coming from the
direction of the city.

"Really? Can I not leave without everything
falling apart?" He groaned.

Not wanting to call attention to himself,
Rayne darted for the closest line of trees and
wove through them until he reached the top of
the rise. There, far in the distance, he could
make out an army assaulting the walls. To his
astonishment, they didn't appear to be doing
very well.

   Spells launched from the army, but instead
of splashing into the defenders, they slammed
into a barrier. Rayne didn't know what
happened here, but he was already grateful for
whatever that defense was.

   *Wait a minute… What happened to my friends
if the Dark Elf army is at Alurian? Did they
die in the attack? Retreat to the city?*

   His thoughts warred with him as despair
slowly crept into his being. It took him a few
moments to marshal his feelings and clear his
head.

   *I can't think like that. There's no way
they died in the fight. They must've retreated
before the battle or were attacked before they
could march out.* Rayne reasoned with himself.

   He needed to get back into the city. Before
that, Rayne wanted to poke around the Dark Elf
army and see if he could discover anything.
While monumentally foolish, it was the kind of
challenge he lived for.

   Backtracking down the hill, he continued
until he was out of the attacking army's line
of sight. From there, he crossed the meadow
and circled around until he approached through
the trees behind the Dark Elf army.

   Snippets of conversation drifted to his
ears, but he was unfamiliar with their
language and couldn't make heads or tails of
it. He knew he was at a severe disadvantage
trying to spy on them and discover anything
useful considering he couldn't read or even
understand their language.

   *If nothing else, I should be able to steal
some documents that one of our Dark Elf allies
in the city can translate that might be
helpful.*

Rayne was quite disappointed with the lack of sentries at the rear of the army. He'd only spotted two Dark Elves, nestled high in trees and half asleep. No ground level guards of any kind and the underbrush was thick enough to hide his presence.

His skills revolved around city life and would never hold up to a skilled elf that was fully alert, but against these low-class examples, it would suffice.

A slow and painstaking travel through the brush finally brought him within sight of the nearest tent. They were camped with their tents only a dozen yards from the forest's edge. A horrible decision from a tactical perspective, but Rayne assumed their nature as elves made it more comforting to them.

Rayne skirted the edge of the encampment, looking for anything that looked like a command pavilion. It took him nearly an hour of slow and methodical skulking, but he finally spotted a large tent that could easily house a dozen people with extreme comfort. In a pinch, it could probably sleep near to forty in it at once.

He pressed up to the back of the tent and listened for any sound inside. After a few minutes, he was satisfied that no one was within. Withdrawing his knife, he cut one of the corner seams toward the bottom of the tent. Too large and they would easily see it. He sliced the minimum distance until he could squeeze through and emerge inside the spacious pavilion.

Once inside, Rayne took a quick look around to verify the tent was unoccupied. Relief sank in as he saw an empty space. He noticed a large table in the center of the tent with papers scattered across its surface. Rayne quickly scanned through the documents, but struggled to make out anything useful. The foreign script eluded him and made it nearly impossible to see what was important and what wasn't.

This is hopeless. I have no chance of finding anything useful here.

The doubts attacked his sense of duty, but he persevered.

It took some digging, but he finally uncovered a few promising maps at the bottom of the pile of documents. While he couldn't read the writing on it, he noticed the overall landmarks. One of them represented the outline of Alurian. The detail on the walls was impressive, but the inside of them was less so. The only landmarks they had on the map were ones you could see in the distance from the wall. As such, the scale was off to Rayne's eye. Some distances were wildly wrong. A couple of other maps on the pile alarmed him.

Why would they carry maps of Calzas with them while out in the field? That's utter foolishness.

These other maps showed the layout of the Dark Elf city and its defenses. There were arrows drawn over it and small scribbles everywhere. Rayne hoped it was something important. He could only be so lucky to find a map detailing the guard patrols and travel routes. One map even showed the forest in the surrounding area of their capital and had a plan for some kind of ambush attack.

As he searched, he heard footsteps approaching the tent. Quickly, he cast aside his doubts and scraped everything into his storage bag. One way or another, he'd find out if anything important or useful was here. He then made his way back to the hole he had cut in the tent and squeezed through, disappearing into the brush outside.

The muted noise of the battlefield returned as he wove his way back through the forest. Explosions still shook the air as he backtracked to the small rise on the horizon. He headed back over the hill and crossed the open field again to his original location. Hugging the trees, he skirted the open space and circled around to the side of the encampment and to the north side of Alurian. He hoped to approach the city from the opposite side of the army to gain access.

While there were no Dark Elves in force, he spotted a few patrols ranging around the perimeter. Rayne was willing to bet they were there looking for people trying to flee from the city or to alert the army if a group of soldiers left to try and flank the main army.

His progress was swift, since all attention was toward Alurian and not back in his direction. When he reached the northern gate of the city, he stopped and watched the patrols. Timing was critical and he could use his stealth ability to cross much of the space. Unfortunately, the limited time he had available was probably not enough to sprint the distance to the wall.

With time ticking away and the spells still exploding near the eastern wall, he decided he'd have to chance it and make a break for it. He took a step forward and glanced each way to see if he was clear and then froze.

What is that?

Squinting at the sky to the west, he noticed a blur that was slowly growing. He backed up and took cover behind a nearby tree so the patrols had no chance of seeing him, but he could monitor this spot in the sky.

It took another two minutes before the speck grew big enough to make out. When it did, Rayne felt a cheer rise in his chest, but he suppressed it to prevent the unnecessary noise.

That's Calfuray! I'm sure of it. If she's alive, Arthur is as well, or the bond would've killed her.

He continued to watch until it was obvious there was another form on her back. The distance made it impossible to make out any details except an indistinct blur. Surprise hit him as he saw another dragon emerge from Calfuray's shadow and they both flew in small circles, surveying the situation.

Did they recruit another dragon? Is that why they left?

The orange and red dragon was smaller than Calfuray, so Rayne assumed it was a younger one. A figure also rested on its back, though.

Is Allendria riding the other?

Rayne watched as both dragons lazily circled and slowly got closer to the ground. He assumed they planned to land and take stock of the scenario before entering the city. Abandoning caution, Rayne sprinted for their general direction. He planned on meeting them on the ground to find out what happened and then to proceed into the city with them. Relief settled over him and some of the hope he didn't realize he'd lost returned.

There might be a chance, after all.

Chapter 30

Breaking a Siege

"And that's the quick summary of what happened," Arthur told Rayne.

"Vana… is gone?" He asked in disbelief.

"I'm sorry to say it's true," Allendria assured him with a pat on his shoulder.

"She lost her life protecting a friend and member of her team. I miss her, as do many others, but I also refuse to tarnish her memory with sorrow. It's not what she would've wanted." Arthur said solemnly.

"I… uh… I think you're right. I'm sorry… I think it will just take some time for me to process that." Rayne said.

"Understandable," Balair told him, "We all miss her."

"Balair, you can talk now?" Rayne asked.

"Of course. Full-fledged dragon now. Not only that, watch this," Balair told him before a flash of gray smoke enveloped him and Balair emerged in his human form with a cocky grin plastering his face.

"For the love of all that's holy, he can turn into a human now as well," Rayne grumbled. "He was bad enough before. Now he's gonna be a nightmare."

Everyone but Balair chuckled at that while Balair just grumbled about being disrespected. Rayne walked over to the bard and extended a hand.

"Wesley, I believe? Arthur told me about you when he ran into you near Seora. It's a pleasure to finally meet you. I'm Rayne."

"Well met, Rayne. I've heard Arthur brag about your skills a few times and outwardly wishing you were around for a couple of our latest trials. Good to put a face to the name."

The two shook hands and smiled at one another.

"I told you our story. Do you have any news about that?" Arthur asked, pointing at the Dark Elf army.

"Yes, and no," Rayne answered cryptically. Arthur opened his mouth, but Rayne held up his hand to tell him to wait.

"I just arrived here from Seora earlier today to find this siege in progress, so I don't have any details from inside the city. The army itself is another matter. I took it upon myself to, uh, borrow some of their documents," Rayne said as he pulled out the stack of papers he'd dumped into his bag and handed them to Allendria. "I don't know if they are of any use since I can't read them, but the maps should at least prove beneficial."

"Good thinking." Arthur praised. "Not sure how smart it was to go into the camp alone, but I guess I'll have to trust your judgment. You are the spy master, after all."

"I have to admit, it might not have been carefully thought out or planned. I'm a little ashamed to admit that I feared something had happened to you," Rayne said.

"I'm sorry you felt that way. Sadly, in this world, things like that are bound to happen. Let's hope it isn't for a long time." Arthur said.

"This is great work," Allendria told him as she browsed the papers. "There are orders from Gliran in here, forcing their attack. It's obvious that a majority of people are not fond of the approach he is taking to the situation. The map itself also shows their complete lack of strategy. They couldn't even bother to fully map out Alurian as is proper. I guess it doesn't hurt that we haven't let them past the wall. Their battle plan for the ambush was rather elegant, and it's honestly a miracle that we didn't lose far more than we did."

"I guess our best bet is to get into the city and figure everything out from there. Balair, you think you can carry Wesley and Rayne?" Arthur asked.

"Sure. It's not far, so it shouldn't be a problem." Balair said.

"Perfect. Break time is up, everyone. Balair, take them straight to the city and land near the inn. We will meet you there. We are going to strafe them with fire to stop their attack and give us some breathing room to talk with the council and sort out the situation." Arthur said.

Everyone nodded in agreement as Balair shifted back to a dragon. They all mounted their appropriate dragons and launched into the air. Arthur held on tight to one of Cal's ridges as they darted for the attacking force. It wasn't long before they were within range and Calfuray dove for the army. A notification popped up.

Resistance	
Requirements: Participate in actions to directly or indirectly influence the outcome of the raid. Rewards: 40,000 Experience, 4,000 Unassigned Skill Experience, 2 Talent Points	Description: A new raid has started near Alurian. Aid either side in the fight. If the side you assist survives the raid, you receive the rewards.

The last spell had just left their mages and hurtled toward the wall when Calfuray dove low and sprayed fire over a large swath of the army. Arthur added a little fury to it and dropped one of his Fireblast orbs on top of them, rocking the space with a blast of fire and air magic.

He saw magical shields spring to life throughout their army and protect many of the elves, but a lot of the fire still spread to the outer ranks. Men and women screamed as their flesh melted and the concussive blast of his spell knocked many others down.

That should be enough. Let's not overdo it. Arthur told Calfuray.

She shook her head, and they turned toward Alurian. The walls came alive as they flew toward the gate. Their low trajectory carried them near the men to bolster their forces before they turned into a steep climb to avoid the barrier. Cheering echoed down the walls as they flew above the zenith of the barrier and flattened out to continue toward the city.

Life inside the barrier looked normal. There were carts headed toward the gate that Arthur assumed carried supplies and food for those on watch and guarding the walls. Construction crews labored at the partially complete buildings and people milled about the city on their normal errands. It was obvious to Arthur that they felt safe inside the barrier.

They landed in the open field near the inn and walked to the road. Cal shifted to her human form and followed along as they walked toward the inn. Allendria walked beside him, hand in hand. People smiled and waved as they passed, and Arthur couldn't help but do the same.

Even the spirits of the people here are high during this attack. He noted.

Wesley, Rayne, and Balair greeted them at the entrance to the inn. Balair had assumed his human form as well and strutted around. Arthur waved for them to follow and he entered the inn. Their footsteps told him they were on his heels.

He found the city council already gathered at their customary meeting table and headed for the group. Arthur noted that none of them looked overly concerned about their current situation and sat around, visiting with a casual air. When they spotted him, they all stood at his approach.

"Looks like trouble found us when I left. I hoped it wouldn't."

"Sure did. They've been out there for two days hammering at the shield, to no avail. Pretty sure they are burning their mana as fast as they regenerate it." Daniel said with a chuckle.

There was one person there that caused him to stop and stare.

"Samson, are you fit to help defend Alurian with us? I don't want you back sooner than you feel ready." Arthur told him in a low tone.

The paladin straightened his stance and took on a hard glint to his eye. "I'm ready for duty. I'll not let our city fall to these intruders."

"Glad to have you back, my friend," Allendria said as she walked over and patted him on the shoulder.

"I also found a straggler," Arthur said as he motioned toward Rayne.

"Rayne! It's good to have you back," Katherine said. "Your sister will be happy to see you."

Almost on cue, his sister emerged from the kitchen carrying drinks on a tray and walked to their table. She sat the drinks down and passed them out before looking at the assembled group, spotting her brother, and dashing to him.

He wrapped her in a tight hug and held on for a few moments before backing away.

"You're looking good. Guess the work is treating you well?" He asked.

"It's honest work and I like the people here." She said.

"Don't let me distract you, then. We also have work to attend to." Rayne told her.

She looked around and spotted Arthur and company all returned and flushed a deep red. Hurrying back to the tray, she handed out the rest of the drinks before hastily inquiring if anyone in Arthur's party needed anything. She disappeared into the kitchen to fetch their food.

"So, who wants to give me the status report?" Arthur asked as he walked to his chair and sat. Everyone else found a seat and looked on in anticipation. The council all looked at each other for a few moments before Kat spoke up.

"Our scouts spotted them four days ago. They were headed in our direction, so our scouts shadowed them on rotation. The runners came back to alert us to the issue and keep us appraised of their progress." Kat said.

Allendria raised an eyebrow at that. "The scouts shadowed their main force for that long without discovery? Impressive."

"They were trained by the best," Kat said with a slight note of sorrow in her voice. "Luckily, we instituted the recharging policy a few days prior to finding them, so our people have steadily been charging the defense orb. With the current charge level and the amount of mana we add each day, we can keep this defense up indefinitely."

"It's that efficient?" Allendria asked in surprise.

"Right now, it is. If they had more attackers to contribute to the magical assault, it would strain our resources more. With the protections and recharge protocols in place, we are producing more than we consume."

"What kind of threshold are we talking about on the increased damage? 25% more? 50% More?" Arthur asked.

"Daranth, you're better with the magical calculations. Care to answer?" Kat asked.

"Of course," he agreed. "We could sustain almost twice the damage we are taking now and still not lose more than we add in. Much more than that and the flow would even out."

"Better than I hoped for," Arthur said. "Great work on watching over the levels."

"Have there been any negotiations with the army?" Allendria asked.

"None. They just showed up, set a camp, and started blasting at the walls. The barrier thoroughly surprised them, based on most of their reactions. They were suspicious of it for a while and were cautious about their attacks. Now they just hammer away at it, hoping it will fall." Samson informed her.

"Morale seems to be doing well in the city," Arthur observed.

"People were very nervous and anxious when we first announced the approaching army. When we raised the shield and they saw the outside army had no effect, they have been thrilled. This city functions almost entirely on its own. The only thing we lack is a local source of ore that we can get while under siege. Everything else can be obtained within the walls. People have been eager to share their mana with the defensive enchantment. Most do it more than the minimum prescribed." Kat said.

"Makes me feel a little better about the situation," Rayne admitted. "I was concerned when I returned and found the city under siege. The barrier is a nice touch, though."

"That was something I made sure was in place before I left," Arthur agreed. "Now the question becomes, what do we do from here?"

"That's what we were discussing as you returned. They've not approached to talk, so there have been no demands made. We've tried to not waste mana attacking them. I know previously you wanted to keep deaths to a minimum, if possible. Honestly, our current approach was to monitor things and wait for you to return to decide." Daniel said.

"Sheesh, some council you guys are." Arthur said mockingly, before they all chuckled. "I've been thinking about this a lot since our last fight. As much as it pains me, it's time to take off the kid gloves."

The group all looked at him, confused. He caught Wesley's eye, and the dwarf nodded in understanding.

"We can't keep playing it safe and pulling back our power to prevent hurting them. They made this choice and I can't risk the safety of my people over theirs. I'm sorry Allendria and Daranth. I know a lot of them are friends and possibly family. I can't risk my people's lives by taking it easy on them. If they will surrender and pledge loyalty to Allendria, I will let them go peacefully, or even join us here."

The group nodded along as he spoke, and when he finished, they sat in silence for a few moments.

"I agree," Daranth said, with a slight pain in his voice. "They are misguided, but stubborn. I only ask that you give them the chance to surrender. If you promise me that, I won't object to what you need to do."

Arthur shook his head. "It wasn't a choice, if I'm being honest. I value your opinion on the matter, but this is final. No more holding back." Daranth looked as if he would respond, but Arthur held up his hand. "I still plan on giving them the chance to surrender and we won't attack helpless fighters. I'm merely stating this is the path forward regardless of the outcome. The battlefield is about to change drastically. We are upping the ante here."

"It's about time," Samson grumbled. "What are my orders?"

"Assemble our twenty finest and best armored warriors and ten of our best mages. Allendria and I will address their army directly and give them terms of our own. I'll give them a one-day grace period to decide and then I'm going to rain down hell on anyone left."

Shocked silence filled the room until Samson stood up and saluted. "I'll take care of it immediately."

The warrior hurried from the room and the rest of the council all stood. Arthur and his group joined the crowd, and they walked out of the inn and into the streets.

"I'm not sure this is the best choice, but we will stand with you," Daniel told Arthur.

"I know it isn't the best choice, but I'm tired of trading the lives of those I care about just to save people too stubborn to save themselves." Arthur agreed.

"Well, if you need anything, let me know," he said before squeezing on Arthur's pauldron. The group of council members all dispersed to handle their day-to-day business while Arthur and his party waited in the street outside of the inn.

"Are you committed to this path?" Cal
asked. "There is no turning back once that
decision is made."

Arthur reached over and grabbed her hand.
"I'm sure. Are you okay with standing by my
side if I choose this path?"

She grinned at him. "My only concern is for
you and me. This works for us. I also agree.
I'm a dragon, after all. We all believe in our
clans and our flights first. Screw anyone else
who gets in the way."

He nodded at her before turning to
Allendria. Her eyes were puffy and red, but
she stared back at him with a steely gaze. A
nod from her told him she agreed, although her
face showed she was struggling with the
necessity.

It only took half an hour for Samson to
gather his warriors and the group to form up
in the space near the inn. Gleaming armor that
marked them as city guards flashed in the
sunlight while all their mages wore a deep red
robe with purple trim. It was something new
that Arthur hadn't seen and wasn't sure what
to think about it.

"They are official city robes for the mage
corps," Samson informed him, guessing at his
stare. "We wanted to keep all city military
forces easily visible. The guards have their
red and purple tabards, and the mages have
their robes."

"Makes sense. Who decided the color
scheme?" Arthur asked.

"The council, of course. They wanted red
for the Kingdom of Fire and Purple to honor
Cal." Samson said.

Arthur saw a blush cross Cal's face, but she recovered quickly. He looked over at Allendria and saw her standing straight and walking toward him. All traces of doubt and sorrow were wiped from her face, and the stoic princess took her place next to him.

Samson signaled for the group to head out and they walked at a steady pace to the wall. This wasn't a meaningful march of any kind and was instead just a brisk walk in a loose formation.

When they made it to the gate, Samson called a halt and had everyone form up. He settled on four ranks of five soldiers and two ranks of five mages.

"Samson, can you get our standard bearer into formation?" Arthur asked.

"Of course," the paladin said as he waved over a nearby soldier carrying a large white flag on a tall pole.

"Send the signal!" Samson called to the wall.

A large ball of fire streaked into the sky behind the wall and toward the city. It shrunk as it continued until the power dissipated and nothing remained.

"The barrier will be down in a few moments and we can continue," Samson told Arthur.

It was almost a minute before Arthur felt the magical shield fade and looked at Samson. The soldier nodded and called for the guards to open the gate. The behemoth contraption swung open on silent hinges and the party strode through in a confident march.

Arthur, Allendria, Samson, Cal, and Balair all walked in front of the assembled force while the standard bearer kept step with them. They walked to a point roughly halfway between the attacking army and the wall before Arthur employed his magic and created a small stone platform. To show off, he also created a dozen stone chairs on the stage in a circle.

Their main party took the seats facing the Dark Elf army and waited.

"You think they'll come out?" Arthur asked.

"Of course. They're too proud not to." Allendria affirmed.

The group all sat and chatted for a while. Balair was tickled at his new human form and kept talking about all the things he wasn't aware humans could do with their odd bodies. Apparently, he'd discovered peeing as a human and naturally found it amusing.

Arthur wasn't sure, but it felt like a half hour passed when he finally saw a group of people approaching from the army. They had the good grace to match his party size as they marched toward their location. Arthur's forces stood in loose formation behind them and were fifty yards away.

The Dark Elf army mirrored them, and the primary force stopped some distance from the meeting area before their commanders continued forward. They had five Dark Elves that joined them on the stage, and Arthur and his group rose as they approached.

"Greetings. I'm King Arthur Firebrand and I wish to discuss terms with your army."

"You're the famous King Arthur we keep hearing about," one elf commented. "If you're looking to surrender, I'm sure we can come up with an acceptable agreement."

"I'm afraid you misunderstand me," Arthur told them. "I'm here to deliver terms for you to surrender to me."

They all froze in place before reaching their seats. True to their pride, they continued after a brief pause and each stood at a chair.

"Before we get to that, I think introductions are in order." Arthur said. "I've introduced myself and I'm sure all of you know Princess Allendria."

"I also have with me my companions Calfuray and Balair and well as the general of the Kingdom of Fire and captain of my guard, Samson." Arthur said as he pointed out each.

The cocky man from earlier spoke up. "All names we've heard and good to finally place a face to them. It was hard to match some of them as we chased you during your retreat."

Arthur gripped the hilt of his sword and had to calm himself before he killed the arrogant man.

"I'm Magistrate Dahna, right hand of the rightful king, Gliran. With me are three of my advisers and the soldier general Tirithan, who I'm sure you know."

"Now that introductions are out of the way, who do you think you are trying to demand our surrender? We have every advantage here and have chased you back to your city and held you captive. We can keep you here until you all starve if necessary." Dahna sneered.

"I assume you're not a military man," Samson commented. "Have you asked your actual military commanders how well your plan is working?"

Dahna glanced at Tirithan briefly before glaring back at Samson. "I have nothing to worry about. You've barely done any damage to our army so far, and I doubt you even can."

Samson looked ready to respond again, but Arthur rose to his feet and held up a hand to the warrior. He then paced back and forth as he addressed the adviser.

"There's no point in Samson trying to convince you of your folly. That is obvious by your attitude, so I'll make this simple. All of you have 24 hours. At the end of that time, we set your fate. I give you three options to choose from. Option one," Arthur punctuated by lifting a single finger. "Is you surrender and name Allendria as your rightful queen. When this minor battle has concluded, we will quickly prepare and march back on your capital. When we kill Gliran, all his loyal subjects go with him to the grave."

"Option two," Arthur said as he raised another finger. "You leave this battlefield and don't harass my city or my soldiers. I will leave you in peace. Make no mistake, we've been very careful about how we waged war against you so far. I've done what I can to minimize casualties to your people in respect to my betrothed and to my conscious. That ends today."

"Your last option is to stay here and continue this silly fight." Arthur's voice shifted into a dark and sinister tone as he continued. "Any left standing here in twenty-four hours and not ready to surrender will die. No more games. My leniency is at an end."

The Dark Elves looked on with pure shock on their faces. Tirithan looked visibly shaken and his purple skin even flushed a slightly whiter shade. Dahna looked ready to spit nails and his purple skin flashed with scarlet heat.

"Who do you think you are to insult us so?" One adviser spat as he jumped up from his seat. "I'll put you where you belong, you little upstart!"

The elf dashed forward and pulled a dagger from his belt as he lunged at Arthur. Sensing no magic in the item short of basic enchantments, Arthur only smiled and let the blade stab into the center of his chest piece. It rebounded from the metal without a scratch and Arthur's grin morphed to anger as he reached out and grabbed hold of the elf's wrist.

"Now my turn," Arthur growled.

Arthur dumped a copious amount of Fire Magic into the man and pushed it toward his core. He didn't try to direct it in any specific way and instead just overloaded the man. All the elf's veins started glowing red, and then his eyes followed suit. The man screamed before even that sound ceased and he crumpled to the ground.

The broken body of the elf was covered in burns and flesh peeled away like ash. Smoke curled out of his eyes and mouth.

"Anyone else want to break the truce of the battle? I'm more than happy to end your worthless lives now." Arthur said.

The rest all shook their heads as they cowered under his gaze. Even Dahna looked shaken at the display of raw power.

"You can see our city shield. That is but the start of power we have been holding back. You haven't seen us in a true offensive. Don't make me bring it out." Arthur said.

Allendria took that chance to step forward.

"Tirithan, please take the offer. Don't let our people die for no reason. Arthur is serious and so am I. No more chances. No more holding back. As much as it pains me, you either stand up to this oppression and join my side, or there is no place for you in our future society."

Tirithan was quiet for a few moments before he looked at her with tears in his eyes. "I can't, my Princess. Honor doesn't allow it."

Allendria looked crestfallen as the warrior turned and walked away from the group and back toward the army.

"You might consider this," Samson called after him. "Is it honorable to serve one who would see his own people dead for personal gain? How about wasting the lives of those he's sworn to protect?"

The warrior's steps faltered for a moment and he paused before taking a deep breath and continuing.

"You'll regret this," Dahna hissed as he waved for his other advisers to follow and they scurried from the platform after Tirithan.

"It was worth a shot." Balair sighed.

"We will see if it made a difference." Cal agreed.

Arthur pushed his magic out and dropped all the chairs back into the ground before smoothing the platform out and also making it a level stone patch on the dirt.

    They joined their escort and everyone
marched back to the city, nothing but a
smoking corpse left in the center of the
stone.

Chapter 31

Eradication

Arthur sat on the wooden couch of their house with Allendria in his arms. She snuggled up to him tightly, her head in the fold of his shoulder. He caressed her hair as she took slow and steady breaths.

"I hope he changes his mind," she murmured.

Arthur gripped her tighter. "I hope so as well. Blind honor and pride are useless. It needs a strong moral compass to guide it or it can do more harm than good."

Allendria slowly sat up before standing to her feet. "I think I'll go to bed early. You going to tuck in?"

"Soon. My mind is still spinning from everything, and I need some time to wind down."

She bent over and kissed him on the cheek before bidding him goodnight and walking to bed. Arthur remained in his spot on the couch, staring at a featureless portion of the wall ahead as he contemplated everything that happened recently. The events of the day swirled in his mind, and the idea of having to live up to his promise somewhat revolted him.

Can I really just wipe them out? Will I be able to live with myself?

A hand jolted him out of his contemplation as it landed on his shoulder, and someone took a seat next to him. Purple eyes met his as he gazed at his fellow occupant.

"It'll be okay," she assured him. "We are with you in this."

He smiled at her before reaching up and taking her hand in his. A gentle squeeze was all he offered before the two of them sat in silence again.

A few minutes passed before Cal spoke up. "Thank you again for the trial and for getting me back to my true self."

"I told you, we're family. I'll always do everything I can to protect you and those I care about."

"People like to say that, but not all can live up to it. I was hesitant about the type of man you'd become when I first made the promise to renew our bond. I'm happy you ended up the kind of man that deserves it." Cal said.

"I appreciate the confidence. Now it's just up to me to live up to it. We'll see if that burden is too much to bear."

Calfuray stood up and brushed off the front of her pants before turning to him. "I have faith you'll do fine. Just keep following your heart."

He nodded in agreement, and she bid him goodnight. Her footsteps down the hallway echoed in his ears for a few moments before fading back to silence.

Arthur placed his hands on the couch on each side of him and began to push himself to his feet when another voice interrupted him.

"Have a minute to talk?" Balair asked.

"Of course," Arthur agreed as he lowered himself back to the seat.

Balair walked over and took the chair opposite the couch before he sat and stared at Arthur.

"I'd like to continue traveling with you for now, if you'll have me." Balair said.

"Well, of course you can. Why would you not…," Arthur said, but his response was interrupted as he realized the truth of the matter.

Balair was a full-fledged dragon now. He was no longer bound to Arthur as a familiar. They also didn't share a soul bond like him and Calfuray, so Balair was technically free to do anything he wished.

"Oh," was all Arthur could manage after the revelation.

"I want to go out and explore the world now that I'm free to do so, but not just yet. I feel obligated to stick around with you. It's only because of you I'm like this, anyway."

"Well, I'm definitely not going to say you can't stay," Arthur said with a laugh.

"Balair, you're family and you always will be, no matter what happens. If you decide it's time for you to go off on your own adventure, you just let me know. I'll be happy to help you prepare anything you need and the only thing I ask is that you check back in from time to time to visit. Until then, I look forward to standing side by side with you in our mutual struggle."

Balair stood, and Arthur mirrored his movement. The young dragon walked over and extended his hand. Arthur smiled and shook it before Balair surprised him and wrapped an arm around him, bringing him into a one arm hug.

Balair backed up and gave him a crooked grin. "Thanks, Arthur. I guess I'll head to bed."

The young dragon turned and walked straight for his room down the hallway.

Did you need anything else for the evening? Zoe asked from the kitchen area.

No, thanks. Feel free to head home. Arthur said.

Arthur, she started. *Can I go to battle with you when you march on the Dark Elves? I think my place might be on the battlefield.*

I'm not going to tell you no, but are you sure? I've only taught you basic magic so far. Arthur sent.

I've been working hard. I made it to level ten in Earth Magic. Can you show me the One with the Ground spell? That should help me feel things nearby. I'm only level five in Air Magic.

Arthur agreed and explained channeling mana through him to learn magic. He cast the One with the Ground spell and in a few moments, she learned it.

Thanks. I need to practice with this in town. I can use it to get a picture of things around me when I can't hear them.

That's the idea. Find Rayne if you can. He can teach you spells the same way. He might have developed a spell that does the same thing with Air Magic by now. That would help you more.

I'll try and find him tomorrow. She agreed. *Goodnight.*

Arthur stood in place for a few more moments before shaking his head and trudged down the hallway. He entered his room and climbed into bed with Allendria, bringing her in close and smelling the woodsy scent of her hair. He drifted off into sleep with her aroma filling his head.

* * *

Arthur stared at the item on the counter in front of him. Nerves fluttered in his chest as he slowly picked it up and turned it over in his hands. His gaze drifted to the table covered with the items and the two large bins nearby that housed even more. The description popped up in his view.

Item: Improved Timed Hellfire Arrow	Attack: +5
	Durability: 40/40
	Rarity: Rare
	Quality: Well Crafted
	Weight: 0.1 kg
	Slot: Arrow
	Traits: A specially enchanted steel arrow. 10 seconds after activation, arrow explodes and deals fire damage to any near it. Damage done is based on the distance from the explosion.
	Explosion Damage: • Deals 300 fire damage to anything within 5 yards of the blast.

	<ul><li>Deals 220 fire damage to anything between 6 and 20 yards of the blast.</li><li>Deals 180 fire damage to anything between 21 and 30 yards of the blast.</li><li>Has a chance to inflict burn status on any enemies hit with the arrow's effect.</li></ul>

It had taken the entire day, but he'd spent his time well. The initial bundle was the normal version with reduced stats but he improved the process and the materials used in each arrow which created the 'Improved' version of the item.

Am I really going to unleash this level of destruction in this world? I know we've used dragon fire, which is nearly on the level of a full-scale bomb, but this is a rapidly produce-able item that can cause immense destruction.

He stood in contemplation for a while longer before shaking his head and committing to the path ahead. He opened a Dimensional Storage Space and had the assistants at the blacksmith carefully load the items in.

His trek back to the inn was a somber matter, but when he arrived, he noticed the party was all dressed for war. Allendria stood near Samson and wore one of their standard sets of mail absorption armor. Samson stood in his special plate armor with Divine Fury strapped to his back. The embossed face staring at all who were brave enough to look.

Balair and Cal looked bored in their human forms and sat on barrels near the entrance to the inn. Arthur felt a pang of regret at the thought of their missing party member.

She would've loved this attack. He mused.

An unexpected face emerged from the inn and came to stand near him.

"Anything I can do to help?" Wesley asked.

"I appreciate it, but this isn't your fight." Arthur told him.

"I know, but it's what I want to do. I've had more fun and actually enjoyed my time in this world for the first time since coming here, and that only happened when I went on your last quest with you. Maybe us earthlings need to stick together. Either way, I feel more welcomed with your group and would like to stick around for now." Wesley said.

"I won't turn you away if you wish to stay. Always good to have more friends around." Arthur agreed.

"Appreciate it. I'll make myself useful while traveling with you. That I promise."

The group took one last look at all their equipment and checked on everything's condition before Samson turned to a small army that was loosely assembled farther down the street.

"Soldiers! Form up in ranks and prepare to march." Samson called to the group.

The assembled warriors snapped into action and quickly sorted themselves into proper ranks. Each stood at attention and waited for orders in a matter of moments.

"Care to address them?" Samson asked Arthur in a low tone.

"That's a good idea," Arthur agreed.

Arthur walked down the street until he walked beside the assembled formation.

"Warriors of Alurian! I appreciate your participation in keeping our city safe. All those who live in this city owe you a debt of gratitude. I've promised these invaders that we will greet them with a harsh death, and I intend to keep that promise. We will still honor any surrenders, but otherwise, we will obliterate any who stand before us.

"Most of you will not even engage in this fight if it goes according to plan. Our ranged fighters should shoulder the brunt of this fight, but we count on everyone to hold their place and protect those near them. Let's show these invaders that they messed with the wrong people. For the Kingdom of Fire!" Arthur yelled as he withdrew Ember and caused flames to dance along the blade overhead.

The army cheered and Samson called for them to head out. Arthur and the party moved to the front of the line as they marched and continued to lead the pack down the road and to the gates of the outer wall. Wesley struck up a fine marching tune, and the army received a morale boost to go with a march speed increase of ten percent that lasted for a full hour.

Samson called the formation to a halt and Arthur walked to the stairs and climbed the battlement. At the top, he gazed over the field and spotted the assembled army. A deep sigh escaped him as he saw them arrayed in battle formation.

I really hoped they would reconsider.

Footsteps approached, and he felt an arm weave into his own. He leaned his head over and rested it on her shoulder.

"I'm sorry, my love." Arthur told her in a soft whisper.

He heard her sniffle, but felt her nod.

"I hoped Tirithan would be reasonable, but stubbornest will literally be the death of him." She said.

"Do you need time before we march out?" Arthur asked.

"No, let's get this over with. No amount of time is going to make it any better."

Arthur turned toward her, held on to her hands, and kissed her on the forehead before turning and walking with her down the stairs. They continued until they were at the head of the army again.

At the base of the wall, Arthur opened up his dimensional storage space and called the archer units forward. He handed each a small load of the exploding arrows.

When the ammunition was distributed, he instructed the units on their use while explaining their battle plan. The group would simply stand in formation with the melee units guarding their front while the archers rained down destruction on the army. Straight forward and simple.

Samson called a command and a red flare launched from their forces and toward the central fortress. They waited patiently until Arthur felt the magic fade from the barrier wall. The gate swung open and their force marched from the wall.

"Are you sure it's smart leaving a perfectly sound defensive wall to fight in the open with an enemy?" Wesley whispered to Arthur as he walked near him.

"Normally, no. We plan on showcasing an overwhelming force and putting an end to this quickly." Arthur explained.

"If you say so. Think I'm going to hang out in the back." The bard said.

Arthur laughed. "We need you in a support role, so go ahead."

The dwarf shuffled around the side of the formation as they marched forward. The army came to a halt roughly one hundred yards from the Dark Elf forces.

A flash of red caught his attention and Arthur turned to see a standard bearer holding a flag of red with a purple dragon head in the center. The color scheme closely matched that of the mage corp.

I really need to discuss that with someone. The color combination feels odd.

Arthur studied the assembled army in front of them. The Dark Elves all stood in formation. Their mages were in the back with the archers in front of them. Soldiers with tall shields guarded the front of the forces. He could feel magical items scattered through the forces, and the magic he felt from them suggested they might be some kind of shield spells.

Not that it will do them much good.

The Dark Elf forces were arranged in two primary columns of fighters. There were blocks of soldiers in each of the primary columns, separated by narrow gaps. Their plate wearers carried tower shields and work black tabards on their armor. The rest of the army appeared to wear leather armor, even those he considered mages.

Could it be? Will he do it? Arthur thought.

Cal and Balair, prepare to blast the force on the left side of that formation as soon as I ask. Our left, not theirs. He added quickly.

Trying to force them to flee into their other column? Balair asked.

Not exactly. Do you see where the units split in the formation line? The small gap? Don't harm anyone on the other side of that. Leave the larger force standing with Tirithan alone.

Want to save those for yourself? Cal asked.

No, they are going to join us. Arthur told them confidently.

What? They both echoed in unison.

Just trust me. I'll say when.

"If my hunch is correct, your wish may come true." Arthur told Allendria in a hushed tone.

He looked at her and saw confusion in her expression before flashing her a smile. "Just watch."

Arthur took a dozen steps forward and used his Air Magic to amplify his voice.

"Your twenty-four-hour grace period is over. All who do not surrender or leave the field now will die." Arthur said.

Tirithan's voice sounded in the distance as he called his forces to attention. The entire column lifted weapons to the ready.

The Dark Elf commander called out "Shift!" and Arthur watched in delight as the entire army, save for the small portion that Arthur identified on the left, peel away and sheath their weapons. They marched away from the smaller column and the formation moved until they were nearly fifty yards away and also facing the rest of the
Dark Elf army.

"Thank you, General Tirithan. You are a shining symbol of honor for your people," Arthur told the man before turning to the remaining army. "Last chance before we eliminate you. Surrender."

The Dark Elves left in battle looked around in confusion. They all stared at the other assembled group of Dark Elves, now facing them and ready for battle.

"I can't believe he actually did it," Allendria whispered.

"I think Samson got through to him where we couldn't." Arthur said.

Arthur could barely pick out Dahna's voice at this distance, but he heard the man spluttering in disbelief before he finally said, "How dare they? Kill them all."

Arthur could only shake his head in resignation before turning and walking back toward his army. He heard the fighters roar and felt the vibrations in the ground as they charged his army. Arthur looked up and nodded to Samson. The paladin called out a single command. "Loose volley one."

Arrows streaked overhead, but they weren't ordinary ones. Each was one of the Hellfire Arrows. He instructed them to use the originals first and they could use the improved version later. He doubted they would need to resort to that. More than one hundred arrows streaked overhead and when Arthur reach his position at the front of the formation, he turned to see them land amongst the forces as they charged at them.

The Dark Elves' screams of rage turned into screams of horror as the entire battlefield turned into one large ball of fire. Arrows detonated everywhere and Arthur saw Calfuray and Balair also streak overhead and blast a row of fire along each edge of the charging force.

Men and women screamed in pain as the flames engulfed everything. A few spots escaped the blasts and the people in them cowered down in fear and covered their faces from the heat. As the intensity died down, Arthur heard Samson.

"Ready volley two!"

Arthur held up a hand to stop the order.

"Hold on string." Samson called, and the archers lowered their arrows.

The few survivors Arthur could see were in a panic. They dropped weapons and tried to run, but everywhere was still smoldering and hot. Crispy, black corpses dotted the landscape and Arthur felt a pang of regret as soon as he watched panicked survivors try to flee through the flames. They ran with no sense of direction, fueled by pure terror. Unable to watch them suffer any longer, he called an order.

"Mage Unit One, Downpour!" Arthur yelled with magical enhancement.

Magical energy built in the area and clouds formed over the burning area. In short order, rain poured from the clouds and stifled the flames. Everyone still alive froze in place and looked up in relief. Many held out their arms and let the rain splash across their bodies to cool them down.

"Paladin Samson. Have our fighters round up the survivors and keep them under guard." Arthur told him.

Samson barked orders and a section of their forces broke free and marched on the smoldering remains of the battlefield. Arthur turned to Allendria and saw tears in her eyes and her hand over her mouth at the sheer destruction. She looked at him and fear was all he saw.

That look hurt him more than any attack could.

"You plan to do this to my city?" She asked in disbelief.

"I truly hope it doesn't come to that. With Tirithan on our side, maybe we can make this a somewhat peaceful takeover." Arthur offered.

"But you will do it if you must?" She asked.

"Yes, I will." He told her somberly.

"Why?"

"It's war," he said with a shrug. "Can you stand there and honestly say that Gliran wouldn't do the same thing to us if he had the chance?"

She opened her mouth as if to argue, but then stopped. She looked down at her feet. "I'm sure he would."

"We save all we can, but not at the expense of those on our side. It will be up to you to help make this a better place and prevent this from happening again. Your fellow Dark Elves need you to stand strong. There's a small army of them right there who need your guidance."

She nodded in agreement and he walked over and held onto her hand.

"Want to go greet Tirithan? I'm hoping he swears to your cause and didn't want to just sit out and march home."

"Let's go find out," she agreed.

Will you two join us by the remaining army? We want to meet Tirithan.

Both dragons agreed, and Arthur and Allendria walked toward the other Dark Elf army. They were halfway there when Tirithan wove through the forces and headed for them. Calfuray and Balair thudded to the ground near Arthur and Allendria and walked with them. He was pleased to see them stay in their dragon form. He suspected the intimidation would work out in his favor.

The dark elves faltered at the sight of the dragons, and a few of them drew weapons. Tirithan froze mid stride and looked around for a few moments before he called out a command and everyone sheathed their weapons again. He resumed his trek and met with Arthur and Allendria in front of the assembled force.

Allendria couldn't resist, and she walked up to him and hugged him. "Thank you for saving our people." She whispered.

The warrior looked shocked before he wrapped arms around her as well. "I'm sorry it took me so long to come to my senses. After seeing your display, I can honestly say I am extremely grateful for the words of your paladin. In the end, his final parting statement was what swayed me." Tirithan said.

"I think I speak for all of us when I say thank you for making that choice. None of us wanted to see that happen, but this fight has gone on long enough. It's time to remove the corruption and get back to peace." Arthur said.

Tirithan looked skeptical. "I'm not sure it's that easy. We have always had tension between us and the humans. Even when Allendria's father ruled."

"We will make it work. I don't recall if I told you during our last encounter, but Allendria and I are engaged to marry. She will become the queen of the Kingdom of Fire. While I understand that may also cause some strife in different areas, we will not let that stop us," Arthur said.

"I'd heard rumors," Tirithan agreed. "I don't mean to sound rude, but what are your plans with the Dark Elves once you're married? That idea is part of what has fueled much of the resistance against your kingdom in the eyes of those who don't support Gliran."

"Understandable concern," Arthur agreed. "I have no intentions of doing anything. Allendria will be the queen of the dark elves. I will not press for any official title among your people. I will assist my wife if she requests, but I leave the governance to the Dark Elves. I only ask that any future children of ours be allowed to prove themselves for a chance at succession, nothing more."

Tirithan visibly relaxed at the statement before extending a hand. "I can accept a man with your level of honor. We will pledge to our queen."

Arthur nodded and gestured toward Allendria. Tirithan fell to a knee, and the assembled force behind him followed suit.

"We pledge our life and loyalty to Queen Allendria." They all stated in unison.

"I accept your pledge and will swear to protect and serve my people." She answered back.

Arthur felt a snap of tension in the air that he couldn't quite explain. He assumed the words were some standard ritual that he didn't know, and an agreement was now officially in place.

Samson approached and Arthur waved for him to come forward.

"Paladin Samson, General Tirithan credits your words with their salvation and for that, I thank you," Arthur said. "At least I assume he will maintain the general title," Arthur said as he looked at Allendria.

"Of course he will. We need our honorable men as just leaders." She said.

Samson bowed to the general. "I'm happy we could save so many with just words. That doesn't finish our problem here, though."

Samson gestured behind him as a group of nearly fifty people were marched toward them. Many of them were burned and their clothes were singed or even missing in places.

"What do you wish to do with them, Queen Allendria?" Samson asked with a quick bow.

She stood up straight at the title. She realized he had shifted into his formal tone for serious matters. The people were her own, and it was up to her to dispense justice. She walked toward the group as they brought them to a halt.

"Fellow Dark Elves. You've seen the power we possess. I asked you multiple times to quit the field or join us. Out of mercy, I'll give you one last chance to swear allegiance to me now. We have people who can tend your wounds and you'll be treated the same as any of Tirithan's forces. Any who refuse, will be executed," she said with finality.

As one, the group fell to their knees. Some of them wept openly as they bowed their heads and recited the pledge that Tirithan's group had. A face in the back caused Arthur to wave his hand down low to get Allendria's attention. She looked at him and he gestured toward the back of the crowd with a tilt of his head. She scanned the people until she finally saw who he had and her features hardened to stone.

She addressed the crowd, "I accept your pledge and will swear to protect and serve my people, except for that sniveling excuse for a Dark Elf. Guards, seize that man," Allendria said as she pointed out Dahna.

The Dark Elf jumped to his feet and tried to run away, but the guards captured him with ease and brought him up to Allendria.

"Not so cocky now as you try to hide in the back," Allendria said. "You don't get the choice of salvation that these had. I sentence you to death. The only question is how it shall be carried out."

Allendria paced back and forth as she lightly tapped on her chin and looked skyward.

"I could set him on fire like Arthur did," she said before she waved that idea away.

"Can't repeat that. Loses its flair."

"Ooh, Balair," she began as she turned toward the dragon.

"Yes, Queen Allendria?"

"Can you eat him for me?" She asked in an innocent tone.

"I mean, I could. Do I have to, though? No offense, but people taste pretty nasty. Although I can see how it'd make a flashy statement for you." Balair said.

"Hmm. Maybe just chew him up a little and spit him out? As long as he dies, I don't care." Allendria said with a wave.

"I can do that. I'll make it flashy in your honor," Balair agreed before taking a few quick steps and snatching the man up in his jaws. Per her instructions, he chewed around a few times and audible crunches and cracks punctuated the nearby area before Balair lifted his head skyward and wedged the body in his teeth. He spread his mouth open just enough to create a gap and a vent of fire burst forth. He kept the pillar of flame burning for a few seconds before dropping his head down and spitting out the charred corpse.

"Pretty sure he's dead." Balair said. "Figured I'd honor your pyromancer skill with a little fire."

"Thank you, noble Balair."

Allendria turned back to face the crowd. “That’s what awaits traitors.”

Chapter 32

Time to End This

Arthur watched Allendria pace in front of the remaining Dark Elves as they kneeled in subjugation to her.

"We'll call this a lesson to any who would think of betraying me. General Tirithan," Allendria said while turning to address the man, "Have these elves kept under supervision until you're satisfied they can be trusted within our force. If any try to betray us, end them."

"It will be done, Your Majesty," Tirithan said with a salute. He began issuing order to some of his nearby warriors. They rounded up the kneeling elves and move them into separate areas.

Congratulations! You have completed an active raid. Your actions have supported the winning side of the Kingdom of Fire.

Resistance	
Requirements: Participate in actions to directly or indirectly influence the outcome of the raid.	Description: A new raid has started near Alurian. Aid either side in the fight. If the side you assist survives the raid, you receive the rewards.

Rewards: 40,000 Experience, 4,000 Unassigned Skill Experience, 2 Talent Points	

Arthur ignored the notifications and resolved to review them later. He had a mountain of them to catch up on with the crafting earlier in the day. Instead, he turned to face Allendria.

"You ready to head back into the city? I think our new allies need a break from sitting in a camp for so long. Let's show them proper hospitality," Arthur suggested as he nodded toward her newly pledged soldiers.

"That sounds marvelous," she agreed. "General Tirithan, please allow your soldiers some leave to enjoy our fair city. We welcome you with open arms and wish for you to join us. I'm sure we can find some accommodation as well for you to rest in comfort."

Tirithan bowed, "As you wish, Your Majesty."

Arthur stretched his arm out to Allendria, and she took his hand. He pulled her in and she hooked her arm into his. They walked toward the gate as Samson started barking orders of his own and directing their own forces back inside. They made it less than a dozen yards before a sound caused Arthur to groan.

He turned to the side and yelled at Balair, "Not the damn time. Put it up and learn some privacy!"

The dragon, now back in human form, was startled by the command and swore as he quickly gathered up his pants. Arthur chuckled and continued on his way through the gate.

That'll teach him to pay better attention.

They continued through the gate and Samson called out the order for their forces to stand down and go about their business. He identified which group he wanted on guard duty at the wall, and the rest dispersed.

Allendria turned to General Tirithan, "Would you walk with me, my friend, as we continue into the city?"

"It'd be a pleasure," he agreed with a smile, and he walked over to join them. He stopped a few steps before reaching them to turn and look at his soldiers. "If anyone causes any issues in the city, there will be hell to pay. Be on your best behavior or I'll have you on permanent cleanup duty."

With his final warning issued, he joined Allendria and Arthur, and they walked down the road toward Alurian. Arthur took the time while Allendria and Tirithan reminisced on old times to review his experience gains since he'd returned.

You have gained 40,000 Experience, 4,000 Unassigned Skill Experience, and 2 Talent Points for completing the Raid Event: Resistance.

Congratulations, you have reached level 31! You now have 5 available skill points. That was an impressive end to that raid!

You have gained 53,110 total experience in Earth Magic.

You have gained 40,140 total experience in Fire Magic.

Congratulations, you have reached level 27 in Fire Magic. Increases the effect of your fire magic spells by 78%. More Enchanting. Uh… set something on fire instead?

You have gained 16,170 total experience in Water Magic.

Congratulations, you have reached levels 13 and 14 in Water Magic. Increases the effect of your Water Magic spells by 30%. A little wetness always helps.

You have gained 22,080 total experience in Arcane Smithing.

You have gained 22,080 total experience in Blacksmithing.

Congratulations, you have reached level 21 in Blacksmithing. You are granted a 60% bonus to forging speed. You should outsource more.

You have gained 18,910 total experience in Metal Construction.

Congratulations, you have reached levels 5, 6, 7, 8, 9, and 10 in Metal Construction. Decreases the time it takes to assemble metal constructions by 27%. That's a lot of metalwork for a day.

You have gained 18,910 total experience in Arcane Metal Construction.
Congratulations, you have reached levels 5, 6, 7, 8, 9, and 10 in Arcane Metal Construction. Increases the effectiveness of metal constructions created with magic by 27%. This kinda feel like cheating… right?

You have gained 18,650 total experience in Enchanting.

You have gained 7,115 total experience.

Arthur considered his five new attribute points. Most of his stats were already super impressive compared to anyone near his level. His biggest concern now was being a leader. With that in mind, he dropped all five into Charisma, bringing it to 26. If it would help him avoid even one battle and lead him to a diplomatic victory, those points would be well spent.

He held off on the unallocated points. Nothing in his skill list was really lagging that was important. He may discover a new skill in the future that would be beneficial to level up quickly.

Arthur pulled up the Tier 1 talents for Arcane Metal Construction.

You have 12 unspent Talent Points.

Tier 1	
Mana Conservation (0/10)	*Each point decreases the mana needed to sustain your constructs.*
Magical Discovery (0/1)	*Grants you a passive ability that lets you randomly loot mechanical parts.*
Enchantment Enhancements (0/10)	*Each point increases the effectiveness of enchantments. Increases the strength and durability of your constructs.*

The options didn't seem very useful when he first reviewed them. The Magical Discovery was a no-brainer, and he put a point in that immediately. Randomly looting parts he could use to support his skill was awesome. The others didn't appear useful at all. Neither would really support his arrows he currently made.

They seem tailormade for this skill and focus heavily on the magical aspect, but why? Arthur asked himself.

I understand wanting to make sure things I make are sturdy, but what's the point? Unless… golems!

His realization sparked interest in the skill. So far, it'd only been used for arrows, but if he could develop mechanical golems, this skill would improve their abilities and sturdiness. An entire force of them could be made and used as guards.

With that thought in mind, he spent five points in Enchantment Enhancements and pulled up Tier 2 options before investing anything further.

Tier 2	
Mechanical Overload (0/1)	*Allows you to overload the magical energy in mechanical creations you made to discharge their energy and cause a damaging explosion. The explosion size and damage is based on the materials and amount of magic present in the device.*

Mechanical Healing *(0/10)*	*Investing all ten points in this skill grants your constructs the ability to self-heal using their built-in mana and the mana in the air around them.*

There it is!

Mechanical Healing was the answer. That would allow him to create constructs that could last nearly forever. With their healing ability, it would allow them to always stay intact. They would just need to be recharged from time to time. His thoughts shifted to the idea of a city filled with these guards on the corners, policing and keeping order.

Deep down, Arthur knew he still had a way to go until he reached anything near that point. Mechanical Overload was very beneficial, though. It would work perfectly with his arrows and allow him to set them off at any moment without having to wait for the full timeout. It could save his life when time is critical.

Arthur put a point in Mechanical Overload and maxed out Enchantment Enhancements to finish his points. He then turned his attention to the Tier 1 options for Metal Construction.

You have 12 unspent Talent Points.

Tier 1	
Material Salvaging *(0/10)*	*Each point gives a small boost to salvage mechanical parts retrieved during scavenging.*

Ingenuity (0/1)	Grants you a large boost to production speed for 15 minutes. During this time, you have a chance to be Inspired and discover a new recipe you can build.
A Keen Eye (0/10)	Each point in this skill increases the chance that something you see will trigger Inspiration and reveal a new recipe you can build.

Ingenuity was another auto-include here. The biggest downfall of this skill was his lack of projects that used it. If he could spark new recipes to use, it would allow him to build on his skill. The other two both had merit, but Arthur put five points in A Keen Eye for the same reason and then looked into Tier 2.

Tier 2	
(Hidden Talent) Magical Augmentation (0/10) Requirements: • Blacksmithing > 10 • Arcane Smithing > 10 • Metal Construction > 8 • Arcane Metal Construction > 1	Each point increases the durability and effectiveness of all metal constructs you make by 5%.

| Spring Loaded (0/1) | Teaches you the schematic to make springs. |
| Magical Alloys (0/10) | Every 2 points invested in this talent increases the effectiveness of constructs built using magical alloys by 5%. |

Ha! Success.

These skills all leaned heavily into his idea of golems. Not only that, but it held great merit for magical versions of transportation. While it appeared the least interesting skill, Spring Loaded was one he was excited to see.

Springs were an integral part of almost everything mechanical. He could even use them to improve his arrow design and make it more functional. Having some experience working with them on Earth with his novice blacksmithing hobby, he had a good understanding of them, but they were notoriously tricky to create. Just spinning metal into the shape doesn't do the trick. The metal has to be hardened just right and the alloy of the metal can affect its strength and flexibility. This skill should help him cut past months of experimentation to sort through those roadblocks. He dumped a point in there immediately.

The other two would be great options but weren't truly useful for him yet, so he dropped his other five points into A Keen Eye to max it out. Learning new recipes was far more important than increasing the power and durability of his constructs. Especially considering arrows was all he had right now.

Next up was his Water Magic. He put his four available points into Soothing.

Soothing (8/10)	Water Magic suffuses your body and constantly improves it. Every point grants 0.5 HP and 0.5 MP regeneration per second. Every 5 points increases all your stats by 1.

Arthur snapped back into focus as he finished going through his notifications and talents to discover the city was quickly approaching. On the edge of the nearest buildings, he could see a line of people waiting on their arrival.

"It appears the city council has come out to greet us as we enter," Allendria said.

"You have a council here? That's an interesting concept. I thought this was a kingdom?" Tirithan asked.

"It is, and I'm the king," Arthur agreed, "but I don't care to micromanage the city. I prefer to let people I can trust handle the day-to-day business. They have the specialized knowledge in all the different areas to make it successful. I know just enough about each subject to be dangerous."

"I see, Your Majesty. It's a rather enlightened view on society." Tirithan said.

"Please call me Arthur. I understand decorum when we are in a formal situation, but otherwise, informal is preferred. I'd appreciate it." Arthur told him.

"Very well, Arthur. I'm really impressed by your stonework here. You don't have dwarven masons floating about, do you?" Tirithan asked.

"Nope, purely magical. Our construction crews have been at work building as fast as their magic allows. As their craft has improved, they've taken it upon themselves to make more intricate designs. We originally started with very basic buildings so we could crank out new housing as quick as possible. Now, I think they take it upon themselves to have competitions about who makes the best design each round." Arthur said with a chuckle.

"I hadn't noticed that myself, but now that you mention it, I think you're right." Allendria agreed.

"Is that… Daranth?" Tirithan asked.

Allendria smiled, "Of course. He's on the city council."

"I wondered where they disappeared to when Gliran chased them out. Did all of his group stay here?"

"Pretty much. They are free to travel as they wish, so some may not be here currently." Allendria said. "We even have an entire section of the city designated as the Dark Elf Quarter, and there is an embassy there. Many of them live in that part of town. They create and supply much of the city's furniture."

The group neared the council members and Daniel stepped forward.

"Welcome back, King Arthur," he said with a curt bow. "I hope all is well?"

"Everything is in hand. General Tirithan has pledged his allegiance to Queen Allendria of the Dark Elves and joined in our fight against Gliran. Most of the army came with him. Those that didn't were… neutralized." Arthur said, carefully choosing his wording.

"So, the siege is over?" Daniel asked.

"It is over." Allendria agreed.

Arthur saw everyone relax as shoulders sunk down lower and smiles bloomed across their faces.

"General Tirithan, I invite you to join us in council at the inn so we can discuss next steps. Your men are free to explore the city, and you can join them after our discussion." Arthur said.

"Of course, Your Majesty."

"Councilwoman Katherine, can you assign someone to help find accommodations for our guests?" Arthur asked.

"Of course, Your Majesty. We may have to erect some of the temporary housing. I'm not sure that is appropriate for true guests." She added.

"I'm sure they will welcome that over sleeping in a military camp. Provide better rooms for the higher rank members and work your way down." Arthur said.

"They will be happy with whatever they get or they can answer to me," Tirithan said, with a touch of steel in his voice.

Katherine flinched at his tone before she nodded in agreement and scribbled on her papers. The party continued down the street and the group of council members headed for the inn. Each took turns walking close to them and introducing themselves to Tirithan as they traveled. Daranth was the last to approach, and the two of them reminisced about home.

Once inside the inn, each of them found seats and Tirithan sat next to Allendria. Daniel disappeared into the back, and Trisha and Paula emerged with plates of food. They quickly set out a hearty slab of steak that Arthur was positive was venison. Each plate also held a large baked potato and a small salad. It was arguably Arthur's favorite dish possible.

Tirithan looked nervous and out of place. He glanced around in confusion at the casual manner in which everyone ate. Arthur grabbed his attention with a few hand gestures and motioned for him to eat. The general nodded and began on his food.

It wasn't long before everyone finished and sat back in their chairs. Arthur waited for Daniel to emerge from the kitchens and join them before he started.

"Alright everyone. The city is safe again. It's time to change focus." Arthur looked around the table until he settled on the face he was looking for. "Rayne, I apologize for not letting you address the council before, but it was a bit of a crisis. Care to fill everyone in on your mission to Seora?"

"I returned to Seora to find it on a decline," Rayne began. Arthur watched some of the council members as their expressions turned to frowns.

"A part of the criminal underground had turned and was slowly taking over the city. They'd disrupted all the resource allocation and goods delivery." Rayne said.

"What was Lady Dalia doing to prevent this?" Katherine asked.

"From what I could tell, nothing." Rayne answered.

"How could she do nothing?" Rowan asked. His tone carried some heat with his words.

"I'm not sure. She knew of the problems. Lords Tripp and Ealin, along with Lady Gemmalin, were all constantly reporting them to her, but she wasn't offering any assistance in fixing it. They were doing what they could but she also wouldn't allow them to call upon city guards to assist in the transportation or distribution to prevent the theft."

"That's unacceptable. I move to suggest you revoke Lady Dalia's command of Seora," Daranth proposed.

"Rayne, what's your opinion on the matter?" Arthur asked.

"I agree with Councilman Daranth. I find it hard to believe she wouldn't assist, which is bad enough. Another concern was everyone I talked to insinuated the trouble began shortly after she arrived and her lack of action makes it feel as though she somehow had a hand in it." Rayne said.

"I agree with the proposal. Lady Dalia will be stripped of command of Seora. I'll appoint Lady Gemmalin as its leader in her stead. Is that acceptable, Rayne?" Arthur asked.

"I think that's the best option. Lady Gemmalin was running almost everything there anyway, even with Dalia around. She was the true driving force in trying to fix the issue and even assisted me while I took care of it."

"Perfect. I'll write up orders stripping Dalia of her duty and another granting Lady Gemmalin the authority over the city. Samson, detail a group of guardsmen to deliver the orders. Have them escort Lady Dalia back to answer for her actions." Arthur said.

"It will be done," Samson agreed.

"Thank you for the hard work, Rayne. Next matter of business is the city itself. How are we holding up?" Arthur asked.

Katherine was the first to answer. "Everything is stocked and ready for another surprise attack. Our mana reserve is higher than ever, and our food supplies are abundant. Construction moves at a rapid pace and the city is expanding fast. The first shipment of food to the dwarves has been procured and is already packed into multiple wagons and ready to leave when Master Wesley is ready to return."

"Fantastic work, everyone. It warms my heart to see the city flourish without my help. I've seen the recent work and the detail going into the city and appreciate all of it. Never let this city fall into disrepair or poor leadership, no matter the reason." Arthur said.

"There is one major concern," Daniel chimed in.

"What's that?" Arthur asked.

"Resources. Plain and simply, we are
growing so fast, we can't keep up with demand.
We were running low on wood, but that was due
to everyone being locked in here and us not
sending out logging crews. Now that we can
resume that, it should restock quickly. Ores
are another issue. Metal takes time to mine
and our smiths go through it at extreme
speeds. Not complaining, mind you, but it
makes it near impossible to keep up with."

"Good to know," Arthur said. "What is the
major challenge with these resources? Not
enough in the local area? The amount of
workforce? Transportation? Or something else?"

The group grew silent for a few moments and
Arthur heard the tapping drone of Rowan's
fingers on the table.

"I know storage and transportation are the
main issues for the ore trade. They can only
haul so much at a time with their carts and
then processed metals take up lots of space in
my shop." Rowan said.

"I believe the logging situation is
similar. They can chop them down quickly, but
transporting large numbers back to the city is
no simple task. They have crafted a couple of
wagons to help, but the animals required to
pull them need feed and rest. So do the work
crews." Daniel said.

"Hmm…," Arthur said as he tapped on the
table. "Transportation should be easy to
solve. We have all the tools necessary.
Between my dimensional spaces and
enchantments, I should be able to craft
something to solve that. It should be
adaptable to both problems. The ability can
also be adapted for storage of goods in town.
You said our wood supply was low since you
halted logging?"

"Yes," Katherine confirmed. "We could have stopped some production and rationed it better, but with enchanted stoves and your temperature controls, most places don't need wood for anything."

"Okay. City council. I am asking for you to create a supply plan for the city. I want to ensure there are sufficient stockpiles of all critical resources for a minimum of six months." Arthur said.

Voices raised in commotion as multiple people started talking. Arthur waved his hands and motioned for everyone to calm down.

"I understand the concerns," he assured them. "I plan on remedying the problems. Most of you immediately asked how I expect you to store that kind of surplus. I plan on making a lot of storage caches scattered through all the major buildings of the city. I'll create them using large dimensional enchantments, similar to my own. They anchor to small spaces and take up very little physical room. I'll do the same for you around the blacksmith, Rowan."

"Any major buildings that house important items need this. The armory, for instance. A major benefit of the spaces is not only can we store a large quantity in such a small space, but they never deteriorate. Food doesn't spoil, metals don't rust, and wood doesn't rot. We need to have equal amounts of all items in each location in case something damages one. We can't have all of our food stored at the inn and it catch on fire and we lose access." Arthur finished.

The room was quiet as everyone contemplated the situation.

"Do you even have time for that?" Samson asked. "I thought you planned on assaulting the Dark Elves?"

"It's on the list and coming soon. We have to take time to secure our home before marching away again. I'm not making that mistake… again.

"I also plan on us putting together a more detailed plan. We can discuss that in a moment." Arthur said. "I'll also ask the council to source any of the current transportation carts in the city. I'll modify them with similar storage spaces so the people transporting can also haul much greater loads with almost no strain."

"Wouldn't it still be just as heavy?" Daniel asked. "The material is all loaded into the space, even if it is scrunched down into a smaller space."

"No, it doesn't. The material isn't truly there. Look at my storage spaces as only doorways. The rooms within are actually totally separate places that are an unmeasurable distance away. I carve out a void in it and we place items there. The openings are just portals for us to access those preset spaces. Nothing is truly here for the spell other than our doorway."

"If that's the case, then I think that would solve our pressing issue." Daniel agreed.

"Great. Next item for business. Daranth, how fares the Dark Elves within the city?" Arthur asked.

Daranth sat up straight as he faced Arthur. "Morale is high. Everyone seems happy to be treated with respect and kindness. Very few issues or arguments are reported."

"Arguments? With who?" Arthur asked.

"Oh, it's nothing. There've been a few Dark Elf haters that cause trouble here and there. Nothing to concern yourself with." Daranth waved away.

"Oh, I will. City Council, I want you to issue a decree that any prejudices or injustices because of different races in this city will be met with swift punishments. Start with small fines or community service and work your way up to exile from the kingdom for multiple repeat offenders." Arthur said.

"Uh, are you sure that is wise?" Daniel asked.

"There's no place for that in this kingdom. We already welcome the Dark Elves, who are on our side. We also have a treaty with the dwarves. There's a chance we can meet others in time. I expect every person to treat others with at least a modicum of respect, as long as they deserve it, anyway. This in no way means people still can't dislike others for their attitudes or behaviors." Arthur clarified.

He watched the crowd to see if anyone had anything to add, but was met with silence.

"I guess it's time to get to the big topic. King Gliran," Arthur said. "Our last assault wasn't planned well enough and I take full responsibility for that. I think we have what we need now to make this a quick and hopefully somewhat bloodless fight. General Tirithan, can you tell us how many fighting men and women Gliran has left at his command?"

"I'd estimate around two thousand. It's hard to be exact depending on if he forces conscription." Tirithan answered.

    "As I told you, we are no longer playing nice and I won't hesitate to blast the city apart while getting to Gliran, but I'd prefer to avoid that if possible. If we launched an assault soon enough, do you think you could open the way?" Arthur asked.

    "What do you mean, Your Majesty?" Tirithan asked.

    "Well, the way I see it is that Gliran shouldn't know that you changed sides. When was the last message that was sent back via scout and what was reported?" Arthur asked.

    "Oh, that was yesterday and we just reported we were at a stalemate trying to bring down your shield." Tirithan said. He nodded as he must've realized what Arthur was insinuating.

    "Good. That means you should be able to return to the city. You can tell them we mustered a force that you felt was too large to combat and retreated. Make up an excuse about Dahna and why he and some of his people are gone. We will arrive a day or two after you and you can assume defensive positions. When we charge the city, you can quietly remove those loyal to Gliran and open the gates. It will help eliminate casualties and prevent unnecessary damage. We can split into parties and subdue the remaining guards loyal to Gliran. Queen Allendria can deal with them afterward. However she sees fit. I'll stress that any resistance will be met swiftly and without mercy. Do you think you can do it?" Arthur asked.

    "It doesn't seem very honorable…," Tirithan said slowly.

"Possibly not, but I see it as the best approach to rid the world of a major evil and not kill too many of either of our people at the same time." Arthur said.

"I agree with that plan, if you can make it happen. We could work together to help identify the places to send squads of fighters. You could organize the civilians within to keep out of harm's way." Allendria said.

"I'll make it happen then. When do you want to proceed?" Tirithan asked.

"I need four or five days to wrap up the projects I have here. You can march out then." Arthur said.

The party all adjourned and went about their daily tasks. Arthur was sitting at the table discussing the plan with Allendria when Tirithan approached.

"Something I can do for you, General?" Allendria asked.

"I'm not sure, Your Majesty. I felt obliged to warn you. I heard rumors before we left that King Gliran was making a deal with another foreign nation for assistance. I'm not sure who it could be, but they kept mentioning the dragons. I wonder if they may end up recruiting a dragon to their side." He said.

Arthur considered the situation and saw Calfuray sitting nearby. He motioned for her to join them and repeated what Tirithan told them.

"It's possible," she said begrudgingly. "There are large rifts in the beliefs of the different clans. We might have to fight another of the dragons. I doubt it'd be more than one or two since our lives are valued so heavily."

"Great, looks like something else we need to plan for." Arthur sighed.

Chapter 33

More Enchanting

Arthur rolled over and draped an arm across Allendria. He wrapped his hand around her and pulled her in close while burying his head into her hair.

"I don't want to get up," he whined.

"Don't," she mumbled.

"Too much to do. If this stupid fighting would ever end, we could sleep late every day. Kings get to do that, right?" Arthur asked with hope in his voice.

"I'll not complain. I'm sure we could make it a royal decree or something. We could both turn our cities over to councils and just lounge around." She suggested.

"I like the way you think," he said, brushing her hair to the side and kissing her neck.

"If you're gonna start that nonsense this morning, get up and go to work."

Arthur laughed, but rolled out of bed, groaning on his way as his bones popped.

I feel like an old man in the morning.

"I'll find you later today. The new transportation carts going to be your focus today?" Allendria asked.

"That's the plan. Need to get that taken care of before we march off. What's your plan for the day?" Arthur asked.

Allendria rolled over and smiled at him. "I'm going to sleep late and then go to the Dark Elf embassy with Tirithan to show him around."

"Ass. Didn't have to rub it in," Arthur grumbled as he walked over and gave her one last kiss before leaving.

His trip to the inn was quick, and upon arrival, he found a small army of carts parked nearby. Rowan was outside waiting for him and motioned him over.

"Morning. Ready to get to work?" Rowan asked.

"Yep. Not sure why all these are here, though," Arthur said.

"So you can change them. No need to build everything from scratch."

"That's fine, but I have to get the Enchantment sorted out first. Until then, you could put these to better use."

"Good to know. You sounded like you had it all figured out yesterday, so we arranged this. We can send them back to work for now and call them in when needed. Anything you need to get started on the enchantment?" Rowan asked.

"Probably, Daranth. I'll need him to build me a wooden frame to practice on… and possibly destroy while experimenting. Another reason I don't want to use the wagons yet," Arthur explained.

"Yeah, good call. Don't want to replace them myself. Anything you need from me or the smithy?" Rowan asked.

"Depends on our wood supply. I'm not sure how high of quality our wood is for enchantment yet. If it isn't good enough, I may coat the frame in a thin layer of Magesteel to hold the enchantment power." Arthur said.

"Why not just make the frame out of Magesteel completely?"

"Don't want to waste that much metal, and it increases the weight. Ideally, I want these things to be light enough to use as a push cart if needed. Takes up less space on the streets and prevents excess animal waste in the city."

"You know, I hate to bring this up… but you mentioned making a compendium of enchantments before. Do you plan on doing that before you run off to war again? I don't want to jinx it, but I feel this city would fall apart without your enchantments. The visible ones we can replicate, but some you embedded in the material as you created it." Rowan said.

"Yeah. It's necessary. I'll make sure I add it to the list of stuff to do before I leave. Kat can source me some paper and I can get it down. I'll leave it to her to improve upon."

"Thanks. I was nervous to bring it up but felt it my duty as a council member," Rowan said with a low chuckle.

"I appreciate it. Never worry about doing your job. It only makes me feel better knowing you all truly care about this city."

Arthur reached over and shook his hand to reassure the man. "I'll go meet with Daranth. Can you have one of your assistants bring over a couple of ingots of Magesteel?"

"Sure can. Let me know if you need anything else."

Arthur left the inn and headed for the Dark Elf part of town. He waved to the citizens going about their business as he strolled through the city. After some distance, he noticed some details he hadn't seen before.

The builders have also been improving their existing work.

Many of the early buildings they created in the city now sported new facades with far more detail work on them. Gone were the bland and flat stone walls. Now the stonework resembled stone bricks around the bottom, with carvings of nature designs along the walls. Arthur smiled as he admired each new design he walked past.

It wasn't long before he approached the embassy building of the Dark Elves and found who he was looking for.

"Daranth," Arthur called with a wave, "got some time to help me out?"

"Always. What can I do for you?" Daranth asked as he walked over to join him.

"Need some wooden frames to practice enchantments on."

"I assume these are meant for your transportation solution?"

"They are," Arthur confirmed.

"How large do you need them?"

"It's probably easier if I had some that were only a couple of feet square. I need something to practice on until I get the enchantment right. Scaling up to a larger size is simple."

"Understood. How big is a foot? Do you mean my foot?" Daranth asked as he looked down at his right foot and wiggled it from side to side.

"Sorry about that. We use different measurements where I'm from. Just go with half a meter square."

"That's simple. Any special requests on its construction?"

"For the test pieces? No. When we build the replicas, we want to ensure they are sturdy. I would request you build them out of the most magically sensitive wood you have. It will improve the enchantment and reduce the risk of it blowing up in my face." Arthur said.

"I can see how that would be bad. I have some selection of yew that is decent with enchantment. Should be more than sufficient for your tests."

"I appreciate it. They don't have to be anything special design-wise. I plan on coating them in a thin layer of Magesteel to make the enchanting easier and to give it a lot more strength and protection."

"Almost seems overkill, but I understand the reasoning. Give me half an hour. We have plenty of small scraps over in the woodworking shop that could make a few of these."

"Care if I tag along? Don't have any other tasks and would like to see someone else craft for a change."

"By all means, follow me," Daranth said.

The two wove their way through the crowded space. He was very surprised at the number of people crowding the halls. It had never been this busy in the past, and he idly wondered if they had some kind of event going on. He was about to ask Daranth when he noticed the detail he'd missed. Much of the crowd was wearing fighting armor. They were Dark Elves from the army that were here visiting and checking out their kinsmen's wares.

"Any trouble with the new arrivals?" Arthur
asked.

"Not really. A couple of people grumbling
about prices, but overall, it is going well."

The woodworking shop was easy to decipher.
As soon as they walked through the doorway, a
cloud of sawdust hit him and sent him into a
short coughing fit.

"Sorry about that. I've gotten used to it
and forgot to warn you."

"No problem," Arthur choked out as he waved
a hand in front of his face to both reassure
Daranth and clear the dust.

Daranth moved to one workbench and waved
the man using it away. The other elf didn't
protest and just picked up his pieces and went
in search of another bench to use. Daranth dug
through some large wooden bins at the ends of
the bench and pulled out small pieces of wood.

He arranged them on the bench and sorted
them by size. He placed two separate stacks of
boards that were all within a few inches of
each other before turning his attention to one
stack. The elf lined up the stack so one end
of the boards lined up perfectly. Arthur felt
magic power build up in the Dark Elf and his
hand glowed red. With a quick swipe, the elf
brought his hand down and sliced cleanly
through the boards, making a perfect cut
through them all at equal lengths.

"That's nice," Arthur remarked.

"Tired of using a saw. Faster and a lot
cleaner." Daranth said.

"Felt like Fire and maybe Air Magic?"
Arthur asked.

"It was indeed. I tried with Fire only and kept burning everything. Made it weak and unusable. I tried it with a combination of fire and water next, but they kept canceling each other out. Finally, the air and fire combo allowed the air to rapidly cool the outer barrier as the inside flames sliced through." Daranth explained.

"Care to teach it to me?" Arthur asked.

"By all means."

Daranth arranged the second stack of items on the table, and Arthur walked over and put his hand on his shoulder. He fed Air and Fire Magic into the elf, and Daranth funneled the power through him and combined it with his own in his hands. Arthur watched the energies swirl and could visualize the magic as the air enveloped the hand in a tight bundle while the fire coursed through the center at high heat. In one swift motion, Daranth brought the hand down, cleanly slicing this stack.

Congratulations, you have discovered the Combination Spell: Wood Slicer. You have gained 250 experience in Air Magic and Fire Magic for discovering a known spell.

Wood Slicer	
Requirements: Air Magic and Fire Magic Mana Cost: 30 MP Cast Time: 1 second	Description: Envelops the target in a super-heated flame with an air buffer to slice through wood.
Mastery Level: 1	

"Who named that spell?" Arthur mumbled to himself.

"I did," Daranth said in a cheerful tone. "I was fortunate enough to create it myself, so I kept it simple and to the point."

"Well, great work. Usually can get a good bonus when creating new spells."

"You do, indeed. Let me get these assembled for you now that everything is cut."

Arthur watched the Dark Elf arrange the boards into rectangular shapes and grab a small metal drill. It was designed similarly to the swing-bit style hand drills from Earth. The man carefully drilled holes in the different sections and ensured they were lined up using a piece of coal to mark locations.

Fishing in a basket near the desk, Daranth retrieved small wooden rods. Magic filled the air again as the elf sliced the rods into small pieces. Arthur realized he was making dowels to connect the pieces.

A little jar on the back of the table revealed a glue that smelled strongly of something resin based. Daranth used a thin piece of wood nearby to scoop out small amounts and spread them over the dowels and the holes before pulling everything together. The dowel rods slid into their places with ease and the fully assembled frame sat on the desk.

"How long does it take that glue to dry?" Arthur asked.

Daranth looked at the piece and put a hand to his chin. "It should be dry enough to move in about five minutes. I'd give it a half hour before you start with the enchantment work, though."

"That's pretty fast. Thought I was going to have to wait much longer."

"It's a powerful blend we use that dries fast. We make it from local plants so it naturally bonds with the native woods easier and stronger."

Arthur sat down in a nearby chair and just enjoyed the time watching a master at his craft. Daranth zipped through the work until he ran out of small scrap pieces. In the end, eight completed frames sat on the table.

"That enough, or should I look for more pieces?" Daranth asked.

Arthur shook himself out of his reverie and looked over the frames. "Those should work perfectly. Thanks for your help. Any chance you can make a dozen or more larger frames? I'll need them as soon as I get this enchantment figured out."

"We can handle that. Any idea of the size?" Daranth asked.

"They need to be big enough to place larger items in, so let's say two meters by a meter and a half. If you could make a couple of them larger than that for bigger items, such as lumber, that would be great. If you have the time and people, you could build them out as hand carts. Focus more on strength, but try to keep them light. Make sure the back of the cart has a wide base. The idea here is they stand the cart on its back end so it looks like a doorway and open the storage to place items in. Then they just pull it back down and continue on their way."

"I can work with that. I'll get a team together and get it started now. I know this is a top priority for everyone here in the city, so I'll have as many as I can spare on it."

Arthur clapped the man on the shoulder. "Thanks for all the work you do. This city owes all of your people a debt for how well it has prospered."

"No, you don't. I'm grateful, but you took us in when we had to flee. We are only doing our part to contribute, just like everyone else," Daranth answered with a smile.

"It's appreciated either way." Arthur returned with a smile of his own before opening up his Dimensional Storage and placing the completed frames inside. He wouldn't do this experimentation anywhere near a building in the city. Unpleasant experiences taught him that lesson.

Arthur said his goodbyes and walked out of the building. Back on the street, a young man pushing a cart rolled up to him, out of breath.

"Your Majesty," the young man said as he gulped in air, "your magesteel."

"Thank you, young man." Arthur said.

Half a dozen ingots sat on the cart and Arthur waved a hand. The air shimmered beside him as the space turned into the black doorway. He grabbed each ingot and stacked them on the floor inside the portal. When finished, the blackness collapsed on itself and winked out of existence as he dismissed the storage space.

"You're free to go back to work," he told the kid with a wave. The youngster nodded in agreement and rushed off toward the blacksmith.

Arthur followed him at a much slower pace.
The streets were bustling with activity, so he
took his time and enjoyed the sights. The
scent of freshly cut wood filled his nostrils
until he exited the Dark Elf Quarter of the
city. It wasn't long after that the smell of
food from the inn tickled his nose. There was
a hint of water, almost like the smell of rain
mixed with it. People laughed and talked as
they entered and exited the bathhouse.

The last portion of his trip brought him to
the blacksmith and brought with it the smell
of coal and steel. The smaller workshop that
he typically used was clear of people, so he
opened his storage space beside the outdoor
work area. His priority was coating these
frames in a layer of Magesteel. After he
prepped all of them, he could begin the
enchanting work.

Arthur took the frames out and stacked them
against one wall. Wanting to save a little
mana, he used the forge to heat the first
ingot of Magesteel. His Arcane Forging skill
made quick work of the metal and it became a
thin sheet of Magesteel.

His progress hit a snag when he tried to
wrap it around the wooden frame. The metal
could not bend unless he heated it close to
forging temperature. When this happened, the
wood immediately combusted as it came in
contact.

After a bit of scrambling, he finally found
a bucket of sand. With the frame on the dirt
floor, he dumped the sand and smothered the
flame. He used his magic to levitate the
charred wooden frame and examined the damage.

| Item: | **Durability:** 12/20 |
| Sturdy Wooden Frame | |

	Rarity: Common
	Quality: Well Crafted
	Weight: 2.0 kg
	Slot: Crafting Item
	Traits: A small frame built of wood. Commonly used for construction.

Ouch. That did some damage.

The durability hit was a problem, but Arthur didn't want to repeat the mistake on a fresh frame, so he continued his experimentation on this one. When he figured out how to case the wood, he'd use a new frame for the enchanting practice and throw this one away.

Now how do I put hot metal onto a wooden frame?

"What ya up to, Arthur?" Balair asked as he strolled over in his human form.

"Trying to figure out how to wrap these wooden frames in a thin sheet of metal." Arthur said.

"So, what's the problem?"

Arthur motioned at the charred frame floating in the air in front of him. "The hot metal immediately ignites the wood."

"So why keep it hot?" Balair asked.

"How else would I bend it?"

"I think you're looking at this the wrong way," Balair began. "Why would you need all of it hot?"

"Still not following," Arthur said as he threw his hands up in frustration.

"Use your Arcane Forging to turn it into a thin sheet that is the correct length. Cool the metal and place it against the wood. Mark the seam along the edge and remove it. Your control should be good enough to only heat the seam and bend it at a square angle. Repeat the process until the last seam. I'd wrap the surrounding metal on all sides and then weld the final seam with your magic. It might char the corner of the wood a little, but if you did a quick weld and immediately pulled out the heat, the damage would be minor. The corners would be tricky to navigate, but I'm sure you could figure it out."

"That's outstanding. I guess you can still surprise me from time to time. I'll see what I can do."

"Think I'll stick around and watch. Have nothing better to do." Balair said.

Arthur resumed his work and took Balair's advice. The process was slow since he had to stop and mark the seam on each step. The corners didn't perfectly line up on the metal and he decided against trying to join them together for fear the heat would further damage the underlying frame.

He completed his original damaged frame and looked it over. Grabbing it on the sides, he did multiple strength tests, pushing and pulling on it to check for instability. Despite the damage to the wooden core, the piece was sturdy and had little give.

"I think I'll just try the enchantment on this one. Appears to be good." Arthur told Balair.

"I'm just an observer. I'm here to give sage advice and laugh at you when you fail," Balair assured him with a grin.

"Ass," Arthur muttered before turning his attention back to the frame. Luckily, he already knew the enchantment he needed. He'd used it to make the bags of holding multiple times. The tricky part was the keyword. The bags he'd used the Soul Bind ability on but didn't think that would work the same on carts. They would also be too tempting of a target to steal if anyone could use them at will.

Thinking through the issue, he pictured the pattern in his mind. He would add in the keyword toward the beginning as a trigger to activate the spell.

Magic built in the area as Arthur channeled power. He used fine control of his fire magic to char the pattern into the compact frame in front of him.

Arthur carefully wove the intricate design around the surface of the metal until it covered the entire frame and melded back to itself. The new pattern was identical to the one with the bags, only this one had the keyword activation at the beginning of the enchantment.

When the power ebbed, Arthur examined his work. He found two spots that he made a mistake and used a small chisel and hammer to correct it. Satisfied with his work, he dumped in mana to fuel the enchantment. Power rushed out of him and into the frame in a gush before slowing to a steady pour. When it became a trickle, Arthur waited for the final prompt.

You have gained 420 experience in Enchanting.

Sweet!

Arthur took the newfound item in hand and examined it.

<table>
<tr><td>Item:
Magesteel Coated
Storage Frame</td><td>Durability: 155/180

Rarity: Epic

Quality: Well Crafted

Weight: 12.0 kg

Slot: Crafting Item

Traits: A small frame, coated in Magesteel, and enchanted to a Dimensional Storage Space.</td></tr>
</table>

Arthur carried the frame out into the field and stood it on its side. He propped it up using a few pieces of scrap wood and stared at it. Reaching out, he laid a hand on it and said, "Open Sesame" in English.

The script on the frame lit up and glowed white. Arthur felt the power build as the square glowed brighter. Blackness filled in the center of the object and grew outward. The runes began flashing with hints of red and blue, and Arthur frowned.

That doesn't seem right…

"Arthur! Get away from it!" Balair yelled.

Arthur turned to see Balair running from the location at full speed. It confused Arthur for an instant before he caught on. Realizing the enchantment would fail, he raced after Balair. A dozen steps later and Arthur heard a loud explosion followed by a ripple of mana coursing through his body. The power brought pain, but it was the least of his worries as the shock wave of the blast blew him from his feet. He tumbled across the ground before slamming into the wooden planks on the side of the workshop. Wood splintered from the impact and sent slivers and sawdust everywhere.

The area quickly calmed, and Arthur surveyed the damage. Propping himself up on one arm, he winced as he felt a pain in his side. Looking down, a small chunk of wood protruded from him. With a grimace, he pulled it free and quickly cast Minor Heal. The pain subsided, and he stood to his feet. Where the frame once stood now resembled a dried-up pond. A five-foot deep crater with charred edges was all that remained of his work.

Glad I got away from there. That would've been deadly.

Footsteps pounding nearby drew his attention, and Arthur turned to see Balair running his way with Rowan and a handful of assistants. They saw Arthur on his feet and came to a halt.

"You okay?" Rowan asked.

"Yeah. I'm fine. My enchantment wasn't so lucky."

"Why do you always have to blow shit up?" Balair asked.

"Price of progress, I guess." Arthur said.

"Anyone hurt?" Rowan asked as he looked around.

"Balair and I were the only ones here, so everyone should be fine."

"Need any help cleaning up this mess?" Rowan asked.

"I can manage it. I made the mess. I'll clean it up."

"Fine by me. Everyone return to work," Rowan told the workers. They turned and headed for the other buildings. "If you need any help, let me know."

With that, the blacksmith trudged back to his forge and left Arthur standing near the scorched and ruined area.

Arthur sighed, but then got to work. He spent some time fixing the ground and getting everything back in order. He had to flag down one of Rowan's apprentices and get them to send for some replacement planks from the Dark Elves. The few that he broke needed to be replaced. Nearly an hour later, Arthur finally sat at the workbench where his remaining metal frames were.

"Any idea what went wrong?" Balair asked.

Arthur turned to find the dragon leaning against the opening.

"Not entirely sure. I'm positive it has something to do with the activation word. Everything else is from a working enchantment."

"Did you set the same word as the opening and closing, or pick a different one?"

Arthur slapped himself on the forehead. "I'm an idiot."

"Not that I'm arguing with you, but why?" Balair asked.

"I didn't set a closing phrase at all. I just will my storage shut so didn't think about it. The power just kept building as it continued to activate in a loop until it exploded. I'll make sure I use the same phrase to open and close it instead."

"Probably a good idea. I don't think I'll stick around for the fireworks this time. I'm going to go find some other way to waste my time."

"Don't cause any trouble… and don't pee in public!" Arthur yelled at him as he walked off.

Arthur repeated the process with the first frame, this time including the deactivation command as well. He breathed a small sigh of relief as the enchantment sucked out less mana than the previous one. More efficient spells always cost him less, so it was a good sign.

This frame rested in the same place as the last, propped up by new pieces of scrap. He was a little more cautious as he approached, carrying a spare tower shield he found in the shop. "Open Sesame," he said as he touched the frame.

The familiar glow lit up the runes but remained steady and strong this time. No continual building of power. The black dimensional portal popped into place, and Arthur watched it from behind the shield. After a solid minute of no issues, he finally took the time to examine the portal.

This space mirrored those he used for his storage locations. He reached in through the slight frame and could feel the floor and one wall. The space was too large for him to reach the top and the other wall with such a limited area to reach through. Arthur wouldn't try to squeeze through the space either. His last test was to close it using the activation, and it snapped shut without an issue.

Relief flooded him as he realized he'd succeeded. Arthur sat in the open field and basked in his moment of triumph. He couldn't wait too long because he had things to do, so he gathered up the remaining items and tossed them into his storage. He left the frame that he successfully enchanted out for fear placing a pocket inside a pocket might cause some strange reaction.

Arthur made a stop at Rowan's forge to inform him of his success and left the enchanted frame in his care. The man could use it as an enchanting pattern to replicate the process. Arthur planned to do the full-size ones with his arcane forging and inlay them on the inside to make it harder to copy if stolen.

The inn was busy as he approached. Arthur continued inside and found Daniel and Kat. After some discussion, they organized to have the existing carts that could make it back to return to the inn to be fit with the new enchantment.

It took the rest of the day, but the Dark
Elves worked their magic to supply him with
the larger frames. He enchanted them as they
came in and attached them to the next cart in
line. By the time he collapsed at their table
in the inn to eat dinner, he'd retrofitted
eighty percent of their carts with the large
storage enchantments. As he took a bite of the
delicious seared deer steak, he checked over
the experience from his work.

*You have gained 14,110 total experience in
Arcane Smithing.*
*Congratulations, you have reached level 21
in Arcane Smithing. Increases the stats on
items created using this ability by 42%.
Bending metal? That all you can do?*
*You have gained 14,110 total experience in
Blacksmithing.*
*You have gained 2,990 total experience in
Earth and Fire Magic.*
*You have gained 15,770 total experience in
Enchanting.*

*A respectable amount for a day's work.
Guess I can't complain.*
His constant skilling reminded him he'd
forgotten to check his level twenty skills for
Blacksmithing and Arcane Smithing.

*Congratulations, you have reached level 20
in Blacksmithing and have been promoted to
Journeyman in the skill. Please choose one of
the following as a bonus for this achievement:*

Ability: Weaponsmith Specialization	
Requirements: Blacksmithing Type: Passive Ability	Description: Gain an innate understanding of weapons. All weapons you make get the following permanent buffs: • +8 to base attack per rarity level. • +5 to two random stats. • 25% chance for a random enchantment.

Ability: Armorsmith Specialization	
Requirements: Blacksmithing Type: Passive Ability	Description: Gain an innate understanding of armor. All armor you make gets the following permanent buffs: • +8 to base defense per rarity level. • +5 to two random stats. • 25% chance for a random enchantment.
Mastery Level: 1	

Ability: Arcane Metallurgist	
Requirements: Blacksmithing Type: Passive Ability	Description: Gain an innate understanding of magical metals and their alloys. You can sense what metals would make beneficial magical alloys based on your level in Blacksmithing and the level of the materials. This has the potential to discover new and unknown materials.
Mastery Level: 1	

The options all had definite benefits. Either weapon or armor would be great. The raw stats alone would beef up everything he made. While he considered both options, his attention kept going back to the metallurgist passive.

So far, he'd seen nor barely even heard of any metal better than magesteel. While it must exist somewhere, there was no telling how or where it would pop up. Being able to combine magesteel into an alloy with other materials may prove pivotal in moving their metal manufacturing forward. He selected Arcane Metallurgist and moved onto Arcane Smithing's option.

Congratulations, you have reached level 20 in Arcane Smithing and have been promoted to Journeyman in the skill. Please choose one of the following as a bonus for this achievement:

Ability: Natural Enchantments	
Requirements: Arcane Smithing Type: Passive Ability	Description: All items you create with Arcane Smithing have a 25% chance to proc a random enchantment.

Ability: Divine Intervention	
Requirements: Arcane Smithing, Arcane Artificer Class Type: Passive Ability	Description: Enhance the benefits of your Arcane Artificer class as follows: • Ability to create two unique items every seven days. (This requires materials and craftsmanship of exquisite quality to activate) • All weapons created by an Arcane Artificer will have 18% higher damage and +3 additional points to two random stats. • All armor created by an Arcane Artificer will have 18% higher defense and +3 additional points to two random stats.

Spell: Steady Hand	
Requirements: Arcane Smithing Mana Cost: 80 MP Cast Time: 2 seconds Cooldown: 2 hours	Description: The next two items you create after casting this spell have a 90% chance to increase in quality and rarity by 1 level and a 45% chance to increase in quality and rarity by 2 levels.
Mastery Level: 1	

Well, damn. Now what? Arthur asked himself.

The abilities all had merit. He dismissed Divine Intervention right away. The proc rate was so low that he'd created thousands of pieces and only managed a few unique items. The odds of him being lucky enough to ever get two in one week was almost a joke, anyway.

Natural Enchantments was tempting. Being able to randomly create new ones by accident would be outstanding. It also meant he would learn how to make that enchantment, since he was sure they'd come with the necessary script and pattern on them.

In the end, he went with Steady Hand. His biggest issue when crafting now was hitting a ceiling on quality and rarity because of their limited material availability. If he couldn't increase their material quality, the next best thing was an almost guaranteed proc to upgrade.

Happy with his options, he turned his focus back to the few tiny pieces of cold steak on his plate.

Tomorrow, we prepare for war.

Chapter 34

Planning an Overthrow

Arthur surveyed the room. It was early morning, but the inn was nearly empty, save for the council members and select attendees of this meeting. Daniel closed the place for them to keep this private.

He considered having it at the new defensive fortress, but decided he liked the privacy and comfort of the inn. It had been a staple for him since he arrived on this world and, while it had undergone many changes, it still felt like home.

Samson sat to his right while Allendria was on his left. They stacked multiple tables end to end to provide enough space for all the attendees. Tirithan was next to Allendria, and all the council members were present. There was also a select delegation from the city guard and representation from the Dark Elves. Calfuray and Balair rounded out the group in human form.

"I'm pleased everyone could make it," Arthur began. "This is a serious subject that I want to make sure all parties present have a say in. We all know what's at stake here, so let's get right to business. Paladin Samson, status of our forces?"

Samson stood from his chair and addressed the room.

"Our standing force for the mission numbers close to eight hundred. We were fortunate our losses were minimal during our last attack."

He delivered the report easily, but Arthur could feel the pain in that statement.

"All of our men have the newest armor variant to absorb damage. Supplies are ready to move out when needed through storage spaces." Samson said before returning to his seat.

"Did the retrofit work for our leather and cloth wearers?" Arthur asked.

Samson nodded. "The enchantments are working for them as well. They aren't as strong as the mail, but do offer additional protection. The cloth actually fares better than leather right now."

"Why is that?" Arthur asked.

Samson pointed to Katherine. Arthur looked at her, the question in his eyes.

"A new type of cloth. I discovered how to make Mageweave. I invested my talents to unlock it and have passed it on to our tailors. It is more durable and naturally mana infused, so it takes better to enchantments. We don't have an equivalent leather that has the same properties." Kat said.

"Great work, and I applaud your dedication to the city and the craft by helping with the breakthrough." Arthur told her. "That will probably save a lot of lives."

"Thank you, Your Majesty," Kat replied.

"It sounds like our forces are ready for battle. I turn this over to Queen Allendria to confirm her part." Arthur said.

"General Tirithan, status of the Dark Elf forces under your command?" Allendria asked.

Tirithan stood and also delivered his report to the group. "My forces are all well fed and ready for battle. The few injuries we sustained are now healed. Our weaponry and armor are standard, with a few of the officers having better equipment. We also have the provisions for our return trip."

"I apologize, General, but you will have to make do with the armor you have for now. Once the battle is settled, we will retrofit your forces with the better armaments of the kingdom, but if you returned to the city now wearing them, they'd be suspicious." Allendria said.

"I appreciate your concern, Queen Allendria. We will accomplish our mission with what we have."

"That brings us back to the actual battle plan," Arthur interjected.

"The forces under Samson's control will march as we did before when confronting the elves. We will array ourselves in the same battle formations and approach from the same place. We want to make it look like we are making the same mistake twice and rushing in without a plan. Scouts from the rangers will keep an eye out for us and warn us if they try the same trick. It shouldn't be an issue this time, though. General Tirithan's forces will be inside the city and will open the gates for us to gain quick access. Queen Allendria, I leave it to you to assign General Tirithan his engagement orders inside the city." Arthur said.

Arthur and Allendria had both discussed these items and came to the decisions on these matters prior to the meeting. For public appearance, Arthur wanted everyone to know that Allendria was solely in charge of the Dark Elves, and he wouldn't interfere unless asked. Keeping their roles this way helped strengthen both of their ties to their respective people.

"General, the human forces are due to arrive around midday. At daylight, I want your forces to move the citizens to safe locations so they will avoid the fighting. Any people known to be loyal to my uncle are to be kept separate from the others or left in place without being sanctioned away. I will pass judgment on them after we retake the city on a case-by-case basis. Any loyal to my uncle who resists, are to be dealt with swiftly and without mercy. Those who resist but do so out of honor, disarm them and show them mercy. I will also judge their actions before deciding for them. Forces on both sides will do all we can to minimize casualties of non-combatants."

"Understood, Your Majesty." Tirithan said.

"Are there any objections to the proposal?" Arthur asked.

A few murmurs of sound passed through the room as some people talked amongst themselves, but no one spoke up.

"Any suggestions or anything to add?" Arthur asked.

One of the Dark Elves stepped forward with a hand raised, and Arthur nodded to acknowledge him.

"Your Majesty, what's to become of the Dark Elves here? Do we have to return to our old city?"

"All matters of your people fall on your queen, so I'll defer to her."

"Any who wish to stay here are free to do so. When I take over, I hope our people are no longer shut off from the world. I'll encourage them to travel. We need to rejoin civilization and build better relationships," Allendria answered.

"Thank you, my Queen." The man said with a bow.

A woman was the next to step forward. She looked to be in her mid-thirties with dark brunette hair.

"Your Majesty, not to be presumptuous, but what's the plan to end our other war?"

"Not an inappropriate question. Our other opponent has been quiet so far. We might run into some of his forces at the Dark Elf capital, but that's currently unknown. After we have the kingdom of the Dark Elves handed over to Allendria, I plan on marching for King Wailyn as quickly as possible and ending his reign as well. The state of the cities I've traveled to and the forces of theirs I've fought don't worry me too much. I plan on being cautious, but I want to end this all in one fell swoop and begin a time of peace and prosperity for the kingdoms," Arthur said.

The room went quiet after his explanation, and no one else stepped forward.

"Looks like we are ready. General Tirithan, your men return home tomorrow morning. We will follow the morning after, so you have a full day to prepare for our 'pursuit' of your forces. I wish everyone luck." Arthur said.

Everyone stirred from their spots and filtered out of the inn. Arthur and Allendria emerged from the darker interior into the bright sunlight amongst the crowd and headed for their house. Balair and Calfuray came up beside them to follow.

"What is our role in the fighting?" Balair asked.

"Backup and support. We'll have you monitor the flanks to prevent them from surrounding us again. I hope you're not needed in the main fight. It would cause way too much damage and loss of life. I will not hesitate to make that decision if I feel it is necessary, though." Arthur said.

"That okay with you?" Calfuray asked Allendria.

"I agree with Arthur. We've gone over this and both decided to save our forces first. Try to prevent unnecessary damage and loss of life, but don't spare our enemies if push comes to shove." Allendria said.

"Then it is settled," Cal said.

"I'm going to run a few errands and check in with people before we see the Dark Elf army off tomorrow. I'll catch you later." Arthur told them. He leaned over and kissed Allendria on the cheek before he turned and walked off.

His first stop was at the carpenters' workshop for the Dark Elves. Daranth arrived shortly after he did and Arthur spent some time enchanting their latest transportation frames. He also had Arthur put enchantments on some of the equipment around the shop. They'd crafted kilns to dry wood and even steaming boxes to help naturally bend it. Arthur added the needed enchantments to make these work quickly and efficiently.

As he left, Daranth thanked him for his time and wished him luck in the upcoming campaign. Arthur checked on the fields and was amazed. This was one area he always neglected now that he handed off the responsibility. They always praised the construction crews for their work because it was on display all the time. Each day you could watch them as they completed something new and intricate. The farmers worked outside of town and although you could see the farmlands from the city, the sheer scope was hard to grasp. Up close, the plants were monstrous, and the workers wove through the rows, pulling off plump vegetables and loading them into a storage cart. Arthur was happy to see the new carts already put to good use.

That would be tiring to have to load all of this food in baskets or push carts and keep traveling to and from the fields to drop it off. Arthur didn't have an agenda out in the farmlands. He was just enjoying the atmosphere and watching people work. It was rewarding in its own way.

Walking down one row, Arthur brushed his hand along the leaves of the squash plants. The bushes had grown so large they were up to his waist and the rough texture of them scraped against his fingertips. A wooden trellis held up a row of tomato plants, and he walked over and plucked a small red one free before tossing it in his mouth. It burst with flavorful juices before he quickly swallowed the snack.

"Ah, refreshing."

The sun was slowly creeping toward the horizon as he toured the fields, so he headed back toward town. There was one person he wanted to talk to and figured now was as good of a time as any. Winding through the streets, he waved at people as he passed, and finally came to a stop. He knocked on the door and the young man he needed to see answered.

"Hey Rayne," Arthur said with a wave and a smile.

"What's up?"

"Got a few minutes? Just wanted to visit."

"Of course, come on in," Rayne said as he stepped aside and motioned for him to enter.

Arthur entered and walked over to the couch in the room before taking a seat. Rayne followed behind and sat on the small chair across from him.

"How've you been? I've had little time to check in with you since you returned."

"I'm good. Taking it easy. Done a lot of work on my Alchemy lately. Had my fill of fighting back in Seora, so wanted to slow down."

"Good to hear. Getting lost in the conflict and battle for too long is never good. Anything interesting with your Alchemy?" Arthur asked.

"As a matter of fact, yes. Check this out." Rayne said as he stood and walked over to the kitchen area. He grabbed his Bag of Holding off the chair and returned. Fishing inside, he pulled free a vial.

The contents of it were something truly marvelous to view. A silvery liquid constantly swirled inside and as he continued to watch, specks of different colors would appear in the swirl and then dissipate back to silver. Reds, blues, greens, and more flashed through the liquid in a never-ending pattern.

"Take a look," Rayne said as he handed it to him. Arthur cradled it and looked at its properties.

Item: Miracle Chromatic Potion	**Durability**: 40/40 **Rarity**: Unique (20) **Quality**: Masterful **Weight**: 0.8 kg **Slot**: Consumable **Traits**: An extraordinarily rare potion that has the ability to revive even those on the very brink of death.

"That's impressive. You made that?" Arthur asked.

"Yeah, but it was one of those luck of the draw things. I think it's like you making a legendary item with your crafting. I gained a special class with it that made it possible for me to gain Miracle type potions." Rayne explained.

"Super handy skill for sure. Make sure to keep that one safe and only use it in an emergency. Judging by the description, it could literally save a life. Any idea what the twenty means next to Unique?" Arthur asked.

"Not one-hundred percent sure, but I assume it means only twenty of that potion can exist at any one time in the world."

"As good of a guess as I can think of."

"I actually planned on giving it to you and Allendria as a wedding present. Figured it'd make a fitting gift for a king and queen." Rayne told him.

Arthur smiled at him and reached over and patted him on the leg.

"I truly appreciate the gesture, but I think it's safer with you. At least until we finish with the wars and get back to peace. Besides, your Stealth skills make you the best option to save someone in a pinch. You can get to them faster than anyone and usually without being seen or noticed."

"I see your point. You do suck at Stealth," Rayne said with a laugh.

"Sure. Rub it in. Some friend you are," Arthur said while grinning. "I would like to discuss the battle, though. I know we haven't really talked about your part in the fight and I was hoping you'd agree to be by my side for the face-off with Gliran. There is no one, save Allendria, that I trust more at my side and, let's be honest, you're a better fighter than her in one-on-one combat."

Rayne stood up and paced back and forth for a few moments, fiddling with his bracers in some nervous habit Arthur didn't recognize.

"I was afraid you'd ask me that. I guess it is my job to keep you safe."

"Something wrong with your sister? Usually, you have no issue jumping into a fight as long as she's safe." Arthur said.

"No. She's doing great and loves her job. I'm happy she could find some peace here," Rayne said as he waved off Arthur's statement.

Arthur remained quiet and considered his words for a few moments before a grin broke over his face. "What's her name?"

Rayne sighed. "That easy to figure out?"

"Well, people stick with what they are good at. That only changes under a few circumstances, mostly. While I'm sure you're beginning to burn out on the violence and all the fighting, I doubt it's enough to make you turn down the drive for the cause. The second most obvious thing would be you found someone new that you want to be around for." Arthur said.

"Yeah. Guess you're right. The cause still matters to me and I'll do anything you need me to for my duty to the kingdom. I have found someone who I think could make a good partner for me. Her name is Scarlett. She is in the same line of work I am."

"Never pegged you as one to find comfort in the thought of being with a spy. Seems like a lot of deception might be involved and could cause trust issues. I'm sure you have your reasons and if you're happy, then go for it. I won't stop you. I just hope you find happiness in the end."

"Me too. My previous relationships haven't been the best," Rayne mumbled.

Arthur stood and walked up to Rayne, placing his hand on the man's shoulder and holding him still. "I need your help. Not just as the king, but as your friend."

"I couldn't turn you down if I wanted.
Let's finish this fight and take out Gliran
and Wailyn. I look forward to a quiet bit of
reflection when it is all settled."

"Start looking for a replacement, or at
least some underlings, to take over your
position as spy master, then." Arthur
suggested.

"I don't fear that job. Who knows, I may
end up with Scarlett and we run it as a team."

"Okay, lover boy. How about you take it one
step at a time? I also would need to meet and
approve of her, if that's the case."

"Yeah, yeah. If it helps, she withstood
torture and held to our side during the
problems in Seora. She kept advocating to stay
loyal to you."

"Definitely helps. I'll keep it in mind."
Arthur said as he gave Rayne one last pat on
the shoulder. "I'm going to head out so you
can start planning your wedding. Still have
preparations to make."

Rayne punched him on the shoulder. "Fine.
See if you're invited." Before laughing and
saying his goodbyes.

Arthur returned to the streets and
continued his journey around the city.

* * *

King Wailyn paced through his private office. His latest report from the Dark Elves offered some hope. He was ecstatic that they drove Arthur's army from the city and even cursed his dragon. Unfortunately, almost all of his army still survived the withdraw and they couldn't penetrate some new barrier over Alurian. This part worried him more than anything else. That type of magic would draw the wrong attention.

"That bastard will ruin everything," Wailyn grumbled as he slammed a fist on the edge of his desk.

"It would indeed," a low voice said from the corner of the room.

Wailyn jerked his head toward the sound and watched a narrow figure emerge. A cloak hid their large form, and a hood covered their face, but he could see the trademark blue skin on the hands and understood the deeper meaning of the message.

"My apologies, ambassador. If I knew to expect you, I would've prepared a better welcome."

"You and I both know why I'm here, and it isn't for a pompous ceremony. This issue needs to be dealt with. Now. If you can't handle it, we will step in. That won't bode well for you."

"I've been nothing but faithful to the empire this entire time. I'll deal with it. One of my allies has a plan and has gathered additional forces of his own. The issue should be resolved shortly." Wailyn said.

"For your sake, it better. You're only allowed to keep this position because of your work so far. Screwing up on this level can be a quick way to a demotion. I'm sure you're aware of what a demotion under the empire means?" The ambassador asked.

"I am. I will fix this," Wailyn reiterated.

"We shall see," the ambassador said before a flash of light enveloped him and his form disappeared.

"Damn Ar'Tookans. This is my kingdom. Not theirs." Wailyn raged. "Gliran's plan better succeed. If not, he better hope he dies before I get him."

Chapter 35

Unexpected Allies

Arthur surveyed the gathered force. Heavy plate armor and kite shields adorned the first row of fighters. Their front line protected most of the army from heavy attacks, and their shields projected a field out to intercept magical spells.

Behind them stood a contingent of archers, mostly clad in chain and leather. The trademark feathers of Hellfire Arrows stuck out of many of their quivers. Others contained deadly steel arrows, ready to fly into enemies.

Taking up the rear of the formation was the mage corp. Clad in their robes, now complete with some underlying metal enchantment plates, they were ready for battle. Arthur could feel the power emanating from some of the higher-level ones as they slowly built their strength to prepare for the attack.

The last group of fighters was nowhere to be found. By design. Their newly formed squad of infiltrators would use stealth to infiltrate the city and assist their Dark Elf allies with holding the enemy forces in place.

Samson stood by his side. His paladin armor having an impressive effect on those assembled before them. Allendria looked radiant in her newest outfit. They'd taken her damage absorption armor and added purple fabrics to give it a more feminine, yet still fierce, look. Her dark hair flowed down her back and her eyes glowed with power.

"Fellow warriors. Today we are here to right a wrong. The evil tyrant who holds this city has murdered innocents to gain his position and has taken the rightful crown from my soon to be queen. They also made the mistake of declaring war on our kingdom. If we wish there to be peace in Dravincia, it's time for us to cross this first major hurdle. If all goes according to plan, there shouldn't be a lot of fighting and minimal death. Spare those you can, but show no mercy to those aligned with our enemy. When those gates open," Arthur said, pointing toward the large wooden gates in the wall of woven branches, "we charge in and fill the breach. Allied Dark Elf forces are wearing purple armbands. Wait for Paladin Samson to give the signal and let's end this war!"

A cheer rose from the gathered soldiers. Arthur turned toward the wall and watched in satisfaction as the Dark Elves manning it shuffled their feet in a fit of nervousness. He glanced at the Raid notice.

Raiding the Capital… Again	
Requirements: Participate in actions to directly or indirectly influence the outcome of the raid.	Description: A new started near Calzas either side in the the side you assist the raid, you recei rewards.

Rewards: 48,000 experience,
5 Talent Points, 3 Spell
Blade Talent Points

"You ready for this?" Arthur asked as he turned to face Allendria.

"As ready as I can be. I hope the plan works as we hoped and we can avoid death, but I'll not make the same mistake twice. This ends today. One way or another." She said.

"Samson. You ready?" Arthur asked, turning toward the paladin.

"The Goddess will protect us today. I have faith in that. It's time to root out this evil." Samson said.

"How about you, Rayne?" Arthur asked.

"You guys make this feel like we are attending a funeral. So dreary and serious. I'm just ready for you to chill out. Let's get this over with and maybe it'll do the job." Rayne said.

Arthur chuckled at his friend and watched the wall in silence. They observed the enemy forces for a few minutes. The slow creaking of armor was the only sound they could hear from the surrounding forces.

"Well damn. No one bothers to ask how I'm doing or if I'm ready. Makes me feel a little left out," Wesley grumbled.

"You're still here?" Arthur asked with a grin.

"Of course I am. Without me here, you're sure to run out of luck and die horribly. My dashing good looks and killer instrument will sway this battle."

"Just don't die. It's nice having someone I can talk to from back home." Arthur said.

"Noted. I prefer that as well."

The sun slowly rose on the horizon and gently drifted overhead. Arthur saw the flash of red and orange to the east and knew that Balair patrolled that side looking for enemies. Looking west, he spotted the purple scales of Calfuray glistening in the rays of the sun. Hopefully, their presence would prevent an attack like last time. Even if the army tried to box them in, they just had to reach the gate first and take the city. It would be much easier playing defense and forcing the Dark Elves to siege their own fortifications.

"Everyone look alive," Samson shouted. "Time for one last check on your gear. Make sure you have your emergency potions handy and your armor is trussed."

Arthur watched the gates slowly creep open. The few guards he could make out on the wall saw the movement and focused on the gate. It was difficult from this distance to see their expressions, but judging by the yelling he heard across the space, he knew it was a mixture of rage and fear.

"Soldiers. Charge and maintain formation until we breach the gate. Spread out to your defined section of the city and begin assisting our allies." Samson called over the group.

Arthur drew Ember and bellowed a war cry. The adrenaline rush fueled him forward in a light jog. He wasn't able to run full speed or he would outpace the rest of the formation and be on his own.

The distance closed much faster than Arthur expected, and within moments, many of the defenders registered what was happening. Some had the presence of mind to fight against their force. Arrows flew and spells crackled through the air. Arthur watched Samson catch a sizzling bolt on his shield and bat it away as if it was a baseball. Allendria blasted an orb of fire from her palm that intercepting another spell from the defenders. Arthur didn't know exactly what it was, but he could feel the primary element was Earth Magic.

Arthur ducked under an incoming arrow and twisted to the side to avoid another aimed for his head. He wasn't truly worried about them. His armor would absorb the damage, but he wanted to preserve as much power as he could for this fight. Taking down Gliran wouldn't be simple.

We've got company. They are trying the flanking maneuver from last time again. Calfuray warned.

They are moving on my side as well. Balair confirmed.

Thanks for the warning. Hold to your sides. We may have you rain fire on them if we feel it is necessary. We should be firmly entrenched on the wall before they can arrive.

"Samson. Flanking maneuver has begun." Arthur said.

Samson nodded and called out. "All reserve units assist the wall teams in clearing out. Prepare to defend against a rear assault."

A chorus of acknowledgments filled the air as they continued to dodge projectiles and spells. A handful of their forces launched return spells and arrows, but none were aiming for serious damage. It was primarily cover fire to distract the defenders.

Their group funneled through the gate, and Arthur spotted General Tirithan waiting for him and Allendria. They approached the elf for his report.

"My Queen," he said with a bow. "We have the civilians secluded in safe areas. There are a few malcontents still out, but nothing dangerous. Some of Gliran's loyal retainers are secluded in the main keep with him. Our teams are waiting on your forces to take the walls."

"Thank you, General. Our teams are on route to your forces. We received word they began the flanking maneuver from before. We want to be firmly entrenched and ready to defend. Order your forces to close the gate when the last of our army makes it through."

"Do you really want to cut off a possible exit?" He asked.

"This ends today. I have faith we will prevail." Allendria said.

"As you wish," Tirithan said and called orders to some of his nearby lieutenants.

Arthur saw the nearly silent gates start moving in the other direction.

Their engineering must be fantastic for the lack of noise.

"General, we are heading for the main keep. Do you need help with anything?" Arthur asked.

"No, but I'm going with you. I have to see the tyrant fall myself."

"I'm not going to stop you. We can…" A giant crash sounded outside the wall and Arthur turned to see a plume of dust and dirt fill the sky.

"What the f…" Arthur said before an urgent call entered his thoughts.

We have trouble. They have a dragon. He just knocked Balair from the sky.

He? You know him? Arthur asked.

Of course. His name is Garthool. He's from the Aspect of Rage clan.

Can you handle him? Arthur asked.

If Balair will get off his scaly ass, we should be able to take him.

Hey! That fucking hurt. Bastard sucker punched me. Balair groaned.

Dust off your skirt, princess, and get back in the air. Calfuray said.

I won't risk it. I'm coming to help. Balair, I'll meet you at your nap site. Arthur sent.

Dick. Balair sent.

"Change of plans," Arthur told Tirithan and Allendria. "Looks like Gliran recruited a dragon. I'm going to go assist in the fight. You two head for Gliran. I'll catch up as soon as I finish."

"Be careful," Allendria said as she grabbed his arm and kissed his cheek.

"I'm always careful," Arthur said with a grin before turning to Rayne. "Keep her safe."

"Always." The young man answered.

"Let's go," Allendria said.

Heeding Allendria's orders, the group marched forward.

"Think I'll head for the walls. Not every day a bard gets to witness a dragon fight. I can imagine the epic ballad about it." Wesley said.

"Feel free. Keep your head down." Arthur said as he charged toward the gate.

No longer restricted in his speed, he zipped through the entrance and found Balair seated like a dog and waiting for him. Cratered ground surrounded him, and he looked like a scolded puppy.

"Head up. We are going to go kick his ass."
Arthur said as he ran over and leaped on
Balair's back. "Hi-yo, Silver, away!"

"What the hell is that?" Balair asked.

"Just go." Arthur said.

Balair launched from the ground and Arthur
felt the pressure force him onto his back. A
cry of pain worried him and he turned to see
Garthool and Calfuray locked in midair. She
had her mouth around his neck and his claws
were scraping one of her rear legs, leaving
gouges and trails of blood.

*If I crash into them, I'm bound to hurt
Cal. Not sure I can engage as the situation
is.* Balair said.

*Can you disengage so we can swoop in for an
attack?* Arthur asked Cal.

*Yeah. This asshole is clawing the shit out
of my leg.*

Balair pumped his wings to gain speed, and
Arthur readied his weapon. He activated the
flame ability and also charged it with his
Spellblade lightning power.

*I'm going to do something stupid. One of
you catch me.* Arthur told them.

*I know good and damn well Allendria told
you not to.* Cal said.

She's not here to stop me.

*I'm going on the record as being opposed to
this when she kicks your ass.* Balair said.

Arthur stood on Balair's back and used his
free hand to hold on to one of the spine
ridges. The wind whipped at him and threatened
to blow him off, but he held on tight.

Instead of letting it deter him, he changed tactics. Arthur summoned his mana and began weaving Air Magic. He encapsulated himself in the power and made a small downward force push on him. This stopped most of the air from in front of him and also allowed him to stand much easier. To test it, he even removed his hand from the spine and took a few steps. It felt almost identical to walking on the ground and it pleased him he could move freely.

Congratulations, you have discovered the Air Magic Spell: Aerial Footing. You have gained 250 experience in Air Magic for discovering a known spell.

Spell: Aerial Footing	
Requirements: Air Magic Mana Cost: 2 MP/second channeled Cast Time: 1 seconds Distance: Self	Description: Use the power of air to hold yourself to a solid object.
Mastery Level: 1	

The enemy dragon's form grew larger as they approached the aerial battle. From a distance it was difficult to tell, but up close, this dragon was definitely bigger than Cal, which meant he was massive compared to Balair.

Black scales covered the beast, and spikes swooped backward from his head, appearing like a spiky mane. Arthur was happy that the head itself was relatively smooth.

Balair extending his claws toward the creature and Calfuray released her bite. She dropped straight down and out of the way as Balair slammed into the dragon and dug claws into his chest. Arthur jumped at the dragon's face and poured mana into Aerial Footing as he landed to hold him in place. He saw the dragon's eyes widen as he stared at the small human resting on his snout.

"No one hurts my friends." Arthur said.

Arthur took a step forward before Garthool jerked his head upward. The movement caught him off guard and he lost control of his Aerial Footing spell. He flew up in the air before he pushed a burst of Air Magic over himself that sent him downward with a lot of force. With both hands around Ember's hilt, he pointed it downward and the power behind the thrust caused the blade to crunch through the top layer of scales and punch farther down into its skull.

Electricity sizzled through the beast, and Arthur watched one of his eyes twitch in response to the current. The flame on the sword also went to work and the smell of burning flesh filled the air as the scales near the entry blackened.

You have dealt 425 damage to Garthool with Ember. (Critical Hit) (Crushing Blow)

A roar of anguish filled the air as the electricity effect faded and Arthur felt as though his eardrums may burst. Knowing his sword could only penetrate the dragon's skull so far, he twisted and rocked on the blade to open the wound and enlarge it. The dragon tried to buck him off again, but Arthur held firm on Ember and his spell. The movements did more to help him widen the wound than dislodge him.

The sword slipped free as the wound grew and Arthur deactivated its powers. He slid it back in its scabbard and built up more mana. A small red ball of swirling energy formed in each of his hands and he continued to pump power into them. The spinning power grew more frantic and moved quicker with each rotation. He clapped his hands together and the balls of power merged, becoming one large orb of energy.

Fifteen feet in front of him, the dragon's enormous eyes narrowed. A claw swiped forward and crashed into Arthur's chest. The thick nails scraped across his metal armor and he fell backward, landing on the tip of its nose.

Garthool dealt 0 damage to you with Claw. (210 negated)

Arthur rolled back to his stomach and pushed back to his feet. His spell fizzled during the attack, causing backlash.

You have suffered 80 damage from Magical Backlash. (215 negated)

His head ached from the backlash effects, which was why he assumed his armor didn't absorb all the damage. Some of it was purely internal.

Garthool rolled in flight and Arthur crouched down, making it easier for him to stay anchored with his magic as the world spun.

His spell was on cooldown now from the backlash, so he pulled Ember free again and reactivated his electricity enchantment on it. Bringing his Enchanted Magesteel Dagger into his other hand, he slashed it into a groove in the scales. It took three swiped and two heavy stabs to break through the scales and tough hide, but as soon as it was exposed, he followed with Ember.

Arthur conjured an Ice Spear and plucked it out of the air before removing Ember and stabbing with the ice.

You have dealt 15 damage to Garthool with Enchanted Magesteel Dagger. (x3)
You have dealt 24 damage to Garthool with Enchanted Magesteel Dagger. (x2)
You have dealt 110 damage to Garthool with Ember. (Crushing Blow)
You have dealt 210 damage to Garthool with Ice Spear. (Elemental Weakness)

Another claw swooped over the snout and Arthur ducked to the side, narrowly avoiding the long talon as it passed inches from his face.

A red arm gouged a furrow near his foot as Balair continued to fight against the larger foe.

Time for the original plan.

Arthur quickly spun up another Dual Cast Fireblast.

"This is going to hurt." He told the dragon before launching it directly at the wound. As soon as it left his hand, he turned and took three long strides.

Disengage and back off. He called to his companions as he hurtled off the dragon's snout. A concussive blast filled the air and launched him farther away, causing him to lose a grip on his Air Magic and begin tumbling. Something hard slammed into his shoulder and sent him spinning faster.

You have dealt 885 damage to Garthool with Dual Cast Fireblast. (Critical Hit) (Mortal Blow)

You have taken 0 damage from Concussive Blast. (35 negated)

You have taken 0 damage from Projectile Dragon Scale. (65 negated)

His vision became a blur of color as his view shifted from sky to ground in rapid succession. Wrestling with his control, he gauged his spin and sent out two quick bursts of Air Magic that helped slow his rotation. He couldn't stop it completely, but he also no longer felt like he wanted to vomit.

The ground grew closer as he continued his efforts to manipulate Air Magic and slow his fall while stopping the rest of his spin. Panic set in as time moved. His heart thundered in his chest as his view of the ground grew in clarity. The closer it became, the more details he could see.

Making out the forms of the elven forces trying to attack them from behind was a simple task, but as he grew closer, he noticed the styles of their armor and weapons. The added clarity did nothing for his sense of safety and caused his panic to rise.

A little help here! Arthur screamed into their bond.

The ground was close enough for him to see the swaying of grass in the breeze when a pair of talons wrapped around his body. A flap of wings buffeted him with air while the change in momentum reminded him of hitting the bottom arc of a roller coaster right as it rose again.

What the hell took you so long? I could almost count the buttons on the elves uniforms I was so close to the ground. Arthur said.

Your explosion knocked us backward as well, and we had to regain our own balance and right ourselves first. Cal said.

Oh. Didn't think about that. Probably should've given you more of a heads up, huh?

Well, you told us you were going to do something stupid, so mission accomplished. Balair said.

Balair dropped him the last few feet to land on his side with a thud before landing beside him.

You have taken 0 damage from Fall. (20 negated)

You are afflicted with Lost Air for 3 seconds.

Arthur gasped as his breath left him from the impact and rolled to his stomach. He pushed himself up to a kneeling position and tried to stretch his arms over his head to help him breathe.

"What was that for?" Arthur wheezed.

"Because you're a dumbass." Balair answered.

"Guess that's fair enough." Arthur said.

The enemy dragon wasn't visible in the sky. Confused, he looked around, trying to ensure he was looking the right direction after all the action. Movement on the ground caught his eye, and he stopped to focus on it. The large black dragon stood and shook the dirt and debris off itself and swung its head in his direction. Blazing fire filled its eyes, and Arthur gulped at the sight.

"I think I pissed him off." Arthur said.

"Without a doubt. That's usually Balair's job." Calfuray said as she landed near them.

After he shook off the initial batch of fear, Arthur noticed the damage. A large chunk of flesh was missing from the dragon's face. Shards of bone protruded from a shattered snout. Thick blood oozed from much of the damage and charred flesh and scales covered the parts that weren't bleeding. Arthur activated Scan.

Name: Garthool	
Level: 45	
Type: Dragon	
Rarity: Rare	
HP: 10191/14000	
MP: 2910/3000	
Stamina: 4820/6000	
Strength: ?	Experience: N/A
Agility: ?	Skills

Intellect: ?	Combat Skills:
Wisdom: ?	
Endurance: ?	?: ? (???/???)
Charisma: ?	?: ? (???/???)
Luck: ?	

Damn. He's too high of a level to see any of his abilities. Luckily, he's taking bleed damage from the attacks and his fight with Balair and Allendria also lost him additional health.

"That's a lot of health to chip away." Arthur mused.

"What's the plan? Are we trying to kill him or just damage him enough for him to flee?" Cal asked.

"Good question. I rarely like leaving enemies alive. That's a good way for them to come back and attack you at a worse moment. Any objections to finishing him?" Arthur asked.

"I'm game." Balair said.

"He started this. Let's end it." Cal agreed.

"I'll keep attacking the damaged part of his face. You two keep him distracted and do whatever damage you can," Arthur said.

Both grumbled in agreement and launched forward with growls. Balair stayed on the ground and galloped forward on all four legs, accumulating speed. Calfuray took to the air but remained low to the ground, also on a collision course.

Arthur followed as close as he could, but he couldn't match their speed as a human. Garthool watched them approach and crouched down with his tail up in the air, as though a cat waiting to pounce. His gaze lingered on both before he locked onto Calfuray, apparently choosing her as the larger threat.

Arthur chuckled at the reaction. Although it was probably the correct one, he knew Balair was tenacious, even if he was small. His Fireblast spell was on cooldown so he drew Ember again and activated its flame ability and charged it with lightning.

A gesture and a thought with his off-hand produced a rift in the air and he stabbed through it with all his power. He felt the resistance as he looked at Garthool and saw the corresponding portal hovering on the edge of the gaping wound. His blade stuck deep and scraped along the edge of exposed bone. The dragon howled in fury as the electricity spread through his face.

At the same time, Balair neared him and leaped forward. He used his wings for one last push to speed up even faster and passed right by his face. Balair's right claw caught the damaged snout and ripped a large gash down the side.

Calfuray followed this by diving for him and swinging her body around in an arc. She smashed her tail directly into his back, creating a loud thud as Garthool collapsed face first into the dirt. Dust and leaves clouded the space as clumps of dirt pelted the immediate area.

Arthur maintained a grip on Ember and it slid free as the dragon toppled. He pulled it back and closed the small rift.

*You have dealt 315 damage to Garthool with
Ember. (Critical Hit)*

Arthur checked his hidden logs to see what
Balair and Cal inflicted on Garthool.

*Balair dealt 495 damage to Garthool with
Claw Swipe. (Critical Hit)*
*Calfuray dealt 625 damage to Garthool with
Tail Smash.*

Don't hold back now. Keep hammering at him.
Arthur said.

Balair turned in a large arc to maintain
his momentum and charged for another attack.
The small dragon jumped onto Garthool's head
and pushed down with all his weight. Claws dug
through scales and Balair jumped again,
ripping free chunks as flesh and scales
showered the air.

Calfuray followed by landing on the beast's
body and pinning his neck down with her front
claw. She reared back and sucked in a large
gulp of air before leaning forward and spewing
fire directly onto his head. The flames burned
hot and Arthur had to stop his approach even
with his heat resistance from Fire Magic.

The ground around the attack blackened and
cracked. Smoke poured from the burning
vegetation and obscured the air. Calfuray
ceased the onslaught as her breath ran out.

Garthool's black scales were glowing with a
super-heated red light, the ones near the
glowing portions looked dull and streaked with
gray ash. A swipe from Calfuray caused another
shower of partially molten scales to fill the
air, and Garthool's flesh separated down to
the bone as her claws dug massive furrows.

Arthur capitalized on Cal's attack with one of his own. He considered piling on more fire, but his best attack was still on cooldown from the dual use. Instead, he opted for the opposite. Mana poured through him as he gathered an enormous bubble of water to hover over the dragon's head. When it reached the size of a smart car, he used his Fire Magic to suck all the heat out and flash freeze it. The shape resembled a stake pointed directly downward.

He released his hold on the magic, and the spike plummeted toward Garthool. Calfuray spotted the attack and disengaged. The spike gained speed as it fell before crunching into the side of his jaw, sending shards of glittering ice in all directions.

You have dealt 1,235 damage to Garthool with Ice Spike. (Critical Hit) (Elemental Weakness) (Mortal Blow)

Garthool flailed at the impact and tried to stand before Balair jumped forward and landed on the remnants of the ice spike, driving it deeper. Garthool's wings snapped out and connected with Balair. The impact sent him flying a few dozen yards from the fight as he crashed into the dirt.

Arthur did another quick Scan to see the total of the damage, ignoring the worthless parts of the screen.

```
Name: Garthool
Level: 45
Type: Dragon
Rarity: Rare
HP: 5244/14000
MP: 2650/3000
```

"Do you yield!" Arthur yelled to Garthool.

The enormous dragon pushed back to a standing position and glared at Arthur. Blood and gore hung from his face in loose strands. Much of his upper snout was destroyed and Arthur could see into his throat from the gaping hole in the middle.

"I'll never surrender to human filth." Garthool grumbled.

"But you'll side with the Dark Elves? Doesn't seem very noble of a dragon." Calfuray hissed.

"Don't speak of nobility to me when you reawakened the bond with the humans."

"I upheld my honor and my family's oath. You are here out of spite. Pathetic for a so-called noble clan of dragons." Cal said.

"You won't win. The other dragon families won't allow it." Garthool said.

"She's not alone," Arthur said. "We will end this once and for all."

Everyone sprang back to action in an instant. Arthur powered Ember with fire and electricity and gestured to pop open a rift. He set the exit portal for a space next to Garthool's eye. In a quick thrust, he popped Ember through the portal and into Garthool's fiery orb. The dragon roared with rage and hot fluid splashed back through the rift to coat Arthur's arm in slimy goo.

You have dealt 385 damage to Garthool with Ember. (Critical Hit) (Blinding Strike)

Balair followed with another slash of claws while Calfuray used her tail as a club to bludgeon him again. Garthool crashed to the ground a few yards from the attack.

Arthur felt power building near Garthool. The energy felt dark and malevolent, but he couldn't pinpoint the magic. Thick black smoke poured from the dragon in all directions, blanketing the ground and obscuring the area.

"We'll finish this later." Garthool said before a gust of wind pushed Arthur back. The smoke swirled faster and filled the entire space in front of the city.

Can you see him? Arthur asked into the bond.

No. This smoke is blanketing too far. Cal said.

Damn. I guess we have to let him go. Don't want to take the chance of you chasing him and it being a trap. You two keep an eye out here and try to deter the Dark Elves from attacking our allies. The ones trying to flank us are in this clearing somewhere. I'm going to find Allendria. Arthur said.

"Go get her. We'll coordinate with Samson to get this cleaned up out here." Balair said.

Arthur dropped the fire and electricity from his blade, put it into his scabbard, and dashed toward the castle.

Chapter 36

Taking Down a King

Rayne followed behind Allendria and Tirithan as they walked through the main keep. Both were intimately familiar with the layout, so there was no stopping to question the route or second guessing a turn. Each moved with precision and wasted no time.

His gaze watched everything they didn't examine. Every shadow reached out to his senses as he scanned every nook and cranny he could find along their route. A well-hidden poison arrow from an assassin might end up dooming them.

The interior felt like any normal stone building he'd explored. Light gray rock covered the walls, and the elves decorated the ceilings with intricately carved beams of wood. They made the main floor of an aged wood that Rayne couldn't identify, and it appeared crafted from a single piece of wood. Rayne now knew the elves used magic to meld it together. He'd watched Daranth and his workers perform their woodworking magic and understood that was the only way a feat such as this could work.

"Seems awfully empty in here," Allendria said.

"Would seem so. I'd like to take credit and say we did a thorough job of clearing everyone out, but I know we avoided much of the main castle, so we wouldn't draw suspicion." Tirithan said.

"He seems to be a pretty common bad guy, so I'm going to assume he gathered his most loyal followers to him and we will have to face them in the chamber before his," Allendria said.

Tirithan turned the next corner. "Your Majesty. I'm not sure how him being a bad guy is related to that behavior."

"Sorry, General. I think I've been around Arthur too long. It's something he would say based on his home. He'd called Gliran a textbook bad guy," Allendria said with a smile.

"I'll take your word for it." Tirithan said.

"Are there any magical defenses here we need to worry about?" Rayne asked.

"A few wards, but nothing that can harm us," Tirithan said with a wave of dismissal.

Rayne continued his march behind the group and kept observing their surroundings. The clomp of footsteps drew his attention, and he spun to look behind them, hand on his daggers.

A group of a dozen armored men and women approached. Most wore leather armor, but a handful had chain and two of them wore full plate suits with large kite shields.

"General," the leading warrior said as she stood up straight and brought her right hand to her chest over the heart in a salute. "The entrance to the castle is secure and I have search teams scouring the place as you requested. Figured we should tag along and help with your fight."

"We appreciate the assistance." Tirithan said.

"What's your name, soldier?" Allendria asked.

"Nadeen, Your Majesty," she said with a quick bow.

"It's always nice to have competent people around to orchestrate things. I'll keep you in mind." Allendria said.

Rayne noticed a slight blush on the soldier's cheeks before she nodded and returned to her place in the formation with the rest of the newly arrived fighters.

The group closed into a tighter formation and continued forward. The two plate fighters took the lead, and they marched through the hallways until Tirithan brought them to a halt. He pointed at a corridor opening ahead of them.

"If your guess about his intentions is true, we will face his underlings in the next room." Tirithan told Allendria.

"Everyone, get ready for a fight. Protect each other and end it quickly. No mercy for any who stand and fight in there." Allendria said.

The group unsheathed weapons. Rayne pulled his daggers free, took a few steps away, and melded into the shadows.

You have activated Stealth.

His breathing slowed, and his attention snapped into focus. He was entering a dangerous area and he could feel the anticipation as his heartbeat sped up in direct contrast to his breathing.

Tirithan gave the order, and the assembled force rounded the corner, walking in a tight formation. The way forward appeared clear and Rayne detected no traps or anything suspicious as he took the lead.

Ahead of them was a room that appeared empty. He suspected the others waited in ambush on each side, where they wouldn't be visible to the hall.

Allendria tapped Tirithan on the shoulder and he lifted his hand to call everyone to a halt. She turned toward their group and motioned for them to be silent and cover their eyes. They did as requested, and Rayne smiled as he realized what she would do. He knew she had the benefit of being with Arthur all the time, and he was not shy about teaching her any magic he'd learned.

Rayne dipped his head down and waited for a moment. Light flashed in the room ahead of them and he quickly squeezed his eyes shut to avoid losing his vision. Yells of confusion filled the area. The light faded, and Allendria called for everyone to attack.

His eyes snapped open, and he rushed into the room, still concealed by his stealth. Everywhere he looked, fighters stumbled around and held their hands over their faces. Some of them stood with their jaws slack, frantically blinking, trying to restore vision. Others buried their fists into their eyes, trying to rub them clear.

He picked out a person toward the back that didn't look as disoriented as the rest and threw a knife. In rapid succession, he picked out three other targets and did the same before rushing headfirst into the nearest warrior. When he was within striking distance, he spun to the side and thrust his stiletto dagger into the man's armpit.

Hot blood gushed out as he withdrew the blade, and a line of blood splattered from the weapon. He buried the swordbreaker into the fighter's thigh and gave it a quick twist. The man screamed in pain and crumpled to the ground.

You have dealt 85 damage to Lackey with Enchanted Steel Throwing Dagger. (x4)
You have dealt 215 damage to Lackey with Enchanted Magesteel Stiletto Dagger. (Critical Hit) (Mortal Blow)
You have dealt 115 damage to Lackey with Enchanted Magesteel Swordbreaker. (Crippling Strike) (Critical Hit)

Grunts of pain and screams of rage filled the area as Rayne surveyed the room. Their allied warriors were making quick work of the enemies. A handful were now back in fighting shape and doing their best to attack back. Rayne rushed to one who was currently in a sword fight with Nadeen. He came up behind the man and planted both daggers. The lackey arched his back and stood up straight as he yelled in pain, right before Nadeen removed his head with a swipe of her sword.

You have dealt 185 damage to Lackey with Double Strike. (Critical Hit)

"Thanks for the assist," Nadeen told him.

Rayne nodded and moved to find another target. Allendria faced off with another enemy using her staff, but Rayne dismissed it. He could tell she was toying with him more than anything. *Probably treating it as a warmup.*

Rayne found two more targets and launched more daggers before spinning around the room again and noticing every enemy was down. Tirithan issued orders for them to scour the bodies for weapons and move them to the edges of the room and out of the way. He wanted the path kept clear. Rayne wandered through the bodies and retrieved his daggers from their unsuspecting victims. The shared experience from them wasn't bad.

You have dealt 85 damage to Lackey with Enchanted Steel Throwing Dagger. (x2)

Lackey (x8) has died.

You have gained 1,920 total experience.

You have gained 420 total experience in Throwing Knives.

You have gained 210 total experience in Small Blades.

You have gained 210 total experience in Dual Wield.

You have gained 105 total experience in Stealth.

"That felt a little too easy," Rayne said as he walked up to Allendria.

"Are you trying to jinx this?" Allendria asked as she rolled her eyes at him.

A loud crashing noise reverberated through the halls and caused the ground to tremble. Rayne felt the impact through his boots and shuddered.

"I assume that's the dragon battle right outside the wall. We have to keep moving." Rayne said as he motioned her toward the door.

The group assembled back into formation and continued for the ornate double doors on the other end of the room. Allendria reached it first and ran a hand over the intricate script carved into the wooden structure.

"What does it say?" Rayne asked.

"It's the history of our people. This tells the story of our earliest descendants as they try to conquer the wilds and establish this very city. It continues all the way until my father's rule," she said as she followed the script to its abrupt end. "Thankfully, Gliran hasn't added his story. When we defeat him, I'll see that they do not mention his name on these hallowed artifacts."

Allendria pushed the doors, and they swung open with ease. A lone elf sat on a large throne on the other side of the room. Rayne didn't see anyone else in the surrounding area, but he wouldn't let his guard down.

The man on the throne had the facial features of a middle-aged human man. Small wrinkles covered the edges of his eyes and mouth while his long black hair contained streaks of bright silver. His neatly trimmed mustache and beard mirrored the hair color. Rayne assumed the silver was the equivalent of gray hair in humans.

Allendria strode forward with confidence, boots clacking on the stone floor.

"Your time is over, traitor. I'll end you for what you did to my father." Allendria said.

Gliran sighed and pushed himself to his feet. "Your father was a fool and would have been the end of this world as we know it. His tolerance of the old human king and their dangerous ideas would only lead to doom."

"I'm not interested in your lies and excuses. You were always a backstabbing coward and my father should have removed you from our society long ago. His love of family was a weakness you played well. I'm taking my throne back and returning our people to the world again."

"So be it. I never wanted to kill you, but it's better than losing everything." Gliran said.

A large two-handed axe appeared in his hands and he smirked at them. Rayne wasn't fond of the idea that he may have access to some kind of dimensional space. Orange and red light pulled Rayne's focus back to Allendria as she dumped Fire Magic into both hands.

Rayne smiled when he recognized Arthur's favorite spell and Allendria was ready to dual cast it. The two orbs flashed forward and headed directly for Gliran. He frowned at the approaching spells before raising the metal head of his axe in front of him to block.

Fire exploded as the balls of power hit the axe. The inferno rolled over the king and engulfed the area. Allendria asserted her Pyromancer power and gathered the fire and began moving it in a vortex. The flame burned hotter as it began bright red and shifted to orange. From there, it continued to flare as it turned light blue.

Stone charred near the flame as the fire finally died and Allendria dropped her hands back to her side. Smoke filled the room but was quickly filtering out of a fireplace chimney and a nearby window.

As the smoke thinned, Rayne noticed the stone where the fire had been was solid black, and thick cracks covered the surface. The space immediately surrounding the king appeared untouched. A shimmering field faded and Gliran stood in his original spot, unmoved.

"That all you have?" Gliran asked.

"I'm just getting started," Allendria said as she charged forward, staff in hand.

Rayne rushed after her, and the rest of the fighters followed behind. Rayne felt magic build as Allendria thrust her staff forward. The heat emanating from the room quickly faded, and the excess warmth seeped from the stone around them and melded into a small ball of power at the tip of her staff. A four-foot-long spear of fire launched from the staff and headed for Gliran.

The king charged back at Allendria and batted the bolt of fire to the side as he closed the distance. Rayne fished two daggers out of his belt and launched them at Gliran. The elf sidestepped one of them and deflected the other with his axe before his weapon and Allendria's staff collided. Sparks flew from the impact and Allendria stumbled backward.

Gliran continued forward and slashed at her. Rayne jumped into the attack and kicked the side of the axe's head, knocking it off course. He ducked as he landed and slashed at the king's leg. The blade hit the mail armor and skidded off, doing no visible damage.

You have dealt 0 damage with Enchanted Magesteel Swordbreaker. (40 blocked)

"Shit," Rayne grumbled as he rolled to the side, avoiding the axe coming for him. He heard a grunt and saw Gliran back up with a hand on his side. Allendria twirled her staff and attempted a second hit. Gliran batted it away with his axe and Tirithan slashed down with his sword. Gliran's axe continued its slash until it intercepted the sword. Tirithan kicked at the king, but he was too fast for them. He spun to the side just as Rayne rushed back in. The spymaster stabbed at his back and the stiletto blade pierced into the chain mail. Gliran thrust the butt of his axe backward and it connected with Rayne's midsection, sending him stumbling backward, gasping for air.

"Split!" Came a command from Tirithan and the group all dove to the side. Balls of fire and arrows launched from the other fighters, all concentrated on Gliran. The king ignored all but those aimed for his head. Projectiles splintered on his armor and he let the magic splash across him. The flames washed over the armor and barely singed the cloth tabard covering his chain.

"So that's how we are going to play?" Gliran said as he moved backward, away from the group. "I guess it's time to even the odds."

Shadows swirled around the king. Power coalesced in a vortex of purple and black smoke. Rayne didn't like the look of this, so he launched two mare daggers that disappeared into the energy. Allendria released a jet of flame from her staff. The flames buffeted against the vortex of power, but appeared to do nothing. The group watched the display of power with trepidation.

As the energy slowed, a changed Gliran stood before them. His armor was now covered in jagged spikes of deep purple. The king smiled and his eyes glowed silver.

"Try this on for size," Gliran said.

He extended his hands and black energy shot forward. Rayne raised his blades to deflect the power, but the streams of energy darted past him and the rest of their group. He turned and watched the power flow through the door and into the room behind them.

"You missed." Allendria said.

"No, I didn't."

Noise in the room behind them caused Rayne to shift his focus. It was only a handful of seconds before a figure emerged in the doorway. One of the previously dead lackeys shambled into the room, dragging a sword that scraped along the stone floor.

"We've got company," Rayne told the group.

"Everyone, shift focus to the undead. The queen and I will handle Gliran." Tirithan ordered.

Rayne tensed at the order. He was torn about what his priority was. His job was to protect Allendria, and that order came from Arthur. At the same time, he knew Arthur would want to save the lives of any of their people he could.

Fighters in plate charged forward first to hold back the stream of undead. The rest of the group stood behind and fired carefully placed arrows and magic into the force.

Rayne watched them for a few moments until he heard the clang of metal on metal again. He turned to see Allendria, Tirithan, and Gliran engaged in combat again.

"They can hold them off," Rayne determined as he rushed back to the fight with Gliran.

As bad as it sounded, he could live with letting some of their warriors die. He would never forgive himself if something happened to Allendria on his watch.

Rayne stepped away and activated stealth again. Skirting the edge of the fighting, he moved to a place on Gliran's flank. Step by step, he inched closer, trying to keep his stealth intact and gain the upper hand. Allendria blasted the false king with fire, and Rayne felt the heat wash over him.

It didn't cause any damage, so his stealth didn't fade, but the warmth spurred him to move quicker. Any stray attack could mess up his chance. Tirithan lunged forward with his sword, and Gliran sidestepped it. He locked his arm over the blade and pinned it against his body while returning a slash at the general. Tirithan had the fighting sense to let go of the blade and dodge the attack. Disengaging without a weapon was better than without a head.

Rayne used that chance to lunge forward with both blades leading the charge. He couldn't tell if it was the king's senses or a special ability, but the elf reacted to the attack and attempted to dodge out of the way. The twist of his body caused the swordbreaker to skate off his armor with a screech, but the stiletto found purchase and buried deep in his side.

You have dealt 0 damage to King Gliran with Enchanted Magesteel Swordbreaker. (Glancing Blow) (15 negated)
You have dealt 54 damage to King Gliran with Enchanted Magesteel Stiletto Dagger.

Damn. The twist made me miss anything vital.

Rayne ducked the backhand swing from the king and hopped backward.

"You annoying little bug," Gliran said as he turned and swung again, aiming for his throat.

With a grin, Rayne met the swing by ducking under but bringing his stiletto up and slamming it into the incoming forearm. Gliran yelled in pain and dropped Tirithan's blade as Rayne pulled his dagger free and lunged for another strike.

The dark armor turned his blades as Rayne missed the seams in his hasty attack. Another grunt of pain followed from Gliran, and Rayne smiled when he saw Tirithan standing on his flank. The general had picked up Gliran's dropped sword and stabbed him in the side again.

A burst of darkness filled the area and the force of the mana in it caused Rayne to stumble backward. Visibility was nonexistent for a moment until the power dissipated from the air and Gliran was standing back on his feet, seemingly unharmed and holding Tirithan's sword.

"I guess two can play at this game," Gliran said as he chanted a few words Rayne didn't recognize. The vortex of dark energy returned for a few seconds before vanishing again, revealing three Gliran's standing in the center of them.

"Let's even the odds, shall we?" Gliran said before each copy charged.

Rayne intercepted the one running for him and caught the oncoming slash in a parry with his swordbreaker. He was confident in his strength. If Gliran split into three copies, that must also mean his strength split between them as well.

His notion was quickly dashed as the oncoming sword pushed had against him and Rayne barely swept the blade to the side before it came crashing down, sending pebbles of stone skyward from the impact.

I couldn't even twist the blade to disarm him. It isn't possible he is that strong.

A boot caught Rayne in the gut and sent him stumbling backward.

King Gliran dealt 65 damage to you with Kick.

He didn't lose any speed, either.

Rayne stepped back as Gliran raised the sword to swing again, only for the king to surprise him and twist to charge Tirithan.

Ringing echoed through the room as the steel clashed and Rayne took a moment to glance at the fight with the undead. Their allies had gathers into a tight line and were pushing hard against the mass of undead. Progress was slow since they were forced to chop the creatures into pieces before they quit moving, but they were holding their own for now.

His senses returned just in time to duck under a swing and focus on their fight. He'd forgotten the clones and the one that Tirithan was originally fighting was trying to remove his head. He kicked out and hit the clone in the knee, causing it to buckle and slump to the ground.

A muffled cry of pain pulled his attention to Allendria. A fresh line of blood was running down her left arm. The red liquid flowed freely and dripped from the point of the elbow in a steady rhythm.

Rayne rushed for Allendria to assist as he watched the next swing. She got her staff in the way and blocked most of it, but the blade still stopped an inch into her right shoulder. Gliran's clone raised the blade one more time for a heavy overhand chop.

"No you don't." Rayne said through gritted teeth as he activated Shadow Form.

Darkness swirled to engulf him and he felt his feet carry him faster. Piling Weak Haste on with the effect, he blasted forward. The blade came down in what felt like slow motion as Rayne stopped in front of Allendria and caught the sword with both of his daggers in an X shape. His increased speed and strength from the transformation allowed him to push back on the weapon and he heaved the swordbreaker up, knocking Gliran's sword out of the way and burying his stiletto dagger into the copy's throat. A small splash of blood leaked from the wound before the king's body burst into shadows and dissipated into the dark areas of the room.

"Thanks." Allendria said.

Rayne turned to her and smiled. "It's my job."

"Not sure I can get used to that face," Allendria said with a grimace.

"Don't blame you. Let's get back to work before I lose hold of this and am useless."

She nodded in agreement, and they charged at one of the two Glirans attacking Tirithan. Allendria sent a flaming arrow from her staff and it smashed into the clone's body right as Rayne buried both blades in its back. The figure went motionless for a moment before it burst into shadows.

"Nowhere left to hide, traitor!" Allendria called to the remaining figure.

Gliran disengaged from the fight with Tirithan and faced all of them at an angle.

"I'll admit. I didn't expect you to make it into the city. Never imagined the honorable Tirithan would turn and allow you access. I guess he can be bought." Gliran said.

"Finally paired some of that honor with a
dash of morality. Someone reminded me that
honor, just for the sake of honor, was empty.
I knew you shouldn't have been allowed to take
power but didn't want to fight against it,"
Tirithan said.

"It's irrelevant. We are here to remove
you. Permanently. There will be no forgiveness
after what you did to my father." Allendria
said.

"Your father was a fool. His insistence on
following in the footsteps of Tristan
Firebrand and implementing change would've
been the death of this world and meant
permanent enslavement. Wailyn and I put aside
our differences to prevent the catastrophe.
I'll not apologize for doing what had to be
done."

"What catastrophe?" Allendria asked.

"The Ar'Tookans. Our agreement with them is
the only reason they haven't enslaved this
planet." Gliran said.

"No one on this planet is powerful enough
to conquer it all. Sounds like you are trying
to save your life with lies." Tirithan spat.

Gliran let out a low chuckle. "You're
partially right. They aren't on this planet.
They travel the universe conquering worlds.
Tristan wanted to fight them head on. He
didn't understand their power. We brokered a
deal instead."

"Sounds like Tristan wasn't a coward and my
uncle is. We will fight against any threat to
us and our way of life. You're currently at
the top of the list." Allendria said as she
sent a searing beam of fire.

Gliran deflected it with his axe, while Rayne and Tirithan rushed forward. The general arrived first and his overhead chop was met with the screech of metal on metal. Rayne lunged for the king's exposed side, but Gliran twisted the haft of the axe down and batted his first strike away.

Rayne's speed was still enhanced with his Shadow Form and Weak Haste, so he quickly dove forward, grazing Gliran's back with a blade as he passed. Landing on the other side of the elf, he spun his stiletto around and stabbed backward, driving the blade into the king's hip joint.

Spinning around, he pulled the blade free and ducked as an arm went flying over his head. Another quick stab sent the swordbreaker into Gliran's underarm.

Gliran deflected your attack.
You have dealt 35 damage to Gliran with Enchanted Magesteel Swordbreaker. (Glancing Blow)
You have dodged an attack from Gliran.
You have dealt 65 damage to Gliran with Enchanted Magesteel Stiletto Dagger. (Critical Hit)
You have dealt 122 damage to Gliran with Enchanted Magesteel Swordbreaker. (Critical Hit) (Mortal Blow)

Rayne stepped back as Tirithan and Allendria continued their assault. Rayne glanced over and noticed the other defenders were struggling with some of the undead. Making a quick judgment call, he dashed across the room and went to work on the undead.

His swordbreaker crunched through the skull of one undead and partially coagulated blood spilled out. He slung his arm and let the blood slide off and onto the floor. Rayne never stopped moving as he continued through the crowd of undead, slashing tendons and smashing skulls.

Heavy footfalls in the antechamber drew his attention, and he glanced over to see what new threat would emerge. Arthur clambered through the doorway and froze at the sight of the melee with the undead.

"Survived the dragon, I see!" Rayne yelled and waved.

"What's going on?" Arthur asked.

"Just your garden variety undead party. Help these people fight off the undead. I'm going back to finish this fight with Allendria."

"I'll join you. She might need my help." Arthur said.

Rayne used his enhanced speed to close the distance and stopped next to Arthur.

"This is something she needs to finish without you. It's her people. If you have to step in, it makes her look weak. Tirithan is her general and I'm not as well-known as you, so I look more like a normal soldier to everyone. Let her win this on her own strength. We have worn Gliran down."

Arthur stared into his haunting visage for a few moments before nodding. "Understood. I'll play cleanup. I mean, I got to fight off a dragon, so there is a limit to heroics for the day."

Rayne grinned and rushed back to Allendria and Tirithan.

As he approached, he watched Tirithan
perform a perfect parry and bat the king's axe
out of the path. Allendria stepped into the
opening and slammed the end of her staff
directly into Gliran's chest, causing the
stylized black armor to crack.

Rayne saw that Gliran's dark powers were
fading. The armor was turning a lighter shade
of purple and impacts of weapons caused
spiderweb cracks all over.

Rayne threw two throwing knives back-to-
back. The first hit the side of the king's
armor and bounced off, but it left behind a
damaged section of armor. The next blade hit
the same spot and slipped in through one
crack, widening the fissure and sticking true.

*Gliran blocked your Throwing Knife with
Armor.*
*You have dealt 38 damage to Gliran with
Enchanted MAgesteel Throwing Knife.*

He could feel his grip on the Shadow Form
waning and knew it was time to finish this
fight. Catching Tirithan's gaze, he motioned
for a pincer move and the general gave a
slight nod of acknowledgement. Rayne
positioned himself on the flank as he
approached and waited for his opportunity. It
was only a few seconds later when Tirithan
sidestepped an attack and swung for Gliran's
left side. The king interposed his axe and
Rayne knew it was the perfect chance for him
to strike.

In one swift motion, he lunged forward and used his swordbreaker to stab into the back of the king's armor directly over the king's lung. Before registering the damage, he already had the stiletto following to break through the same spot. It slid in smoothly, with almost no resistance as the plate armor peeled apart.

The blade slipped all the way to the hilt, and the king yelled in pain as Rayne bashed his swordbreaker next to it and then plunged it through the damaged metal.

A hissing noise made him look to the side in time to watch Tirithan's blade break through his armor and slide into the king's side. Blood poured from all the wounds and Gliran froze in place.

"It's over Uncle. I'm taking back my father's throne." Allendria said as she stepped up to face him.

"You've doomed us all," Gliran managed through clenched teeth.

"I'll take my chances," she said as she stabbed the top of her staff through his chest plate.

Rayne watched fire course through the rod and enter the king's body. Red and orange light emitted from Gliran's eyes and mouth as the power burned. Tirithan and Rayne retreated as the flames poured from the wounds they inflicted as well.

Allendria let the fire burn for a full fifteen seconds before stopping the flow of power. A burned husk stood in Gliran's place for a few moments before abruptly crashing to the ground. The entire body dissipated into a cloud of dark gray ash as it scattered across the floor.

“He’s finally dead,” Allendria said, with tears in her eyes.

Chapter 37

Solidifying Rule

Arthur stood near the stage and watched Allendria with adoration. She was regal in her battle armor, although it was now clean and free of blackened soot and blood. Her people stood listening to her every word in rapture as she spoke to the assembled Dark Elves.

"Our struggle doesn't end here. I've removed the traitor and have taken back the throne, but other dangers are sure to come for us in the future. Many of you may be curious about where I've been. Some of you have probably heard the rumors," Allendria said.

Murmurs spread through the crowd. Just loud enough to distort the sound, but not enough to pick up individual words.

"Some of those rumors are true," she pronounced, and the crowd went silent. "I've been living with humans since I escaped. They took me in and have treated me as family. Not only that, they offered asylum to our fellow Dark Elves in the city of Alurian. Their king, Arthur, protected our people when Gliran tried to hunt them down and they still live with us now."

More mumbled sounds filled the space, but these sounded more cheerful in tone.

"Another rumor that is true is I am engaged to marry a human. Their king proposed to me and I accepted. I want to introduce King Arthur Firebrand," Allendria said as she looked at Arthur with a smile.

Arthur recognized his cue and walked onto the stage. A chorus of shouts mixed with cheers assaulted him.

"We can't have a human ruler!"

"That's the man who fought the dragon."

"I refuse to take orders from them."

Arthur understood their sentiments to a degree. Decades of hate were hard to overcome so quickly. He walked up to Allendria and kissed her on the cheek before turning to look over the crowd. Quiet descended from his action and a few of the elves shuffled uncomfortably on their feet.

"Esteemed citizens. I want to make something clear for you. I have no intention of ruling over any of you. My purpose for being here is I love your queen and want to see her succeed. For that reason, I proclaim now that I abdicate any right to wear the crown for the Dark Elves."

King Arthur Firebrand of the Kingdom of Fire has formally abdicated any claim to be the King of the Dark Elves. This rule will be enforced by the gods.

The notification flashed before all the citizens of the Dark Elves, and he was sure all the people in the Kingdom of Fire.

"Your queen will rule for you, and I will only be here if she asks for my advice or assistance. All decisions for your people are hers and hers alone. I do hope we can find a common ground and work together in the years to come."

Arthur stepped back and stood behind Allendria with his arms behind him in a stance resembling parade rest. Allendria took that chance to continue her speech. He knew the gist of what she would say, so he took the time to scan his notifications from the fight.

Raiding the Capital… Again	
Requirements: Participate in actions to directly or indirectly influence the outcome of the raid. Rewards: 48,000 experience, 5 Talent Points, 3 Spell Blade Talent Points	Description: A new r started near Calzas. either side in the f the side you assist the raid, you receiv rewards.

You have completed the Raid Quest Raiding the Capital… Again. You gain 48,000 experience, 5 Talent Points, and 3 Spell Blade Talent Points.

You have gained 3,860 total experience in Air Magic.

You have gained 1,840 total experience in Swords.

Congratulations, you have reached level 13 in Swords. Swing speed with swords increased by 36%. I'll give you credit. That aerial fight was pretty cool.

You have gained 2,150 total experience in Fire Magic.

You have gained 3,105 total experience in Dimensional Magic.

You have gained 1,600 total experience in Small Blades.

You have gained 1,600 total experience in Dual Wield.

You have gained 1,915 total experience in Medium Armor.

You have gained 2,845 total experience.

Arthur opened his Swords talent tree and checked out the Tier 3 options.

You have 4 unspent Talent Points.

Talent	Description
Tier 1	
Powerful Strikes (5/5)	*Increases base damage of swords you use by 1 point per talent point.*
Blade Forms (5/5)	*Each point increases your swing speed with swords by 2%.*
Passata Sotto (1/1)	*A melee ability that allows you to avoid an incoming strike by ducking down low and then counter-attacking with an upward angled thrust.* *Cost: 10 Stamina*
Tier 2	
Heavy Guard (3/10)	*Each point increases your chance to successfully block attacks by 2%. More points also allow you to block stronger attacks.*

Deflection (0/10)	Increases your chance to parry blows with Swords by 2% per point.
Tier 3	
Dual Wield Bonus (0/10)	Each point increases the damage of both weapons by 5% as long as one weapon is a sword.
Keen Edges (0/10)	Each point decreases durability loss by 4% and increases the sharpness of your edge by 3%.

Heavy Guard was temping, but he was working on dodging more than blocking. Deflection was still primarily useless since he parried with his short blade. Durability issues hadn't really bothered him with any of his weapons yet, so he eyed Dual Wield Bonus. The added damage to both weapons was too good to give up. He dropped all four points into it.

A loud cheer filled the area, and Arthur paused to pay attention to the crowd. He saw joy on their faces and some were clapping, so Arthur smiled and give a few quick claps to go along with them before turning his focus back inward.

The next tree to look at was his Spell Blade Talents. Those he hadn't checked since he originally obtained the class, so he was thoroughly surprised by what he saw.

You have 15 unused Talent Points.

Spell Blade	
Tier 1	
Disrupting Blow (1/1)	Coat your blade in magic and deliver a surge of raw mana on impact to disrupt spell casting and magical regeneration. Mana cost: 50 Duration: 2 minutes Duration of Disrupt Effect: 30 seconds
Spell Edges (1/5)	Increases the strength of your weapon enchantments when used on bladed weapons by 10% per point.
Spell Faces (0/5)	Increases the strength of your weapon enchantments when used on blunt weapons by 10% per point.
Shiv (1/1)	A quick, thrusting attack that can only be used when blocking or parrying with your main hand. The ability causes your off-hand weapon enchantment to deal 10% more damage and guarantees at least one status effect is applied when an enchantment that has status effects is used. Mana Cost: 30 Stamina Cooldown: 30 seconds

Mana Channeling (0/10)	Boosts the duration of enchantment spells you cast on weapons by 25% per point.
Imbue (1/1)	Permanently affix weapon enchantments you cast to their designated weapons for the duration of their respective spells. Enchantment won't fade when you drop the weapon.

Fourteen? How the hell do I have so many? I got three from my initial class quest and three from this one. Where are the other twelve coming from?

And they call me the stupid one. Balair grunted.

Was I speaking in our mind communication? Arthur asked.

Sure were. I worry about you sometimes. The explanation for your question is actually easy. Your levels. Classes grant you one talent point for each level starting at twenty. This happens after your first level up following gaining a class. You're level thirty-one, so you have twelve additional points. Balair explained.

Son of a… I've had these the whole time and never checked?

Sure have. How about you fix that before you forget about it again? Balair said with a chuckle.

Arthur agreed and started looking through the options. He'd picked up Disrupting Blow during the quest and learned it naturally, but the others he spent points on. Instead of committing everything, he added one point in Spell Edges and checked the new Tier 2 options.

Tier 2	
Mana Leech Strike (0/5)	*Learn how to properly channel mana. After you commit all five points, you gain the ability, Mana Leech Strike.* *Stamina cost: 25 Effect: Strike the target and leech mana from them. This ability drains mana based on the damage of the attack. Every 3 points of damage drains 1 point of mana from the target.*
Elemental Confluence (0/5) *Requirements: Have at least 1 Combination Spell.*	*Increase your control over elemental enchanting and allow you to weave hybrid spell effects into enchantments. Requires all 5 points to gain the ability.*

Double Discharge (0/1)	Expend enchantments on up to two of your weapons to deal 150% damage to the target. This effect resets any potential enchantment cooldowns.
Pure Damage (0/10)	Boosts damage of your weapons while enchanted. Each point increases their base attack by 2.

Arthur immediately dropped all five points in Mana Leech Strike and Elemental Confluence. Being able to imbue his weapon with ice or stone type of effects would be significant.

Most of his abilities revolved heavily around mana, so the mana leeching effect would be great in those few situations he ran out. He put one point into Double Discharge because that ability sounded like a great option for a finisher. The last three he put into Pure Damage.

There was one other set of notifications that truly surprised him.

You have completed a hidden quest for your Soul Bond. (Dragon Face Off) You've earned 3 Soul Bond Talents.

You have completed a hidden quest for your Soul Bond. (Downfall of a King) You've earned 2 Soul Bond Talent Points.

You have completed a hidden quest for your Divine Power and earned 2 Divine Points. (Downfall of a King)

They didn't spell out exactly what the hidden quests were, but the names they gave were a pretty good indication. Fighting another dragon in combat with Calfuray must have earned that. The Downfall of a King one was probably for defeating Gliran. He may not have done it himself, but he helped in the siege and getting rid of Gliran was a big priority for him with his goddess as well.

Both were so rare to see that he pulled up his skill tree with the Soul Bond to remind him what was even in it.

You have 5 unused Talent Points.

Soul Bond	
Tier 1	
Shared Mana Regeneration (1/1)	*Combines the mana regeneration of both parties to create a higher mana regeneration rate for both. Both mana regeneration rates are added together and then multiplied by 0.8 to reach your final mana regeneration rate.*
Dragon Healing (5/5)	*Grants you the ability to heal HP like a dragon does. Each point after the first increases the healing speed by 10%.*
Hard as Iron (0/5)	*Each point increases your base defense rating of all pieces of armor by 15.*

Feed the Flames (2/5)	*Increases the effectiveness of your special dragon bond abilities by 10% per point and reduces their cooldown by 3 hours.*
Tier 2	
Partial Transformation (1/1)	*Allows you to partially shift into a draconic form. This new form hardens your skin on your arms, legs, and torso to resemble scales and decreases the damage you take. It also increases your Strength by 10%. This effect lasts for 3 minutes.* *Cooldown: 8 hours*
Protect Your Partner (5/5)	*Each point in this ability grants you and your Soul Bond companion the following:* • *2 Strength* • *1 Intellect* • *3 Endurance*
Form of Ferocity (0/5)	*Each point unlocks a new tier of the ability Form of Ferocity.*

	The first tier boosts the speed and combat damage of both partners by 15% for 5 minutes. *Subsequent tiers improve these criteria and can even unlock additional effects.* *Tier 1 Cooldown: 5 hours.*
Tier 3	
Skin of Scales (0/5)	*Causes small dragon scales to form on the edge of your skin. Reduces damage taken by 10% per point while the skill is active.* *Cooldown: 8 Hours* *Duration: 2 Minutes*
All That Glitters (0/5)	*Dragons have an innate sense for treasure. You gain the following for each point of this skill:* *Increase money found during fights by 5%.* *• Increases the chance of finding items of higher rarity by 15%.* *• Gain 10% more*

	resources when gathering or mining.
Dragon Swiftness (5/5)	*Each point increases your base Agility by 2.*
Being of Fire (0/5)	*Increases your resistance to Fire Based effects by 15% per point. If you invest all five points, you become immune to all normal fire attacks.*

The options weighed on him as he scanned the group. He looked over Feed the Flames since Cal mentioned it last time. While the cooldown reduction and power boost sounded great, he tended to not use them. It reminded him of playing old RPG games and hoarding the best items all the way until the end for fear of needing them and not having them.

Hard as Iron was intriguing because he now had decent armor to work with. If he could mitigate most of the damage up front, it would save the mana cost of his damage reduction, making his effective health much higher.

The Tier 3 abilities all had their advantages. Being of Fire really interested him because he was not fond of being hit by Fire Magic. The problem was he needed five points to dedicate to it for it to be truly great. Gaining talents in this tree was very infrequent.

All That Glitters was intriguing for the items, but he rarely ever gained much loot from his fights.

He juggled back and forth with the decision until deciding to max out Feed the Flames as Cal suggested and then spending the last two for All That Glitters. Hopefully, he could get some real loot.

Arthur snapped back to attention in time to see Allendria wrapping up her speech, and the crowd cheered again. She waved at her people before turning and catching his eye. She grinned at him and motioned for him to leave the stage.

He took his cue and turned to walk off while she followed right behind. They headed straight for the castle and didn't stop for any detours. Allendria walked up beside him and took his hand.

"Thank you for this. All of it."

"I'd do anything for you. How does it feel to be back in your rightful place?" Arthur asked.

"Kind of surreal. I wasn't sure this day would ever come. You never knew your legacy, so the transition was probably very different. I was raised my whole life to do this job, even if I was sheltered. When that was taken away, I felt lost and without purpose. Now that fire has returned."

Arthur squeezed her hand and smiled. She returned the gesture, and they continued to a large banquet room off the main hallway. People mingled around the area and visited in hush tones. Arthur noticed his group there as he waved at Samson, Wesley, Rayne, Balair, and Calfuray. Tirithan stood at the right of Allendria's seat and Samson set to the left of Arthur's.

They took their seats and everyone in the room broke off their conversations and sat in the assorted chairs.

"Today is a momentous day for our people," Allendria began. "It took some time, but we have removed the usurper and, hopefully, we can turn things around. My time with the humans has showed me how much we have squandered our potential in the recent years. Even our own people are resurrecting some of the magical means of construction in the city of Alurian. I believe it is time for us to move our civilization forward."

"My lady, I believe there is one more thing left to do." Tirithan told her.

"Yes, general?"

"You're the queen now. You need to declare the war with the Kingdom of Fire over."

"Thank you for reminding me. I, Queen Allendria of the Dark Elves, declare the war between my people and the Kingdom of Fire finished. I also declare the Conclave of Dark Elves and the Kingdom of Fire to be Allies."

The proclamation was met with a notification to Arthur.

The Conclave of Dark Elves has proposed an Alliance with the Kingdom of Fire. Do you Accept? Yes/No.

Arthur accepted, and the hushed murmur across the room told him everyone had received the notification.

"Now the matter moves to planning for the future." Allendria said. "King Arthur, I know you have an ongoing war with King Wailyn. Our alliance now puts us on the same side as you and we are currently at war with him. Do you have a plan?"

"In a manner of speaking. I have a few things to address back in Alurian and would like for my people to have some time at home. From there, I plan to march on the capital and overthrow Wailyn. He's never been overly strong and most of his power is weaker. His army of low-level thugs and bullies won't be any match for our forces. Unless he recruits some unknown allies like Gliran did, there should be no problems."

"When should we plan to march?" Tirithan asked.

"I appreciate the sentiment, but I'm going to request you stay here. Your Queen needs time to solidify her rule and gain the trust of your people. I prefer her to be safe here with her own people while I finish this fight." Arthur said.

"I don't need you to protect me. I can handle myself." Allendria said as her cheeks flushed red.

"I'm more concerned about you gaining the trust of your people. They need someone to guide them and help them back on their feet. You've seen some ways we did it firsthand, so you are the perfect choice to facilitate things here. I truly think we can handle Wailyn with little trouble." Arthur explained.

"Pardon me for saying," Tirithan said. "But I agree with Arthur. I think you're needed here."

Emotions warred on Allendria's face as Arthur worried she might blow up on somebody and burn the room to a crisp, but she slowly wrestled herself back to reality. Arthur could almost feel the temperature of the room spike and then slowly drop to normal.

She finally let out a heavy sigh. "Fine. I see the merit in it. Just wish I was there to finish it with you."

"I'll send for you to join us as soon as the battle is over and we can celebrate." Arthur said.

"When are you leaving?" Allendria asked.

"Tomorrow, unless you need me for something." Arthur said.

She looked a little upset about the news, but merely nodded in agreement.

"General, I would like to make a request," Samson said.

"What can I do for you?" Tirithan asked.

"I'd like to request you establish a Queen's Guard to keep Her Highness safe."

Murmurs traveled around the room, and Arthur felt they were mostly in favor of the idea. Tirithan looked to Allendria, and she offered no opinion on the matter.

"I'll take care of it. I believe it to be a good idea. My Queen, any objections?" Tirithan asked.

"I'm sure I could think of some, but what's the point? The arguments for it would probably outweigh any objections I had. I will request that the woman who fought with us in the keep, Lady Nadeen, be named as the leader of the guard. She had a very level head on her when it came to decision making."

"Agreed. I reviewed reports of her work after the battle and she performed exceptionally. I'll coordinate with her to build out the rest of the guard." Tirithan said.

"Then it is settled. The human contingent will leave tomorrow and head for Alurian. We will stay behind and work toward building up the lost trust of the Dark Elves," Allendria pronounced.

There were a few more issues of business discussed but mostly city related items, so Arthur paid little attention. Eventually, Allendria called for the meeting adjourned.

Everyone filed out of the room in neat order and broke into groups. Arthur watched Balair and Calfuray head off with Rayne and Samson while the Dark Elves congregated together off to the side. Allendria walked up beside him.

"Will you walk with me?" She asked.

"Of course," he told her as he put his arm out and she wrapped hers around it.

They walked through the palace and continued out into the city. Most of their trip was in silence, and she just nuzzled up to his side. When they exited the palace proper, she regained her straight and regal bearing.

"I want you to see the city before you go," Allendria told him as she walked. "I also want to talk to you in private."

"Whatever I screwed up, I'm sorry." He told her.

She laughed at his comment before slapping him lightly on the shoulder.

"Do you have to go so soon?" She asked.

"Have to? Maybe not. Need to? Absolutely." Arthur said.

"Can't you stay a little longer?" she pleaded.

He looked at her and saw a glimmer of fear in her eyes.

"What's wrong?" He asked. "I have total faith you can handle this with your people. As you've said, you've been raised for this."

Tears welled up in her eyes. "It's not that. I don't really want you to go to war. I don't know if I could do this if something happened to you."

"We've been through a lot since we met. I'm harder to kill than that," Arthur said with a sly smile.

Allendria didn't respond, but looked around the immediate area. She grabbed his hand and led him into a small copse of trees. They continued to a small opening before Allendria took a seat on a patch of long grass. Arthur sat with her and took her hand.

"What's really going on?" Arthur asked.

"This isn't how I wanted to have this conversation, but let's get married before you go!" she blurted.

Arthur was shocked at her sudden outburst. It took him a few moments to gather his thoughts before he answered.

"We really should wait until after I take care of Wailyn. I don't want our wedding overshadowed by war. We should usher in our union with a time of peace, not the middle of a war. I don't want your people saying you sold yourself to the humans for help." Arthur said.

She looked red faced for a few moments before letting out a heavy sigh.

"I understand your reason, but there's something else," she said before she reached down and laid an arm across her belly. "I'm pregnant."

Arthur sat with his mouth hanging open for a solid three seconds. His pulse quickened, and his heartbeat thundered in his head. He finally pulled himself together as tears welled in the corner of his eyes.

"I'm going to be a dad? We're going to have a baby?" He asked with a tremble in his voice.

She gripped his hands and squeezed tight.

"Yes. I wanted to wait a little longer for the perfect time to tell you, but with you leaving, it couldn't wait."

"I'm thrilled you told me, but I'm sorry to say I don't think it changes anything. As much as I'd like to put everything on hold and go through with the wedding, now I have even more of a burning desire to end this war and have our peaceful life start. I don't want our future son or daughter born into this trouble." Arthur said.

"Then let me come with you. I want our child to have a father. Let's finish this together." Allendria pleaded.

"I love you, but I'm going to beg you to stay here. I wouldn't be able to think straight if you were there. The entire time, I would stress over your safety. I'd be more likely to make a mistake that could doom us both." Arthur said somberly.

"Damn it. I know that but I just…" she couldn't finish the statement and just growled in anger.

"I'll survive. I promise. We have a terrific life waiting for us."

"I hope so. It's just, I worry. Maybe it's just the hormones going crazy, but something feels wrong about the whole thing." Allendria said.

Arthur stood up and reached down for her hand. She slowly placed hers in his and he lifted her back to her feet.

"Let's not mar this joyous occasion. You can show me around and give me a proper tour. I expect you to explain all the important places to me and give me their story as well. Tonight is just for us and nothing more. Tomorrow, I go to finish this. I promise you, as soon as Wailyn is gone, we plan the wedding. It'll be a big affair with all our friends. None of this month's long delay. Let's say one month for preparation and call it done." Arthur said.

Allendria smiled, tears still shimmering in her eyes. "I'll hold you to that promise. One month after the king is dead and you're mine at the altar. Now let's go. I have a lot of talking to do as we walk."

She grabbed his arm and pulled him back to the streets. They walked through the city for the rest of the evening, stopping to look at different monuments and buildings. Their trip lasted long into the evening before finally retiring to their room at the palace.

Arthur wrapped her in his arms, kissed her deeply, and pulled her to the bed with him.

Chapter 38

Final Preparations

The next day passed quickly as everyone made ready to march out. Samson was up with the daylight and ordered his men around while Arthur strolled the grounds, offering praise to the men and women who followed him and performed well in the attack.

Arthur felt it necessary to be seen with his army and to help them with some of their preparation to leave. He couldn't stay for the entire process, however.

Later in the morning, he met with Allendria and her advisors. He smiled when he spotted two female elves flanking Allendria. Both were from the last battle in the palace, so Arthur assumed one of them was her new head of security, Nadeen.

"Good morning, everyone," Allendria started. "I know there is a laundry list of stuff for us to finish today, but I felt it necessary to convene this meeting before our allies left."

Allendria looked at Arthur and nodded.

"What can I do for you, Your Majesty?" Arthur asked with a formal bow, showing deference to her station in her city.

"This isn't that formal of a meeting," Allendria laughed as she waved for everyone to find a seat.

"I'm sure our esteemed advisers here have heard the tale of the fall of Gliran? My focus for this meeting is on one particular point of interest. Has anyone here heard of the Ar'Tookan he mentioned?" Allendria asked.

The room was silent as everyone looked at each other and shook their heads slowly. General Tirithan appeared to contemplate something as he looked at the ceiling and rubbed his jaw.

"Possibly." Tirithan said.

Allendria's eyebrows raised at that. "When?"

"I haven't heard the actual name before, but I recall seeing a strange figure entering or leaving Gliran's office from time to time. It was very rare and I only truly remember seeing them twice. Normally I wouldn't bother, but the figure stood out. It was a little larger than the average Dark Elf, and on one occasion, its hand slipped from the robes that always concealed it. The hand was blue. I dismissed it as me seeing things, but that might be the link." Tirithan explained.

"Interesting," Allendria said as she tapped the large wooden conference table.

"Whatever the case, I'm sure this same 'ambassador' visited Wailyn as well. Gliran confirmed they both had an agreement with it." Arthur reminded.

"So, what do we do about them?" Allendria asked.

Another round of silence before Samson raised his hand.

"Yes, Paladin Samson?" Allendria asked.

"My apologies, Your Majesty. Wasn't sure if it was my place to speak here." Samson said.

"You're always welcome to speak. You are a friend of the Dark Elves, and more importantly a friend of mine. What advice do you have?"

Samson's back straightened to his normal military bearing before he spoke. "As with any unknown enemy, the best you can do is prepare. Dust off your magic, train up your skills, and make sure you stock food and other supplies. For all we know, it could be years before they do anything. Gliran said himself they traveled the universe. No point in trying to plan anything beyond the basics for an unknown enemy. Just focus on helping your people improve in all aspects of their life."

Tirithan smiled warmly at the warrior before joining. "I agree with Paladin Samson. Let's focus on our people and see where everything lands. I think we have time."

Allendria looked at Arthur, and he nodded in agreement.

"I guess that's settled. We can table the matter until they show their face and then focus our efforts. In the meantime, I think we should properly send our allies off so they can prepare for the next step in their war." Allendria said.

"Agreed," Tirithan smiled. "We have some of our forces gathering the Dark Elf citizens so we can have a proper parade through the city. We'd be honored if you'd join the procession, Queen Allendria."

"I wouldn't miss it. Let's adjourn and get ready for the parade." Allendria said.

The group stood and filed out of the room. Each talking in quiet conversations. Arthur followed behind and grabbed Allendria's hand to walk with her.

* * *

Allendria separated from Arthur and bid him to go check on his men and coordinate their exit with Samson. She kissed him on the cheek. "I'll see you soon."

He squeezed her hand and walked off to join the paladin.

Allendria caught Tirithan's eye and motioned for him to come to her. The general politely excused himself from his conversation and Allendria walked with him to a secluded corner in the hall.

"I need you to do something, and Arthur can't find out about it." She said.

"That sounds ominous, but you're the queen." Tirithan said.

"I don't like this. Something feels wrong. I need you to make preparations." Allendria said and then she leaned in and continued her explanation in low tones. The general nodded along before he looked up.

"Are you sure?" He asked. Staring into her eyes.

"Absolutely." She confirmed.

Tirithan ran a hand through his long hair before sighing. "As you command. We'll be ready in two days."

"That will do."

★ ★ ★

King Wailyn fumed as he stalked around his office. A bloodstain decorated the floor near the door, where the last unfortunate messenger interrupted him. His gaze kept returning to the floating notifications he refused to dismiss.

King Gliran of the Dark Elves is dead. Queen Allendria has ascended the throne.

The Conclave of Dark Elves has entered an Alliance with the Kingdom of Fire.

"He assured me he couldn't lose. He even had that blasted wyrm on his side and still couldn't secure victory. How pathetic is he?" Wailyn mumbled.

"There was some trickery involved. It was rather refreshing, if I'm being honest. That said, we are disappointed in you and your so-called ally." A voice said from the shadow. A figure stepped forth in their long black robe. It always annoyed Wailyn how they just appeared.

"I'll take care of it myself. I've been nothing but loyal to the empire." Wailyn grumbled.

"You have, and I'll admit your foe is better than I expected. We had to pull some strings to get Garthool's help." The figure grumbled.

"That didn't do much good. Even he fell."

"He lives. They defeated him in battle, but he escaped. It seems Arthur evolved his dragonling all the way to a dragon, so now he has two dragon allies."

"Damn. I don't have the power to stop two of them. Even if I call on Isabelle, I couldn't take him and the dragons." Wailyn cursed.

"Garthool will return to fight with you. He
should be here in a day or so. I've sent for
additional reinforcements. As long as you can
hold the city wall long enough for me to get
our surprise in place, victory will be yours.
I hope you realize this isn't something I'd do
for everybody. I expect something in return."
The figure said.

"Whatever you need, I'll figure out a way
to get it. Help me win this and stop your
people from invading and it'll be worth the
cost. Not keen to be a slave."

"There are many forms of slavery, but I see
your point. You could argue you're already a
slave. That said, you'll have your help. Stay
alive and win." The figure said before it
retreated to the shadows and disappeared.

Wailyn sat back in his chair and let out a
breath. His hand shook from the fear of
failure and reprisal. His initial instinct
yelled he was about to be killed and invaded,
but it appeared he had one more chance.

"I'll not waste it."

* * *

Arthur saw the gates of Alurian come into
view as they exited the forest. He let out an
involuntary sigh of relief.

"Was that necessary?" Balair asked as he
sauntered along beside him.

"Felt necessary to me. I've grown attached
to the place, and it feels like home." Arthur
said.

*It's growing into a formidable stronghold.
I dare say it is better equipped than the
capital now. Might consider keeping it as the
capital city of the kingdom when you defeat
Wailyn.* Calfuray sent to them.

Her purple form flew through the air and circled the city. She was high enough that Arthur could only make out a vague shape.

I think I will. I have no ties to the current capital, anyway. If it's in as bad of shape as Seora was, it'll take time to fix.

"It's a comforting sight," Samson said.

"Hopefully, we'll be able to celebrate a little peace before long. It'll be nice to have some quiet time to get everything in order and not worry about fighting or war." Arthur said.

"I'm fine with the action. Have nothing else to do but manage guards and our army," Samson grumbled.

Arthur could hear the catch in the man's throat and admonished himself. Surely the statement brought up old wounds and Arthur couldn't blame him. It would be difficult to enjoy peace when the one you wanted to spend it with was gone.

The two continued in silence the rest of the way and arrived to a small amount of fanfare at the gate. A few council members waited to greet them and cheers rose from a few dozen gathered citizens and the guards on the wall.

Arthur smiled and waved before approaching Daniel.

"Small welcoming party?" Arthur asked.

"It seemed like the best thing to do. The city has already been celebrating since the notification went through and quite frankly, half the town is probably too drunk to be trusted in the street." Daniel said while chuckling.

"Good call," Arthur confirmed.

"Is Queen Allendria with you?" Daranth asked as he looked past Arthur and scanned the faces.

"She stayed behind to help the rest of your people. They will have a transition ahead of them as they work to move their civilization forward instead of staying stagnant. I won't hold it against you or any of your fellow Dark Elves if you decide to return home." Arthur confirmed.

"Some may take that offer. I'll probably return from time to time to visit, but I'd be lying if I said that Alurian didn't feel like home now. Besides, someone has to keep this council honest," Daranth said with a small shove against Daniel's shoulder.

"That was one time…" Daniel started before they both broke into laughter.

"Anything pressing to attend?" Arthur asked.

"Other than you preparing for war, I take it?" Daniel asked.

Arthur nodded.

"We have Lady Dalia here for your judgment. I suggest you take care of that as soon as possible." Daniel said.

"Can you call a council meeting and have her present? I want to make sure everyone sees this, so there isn't any confusion about where I stand or what I expect." Arthur said as he ground out the last few words.

"The council members are all waiting for you at the inn. We figured you'd want to meet on your return. I'll send a runner to ensure they bring Lady Dalia." Daniel said.

The innkeeper motioned for a small boy to approach from the side. The young man ran up and Daniel bent down low and whispered something in his ear. He placed a small coin in their hand and they scampered off in a flash.

"The messenger?" Arthur asked.

"Might as well put some kids to work. Teach them early." Daniel said.

Arthur wasn't sure forcing young kids to work was a good idea, but if they had to work, a messenger wouldn't be a bad gig for them. It probably stemmed from his life on Earth before and he had to remind himself that life worked differently here. The inherent dangers of everything made it more difficult to shelter kids, and the need to improve skills matched that assumption. He'd let the council govern the city as agreed, but keeping an eye on child labor rules and regulations would be a priority.

"Need me for anything, or can I go find my sister?" Rayne asked as he walked to match pace with them.

"Council meeting. Can you stick around for it? I have a feeling you'll be needed." Arthur said.

"There a problem?" the younger man asked.

"Kinda. I sent for Lady Dalia to be brought here to answer for her actions, or lack thereof, in Seora. I may need you to testify to what you saw again." Arthur said.

A wide grin split Rayne's face. "I'd love to."

They marched directly into the inn and found the council table occupied in the back corner. It was only a matter of minutes for them to be seated and for food to appear in front of them.

"I missed good food," Balair mumbled through his bites of the seared venison in front of him. The young dragon may look like a human, but he didn't have the manners of one. Calfuray walked in, now in her human form.

"Sky is clear. Oh, is that seared venison with mashed potatoes?" She said as she sat next to Arthur and began eating. She at least had more self-control and used the utensils provided.

The group finished their meal as normal, and Arthur glanced at Daniel. He gave a subtle nod and Daniel mouthed, 'right now?' to him in a silent question.

He tipped his head again and Daniel turned and made a few hand gestures to a guard in his gleaming city armor by the back door. In a matter of moments, three people emerged from the back. Lady Dalia was in the center, and a guard flanked her on each side.

Arthur stood from his seat and the table grew quiet. Dalia locked eyes with him and gave a short bow.

"Your Majesty, how great it is to see you. I fear there has been some mistake. Is there a reason I'm being escorted everywhere by guards?" Lady Dalia asked.

"No mistake, Dalia." Arthur said. He watched her visibly flinch and could swear there was a flash of anger in her face as he left off the 'Lady' part.

"You've been summoned to answer for your neglect." Arthur said. "I was informed of the sad state of affairs of Seora. The thieves running rampant, hijacking shipments and resources. And the Lady placed in charge of the city doing nothing about it despite protests and requests from several other city officials."

Fire flashed in her eyes, and Arthur was sure he saw it that time. Her gaze immediately snapped to Rayne seated near him. If looks could do damage, he was sure that would be a critical hit.

"I believe your reports might not have been entirely accurate, Your Majesty. I tried my best with what I had, but there were limited resources available to me." She said.

"Rayne, when you investigated, and single-handedly solved the problem, did you witness any of this attempt to fix the issue?" Arthur asked.

"No, Your Majesty." Rayne confirmed.

"Did you witness Lord Tremont and Lady Gemmalin plea with Dalia to fix the issue?" Arthur asked.

"I did. I was also approached by Lady Gemmalin personally to ask me to fix the problem because she stated they'd seen no help of any kind despite their pleas. I'd also like to add that Lady Gemmalin was invaluable in assisting me with my mission." Rayne summarized.

"You liar!" Dalia screamed. "How dare you do this to me!"

"Silence," Samson boomed and Dalia snapped her mouth shut.

"Daniel, can you bring me the letters?" Arthur asked.

Daniel walked to the bar and reached behind. He came back with three different sheets of paper rolled up neatly, with a small string tying them shut. Arthur took them, laid two on the table, and opened the other. He scanned the contents before placing it on the table and opening and reading the others.

"Dalia, do you know what these are?" Arthur asked, gesturing toward the papers.

"No, Your Majesty." She said, a slight tremble in her voice.

"These are something I asked for when I sent for you. Statements on your conduct from Lady Gemmalin and Lords Tripp and Ealin." Arthur watched her face pale.

"All of these agree with Rayne's assessment and are nearly identical to the story he recounted to this council already. Your lies are no longer to be tolerated. By all accounts I should have you executed." Arthur said.

Dalia's mouth hung open, and she stared at him in shock. It took her a few moments, but she found her voice.

"Please no, Your Majesty. I have been a faithful servant and tried my best to serve you." Dalia pleaded, but Arthur didn't quite buy it.

"I have no doubt you tried your best to serve you and not me. That said, I feel a little indebted to you since you have done some good. Because of that, I'm not planning to execute you. Instead, I strip you of your noble title and banish you from the kingdom. You have one week to get your affairs in order and leave. We will station guards on you at all times until you leave the city walls. Once you leave, you are not be seen in this kingdom again by punishment of death."

Arthur's proclamation rang through the crowd, and no one said anything. Dalia's face ran through a full range of emotion as sadness took over and tears fell. It wasn't long before those tears and sadness morphed into what Arthur thought of as rage and she clenched her fists. He thought she might try something foolish, but she finally calmed herself and merely turned and stormed out of the room. Arthur didn't feel like dealing with her anymore, so he let the dismissal go.

"My apologies, council members. I didn't want this meeting to be overshadowed by a deed such as that. I felt it was important that you see I won't tolerate that kind of neglect or behavior. I expect our leaders to set an example and work toward fixing problems. Not letting them fester."

Everyone mumbled in agreement.

"Now. Let's talk about war preparation. I'd like to march as soon as we can." Arthur said, and the discussion picked back up.

* * *

"Sister!" the voice boomed across the white space.

"Can you at least try to be civil here? This is my home," Lianna said as she put down a book she'd been reading.

Isabell walked over and stood in front of her sister.

"This has gone far enough," Isabell told her.

"Just because you're losing control of the world is no reason to be an ass. What comes around goes around. You did the same thing to me, if you don't recall." Lianna said in a calm tone.

"That's not the point," Isabell huffed. "You know what will happen if the Ar'Tookan decide the agreement is broken. We have to stop that now or it will be too late. They are already taking a keen interest in the current events."

Lianna hesitated. She knew they were dangerous to be on the wrong side of. While she didn't fear them personally, she wasn't keen on them enslaving any other planets under her power. That would drastically weaken her in the Game of Gods.

"I can tell you see the dilemma here," Isabell said.

"What would you have me do? I can't stop what's in motion. Nor do I really want to. This planet is on the brink of death and destruction from the horrible handling of your minders," Lianna said.

"How about we meet in the middle?" Isabell said.

"I'll consider it. What do you propose?"

"Let me remove Arthur from the mix. He is the real problem here. I'll even agree to wait until after Wailyn is dead. Short of a miracle, or direct intervention, I don't see him winning this fight." Isabell said.

"What good is that going to do?" Lianna asked.

"You and I both know he's the real catalyst. Without him, world development will slow and finally hit a cap. His advanced knowledge of things from his home world allows him to see things differently and work magic in ways others haven't thought of. That kind of thinking is dangerous around the Ar'Tookan. If we remove him, there might be a chance to broker a new peace. Also, if they find out Arthur has Dimensional Magic, there will be hell to pay. They might even enslave him to use in their war." Isabell said.

Lianna bit her lip and thought about the problem. *What she says is correct. I just can't waste this opportunity.*

"I'll consider it," she told her. "I'm tempted to decline outright just for your temerity, and because I want the power from the world. I won't overlook the potential for catastrophe, though. Let's see how this fight goes. It may be a simple transition and there could be a possibility of a deal with the Ar'Tookans from Arthur. I'll intervene personally with him if necessary.

Isabell looked like she wanted to blow up in anger again, but she pulled herself together. Her face slowly morphed into a look of calm before she responded.

"Fine. I guess that's fair. Thank you, sister." She said before walking away and fading into the vast white.

She must be desperate to thank me…

* * *

The next two days went by in a blur. Arthur didn't want to delay too long, but he also wanted to make sure everything was ready. The trip would take some time and wasn't just a quick day or two march. They needed to go north and east, close to the trail they took for their class quests and even further past. If they kept up a decent pace, he figured they could make it in three weeks.

His time was spent in the blacksmith and doing his enchanting work. The goal was to ensure that everyone marching with them had damage negation armor. So far, all the plate and chain was now complete. Arthur was at the mercy of other crafters to finish the leather and cloth pieces. He spent some time laying in those enchantments but the crafters weren't as fast as he was. That said, he wasn't going to spend more time trying to grind those skills.

He also set aside time to prepare his Wizard's Den. Much of it was in order from his previous attempts at decorating, but he'd spent more time pouring mana in and expanding it. He expanded part of the space and blocked it off as its own room. This area he used to dump excess equipment and supplies.

Since the room had a fully functioning kitchen, his inner circle would camp in style. He almost felt bad about that, but then remembered this was a war and he was a king, like it or not. To keep from feeling too guilty, he decided he wouldn't close the space at night and would keep the doorway open inside a small tent. That way, anyone in the army could approach or signal them of oncoming danger.

It would be horrible if he woke one morning, opened the den, and found their camp burned to a crisp and everyone dead.

The council also offered suggestions of their own. They set aside provisions for the march. Some of which would be stored in Dimensional Bags and the rest would be in one of Arthur's Dimensional Storage spaces. They didn't want to risk their people starving if something happened to Arthur and he couldn't summon his space.

They also insisted he fill another Dimensional Storage with food to distribute to the citizens in the capital. If it was in the same state as Seora, they'd need all the help they could get. Arthur was so pleased with the suggestion that he set aside a small window of time to smith a bunch of basic farming and crafting tools out of their leftover lower quality metals. He could hand those out as needed.

At the end of the two days, he met with Samson in a staging area outside of the city.

"Everything ready?" He asked the paladin as he approached.

"Will be by morning. The last of the supplies are being packed and loaded. Gear is being checked and swapped out. Some of our reserve forces who are coming with us needed the newer armor."

"Great work," Arthur said as he clapped the man on the shoulder. "I want you to know I appreciate everything you've done. I know there were some tough times, but I couldn't have done this without you."

Samson was quiet for a moment before his shoulders slumped.

"Thank you. I'm sorry about how I've acted the last few weeks. My head knows Vana's death wasn't your fault, but my heart keeps wanting to lash out at everyone. If not for you, I'd still be some washed up old veteran being kicked around like a lapdog by a group of thieves."

"You have a family now and forever, my friend. Hopefully, we can finally have some peace and quiet after this," Arthur said.

Samson grumbled. "You're trying to curse it, aren't you?"

"Not on purpose. Anything I can do for you before we leave in the morning?"

"I've got this covered. You may do one last check to make sure there are no more pieces or armor or weapons that need enchanting, but we should be ready at daylight." Samson said.

"I'll leave you to it. Let's go finish this once and for all." Arthur said before marching into the camp. Arthur checked over his skill gains from the last two days while he finished the last of his inspections.

You have gained 2,990 total experience in Air Magic.

Congratulations, you have reached level 14 in Air Magic. Air Magic spells now have a 27% increased effect. You're horrible about forgetting some of your skills.

You have gained 8,210 total experience in Earth Magic.

You have gained 7,120 total experience in Fire Magic.

You have gained 3,310 total experience in Water Magic.

You have gained 2,145 total experience in Dimensional Magic.

You have gained 13,120 total experience in Enchanting.

Congratulations, you have reached level 22 in Enchanting. Your enchantments have a 63% decreased mana cost. You should really hand off some of this work.

You have gained 8,110 total experience in Blacksmithing.

You have gained 8,110 total experience in Arcane Smithing.

Arthur looked over his Talents for Air Magic and put his two points in Hasty.

Hasty (3/10)	Boosts speed enhancement effects by 3% per point.

A quick glance at his Enchanting talents led him to add points to Blessing of the Ancients.

Blessing of the Ancients (8/10)	This talent increases the chance any item you create will be Blessed by the Ancients. Each point invested increases this chance by 1%. Blessing of the Ancients: Divine inspiration influences the item to change its properties and improve it. The possibilities are endless and unable to be predicted.

Arthur smiled to himself as he finished up his tour of the fighters and turned for home. *Tomorrow is the beginning of the end.*

Chapter 39

Assault!

Arthur sat up in bed and stretched his arms over his head. He flipped the covers off and stood up. Stumbling into the kitchen area, he reached into his cold storage and pulled out a small pitcher of tea.

The brew was a little stronger than he was used to back on Earth, but he wasn't going to complain. A little bit of sugar mixed in gave it the perfect taste. He finished up his small cup before placing the cup in the sink and walking back to the main room.

Everyone else was stirring and getting ready as he strapped on armor and weapons. Arthur walked over and helped Rayne tighten some straps on the back of his leather armor before Rayne returned the favor and ensured his mail was all secure.

"You ready?" Arthur asked.

"As ready as I can be."

Anything I can do to help? Zoe asked.

Arthur spotted her as she entered the doorway from the campground.

No thanks. I know you wanted to be here at the battle, but I need you to stay in the back with the logistics and reserve forces. Haven't had enough time to train you in your new magical techniques. Arthur said.

I can detect things in the air and on the ground now thanks to Rayne's help. He's an excellent teacher.

"Hi Zoe," Rayne told her with a wave.

She returned the gesture before looking back at Arthur.

Give it some time. I'm sure there will be a chance for you to fight. Until then, help where you can.

She nodded in agreement before turning and leaving the den. Rayne looked confused before shrugging. "When is Cal supposed to be back?"

"Any minute now. She was doing one last flyover to check for any surprises." Arthur said.

Rayne nodded, and they emerged from his Wizard's Den. Samson was already outside, ordering people around and checking on gear and supplies.

"Get all the camping gear stacked over by the logistics cart. I want all of it in the storage pocket within the hour!" Samson barked at the nearby soldiers.

Arthur walked up next to him, Rayne by his side.

"We still on time?" Arthur asked.

"As long as Cal arrives soon, we should be ready to begin the assault." Samson confirmed.

Arthur scanned the camp. The trip was relatively easy and with their advanced gear and equipment they made it in two and a half weeks. The few carts they had were still in perfect working order, and Arthur was tickled that everything held up so well.

They had one small party of goblins that he let the army clear out as a warmup two days ago, and now everyone was eager. He looked over the horizon and spotted the city walls of Esmere. From a distance, they looked imposing. Nearly thirty feet tall with crenelated towers every three-hundred feet.

"Plan still the same?" Rayne asked.

"Unless something changes with Cal's report." Arthur confirmed.

"Sure I can't just take Wailyn out myself?" Rayne asked.

"No. I don't know what powers Isabell may have granted him. Just find him and keep an eye on him. I'll let you know if that changes." Arthur said.

"Takes all the fun out of it," Rayne grumbled.

"Can I light the wall on fire?" Balair asked as he walked over to join them in his human form.

"Depends. I'm inclined to say yes. If they have something to repel dragons, you're the perfect sacrifice," Arthur said with a wry smile.

"I swear you become more of a dick every day. Why do I even hang around anymore?" Balair said.

"Mainly for free food and a warm place to sleep." Samson said.

"Got me there," Balair agreed.

Clear me a spot. Calfuray sent.

Arthur relayed the message and Samson had the soldiers move out of an area beside them. Her purple form landed with a light gust of wind before she shifted down into her human form.

"Looks the same as yesterday. Guards on the walls loaded down with long spears. Looks like a porcupine. City is a mess and half the buildings look run down and dilapidated. If it wasn't for the defenders on the wall, I'd say it was an abandoned ghost town." Cal reported.

"Any signs of the civilians?" Arthur asked.

"Didn't see anyone not in armor or armed with a weapon. They could be anywhere." Cal said.

"Change of plans, Rayne. I want your priority to be to locate the citizens first. I don't doubt he tried to make a trap where we accidentally kill them while trying to breach the walls. Find them and get them out of the line of fire if you can. If not, find some way to signal us and let us know where they are." Arthur said.

"I can think of something," Rayne said.

"Any concerns?" Samson asked Cal.

"It looks simple, and that worries me. I at least expect Garthool to make an appearance and try to redeem himself." Cal said.

"I'm sure there are a few surprises. Samson, you have full command of our forces. You do what you feel is best. I'm going to play reserves and fill in gaps and handle surprises. Use Balair if you need to create openings on the wall. Cal will stay with me in reserve in case anything unexpected happens." Arthur said.

"Understood." Samson said.

"Well, I'm off," Rayne told them.

Arthur turned to the thief and extended his hand. Rayne took it with a smile and Arthur pulled him into a hug.

"Watch your back and stay alive. You're family now. We can't lose any more family." Arthur said before they separated.

"Thank you. I'll try. You better not die. Allendria would kill me if you didn't survive." Rayne said.

"I've no doubt she would go on a rampage. How about we all come out of this one alive?" Arthur said.

"Amen to that," Wesley said.

Arthur turned to look at the bard.

"Where the hell did you come from?" Arthur asked.

"I've been with you the whole time…" Wesley said.

"Have you really? I guess I didn't notice you tagged along for this. Figured you'd stay in Alurian for sure after you played sentry at the Dark Elf Siege." Arthur said.

"Makes for good stories. Have to get experience for my bard class and storytelling goes a long way for that." Wesley said.

"Stay in the back and stay out of the way," Samson ordered. "We don't have extra people to watch your back this time."

"Of course."

Arthur shifted focus back to the Rayne and realized he was gone. He'd taken the time to pull a Batman and just bounce while everyone was distracted.

"Your show, Samson." Arthur said.

***

Arthur stood at the back of the formation. His hands were sweaty as he flexed his fingers in anticipation. The army stood just outside of the defender's range and was lined up to assault the wall.

Clash of Kings	
Requirements: Participate in actions to directly or indirectly influence the outcome of the raid. Rewards: 27,500 experience, 3 Talent Points, 1 Spell Blade Talent Points	Description: A new r started near Esmere. either side in the f the side you assist the raid, you receiv rewards.

Compared to the size of the city, their army looked tiny. Less than a thousand people were all they could bring, but their superior weaponry and armor should make this possible. It also helped because they could focus on one section of the wall and only so many defenders could protect such a small space at one time.

Arthur walked through the crowd to the front of the formation before turning and projecting his voice toward his men.

"Today is the day we right the wrongs of the past. All of you have suffered under the poor leadership of this tyrant. Channel that rage for everything and everyone you've lost. Let's usher in a new age of peace for the Kingdom of Fire!" Arthur announced.

The crowd cheered at his speech before Samson walked up to join him.

"Soldiers of the Kingdom of Fire," the paladin started as he withdrew his weapon. "Attack!"

Arthur stood in place as the army filtered past him in slow and orderly lines. They weren't foolish enough to charge in a haphazard formation and suffer the consequences. Warriors in heavy plate with large tower shields led the formation while the mages in the rear provided spell cover.

Arrows blanketed the sky as the forces closed the distance. The discipline of his army showed brightly as the mages batted the projectiles down, so they fell short. They easily deflected the few stray arrows that made it through with shields.

Other mages lobbed balls of fire from his forces at the people on the wall. Fire rippled along the battlements as each successive ball found a mark. To Arthur's surprise, the defenders seemed largely unaffected by the blast. He didn't know if their mages were shielding them or if there was some kind of enchantment in place.

"Mages?" Balair asked.

"Not sure. Possibly." Arthur said.

"Balair!" Samson called. "You're up."

"This had better not turn into another heroic sacrifice," the dragon grumbled before running some distance and leaping into the air as his body transformed into his dragon form.

Balair flew in lazy circles as he rose higher and higher into the air. In a matter of seconds, he began his dive and headed for the section of wall they were marching for.

His approach signaled panic as Arthur watched the defenders scramble. Flames poured from the dragon as he bathed the walkway with his breath. Arthur heard a few screams from his place on the field, but they were hard to make out at this distance. *If nothing else, he killed a few of them.*

A loud roar echoed across the field, and Arthur turned toward the sound. Black clouds covered the sky in the distance, and Arthur narrowed his eyes.

Garthool has returned.

I'm on it. Calfuray sent.

Calfuray took to the sky and rose to interpose herself between them and the approaching darkness. Balair banked out of his attack and flew to join Calfuray.

A large black head burst from the cloud bank as Garthool sped forward. Cal roared in challenge and Garthool returned it. Unfortunately, another roar joined Garthool's as a dark blue dragon emerged from the darkness.

That's Chillventus. I'm surprised he agreed to be part of this. He notoriously hates other races. Calfuray sent.

Cal, pull back for a second. Balair, come grab me. I'm joining the fight. Arthur said.

Calfuray slowed her flight and banked to the side to maintain her position. Balair turned a quick one-eighty and dashed for Arthur.

"Samson, I'm heading up with Balair. We have two dragons this time." Arthur called to the paladin.

Samson looked toward the approaching enemies and nodded. "Good luck."

Arthur sprinted in the direction at his fastest speed. He activated Weak Haste as he went and his body launched forward. Distance melted in his view until he spotted Balair swooping down low. Balair flew past him and he turned his head to watch the younger dragon bank to come up on his side. Arthur smiled and waited until he was almost to him before leaping high in the air. Balair snatched him with his claws and took him higher in the sky before launching him upward.

Arthur spun once as he flipped through the air, but quickly slowed his spin with Air Magic. Before he did much else, Balair was under him and he landed with a thump on the dragon's back. He bounced once before finding a handhold on one of his back ridges and then activated his Aerial Footing ability. Magic in place, he rose to his feet easily and walked toward the base of Balair's neck.

They caught up with Calfuray in the air and then both dragons continued forward to the enemies. Fighting them away from the city and the armies would be a much better option and reduce the risk of collateral damage on both sides.

Is that a scar? Arthur asked.

On Garthool? Kinda. We have natural healing abilities, but it takes time based on the damage. That was severe damage he had on his face from the attacks. It would normally take a full month or two to heal something that bad. The partially healed wound looks like a scar, though. Calfuray explained.

The scar in question covered the entire snout from the crease of his mouth, at an angle all the way to the tip of the nose.

Chillventus was more comparable in size to Calfuray. He had the sweeping spikes off the back of his head similar to Garthool, but he had what looked like fine silver hair woven into a semblance of a mane around the neck along the spines.

They stopped at a hover when the two sets of dragons grew near.

Arthur amplified his voice. "Came back to let us finish the job this time?"

"I'm here to kill you all. Even found another who agreed with my idea on the matter." Garthool said.

"Must have been a good talk if you convinced Chillventus to come along. What did he promise you for your help?" Calfuray asked.

"I get to kill a bunch of things I already hate. That and take out a human sympathizer. Seemed like a win-win all around." Chillventus answered.

"Seriously? Chillventus, though? What, was Frost Bat already taken as a name?" Balair asked.

"How dare you," Chillventus said before charging at Balair. Garthool was right behind him, but Calfuray interposed herself in his path. Their fight started with flashing claws, and Arthur focused on the danger ahead of him. He scanned both dragons to see what they were dealing with.

<table>
<tr><td colspan="2">

Name: Garthool
Level: 45
Type: Dragon
Rarity: Rare
HP: 12850/14000
MP: 3000/3000
Stamina: 6000/6000

</td></tr>
<tr><td>

Strength: ?
Agility: ?
Intellect: ?
Wisdom: ?
Endurance: ?
Charisma: ?
Luck: ?

</td><td>

Experience: N/A

Skills
Combat Skills:

?: ? (???/???)
?: ? (???/???)

</td></tr>
</table>

Name: Chillventus
Level: 35
Type: Dragon
Rarity: Rare
HP: 11325/11325

| MP: 4500/4500 | |
Stamina: 4200/4200	
Strength: ?	Experience: N/A
Agility: ?	Skills
Intellect: ?	Combat Skills:
Wisdom: ?	
Endurance: ?	?: ? (???/???)
Charisma: ?	?: ? (???/???)
Luck: ?	

Well, this is going to suck.

Arthur drew Ember and his enchanted dagger before adding fire from his Spell Blade Class. He shrugged his shoulders and moved them in circles to loosen up as they closed the last few feet. When Balair collided with Chillventus, Arthur leaped forward and landed on the dragon's back. He activated Aerial Footing again to attach him to the new target and then stood and raced for the base of his neck.

Balair cried out as claws skittered down his side. But he wasn't the only one taking damage. Arthur stopped and hopped backward as one of Balair's claws wrapped around and raked down the back of Chillventus. Scales popped and snapped as pieces littered the air.

Arthur reached the base of the neck and plunged Ember deep into the nearest gap in the scales. He activated the flames from Ember's ability at the same time. The heat from the blade warped the air around it as it entered the dragon's flesh as though a hot knife through butter.

Chillventus roared. Whether in anger or pain, Arthur wasn't entirely sure. Pain seared down his side and he stumbled, nearly losing his footing. If not for the blade still buried in the dragon, he wouldn't have held on.

Chillventus dealt 0 damage to you with Tail Swipe. (85 damage negated)

Well, this trick worked once. Let's try it again.

Arthur grabbed the blade with both hands and braced his feet against the dragon's back. He used all his strength to twist Ember and the wound slowly opened. A small river of blue blood welled up in the gash and began trickling over the edges and running down the dragon's side.

To Arthur's surprise, he realized the blue blood was actually protecting the dragon from his flames and was pushing the heat back from the blade. It even prevented the flesh from cauterizing, as it normally would.

You have dealt 310 damage with Ember to Chillventus. (Critical Hit) (Elemental Weakness)

The blade slid free with ease, and Arthur slung the excess blue liquid off with a quick swipe. He didn't want to risk it damaging his weapon. A quick thought dropped the enchantments and the innate fire, and he slid Ember and his dagger back into their scabbards.

Arthur took a few steps back and spun up his dual cast Fireblast. The small orbs of fire formed in his hands. He timed the rise and fall of the back as the dragon flapped its wings and continued its fight with Balair. Throwing the spells at the wound, he continued to backpedal at a quicker rate. Aerial Footing allowed him to move quickly without as much risk of falling off, but he didn't want to take his eyes from the impact.

The balls shots forward before slamming into the area around the wound. Arthur was disappointed they didn't hit directly inside the injury, but it was hard to get a perfect target with the movement. The orbs exploded and sent waves of fire spinning in small domes of flames.

His Fire Magic kicked in as he used his innate resistance to shield himself from any of the potential damage. Chillventus roared and bucked, violently jerking his body in up and down motions. Arthur assumed he was trying to make him fall off, but all it really did was make him feel like he was on a crazy roller coaster. There was a little queasiness to it that reminded him of seasickness, though.

You have dealt 410 damage to Chillventus with Dual Cast Fireblast. (Elemental Weakness)

As soon as the flames cleared, Arthur rushed forward again, pulling both weapons from their scabbards and lunging at the now sizzling ruined flesh. Fire flashed over both weapons as he activated his Spell Blade skills, and they slid into the charred flesh. The smaller blade sunk to the hilt while his sword punched down almost a foot deep. With a violent jerk, he ripped both out sideways, chunks of flesh breaking free as blood sprayed over the area.

You have dealt 185 damage to Chillventus with Enchanted Magesteel Dagger. (Elemental Weakness)
You have dealt 225 damage to Chillventus with Ember. (Elemental Weakness)
You have dealt 185 damage to Chillventus with Rip. (Elemental Weakness) (Bleed)

The dragon roared again, but this time in obvious anger. Shards of ice formed around its head and shot backward. The first two caught Arthur by surprise, and he took the blasts directly to the chest. Staggering him backward and leaving frost on his breastplate.

Chillventus has dealt 0 damage to you with Icicle Blast. (70 damage negated) (x2)

Arthur dodged the next three icicles as they flew toward him. The fourth he smashed with Ember and it burst into a cloud of glittery dust. Magic gathered around Chillventus' head again, but this time it took on the form of a thick mist as it slowly flowed backward to cover the dragon.

The cold seeped into his bones as the chilling air approached, so Arthur leaned heavily on his Fire Magic to ramp up the heat. A shimmering barrier of red and orange appeared around him as he poured mana in to fight off the attack. He kneeled down to make a smaller zone for him to cover so he could preserve some of his mana. His pool may have been extensive, but there was still a siege to win and another dragon to deal with.

Glancing at the other fight only showed flashes of shadow as Calfuray and Garthool fought in midair. The heavy ice mist obscuring any details from his vision.

A flaming claw struck a few feet from the edge of his barrier and steam sizzled off the limb as Balair ripped flesh down the side of the dragon. Growing tired of this game, Arthur activated Disrupting Blow and stabbed both weapons into the dragon's back. For good measure, he also selected Mana Leech strike and layered it with Double Discharge.

Whether all three could work in conjunction, Arthur wasn't sure. The results of the attack proved that not only was it possible, it was a fantastic option.

You have dealt 1260 damage with Combination Attack. (Critical Hit) (Elemental Weakness)
You have drained 420 mana from Chillventus.

The spell creating the mist dissipated and the air gradually cleared. Arthur could finally see the fight between Cal and Garthool and wasn't pleased with what he saw. Both were injured, but Cal looked to have taken the most damage between the two. She was bleeding in multiple places and her right wing appeared to catch when she flapped it.

This is taking too long. I need to end it, and quick. He did another scan to see the progress they made.

Name: Chillventus
Level: 35
Type: Dragon
Rarity: Rare
HP: 7815/11325
MP: 2754/4500
Stamina: 3415/4200

Have to give it to Balair. He's doing a credible job with the damage. Not sure I can tell him that because I'd never hear the end of it, though.

Arthur hoped for a little less health left than that, but he couldn't complain. Balair was fighting a dragon almost twice his size while Arthur held on to its back and attacked it.

Ending this fight quickly was the top priority, but Arthur was loath to burn his long cooldowns in case of an emergency. He weighed the options and decided that dealing with King Wailyn could be done much easier than fighting two dragons. His mind made up, he reached out to Balair.

Can you get Chillventus to Garthool? I need both of them side by side. Arthur sent.

We can. Calfuray answered. Her mental voice sounded tired and winded.

Let's go. As soon as they are together, I'm blowing through cooldowns to end this. Arthur said.

Brace yourself, Balair sent.

Arthur stayed low and concentrated on his
Aerial Footing spell to ensure he held his
ground. In moments he was rocked violently as
Balair barreled into Chillventus. The young
dragon abandoned all fighting style and went
straight brawler with a tackle that would make
Goldberg proud.

Chillventus tried to stop his momentum as
he flapped his wings and slashed at Balair
with his claws, but it didn't stop their
direction. A few seconds later, they hit hard
and Arthur ducked as one of Garthool's wings
slammed into Chillventus' back.

Arthur activated Call Wrath and targeted
Chillventus to double all his damage to him.
He then activated Retribution and Divine Fury
from his divine tree to deal out continuous
AOE damage to both. Back on his feet, Arthur
walked forward through the storm of damage and
looked down at the wound in the base of the
dragon's neck. He activated Dragonfire.

Flames bubbled up inside of Arthur and the
sheer force of it made him redouble his Aerial
Footing spell to keep from flying backward.
Fire poured from him as he aimed directly at
the gaping hole. The blue blood sizzled and
bubbled as the flames finally charred flesh
and cracked scales.

*You have dealt 1,350 damage to Chillventus
with Dragonfire. (Critical Hit) (Elemental
Weakness)*

The high damage from his Dragonfire ability warmed his heart. He worried its lower base damage would make it next to useless against this dragon, but the elemental weakness couple with critical hit made it formidable. Looking over the damage, he realized that although his divine abilities didn't receive the elemental weakness buff, they were affected by his Agility, making them crit. So far, he was averaging a crit on one out of three ticks of the ability on each target.

Ticks of damage continued to roll in as Arthur turned his attention back to the target. With his biggest abilities on cooldown, it was back to good old fashion stabbing. He used Ember and his dagger to slash and carve chunks of burning and crispy flesh from the dragon's neck. He quickly dug deeper and deeper, through sinew and muscle, trying to find purchase on something more dangerous.

Twice a tail smashed into him, but all it did was flatten him into the puddle of gore he stood in. The mana barrier on his gear absorbed it all without an issue.

Chillventus has dealt 0 damage to you with Tail Smash. (85 damage negated) (x2)

His sword continued to slice until it struck something solid. Arthur felt the reverberation of bone and paused. Using his magic, he amplified his voice.

"Surrender Chillventus or it's time for you to die."

"I'll never surrender to pathetic humans like you. I'm a proud dragon from a noble…"

The statement never finished, as Arthur put away his dagger and activated a Dual Cast Searing Beam. The power burned into the vertebrae as it quickly darkened and the surrounding flesh sizzled. Grabbing Ember with both hands and using all his strength, he plunged it straight down, sliding right between the gap in the vertebrae. Blue blood and clear fluid sprayed from the wound like a geyser, but Arthur ignored it and ripped the sword to the side.

Good. I didn't want to let you live, anyway.

You have dealt 610 damage to Chillventus with Dual Cast Searing Beam. (Critical Hit)
You have dealt 510 damage to Chillventus with Ember. (Critical Hit) (Elemental Weakness) (Decapitating Blow)

The dragon went rigid as its body stopped working. Arthur felt a moment of weightlessness as it plummeted from the sky. Overhead, Balair roared in triumph before he spotted Arthur and dove for him. A glance at the ground and up at Balair told him there was no way he could reach him in time. His mind raced for options to stop his fall and while he was sure his Air Magic could cushion the impact, the distance and speed he was traveling would surely be too much to negate.

An idea flashed through his mind, and he looked at Balair.

Stop there and hover in that spot. You can't reach me in time. I have an idea.

Balair looked hesitant, but obeyed instructions and stopped to hover in place.

Arthur put Ember back in its scabbard, pulled on his mana, and activated his Rift magic. He directed a portal to open right below Balair's claw and then quickly popped another open right above him. In an instance, he jumped from the dragon and reached through the hole, grabbing on to Balair's claw with his right arm. The sudden stop nearly jerked his arm out of socket, but he gritted his teeth and held on.

Water Magic welled up in him as he sent the power to heal the damage to the shoulder. An enormous crashing sound filled the air as Arthur looked down to see Chillventus' body crumbled on the ground. Blood leaked from his wounds and a puddle of the blue liquid formed around him in the crater his body left.

Good job. Now what? Balair asked.

Arthur hung from a small rift, just big enough to fit his arm through, while Balair floated far overhead. If he tried to fly down to him, he'd pass below the rift and Arthur would have to let go or risk breaking his arm over backward. If Balair tried to fly higher, it would pull Arthur forward and likely kill him as his body tried to squeeze through the tiny hole.

Tag, you're it. Calfuray called as she dove past Balair for Arthur. She raced downward and grew close before Arthur spotted Garthool approaching Balair.

Arthur used his magic to cast a Major Heal on Balair.

Evade him, Balair. We'll be back to help in a moment. Arthur sent before letting go. He snapped the rift shut as his arm left and Balair dove immediately after. Instead of racing for Arthur, the small dragon banked hard and circled away from Arthur and Cal.

Smelling easier prey, Garthool followed
Balair instead of chasing Calfuray. She passed
Arthur in her dive and spread her wings to
steady out under him. Arthur landed with a
thud and activated his Aerial Footing spell.

*You have taken 0 damage from Fall. (185
negated)*

He rolled over and pushed himself to his
feet. Remembering Cal's earlier injuries, he
cast Minor Heal. The water magic flowed
through her and began repairing some of the
lesser wounds. If nothing else, it may offer a
brief glimpse of comfort. The long cooldown of
a minute hampered his ability to keep spamming
it on her.
Thanks. It soothers the ache a little.
Calfuray said.
Glad to hear it. Let's go get Garthool.
Arthur said.
Focusing on his Water Magic again, Arthur
wanted to improve the healing. He kneeled down
and placed a hand on her back. Feeling the
flow of her blood, he had his water magic
enhance the liquid in her body. He kept
pumping mana into the spell as it circulated
with her bloodstream. The energy wove through
every inch of the dragon as the veins and
arteries fed the healing power to Cal. He
envisioned the effect lasting for a longer
period of time and released the spell.

*Congratulations, you have discovered the
Water Magic spell Rejuvenation. You have
gained 250 experience for discovering a known
spell.*

<table>
<tr><td colspan="2" align="center">Spell: Rejuvenation</td></tr>
<tr><td>Requirements: Water Magic
Mana Cost: 180 MP
Cast Time: 3 seconds
Cooldown: 45 seconds</td><td>Description: Use the power of Water Magic to speed up the recovery process of the body. Heals target for 50 HP/s for 2 minutes.</td></tr>
<tr><td colspan="2" align="center">Mastery Level: 1</td></tr>
</table>

Calfuray turned and darted after the larger dragon. Balair was leading him on a merry chase around the sky. The smaller dragon didn't have the speed Garthool could manage, but he had more maneuverability. His ability to shift directions on a dime left the larger dragon swooping past and missing his target.

Arthur did a quick scan to see how much damage was done.

<table>
<tr><td>Name: Garthool
Level: 45
Type: Dragon
Rarity: Rare
HP: 6940/14000
MP: 2200/3000
Stamina: 3120/6000</td></tr>
</table>

Great work on Garthool, Cal.

Thanks. Although, I'm afraid I'm spent. The injuries are sapping my strength and he is too powerful for me to handle alone. Calfuray said.

Good thing you're not alone. Arthur said.

She's damn near alone. I don't have much left in me either. Going claw to claw with Chillnuts down there left me drained and injured as well. Thanks for asking. Balair grumbled.

Arthur and Cal both chuckled at his response as they approached the chase.

Same plan as last time? Cal asked.

I want this bastard on the ground. Not looking forward to falling out of the sky on the back of a dead dragon again.

So, what do you need us to do? Balair asked.

Keep him distracted. Throw spells at him. Annoy him. Hell, you're an expert at that. Arthur said.

Oh, I can definitely do that.

Good. I'm going to jump on board like last time, but I'm aiming for his wings instead. Arthur confirmed.

I'll get you close. Cal said.

They continued their chase until Cal was directly behind Garthool. Her approach turned out to be simple. Just crash right into him.

Arthur used the same tactic as last time and jumped right as they collided. His leap carried him over the dragon's back and he nearly missed the mark altogether if he didn't have the foresight to blast himself back toward its body with raw Air Magic.

He used his small dagger to catch himself as it wedged between two scales. Activating Aerial Footing, he put his dagger away and pulled out Ember. Using his new combination ability from Spell Blade, he encased the sword in Ice Magic. He ran along the spine until he reached the closest wing joint. A few more steps carried him onto the wing, and he stopped at the first major joint. With a grin, he plunged Ember in and the magic caused ice crystals to form along the joint. He kept the blade in place and allowed the cold to seep deeper as the ice solidified.

Every time Garthool flapped his wings, part of the ice would break and splinter free, but Arthur was patient. When he felt enough cold seeped in, he withdrew Ember and raced for the joint at the dragon's back. Another stab of the sword, and he allowed the ice to crawl down the ridge of the wing and along Garthool's side.

The wing slowed as the dragon tried to maintain his altitude, but Arthur noticed they were growing closer to the ground. Small fireballs shot from Balair and struck along Garthool's face while Calfuray smashed icicles of her own into the dragon. They were careful to avoid the wings themselves.

Arthur moved to the other wing and repeated the process. First freezing the outer joint and then moving to the inner connection.

"Get off me, you little bug!" Garthool yelled as a shadow covered Arthur and a tail hit him head on. The attack crushed him to the scales on the dragon's back. He lay there dazed for a few moments before seeing the shadow again. Out of instinct, he rolled to the side, and it smashed into its back.

Seeing his opportunity, Arthur raced to the last joint again. As if on cue, the tail's shadow reappeared and Arthur smiled, He jabbed Ember into the joint and then leaped to the side, deftly rolling out of the way as the tail crashed down and drove Ember all the way to the hilt in its shoulder.

You have dealt 185 damage to Garthool with Ember. (Freezing Strike) (x3)
You have dealt 245 damage to Garthool with Ember. (Freezing Strike) (Critical Hit)

Garthool roared in anger, but a grinding noise was all Arthur could hear. Ember must have punched through the edge of the bone in the joint or perfectly wedged in the space because the wing stopped moving. Their altitude dropped quickly as they approached the ground. In seconds, Garthool landed and Arthur immediately saw a face turn to stare at him. Fiery anger reflected in its deep black eyes.

"Hi," Arthur said with a sheepish smile and a wave.

Fire reflected off Garthool's teeth as his mouth cracked open and he bathed his back with flames. Arthur dove to the side, grabbed Ember, and ripped it free. Letting his fall continue until he landed on the ground. The impact of the landing dealt some damage, but it was better than being covered in fire.

You have taken 0 damage from Fall. (60 negated.)

"I'd ask if you just want to give up now and leave, but honestly, I prefer you die. You had your chance to give up this stupid fight and came back instead." Arthur said with his enhanced voice.

"Powers greater than you forced my hand, and I'd rather take my chance of dying to you than facing them." Garthool said.

Arthur stared up at Garthool's face between the towering legs to either side of him. He held his sword up in both hands in front of him and waited for the attack. As the face closed in, he gripped the blade tight and prepared to slash. Purple flashed in his view and Calfuray collided into the head, her jaws snapping down on his neck.

The distraction must have worked perfectly since Balair also hit at nearly the same time, pushing into the dragon's side and toppling him over. Arthur was stunned for a moment as the body collapsed onto its side and he stood staring at the soft underbelly of the beast.

Knowing his friends couldn't hold for long, he activated his ice effect on Ember and stabbed into the belly. The blade sliced through scales and he carved his way toward the chest. Ice crystallized near the wound and blotches of dark red frozen blood turned into pristine shards.

Arthur turned and ran to gain distance from the body while spinning up a Dual Cast Fireblast. The orbs appeared in his hands and he launched them into the gaping wound in his stomach.

Garthool roared in pain as the orbs exploded. A raging inferno of fire churned at his insides and smoke poured out of the long cut in his belly.

You have dealt 1815 damage to Garthool with Dual Cast Fireblast. (Critical Hit) (Mortal Blow) (Fatal Blow)

The dragon stopped thrashing and laid still. Balair and Calfuray released their grip on him and stumbled over the Arthur.

"You haven't won. This is just the beginning." Garthool said.

Arthur felt a disturbance near the battlefield that he didn't recognize. The magic in the area distorted, and he spun to see a large portal appear to the side of his forces.

"Too late now. Your time is up," Garthool grumbled as he laid his head to rest and his breathing stopped.

"What the hell is that?" Arthur asked.

Tall figures marched from the rift, dressed in clothes that closely resembled military gear from Arthur's world. Their bodies were much larger, with many of them being closer to eight feet tall. Most distinct of all was their skin. They had blue skin.

"It can't be…" Arthur said.

His question was quickly answered as the new arrivals formed up and lifted what looked to be firearms to their shoulders.

Interdimensional Warriors	
Requirements: Participate in actions to directly or indirectly influence the outcome of the raid. Rewards: 77,450 experience, 8 Talent Points, 5 Spell Blade Talent Points	Description: A new r started near Calzas. either side in the f the side you assist the raid, you receiv rewards.

    Energy blasted forth out of them and Arthur
felt the bursts of pure mana as the weapons
fired blast after blast into his people.

Chapter 40

Fight for Survival

Arthur vaguely heard Samson yelling commands at their distance from the battle. Blasts of energy assaulted his people, and he heard cries of pain and yells of anger.

"I need to get over there now. Either of you in good enough shape to get me there?" Arthur asked.

"I can do it," Balair confirmed.

Arthur ran over and hopped on his back. Balair took three running steps and jumped into the air as they darted back toward the battle.

Samson was doing an admirable job of getting their people back into formation and facing the new enemy. Those in the city were now forgotten and ignored. From the look of the battlefield, they weren't much of an issue to begin with.

Magic flashed in his view as he spotted small shields of air and walls of stone sprout up to provide cover.

Great work. Arthur thought as pride swelled in him for his people.

Just get me to Samson. I don't want to risk you flying over that army. I'm sure their blasters will do actual damage to you. Arthur sent Balair.

He grunted in agreement, and they dropped low to skim close to the ground. His claws stretched forward as he brought them to a rest at the back of the army.

"Thanks," Arthur said as he patted Balair on the shoulder and vaulted off his back. He looked back to see Balair slumped to the ground, obviously exhausted from his effort.

Weaving through the army, he headed for the sound of Samson's voice. He found the man near the front line arranging shield bearers and standing in their center to hold the line with his own shield, Divine Fury.

"Samson, what can I do?" Arthur asked as he approached.

The paladin glanced backward to see his approach. "Dragons taken care of?"

"Yep. Both dead. I see someone invited more guests."

"I sure as hell didn't. At least now we have an actual glimpse at the Ar'Tookans everyone keeps mentioning. Their magic is powerful." Samson said.

"I think it's actually technology mixed with magic. Something akin to what I've been wrestling with."

"You have some of those weapons?" Samson asked. Hope in his voice.

"No," Arthur said as he shook his head. "I considered making things like that, but decided against it because I thought they might cause more harm than good."

"Not right now, they wouldn't."

"Doesn't help us now. What do you need?" Arthur asked again.

"Breathing room. They surprised us from the side. We have a shield wall here holding off the brunt of the attack, but we could use fortifications to assist. Not enough time to get it done, though, and our mages aren't strong enough." Samson said.

Arthur looked at the battlefield. The span he needed to cover was something he could do fairly quickly with his predefined wall spells. A few minutes of work could fortify them enough to hold the line.

"Is your bulwark ability for Paladin on cooldown?" Arthur asked.

"No," Samson said.

"If you can activate it to give me a few moments, I can get your wall up for you."

"Done," Samson said before raising his voice. "Hold the line at my position. No one move forward without direct orders."

Power surged from Samson as he activated his paladin ability. A translucent wall of power shimmered into place ahead of them, and Arthur dashed forward past the line.

He pulled on his Earth and Fire Magic and cast his Raise Stone Wall spell over and over as he dashed along the span. The work he did on the farming cities helped, since those wall sections were much bigger and more defensible. He used that size for the spell, and sections of stone rose quickly.

It flowed from the ground upward as dust and debris fell. The magic ceased as the wall reached over a dozen feet, just inside the bulwark of magic. Arthur continued casting spells, bringing small towers up on certain spots in the wall. He widened the walkway on the back to accommodate two rows of fighters.

The ends of the wall he had curve backward for two dozen more feet to provide some defense on the sides and prevent them from assaulting the corner. His last step was to add stairs to the back so the defenders could take up position. Work complete, he looked at his stats.

HP: 890/890
Mana Shield: (350/2,500)
MP: 210/1,560
Stamina: 450/850

The stats weren't terrible, but he didn't like his mana. He'd already pulled mana from his necklace, and Ember had used a fair amount of its own as well.

Item Mana:

Necklace: 5,110/10,000
Ember: 1,890/3,500

Arthur siphoned more mana from his necklace and then recharged his armor's mana to bring the shield back to full.

"Take to the wall. Archers up first to the towers. Be watchful of tricks." Samson ordered.

Arthur turned to see people scrambling past him and climbing the stairs. He hurried back over to Samson.

"Anything else?"

"Just join the fight. I think that should do for now. Thanks." Samson said.

Arthur clasped wrists with him and they
both turned to race up the wall. The blasts
from the other side continued, only now he
heard them crack against the stone as they
blasted the new wall.

He reached the top and scanned their enemy,
now able to see them clearly. Their features
all ranged just as much as one human to
another, but each had the distinctive blue
skin. Most of them stood between seven and
nine feet tall. Overall, there were roughly
thirty of them arrayed in formation.

The power of their blasters was unknown to
him, so Arthur did something foolish. He stood
on one battlement in a clear line of fire. It
took only a few seconds before a blast struck
him in the chest and he fell back onto the
stone walkway.

*Ar'Tookan Warrior has dealt 20 damage to
you with Blaster. (110 negated)*

"For fuck's sake. That hurt," Arthur
grumbled as he pushed himself back to his
feet. "How the hell did it do damage through
my armor?"

Arthur was contemplating this revelation
when he saw a commotion brewing toward the
back of the army. One of the rearmost fighters
ducked down low before returning to standing
holding a giant cannon. The metal was deep
gray, and the barrel had a saddle of leather
that sat on his shoulder. A long fore grip on
the front allowed him to steady it and aim.

"Take cover!" Arthur yelled as the soldier
fired.

A ball of purple energy formed at the mouth of the barrel and rocketed forward. It was roughly the size of a cannonball but made of pure energy. In moments, it smashed into a section of the wall and exploded. The energy swirled in a vortex and ripped stone from its place. The power seemed to crumble anything it touched as the stone turned to dust and formed a small pile of the powder on the ground. When the magic dissipated, a hole the size of a person remained.

Arthur grit his teeth at the destruction. *Damn, if they hit a place with a defender, they won't survive.*

Done playing games, Arthur pulled on his magic and formed a Fireblast in each of his hands. Not wanting to waste trying to launch it, he clapped his hands together, and they melded into one larger, roiling ball of fire. With a grin, he gestured with his now empty hand and a small rift formed beside him. He selected a place right next to the cannon wielding warrior and opened the other side.

Their forces panicked and yelled, pointing at the rift. It was too late as Arthur lobbed the overcharged Fireblast through and snapped it closed.

The field lit up as the orb detonated. Small bubbles of power covered their fighters as they activated personal shields. Cannon guy's shield held for less than a second before it popped and the fire consumed him. Flames ate away at his skin as his mouth opened to scream.

Those immediately near him in formation suffered a similar fate as their shields also popped and they burned. Those in the next rows survived with minor burns. It did enough damage to eat the shield, but it was nearly burned out by the time it popped. They just had a few smoldering spots on their uniforms.

A taller man near the back of their formation yelled out something and everyone ceased fire. He walked through the crowd and approached the front. Without slowing down, he took a few more steps forward, so he was halfway between their defensive wall and his army.

"Who's in charge here?" He called in a deeply accented common speech.

Arthur motioned for Samson to join him on the battlement, so he walked over to stand by Arthur.

"I'm King Arthur Firebrand and am in charge of my kingdom. The fight is under the command of my general, Paladin Samson," Arthur said as he motioned at Samson.

"Who just used the forbidden magic?" The figure asked.

"Not sure what you mean? Fire Magic seems pretty common to be forbidden. Unless you insinuate all magic is forbidden." Arthur said.

"Not the fire. The portal." The man clarified.

"That would be me." Arthur said.

"You are hereby under arrest by the Ar'Tookan Empire. You will be taken to our closest prison and evaluated for your skill. If you prove useful, we may allow you to operate our portal array for the transport corp."

"Fuck off. I don't recognize your authority. This is our world and not yours."

"The slave races should know better than to speak to their betters like that. Seems you will need 'rehabilitation' first. I'll see to the first phase personally."

"Hard to do when you're dead. Now that I know your goals, none of your forces will leave here alive." Arthur said.

"We shall see about that," the man said before turning and walking back into formation. Arthur watched him raise a hand and a bright red light flashed upward.

Damn. What is it now? Arthur wondered.

A trumpet blast filled the air, and Arthur turned to look at the castle. The main gate opened and standing inside was who he guessed to be King Wailyn on a somewhat sick-looking horse. His armor was fine and polished, but the horse looked like it was more likely to collapse than charge the field. To each side of him stood three rows of men, fully armed and ready for battle. They all charged forward toward the rear flank of Arthur's army.

"Samson, I'm going to head them off and raise some more stone. Keep an eye on our blue friends." Arthur said as he hopped off the wall and raced across the clearing.

He arrived shortly after and began pouring mana into his magic. Stone rose at a prodigious rate. He didn't make the walls very long and instead focused on boxing them in a small stone fortress. Spreading everyone out to cover more distance left them vulnerable on the other sides.

Adding a couple dozen feet to the end of
the already curved wall allowed him to curve
it again and continue down the side. From
there, it only took one more curved wall to
reach the other side and butt up to the
existing stone.

More stairs appeared as he kept spending
mana lavishly, but he decided against using
anymore for towers this time.

Arthur raced up the wall and watched the
king's forces come within bowshot and stop.
Men in plate armor with shields stood out
front to block any incoming damage while their
archers rained arrows on the fortification. He
ignored the arrows as a few of them came down
and bounced off his armor.

Archer has dealt 0 damage to you with Iron
Arrow. (25 negated) (x3)

Brushing off the danger from this side,
Arthur went back to Samson.

"Could probably put some of our archers on
the other side to harass Wailyn. They are
fighting in the conventional style and doing
minimal damage. Don't think they could get
through the stone if they wanted." Arthur
said.

"I'll move some. They aren't damaging these
Ar'Tookans much, anyway." Samson said.

"Looks like it's time for a Hellfire
Volley," Arthur said.

"Sounds like a plan. I'll move them after."
Samson agreed.

Arthur opened up his storage and pulled a barrel of the projectiles out. He ran up and down the wall, carrying them to the archers arrayed there with instructions to wait for the call to volley. When all were dispersed, he returned to Samson and pulled his own bow out of storage.

"We are ready."

Samson nodded and called out. "Archers, ready arrows."

Everyone set a Hellfire arrow to their string and waited. Arthur did the same and looked at Samson.

"Draw!" Samson called before following it. "Loose!"

Arrows raced across the opening as two dozen Hellfire Arrows descended on the Ar'Tookans. Arthur watched them yell in warning before their shields popped back into place. Explosions ripped the area apart as the myriad of weapons landed amongst the enemies.

Damage notifications poured in to Arthur, but he ignored them. He felt the heat from the explosions at the top of the wall. The mana slowly faded as the hellfire spells ran their course.

The area cleared, and Arthur had a mild moment of panic. Somehow, all of their soldiers stood where they were without a scratch on them.

A command echoed across the field, and the Ar'Tookans raised their weapons and resumed firing. Arthur spotted a few of them carrying a larger weapon that fired small balls of black energy. Where they struck, the walls crumbled to dust in an instant. The damage was limited to an area about four feet in radius, but enough of those and the wall would crumble entirely.

Arthur pulled Ember free and activated his ice enchantment on it. With a gesture, he opened a rift in front of him and then picked his first target. The exit portal appeared right next to one of the larger weapon wielders, and Arthur stabbed forward. His blade pierced the side of the soldier's neck and the man collapsed to the ground.

You have dealt 215 damage to Ar'Tookan Soldier with Ember. (Critical Hit) (Fatal Blow)
Ar'Tookan Soldier has died.

He pulled his hand back and snapped the rift closed before opening another by the man next to the last. This time, he went to thrust his sword, but instead was blasted in the chest by gunfire through the rift. Two shots splashed into his chest before he shut the rift.

Ar'Tookan Soldier has dealt 20 damage to you with Blaster. (110 negated) (x2)

"Those things still hurt." Arthur grumbled.
Their rate of fire intensified as they blasted at the stone wall. Chunks rained down from the battlements as the wall began to deteriorate and fall apart. Arthur scrambled to do something about it and began lobbing spells as fast as he could. He launched Stone Spikes and dropped a giant Orb of Ice, but each time the Ar'Tookans blasted the projectiles out of the air.

Arthur saw red and purple in his peripheral vision and looked to see Cal and Balair approaching the army from the rear. They came in low and strafed the entire force with their fire breath. The attack took them by surprise and those in the line of fire suffered substantial damage without their shields active.

Gunfire followed the two dragons and multiple projectiles smashed into their sides and wings as they swooped past. Both faltered in flight and went down to the ground behind their small fortress.

Are you two alright? Arthur asked.

We'll be fine. Those blasters hurt. Balair said.

I'm fine as well. Cal sent. *You need something to help finish them. You're pinned down right now and can't even make a proper charge. A distraction is in order.*

You're not going to fly over them again. You two have already suffered too much damage. Stay safe and I'll figure something out. Can either of you try to reach Rayne with our telepathic speech and ask him to keep Wailyn busy while we settle this? Arthur said.

I'll find him. Balair agreed.

Arthur hesitantly checked his stats.

HP: 824/890	
Mana Shield: (870/2500)	
MP: 155/1520	
Stamina: 320/890	
Item Mana:	
Necklace: 1,205/10,000	
Ember: 475/3,500	

Damn it. Raising those walls and building this makeshift fort took up almost everything I had. The few spells I tested just drained me further.

Arthur rushed over to Samson.

"Any ideas?" he asked.

"Not really. We are sitting ducks inside this fortress. It's doing a great job of protecting us, but enough sustained fire will break it down in short order. We really need to charge them and fight, but I'm afraid those weapons will cut us down if we try." Samson summarized.

"Do you think another volley of Hellfire…," Arthur said as he trailed off. Movement in the stand of trees behind the Ar'Tookans drew his attention.

"What fresh hell is this?" Arthur asked.

"What is it?" Samson asked.

"There's something in that stand of trees directly behind the Ar'Tookans. Last thing we need is for them to get more reinforcements."

The two watched the area for a couple of minutes before Arthur smiled.

"Time for a distraction. We need to keep their focus on us, but gather a group to strike at them in the clearing on the ground."

"That who I think it is?" Samson asked.

"Appears to be. Bless her and curse her all the same. Shoulda known she would ignore me."

"I'll gather our forces. Can you provide the distraction?" Samson asked.

"I'm running low on mana, but I'll do what I can," Arthur said as he pulled his bow out again. He grabbed a handful of Hellfire Arrows and propped them against the wall in front of him.

Samson scrambled down and began issuing
orders. He had them passed down quietly so it
wouldn't alert their enemies. Arthur placed
the first arrow and launched it into the
crowd.

Cries of warning rose again and shields
flared to life. Arthur ignored the response
and followed it with another arrow. This one
aimed toward the edge of the formation. He
rose to fire a third when a blast hit him in
the chest and rocked him backward.

*Ar'Tookan Soldier has dealt 20 damage to
you with Blaster. (110 negated)*

Finding another location in the
crenelation, he readied to fire again. His
third arrow headed for the other edge, so fire
blanketed the field.

As before, the flames cleared to leave
hardly any damage.

*You have dealt 15 damage to Ar'Tookan
Soldier with Hellfire Arrow. (120 negated)
(x15)*

The Ar'Tookans continued to whittle away at
their stone defense, but Arthur wasn't
concerned. He just needed them to continue
watching them and not turn to look behind
them. A chunk of stone blasted from a nearby
portion of the wall and crashed into his
chest, send him over the walkway and to the
ground inside the fortress.

*Stone Debris has dealt 0 damage to you. (45
negated)*

Running back up the wall, he continued his assault. Three more Hellfire Arrows covered the army and he let their power fade. Their help was nearly upon the enemy, so he poured what he could scrape of his mana into another Dual Cast Fireblast. He launched those and followed them with a Searing Beam and more Earth Spikes.

Arthur ducked behind the stone wall as blasts aimed for his head. Figuring he wasted enough time, he dropped to the ground and joined the rest of the army.

"Let's go," Arthur told Samson.

Samson nodded and commanded everyone to the ground. They formed up, and Arthur used his magic to expand the hole from the blast in the wall until it allowed them to emerge. Arthur drew his weapons and activated each with ice magic. He led them through the gap and the Ar'Tookans looked on in surprise.

Their gunfire had stopped as they stared at his group in disbelief.

"Charge!" Samson yelled as their forces dashed forward.

"Now would be a good time for your magic, Samson!" Arthur yelled.

"Way ahead of you," the paladin responded as magic rushed to him and brilliant wings of silver exploded behind him.

You have been blessed by the Paladin Samson. Increases your attack and defense by 15% for 20 minutes. You will be able to ignore minor wounds and continue fighting.

The gunfire resumed and Arthur took two shots to the chest and one to the leg before the enemies began yelling in panic. Arthur smiled as the Dark Elf army slammed into the rear ranks and began cutting through the fighters.

Arthur leaped forward and stabbed the first Ar'Tookan with Ember. The blade slid easily into his chest, and the man's eyes rolled back as he slumped to the ground. He kept up his movement as he spun and slammed the dagger into the next one's back.

Another blast caught him in the shoulder, and he stumbled to the side, missing his swing. Changing direction, he pivoted in place and slashed at the next warrior. Leaning to the side, he dodged a blast aimed for his face and lunged forward to stab at his attacker. He weaved through two more foes before he came face to face with the leader.

"Told you this would be your end," Arthur said.

"You might be right, but your trouble has just started. The Empire won't tolerate someone killing a patrol squad. This planet is now doomed to invasion."

"We'll see about that. I'll stop them myself if I must," Arthur said.

He slashed down with Ember, but the soldier grinned and pulled out a blade of his own. The slim design looked flimsy, but whatever it was made of was durable. Their blades met and the Ar'Tookan man's strength showed through as he held back Arthur's attack with relative ease.

Arthur thrust forward with his dagger, but his enemy batted that hand to the side with his other arm. A kick to the knee took the fighter by surprise and Arthur tried to follow it with a thrust. The commander parried his blade as it screeched along his own before hitting Arthur in the face with a backhand.

Ar'Tookan Captain has dealt 80 damage to you with Heavy Backhand.

Damn. No more mana left in my shield?
His enemy thrust forward with his own blade and Arthur activated his Passata Soto ability. He dropped to the ground and thrust upward, Ember sinking into the belly of his attacker.

You have dealt 110 damage to Ar'Tookan Captain with Ember.

The man grunted but backed up, pulling the sword free. It didn't affect him much as he swung again. This time, Arthur blocked it with Ember and activated Shiv. The lightning-fast attack caused his dagger to sink into the man's side.

You have dealt 105 damage to Ar'Tookan Captain with Enchanted Magesteel Dagger. (Critical Hit)

Arthur felt good about his accomplishment until a fist crashed into his face. The pain of the blow shook his concentration and his eyes blurred from the impact. He tried to reorient himself, but a slash to his arm caused another burning pain before fire burned through his shoulder.

His vision finally cleared enough to see
the captain's sword sticking through his right
shoulder, causing pain to radiate across his
entire chest.

*Ar'Tookan Captain has dealt 65 damage to
you with Dizzying Punch.*
*You suffer from temporary blindness for 4
seconds.*
*Ar'Tookan Captain has dealt 105 damage to
you with Blackblade.*
*Ar'Tookan Captain has dealt 180 damage to
you with Blackblade. (Critical Hit)*

"So, who's going to die today, human?" The
captain said as he leaned closer to Arthur.
"Who do you think you are, standing up to the
Empire?"
"He's my future husband," came a low and
sinister voice.
Confusion flashed across the captain's face
before he stood straight and yelled in pain.
Red light shone from his mouth and then moved
to his eyes. Arthur watched in morbid
satisfaction as fire ripped him apart from the
inside.
In moments, his smoking corpse collapsed to
the ground, Allendria standing behind him with
her staff pointed forward.
"I'm both thrilled to see you and furious
that you refused to listen to reason." Arthur
said with a heavy sigh.
"I listened. I just made my own decision in
the end." She said.
She walked over and gently grabbed the
blade stuck in his shoulder before sliding it
free. Arthur winced in pain but activated
Major Heal to let his health tick upward.

"I guess we've seen our new enemy now," Allendria said.

"Sooner than expected. I still have an old enemy to deal with, though." Arthur said as he and Allendria headed for their busted fortress. Arthur bent down and grabbed one of the weapons they used. He put it to his shoulder and pulled the trigger. It hummed for a few moments before Arthur had a bad feeling and threw it to the side.

The weapon exploded in midair, and Arthur suffered minor damage from it.

"Don't try to use their weapons. Gather them somewhere and I'll store them for now. They must have safeguards to prevent enemies from using them." Arthur told Samson as they approached.

"Yeah. We found out the hard way. One of our people tried that already. Luckily, their mana shield absorbed most of the damage, but it took them out of the fight." Samson said.

"Have our people clean up this battlefield. Care to join us in finishing King Wailyn?" Arthur asked.

"I wouldn't miss it," Samson said as he issued orders and then followed them as they walked around the corner of the makeshift fortress.

Allendria stepped to him and kissed him on the cheek before grabbing his hand and placing it on her necklace.

"Take some mana. Looks like you're running low."

"Thanks," he said as he kissed her back and siphoned some out of her amulet.

Arthur smiled at the scene as they rounded the corner. Wailyn's forces were in a panic as the surrounding fighters spun in circles, chasing ghosts. The figure in the dark leather blinked in and out of existence as it attacked person after person. Black shadows pouring from its hood and arms.

"Guess Rayne managed to keep them busy." Arthur said.

"Looks like it." Allendria agreed.

Arthur, Allendria, and Samson approached and stood in a line together in front of their assembled army. Wailyn's people ignored their approach, instead trying to chase the shadow killing their people.

Two loud thuds drew everyone's attention as Calfuray and Balair landed on either side of their army.

"Give up now and we may let you live," Arthur told them.

Most of the normal soldiers dropped weapons and huddled together. A handful that stood near Wailyn looked defiant.

"You must be Arthur," the larger man on the skinny horse said. He swung over the saddle and dropped from the beast before walking forward.

"And you must be Wailyn." Arthur said.

"I'm King Wailyn and you have doomed this entire world with your actions."

"Not interested in your cowardice. It's obvious you sold the livelihood of this planet for some agreement at peace, but all you've done is nearly kill everyone here. It's not better off than being enslaved in your kingdom." Arthur said.

"Looks like you have me here," the king gestured around him. "How about we duel? One on one, to end this."

"Not sure why I need to. You're done for
and this city and kingdom are mine." Arthur
said.

"You haven't taken the city yet, but
killing me would revert everything to your
control, I wager," Wailyn said.

"I'll fight you. I want to kill the man who
betrayed my family. They deserve some
justice."

The onlookers all gathered around and made
space for the two of them. Arthur wasn't sure
about his combat ability, but he drew both
weapons. He put ice on his dagger and fire on
Ember while also activating Ember's own
ability.

The two squared off as they circled each
other. Arthur took the initiative and thrust
first. Wailyn parried the attack and spun his
blade to slash back at Arthur. Arthur twisted
to the side and ducked under the oncoming
blade before his dagger cut across the side of
Wailyn's armor. Frost crystallized where the
blade had nicked him.

*You have dealt 15 damage to King Wailyn
with Enchanted Magesteel Dagger. (Glancing
Blow)*

Arthur kicked out, but Wailyn avoided the
attack. He took a few steps back, and they
reset their pose before resuming their
original circling.

"Not only do you look like your father, you
also fight like him. Inexperienced." Wailyn
said.

Arthur slashed again, aiming for his side,
but Wailyn stepped back to let the blade pass.
He closed the gap and head-butted Arthur.
Arthur staggered backward and shook his head
to clear the pain.

*King Wailyn has dealt 40 damage with
Headbutt.*

Want to play that way, fine.
Arthur grinned as he went on the offensive
again. This time, he raised his dagger as if
to attack but activated his Shine spell. The
bright flash startled Wailyn, and he missed
Arthur's follow up swing with Ember that cut
deep into his shoulder.

*You have dealt 180 damage to King Wailyn
with Ember. (Critical Hit)*

Arthur dove to the side as a stream of
flame poured from Wailyn's hand. Drawing on
what little mana he had left, Arthur created
Stone Spikes from the ground and launched them
at Wailyn.
The king stood firm and deflected the first
two, but the third clipped his leg while the
fourth and fifth crunched into his armor.

*You have dealt 25 damage to King Wailyn
with Stone Spike. (Glancing Blow)*
*You have dealt 95 damage to King Wailyn
with Stone Spike. (x2)*

Arthur smiled as Wailyn sagged to a knee.
His breathing came in heavy and labored.

"Looks like you're out of practice. Guess you don't need to be when all you do is hire worthless thugs to police your people," Arthur said.

"This isn't over yet, boy," Wailyn said as shadows gathered around him. The dark power swirled around his form and it gathered on the king.

Arthur backed away and was getting ready to call on his friends when the shadows ceased and Wailyn remained unchanged. A soft voice filled the clearing.

"You've failed me, Wailyn. I don't take kindly to failure. You're as good as dead already and have no chance of winning. I won't waste my power on a dead man."

The voice faded and Wailyn went pale as a ghost.

"Looks like Isabell decided you were a poor bet. I actually agree with her for once," Arthur said as he stepped forward and slashed at Wailyn.

Ember slid through his neck with ease as the man continued to look shocked and didn't try to dodge. A line of blood formed along his throat and the king still didn't change his expression. When his head slid off his neck, the expression finally morphed from shock to a look of fear before his eyes went vacant.

You have dealt 245 damage to King Wailyn with Ember. (Critical hit) (Decapitating Blow)

King Arthur Firebrand has slain King Wailyn. All lands and subjects owned by King Wailyn are now subjects of the Kingdom of Fire.

    The notifications rolled over him, but he
ignored them. He stood there and reveled in
the feeling of killing the man who betrayed
his parents and robbed him of a family in this
world.

Chapter 41

Cleaning Up

Arthur stored all the gear and items from the Ar'Tookans in a dimensional space to keep anyone from accidentally blowing themselves up.

Loses from the battle were much lower than Arthur feared. The arrival of the Ar'Tookans was to blame for all of them. They hadn't lost a person until that point and suffered only minor injuries. When all was said and done, two dozen fighters were dead and another sixty were injured enough to need recovery time. Three-hundred fighters needed minor medical attention but waited on the mages to finish with the more serious cases.

Arthur toured the city of Esmere. It reminded him of the first time he walked through Seora. Crumbling buildings in all manner of disrepair decorated every street. While Seora had a few nobles who kept their places in decent condition, Esmere had no such luck. Even the noble portion of the city was in ruins.

They found out why as they talked to the few inhabitants left in the city. Apparently, Wailyn had a habit of executing anyone who questioned him and didn't follow his rule explicitly. Over time, the noble houses dwindled and died before the only ones left were those that licked his boots in the castle itself.

The castle was in one piece, but that was the best Arthur could say about it. The few people left alive in the city meant Wailyn didn't have much in the way of castle servants. Litter and refuse lined the unused portion of the castle. Only a select few sleeping quarters, the throne room, and one large assembly hall were clean enough to stay in for any length of time.

Arthur was tempted to burn the entire city to the ground. His sympathy won out, and he didn't want to force anyone from their homes. Instead, he had his forces gather everyone they could find in the city and had them assemble in the main square.

Looking over the crowd, they all appeared malnourished and sickly. There were less than one-hundred people total.

"Greeting citizens of Esmere. I'm King Arthur Firebrand of the Kingdom of Fire. I've taken control of this city and disposed of the traitor, Wailyn. After inspecting your city, I've decided not to invest the time or resources to rebuild it. I'll offer all of you a choice. You can stay here in what you consider home and rebuild on your own. Use anything you see fit from the city to do so," Arthur said before raising a hand. "As long as you don't steal it from someone else here, that is."

The crowd shuffled in place. He could tell a handful of them liked the idea, but the rest just looked dejected and abandoned.

"The second option is to return with me to the capital of my kingdom. The city of Alurian. It is a prosperous place and I will guarantee each of you gets a house nicer than any you've seen. We have plenty of work available and more than enough food to go around for all. I won't force anyone to leave, but I'll take care of any who return with us."

Expressions of hope and even some tears appeared on the faces in front of him. Arthur noticed the handful of families with children all looked eager to leave with him. It warmed his heart to get them out of this squalor.

"If you wish to travel with us, find our general, Paladin Samson. He'll direct you to the correct person who can take down your information and get you to the staging area. We will provide all who elect to stay with basic tools to farm and cultivate land on your own. I'll also leave a small supply of food for each family and seeds for planting your own gardens. Keep in mind my offer doesn't expire and you're welcome to join us in Alurian if you change your mind in the future. It'll be up to you to travel on your own, though. I look forward to seeing many of you on our return march." Arthur said as he waved to the crowd and departed.

"No need to rush. Keep in an orderly line. You have plenty of time to register to leave." Samson called over the crowd.

Arthur smiled to himself as he raced away from the situation. One benefit of being king was allowing others to do the work he didn't want to.

He strolled back toward their camp outside of the city and his Wizard's Den. The portal was left open so he and his friends could access the amenities whenever they needed. While he traveled, he took the time to go over the long list of pertinent notifications from the battle. He collapsed all the experience gains together.

You have gained 7,540 total experience in Air Magic.

You have gained 4,220 total experience in Swords.

You have gained 10,120 total experience in Earth Magic.

Congratulations, you have reached level 28 in Earth Magic. Increases the effect of your earth magic spells by 81%. Those stone spikes were pretty worthless.

You have gained 13,850 total experience in Fire Magic.

You have gained 2,310 total experience in Dimensional Magic.

You have gained 2,920 total experience in Small Blades.

Congratulations, you have reached level 11 in Small Blades. Swing speed with Small Blades increased by 30%. Like the combo enchant.

You have gained 2,920 total experience in Dual Wield.

Congratulations, you have reached level 10 in Dual Wield. Accuracy penalty with off-hand weapons decreased by 27%. Some cool acrobatics.

You have gained 5,775 total experience in Medium Armor.

Congratulations, you have reached levels 9 and 10 in Medium Armor. Armor bonuses granted by medium armor increased by 27%. Not sure I've seen someone stupid enough to jump on a wall to purposefully take a blaster shot.

You have gained 3,110 total experience in Dual Casting.

You have gained 350 total experience in Archery.

Congratulations, you have reached level 11 in Archery. You are granted a 30% bonus to accuracy. Love those Hellfire Arrows.

You have gained 440 total experience in Block.

Congratulations, you have reached level 4 in Bock. You are granted a 9% bonus to Strength while blocking. Badly need to level this.

You have gained 845 total experience in Scan.

You have gained 210 total experience in Light Magic

You have gained 24,990 total experience.

The sheer amount of experience alone boggled his mind. Typically, these fights never amounted to much experience unless it was because of the raid quest. He hadn't even confirmed that one yet. A quick investigation through the experience notifications told him why. The Ar'Tookan soldiers were all worth an exorbitant amount of experience, even after splitting for the group. They alone accounted for ninety percent of the gain.

The rest of his notifications were even more impressive.

You have completed the Raid Quest Clash of Kings. You gain 27,500 experience, 3 Talent Points, and ` Spell Blade Talent Points.

You have completed the Raid Quest Interdimensional Warriors. You gain 77,450 experience, 8 Talent Points, and 5 Spell Blade Talent Points.

Congratulations, you have reached level 32! You now have 5 available skill points. That's probably not good with the blue guys.

You have completed a hidden quest for your Soul Bond. (Dragon Face Off… Again) You've earned 3 Soul Bond Talents.

You have completed a hidden quest for your Soul Bond. (Downfall of a King) You've earned 2 Soul Bond Talent Points.

You have completed a hidden quest for your Soul Bond. (Beat Overwhelming Odds) You've earned 3 Soul Bond Talents.

You have completed a hidden quest for your Divine Power and earned 1 Divine Points. (Downfall of a King)

You have completed a hidden quest for your Divine Power and earned 2 Divine Points. (Righteous Retribution)

You have advanced your Divine Champion rank to Apprentice.

You have advanced your Divine Champion rank to Adept.

About time I advanced that. He dug deeper into the Divine Skills and discovered he gained the first rank for defeating three champions. He could swear he defeated four, but he assumed Gliran wasn't technically a champion of Isabell. The second he gained for fulfilling his vengeance quest, Righteous Retribution. *Nothing like good old fashion vengeance to advance a religious rank.*

With the level advancement, he looked over his stats.

Strength: 33
Agility: 47
Intellect: 51
Wisdom: 31
Endurance: 44
Charisma: 27
Luck: 21

Most of his attributes were abnormally high, so he boosted some of his lower ones. Mana was rarely an issue, so he brushed off Wisdom. He dropped two into Charisma, bringing it to 29. The other three he placed in Luck, bringing it to 24. Hopefully those would pan out for him in the future.

The twenty-five percent boost to a skill he used on his Dimensional Magic netting him an additional 13,000 experience, but it wasn't enough to bump him up a level.

His Small Blades Talent tree was a simple choice. He opted to put two points in Damage Bonus.

Damage Bonus (2/10)	*Every 2 points invested in this talent increases your base and maximum damage with your Small Blades by 1.*

The bonus points he left alone since he didn't want to use them here.

Next, he looked over his Dual Wield Talents. He realized he had four points available in this tree, so he put all four in Main Hand Dexterity, bringing it to nine.

Main Hand Dexterity (9/10)	*Increases swing speed with main hand weapon by 3% per point.*

A glance at his Medium Armor tree pushed him to place one point in Mighty Resist.

Mighty Resist (5/5)	*While wearing at least 4 pieces of Medium Armor, reduces damage dealt to you by spells by 3% per point.*

This was enough to bring out the Tier 2 options for Heavy Armor.

You have 15 Free Talent Points. You have 7 unspent Talent points.

Tier 2	
Articulating Plates (0/10)	*While wearing at least 4 pieces of Medium Armor, decreases speed loss due to the weight of armor by 10% per point.*
Slick Plating (0/5)	*While wearing at least 4 pieces of Medium Armor, raises the chance that hits on you will be Glancing Blows by 3% per point.*
Regenerative Bounceback (0/5)	*While wearing at least 4 pieces of Medium Armor, increases the speed you respond to attacks by 3% per point.*

Arthur didn't have much trouble with movement in his armor because of his higher stats, so he put five points into Slick Plating. The added chance to cause Glancing Blows was great. Regenerative Bounceback got the last two.

It had been a while since he looked over his Archery Tree, so he brought the whole thing up.

Tier 1	

Aim Shot (1/1)	This ability allows the user to slow down the moments ,while being able to see farther and more accurately, to pick the perfect shot. Cost: 25 Stamina
Steady Fire (5/5)	This ability allows the user to fire faster. Each level adds 4% to rate of fire. Maximum of 20%.
Arrow Straightening (1/1)	This ability allows the user to use a small amount of mana to ensure arrows are perfectly straight and true. Cost: 5 Mana
Tier 2	
Sustained Focus (4/4)	This ability decreases the Stamina cost of using Aim Shot by 5 per level, maximum of 20 Stamina reduction.
Sharpened Arrowheads (1/5)	This ability increases the likelihood that critical strikes will also cause mortal damage. Each level increases this chance by 5% for a maximum of 25%.
Tier 3	

Full Draw (0/10)	*Each point allows you to fire arrows 10% farther.*
Magical Arrows (0/5)	*Investing all 5 points in this skill allows you to create arrows of pure magic and fire them from any bow you use. These arrows gain bonus damage based on the magic used and your skill level.*
Redirect (0/3)	*Each point allows you to redirect your arrow while in flight one time.*

The Magical Arrows talent was interesting, but he didn't have enough points to unlock it. Because of that and his infrequent use of a bow, he opted to put his last 2 points into Full Draw.

Arthur examined his Soul Bond Talents again and used 5 points to unlock Skin of Scales. The last 3 he used on All That Glitters.

Skin of Scales (5/5)	*Causes small dragon scales to form on the edge of your skin. Reduces damage taken by 10% per point while skill is active.* *Cooldown: 8 Hours* *Duration: 2 Minutes*

All That Glitters (5/5)	*Dragons have an innate sense for treasure. You gain the following for each point of this skill:* • *Increase money found during fights by 5%. Increases the chance of finding items of higher rarity by 15%. Gain 10% more resources when gathering or mining.*

Finally, he looked into his new Divine Talents. There were plenty of options, with the two new tiers now open.

Novice Skills	
Divine Fury (1/1)	*Channel a raging storm around your body that deals 25 HP/s damage to enemies. Lasts for 30 seconds.* *Mana cost: 600* *Cooldown: 3 days*
Nurtured Growth (0/1)	*Infuse plant life in a 100 square yard space with the power of divinity. Plants will grow 150% faster and produce 100% more usable food.*

	Mana Cost: 800 Mana Cooldown: 2 Weeks
Call Wrath (1/1)	*Marks a target enemy for wrath. All damage you do to a marked enemy is increased by 100% for 5 minutes.* *Mana Cost: 150* *Cooldown: 1 Day*
Retribution (1/1)	*Call upon holy fire to bathe an area and deal damage to all enemies in the space. Cast range of 200 yards. Deals 50 HP/s damage for 10 seconds.* *Mana Cost: 500 mana* *Cooldown: 5 days*
Blessing of Salvation (0/1)	*Send out waves of healing energy to revitalize allies near you. This ability will restore the health, mana, and stamina of all nearby allies by 40%* *Mana Cost: 200* *Cooldown: 7 days*
Apprentice Skills	

Building Prowess (0/1)	Draw on your divine essence to increase the effectiveness and speed while building with magic. Also decreases mana cost of these abilities. Mana cost: 800 Duration: 1 hour Speed Increase: 110% Mana Cost Reduction: 85% Cooldown: 1 day
Summon the Seraph (0/1)	Call upon your connection with the Divine to summon a Seraph to fight for you. Their armor and weapons will be of the same tier as you and their level will be equal to yours plus 5. Mana Cost: 1200 Mana Cooldown: 5 Days
Divine Watch (0/1)	Marks a target and tracks their conversations and actions. Mana Cost: 200 Duration: 8 hours Cooldown: 1 Day
Gift of Flight (0/1)	Wings of holy energy emerge from your back and grant you flight for short distances.

	Mana Cost: 300 mana Duration: 10 minutes Cooldown: 1 day
Adept Skills	
Invincibility (0/1)	Channel divine power into your body to protect you from all damage and remove negative status effect. Mana cost: 600 Duration: 20 seconds Cooldown: 4 days
Divine Avatar (0/1)	Your body is infused with a burst of Divine power. This energy causes the following: Double in size. Double your Strength. Increase your Agility by 50%. Mana Cost: 1400 Mana Duration: 20 minutes Cooldown: 2 Weeks

Master Craftsman (0/1)	Gives any item you create a 5% chance to be blessed by the gods. This blessing can increase their base stats, grant them permanent enchantments, and even trigger them becoming a named item.

As Arthur expected from God level skills, there were great options all around. Some were more useful to him than others, and that was what he focused on. Instead of looking over each skill by their pure ability alone, he considered how it would help his style. For instance, Divine Watch would be an incredible way to sniff out traitors, but would be far more useful to Rayne than Arthur. On the flip side, Gift of Flight was important to him if he was going to have to fight more from dragon-back in the future.

It took some time for him to weight the pros and cons of each option but in the end, he only had 3 points. He chose Invincible, Gift of Flight, and Master Craftsman. The rest all had their uses, but he felt these meshed well with his normal scenarios.

Crafting was always something he enjoyed, so making better gear appealed to him. The other two were 'oh shit buttons' that he could use to save his life. Nearly dying by falling off a dragon instilled a slight bit of fear that the Gift of Wings helped ease.

It took them a week to fully settle things in Esmere. Arthur truly planned to just leave as soon as possible, but he couldn't bring himself to abandon the people that wanted to stay in such poor conditions. He worked his magic and created better housing arrangements for each and even went as far as planting them a garden. Using some of his skills, he could coax some growth out before he left.

They assembled the people who wanted to leave, and Arthur made a few wagons to help transport them. No animals were at hand, so Arthur used his trick from before to create golems to haul them along.

Their trip was smooth as they traversed the countryside back to Alurian. The city was alive and vibrant with activity as they rolled up to the gate. Men and women of Esmere left their wagons to get a glimpse of their new home.

Shock and disbelief covered their faces as they stared at the wall and the city in the distance. The gate was open, so they had a clear look at the buildings.

"Welcome home," Arthur announced.

They walked down the long and winding road to the city and were met with people cheering along the path. The city council waited for them at the edge of time.

"Welcome back, Your Majesty," Daniel said with a bow. "We have prepared a celebration feast for this evening in the Guard Fortress."

"Great idea." Arthur said. "We have some fresh faces that need a place to live."

"I can see that," Daniel commented as he looked at the assembled group.

"Welcome to Alurian, people of Esmere. Everyone come forward one at a time and talk to Lady Katherine," Daranth said as he motioned to the woman. "She will work to get you a residence assigned."

Arthur smiled at the assembled group and waved his goodbyes. He had a lot to do before the feast, starting with him reaching over and grabbing Allendria by the hand.

"I'm ready to get you home," he told her in a low voice.

"Oh, are you really?" Allendria whispered in his ear.

"Let's go," Arthur said as he pulled her to the side of the crowd, ducked behind the nearest house, and rushed home.

★★★

Lianna approached the barrier in the white space. Unlike her sister, she wasn't rude. Using her power, she brushed against the barrier and waited. In a few moments, the barrier dropped, and she entered.

"Welcome sister. What brings you to my part of the realm?" Isabell asked.

"I've decided to accept your offer," she said sullenly.

"Stepping into the dark side with me?" Isabell said with a coo.

"No. I just fear the repercussions. Arthur killed a squad of Ar'Tookan Scouts and their commander. I'm hoping we can avoid trouble if he isn't around anymore. That's it, though. Remove him and I'll cooperate with the plot."

"Fine. I can make it happen. All I need is for you to ensure your paladin doesn't interfere. It will happen tonight, after the feast."

Lianna narrowed her eyes. "That's a quick turnaround. Almost as if you planned this already."

"I always keep agents around important people."

Lianna huffed. "Whatever. I'll assist this one time, but that is it."

"Great to see you as always, sister." Isabell said with a chuckle.

Lianna stood and stormed out.

"Now who's being dramatic," Isabell murmured.

* * *

Music rolled over the guests at the banquet. Arthur saw Wesley standing on the stage with his hurdy-gurdy as the melody soothed everyone present. Purple and red banners hung from the stone walls around the expansive hall.

The celebration was one of peace, so Arthur sat in regal clothing. A tailor in town made a pair of nice black pants with a white shirt and a deep purple vest. He left his armor and Ember in his Wizard's Den. All he carried was his dagger for his food.

Allendria joined him in her attire and wore a long gown of deep green. It hugged her curves just right and dipped down in a low V on the front.

He lifted his mug of ale and took a drink. The liquid held a slight burn as it rolled down his throat, but it was a good hurt. Arthur reached over and grabbed onto Allendria's hand. She squeezed back and the two of them stood.

"Thank you all for being here," Arthur said. "Everyone here is equally responsible for our success. I consider all of you friends, but better yet, I also consider you heroes. It took courage to stand up and fight back. Even in the face of overwhelming odds and foreign enemies, you never backed down. It's important to move forward and remember to never take what we have for granted. Protect what we have at all costs."

He ended his speech to cheers from the crowd. To show his solidarity, he approached the nearest crystal pillar and discharged all his excess mana in, charging up the defensive structure.

Guests followed behind to do the same in their show of loyalty to the city. Arthur stood at the side of the room with Allendria.

"It feels good," he told her.

She leaned her head on his shoulder. "It sure does. The real question is, how do we maintain our rule in two places without always being apart?"

Arthur grimaced. "Good question. I guess we can have constant sleepovers, but that doesn't fix the problem. Maybe it's time for me to look into portals. A quick hop into your bedroom at night would be welcome."

"That's a dangerous proposal if you can just portal into any elf maiden's bedroom whenever you want," she said as she ran a finger down his cheek.

"You're enough trouble as it is. Don't need to find another," Arthur laughed.

* * *

Samson watched the assembled guests as everyone dispersed from the party. He shook hands and waved at people he recognized. Most of those in attendance were people who fought on the front lines recently. Since the hall couldn't fit the entire city, they gave priority to those on the front lines. Other feasts were held throughout the city for the rest of the citizens.

Feeling tired, Samson marched through the building and headed for the exit. Bare stone walls passed by, but he didn't pay much attention. He looked up and saluted a guard as he walked past. The man returned the gesture, and he continued on his path.

The coolness of the outside air brought a little life back to him as he looked at the sky and inhaled the crisp air. The stars were bright without a cloud in the sky and he felt a sense of peace wash over him.

His mind wandered through the recent events until a thought tickled the back of his mind. *The guard. They didn't look familiar.*

Samson knew almost every guard in this city by sight, if not personally. It could be the weariness making him question things. He turned to walk back inside to check it out until a voice called to him. The sound drifted on the wind, but he couldn't find its source. Following the noise, he walked around the side of the building and came to a halt.

"Goddess," Samson breathed.

"Hello Paladin Samson. You've made me proud," Lianna told him.

He dropped to a knee in her presence and stared at the ground.

"None of that. I couldn't have asked for a better warrior to champion my cause. You are a shining example of what you should be."

"Thank you. I don't deserve your praise." He told her.

"You more than deserve it. You embody it. Do me a favor, my paladin."

"Anything, my lady." Samson said.

"Rest. There will be more challenges in the future and you are worn thin. I can feel the fatigue down to your very bones. Go home and sleep. No more work for the evening."

"But the city needs…" Samson said before Lianna cut him off.

"Nonsense. This city has run smoothly the entire time you were gone. It can survive the night without you. Do this for me. I want you ready for your next challenge."

"As you command," Samson said as he clasped his fist to his chest.

"You're a fine man. Make me proud." She said as she faded from sight.

Samson remained on his knee for a few moments as tears flowed down his face. He took the time to wipe them clear and regain his composure before returning to his feet. All other thoughts dismissed, he strode with shoulders high and his confidence soaring to do as bid.

Chapter 42

Downfall

Arthur and Allendria's footsteps echoed off of the walls in the hallway as they strolled through. After so much time fighting, they could finally relax and live their life. The appearance of the Ar'Tookans during the fight was disconcerting, but they'd heard no reports of any sightings elsewhere. For now, they'd take what they could get and enjoy some peace.

Four guards exited the new throne room in the city fortress as they approached the doorway. While they were away, the builders took it upon themselves to add this room for official meetings and functions while they were in residence. This room was adjacent to the main hall where the feast had just finished. The guards came to attention with a salute as the two passed.

Must be the change of the guard, Arthur reflected as he noticed a full contingent lining the walls inside the room. Arthur and Allendria walked up to the two thrones and took a seat.

"Where do we go from here?" Allendria asked.

"Wherever we want. No more evil tyrants breathing down our necks. It's just the two of us. I think we should enjoy what we have for a while. There will always be things to deal with in this world, but we need to cherish the time we have together." Arthur said as he reached over and held her hand.

"That sounds nice. We've been fighting for so long, I'm not sure I know how to relax anymore."

He squeezed her hand at those words. "We'll figure it out together."

The two of them sat in the chairs in silence as they looked around the room. It didn't take long for boredom to set in.

"Throne rooms are pretty bleak, aren't they?" Arthur asked.

Allendria chuckled. "It's almost depressing in here, staring at nothing interesting. Why would rulers ever want to sit in one of these places unless they were in a meeting?"

"Beats me. Want to go for a walk?" Arthur asked.

"Sounds great," she said as she leaned over and kissed him.

They rose to their feet and started walking toward the doorway back into the hall.

* * *

Rayne strolled through the hall. Memories flashed through his mind as he tried to process everything that had happened recently. The fighting was brutal during the siege, and his inner demon showed more of his face than Rayne was comfortable with.

It wasn't so much that the demon that truly
bothered him. The more he considered
everything, the more he realized the inner
demon was nothing more than himself. That
power had no control over him. His soul-
searching during the fight led him to that
revelation. Blaming this dark side of him on
another power was much easier than facing his
own inner demons.

Preying on the fears of those soldiers as
he picked them apart to delay their attack
felt wrong and also so right. The strange
dichotomy to it wouldn't process in his mind.

Rayne melded to the dark hallways in the
fortress as he continued forward. Shadows
latched onto him, and he could almost feel the
cold emptiness. The occasional guard or castle
worker interrupted his musings, scurrying
past.

Stonework changed subtly as he entered the
new section that was added for the throne
room. His stride faltered for half a step as
he saw the guards outside. Neither of them
looked familiar. To anyone else, that wouldn't
be out of the ordinary, but Rayne took pride
in being able to recognize most of them by
sight. Knowing those who worked in the castle
was a matter of duty when you were the kingdom
spymaster. With their recent battles, they
would place only known guards in such a place.

Rayne approached the open doorway, and the two guards turned their attention to him. One of them walked forward, but Rayne could see through the open archway. Arthur and Allendria were hand in hand, walking toward him. Rage burned through his being as he observed the scene. Purple energy cascaded over his body and a Weak Haste spell snapped into place on him. He fished a throwing knife from his belt and hurled it with all the speed he could muster.

* * *

Arthur walked toward the entrance of the throne room. He smiled as he watched Rayne come into view. The young man had been a lifesaver on their journeys. Arthur didn't let the spooky nature of Rayne's magic or abilities distract from the good he saw in him. Everyone wrestled with their inner self. Rayne did the same, but he was making progress.

Purple energy swirled around the rogue and Arthur froze mid-step. Eerie blue wisps of power formed over his face, creating eyes and a mouth over the purple shadows invading his hood. Arthur barely registered the man's speed increase as he grabbed a throwing knife and launched directly for him and Allendria.

Time seemed to slow as he watched the dagger flip end over end and close the distance. The shock of the action was almost too much for him to comprehend.

Rayne would never turn on us, would he?

His alarm shifted to confusion as he noticed Rayne aimed the blade at a space between him and Allendria.

Before the throwing knife passed, he felt
two sharp, burning pains in his lower back.
His breath disappeared in a flash as his body
fought against itself. Notifications flashed
through his vision.

*Unknown Assailant has dealt 175 HP damage
to you with Backstab. (Critical Hit) (Mortal
Blow) (x2)*
*Your flow of Mana has been disrupted and
will not recover for 5 minutes. Unable to cast
any spells for the duration.*
*You have been afflicted by Curse of
Cancellation. All magical healing effects are
nullified for the next 5 minutes.*

Fog filled his mind as weakness overtook
his body. His entire being was focused on the
agony in his lower back. At least it was until
he heard Allendria scream beside him.

His focus snapped back into place, and he
turned to face her. Allendria's face was
locked into a primal scream and Arthur took a
moment to look her way. A figure in a black
robe stood behind her. He strained to look
upon the masked figure, but an unseen force
kept trying to deflect his attention. Two
blades were buried to the hilt in Allendria's
lower back. They slid free in a smooth motion
and blood poured from the wounds, staining her
dark green dress.

   Allendria's eyes flooded with tears.
Arthur's rage ignited, and he leaped for the
assailant. The pain of his injuries wracked
his body, but rage pushed him forward. He only
had his personal dagger, but in his fury, he
didn't even draw it. Instead, he tackled them
to the ground and used pure, raw force to
smash a fist against their face. The dark mask
cracked as his fist crunched into it. With
pain flaring along his back, he lifted his
fist and punched down again. This time
receiving a deep gash in each arm from the
enemy's blades.

   *You dealt 35 HP damage to Unknown Assailant
with Unarmed.*
   *You dealt 35 HP damage to Unknown Assailant
with Unarmed.*
   *Unknown Assailant has dealt 28 HP damage to
you with Dagger of Cancellation.*
   *Unknown Assailant has dealt 26 HP damage to
you with Steel Dagger.*
   *Mortal Bleed has dealt 26 HP damage to you.
(x2)*

   The second punch crashed into the figure's
nose and the edge of his mask. Its durability
expended, it crumbled to dust and fell from
his face. Arthur only vaguely recognized the
man.
   Gallant.
   Arthur's rage rose higher as he realized
Dalia's assistant was a traitor. He slid
upward, pinned both of the small man's arms
with his legs, fished out his dagger, and sunk
it to the hilt in his throat. With a jerk, he
ripped it out the side, nearly separating his
head.

You dealt 220 HP Damage to Gallant with Enchanted Magesteel Dagger. (Critical Hit) (Fatal Blow)
   Gallant has died.

   Arthur looked up as Rayne crossed the distance to him. Two of the guards along the wall interposed themselves in his way and halted his charge.
   "Look out!" Rayne shouted.
   The sound of footsteps caught Arthur's attention, and he turned to see a second masked figure running at him with two bloody blades. The first one was the missing Manastrike Blade. He assumed the other was a Dagger of Cancellation.
   It had been so long that he actually forgot the Manastrike Blade was stolen. Now, the thief had finally shown their hand. As a minor consolation, a large bloody spot covered their left shoulder where Rayne's dagger hit.
   Arthur attempted to jump to his feet, but the action sent spasms through his body and he rolled to the side. Burning fire spread through him as the injury to his back contacted the ground. He screamed in pain before rolling back to a knee. Sweat poured down his face at the exertions. The constant movement wasn't helping his Mortal Bleed condition.

   Mortal Bleed has dealt 26 HP damage to you. (x6)

He lifted his dagger and barely parried the first attack. The assailant was weak compared to him, but his injuries made fighting back a struggle. The second blade struck him with a glancing blow on the arm and refreshed the time on his cancellation poison.

Unknown Assailant has dealt 14 HP damage to you with Dagger of Cancellation. (Glancing Blow)

The attacker didn't relent and Arthur was worried he'd never be able to regain his footing. Another dagger entered his view and smashed into the side of their mask. Shards of white filled the air as the assailant cried out in pain. Arthur recognized the voice when he heard it.

"Dalia? Looks like I should have killed you instead of exiling you."

The figure grabbed her cracked mask and threw it to the ground. Dalia sneered at him.

"I plan to save this world. My Goddess Isabell will ensure we are protected from the invaders as long as we get rid of you. I'll risk execution for the promise of safety."

"As if you care," Allendria began before she grunted in pain and took a breath, "about anyone but yourself, you traitorous bitch."

"Power is always nice as well. I really don't care what happens to the world as long as I'm up top," she agreed with a shrug.

Dalia's eyes widened for a moment before she dove to the side. Another throwing knife passed through the space she just vacated and he heard Rayne curse in frustration.

"You'll never escape. Give up now." Arthur told her.

Dalia laughed. "You fool. I don't need to escape. All the people here belong to me."

Arthur looked around and realized he didn't recognize any of the guard's faces.

How could I miss such a detail?

They all stood with weapons drawn but were split into pairs, covering each of the entrances. The four remaining without a door to guard rushed to fight Rayne and prevent him from entering.

Arthur, what is happening? Calfuray's frantic voice drifted to him.

They have betrayed us. Dalia has turned a large force of the guards and has attacked me and Allendria. I don't see a way out and I'm losing health too fast.

I noticed! Heal yourself.

Not possible. They used a damn dagger that cancels magical healing.

Arthur tried to stand and failed. Dalia yelled in rage as she had to dodge another throwing knife and couldn't get to him.

You don't have any potions? Balair asked as he entered their conversation.

None on me. They are all in my Wizard's Den and I'm also cut off from my magic.

Fuck, this is bad. I'm on my way. Hold on. Calfuray said.

We are in the throne room. Arthur told her.

We both just left the fortress, but we'll turn around. Balair told him.

They have guards on the doors and probably more through the halls. Do whatever you have to and destroy anything you need to get here. Arthur said.

A blast of fire caused Dalia to jump to the side again. Arthur spared a glance and saw Allendria on a knee with her hand outstretched. Orange fire built in her palm for another spell.

"That's enough of that," Dalia said and she threw Manastrike at Allendria. The blade crossed the distance in a flash, sinking into her chest. The fire in her hand winked out as the spell negation took effect, and Allendria stared at it in shock.

"No!" Arthur roared as he jumped to his feet. The pain threatened to drag him back to the ground, but his adrenaline pushed through. Dalia's eyes widened as he approached, and she slashed wildly with her remaining dagger. Arthur parried the blade with his own and stepped forward. Dalia staggered back as his fist connected with her nose. Bones cracked under the force.

You dealt 75 HP damage to Dalia with Unarmed. (Critical Hit)

Tears cascaded down Dalia's face. She lifted her hand and felt her nose. Her blurry eyes blazed with anger.

A thud reached Arthur's ears, and he turned to see Allendria flat on the ground. Forgetting about Dalia, he rushed to her side and slid to a stop on the ground near her.

"A fitting end that the two of you will die together. Good riddance." Dalia cackled.

Footsteps echoed on the stone as she clumsily retreated toward the nearest doorway.

A flash of fire confused him until he looked toward Rayne and saw Balair entering the fight in his human form. More guards rushed into the rooms from the other two exits, but each of them ran straight for Rayne and Balair. None of them tried to help.

How did she turn everyone against us?

Arthur grabbed Allendria's hand as he kneeled by her side.

"Hang on for me. You can't leave me." He said frantically as he searched for options. Her necklace caught his attention, and he reached out to touch it with his other hand. The power of the artifact filled him and in his desperation, he attempted the most powerful heal spell he knew.

Rejuvenation has no effect on Allendria due to Curse of Cancellation.

"Dammit!" He roared as he looked into Allendria's eyes. Tears rolled down her face and his eyes blurred with them as well.

"I'm sorry we couldn't have the life we dreamed of," she whispered to him.

"Don't give up on me yet. We'll figure this out," he pleaded with her.

"We both know that isn't true." She said as she shuddered.

Arthur pulled more mana from the necklace and cast the spell again.

Major Rejuvenation has no effect on Allendria due to Curse of Cancellation.

He slammed his fist on the stone floor in frustration. His draw increased and mana poured in as he cast spell after spell.

*Minor Heal Wounds has no effect on
Allendria due to Curse of Cancellation.*
*Major Heal Wounds has no effect on
Allendria due to Curse of Cancellation.*
*Rejuvenation has no effect on Allendria due
to Curse of Cancellation.*
Accelerated Body heals for 0 HP.

His heart soared when the last spell didn't
say it failed, but his despair set in as he
saw it healed for zero HP.

Her hand slowly rose and brushed against
his face.

"I love you."

Tears rolled down his cheeks as he reached
over and grabbed her hand.

"I love you too."

Her hand went limp and her eyes rolled back
in her head. Arthur lowered her hand to the
ground and brushed stray hairs out of her
face. His gaze remained locked on her as he
felt his health tick away.

Mortal Bleed has dealt 26 HP damage to you.
(x8)

A grunt of pain drew his attention, and he
turned to see eight people surrounding Rayne
and Balair. The young man fought valiantly and
his shadowy power was on full display as he
dashed from target to target. Arthur could
tell he was running out of power, though.

A roar shook the building as a deep thud
resounded and dust shook from the ceiling. The
sound of tearing stone filled the room as a
corner of the roof crumbled.

I'm almost to you. Calfuray told him.

Arthur looked at his health.

Shit. Not enough time with that bleeding effect.

Cal. I need you to do me a favor.

Not the time, Arthur. I'm going to rip this fucking roof off and get to you before it's too late.

I'm sorry, my friend. It's already too late. I have no way of healing myself and am bleeding out too fast. I'm afraid this is the end of our journey.

I won't let it be! Let me get to you and I'll figure things out. Cal pleaded.

Thank you for everything, Cal, but I refuse to let you die with me. Please do me a favor. Rescue Rayne. He is a good man and has been a loyal friend. Please get him out of here.

The noise above paused for a moment before it increased in ferocity. *No. I refuse to give up on you. If you die, so do I.*

No, you won't. While I can't heal us, I can use the last of the mana in Allendria's necklace to rip myself out of the dimension. It will break the bond and set you free. I'll miss you. Take care of our friends. Arthur said. Pain flared for a moment and he winced before continuing.

Balair, I know you're listening too. I'll miss you as well. Enjoy your life as a true and majestic dragon.

It's been an honor, Arthur. The solemn voice of Balair came through their link. He heard the man roar and watched him try to push through the guards and get to Arthur. They raised pikes and spears to ward him off. His body emitted flames and burned any near him, save for Rayne. Their long spears still allowed them to hold him back at a distance.

Stones fell from the ceiling and crashed into the ground as claws poked through the holes. Arthur looked at Allendria and saw her eyes were now closed. Her body was still, and he brushed her cheek. Rayne continue to fight through the soldiers, still trying desperately to reach him.

"Thank you, Rayne. I'm sorry it had to end this way." Arthur said as he wove a small amount of Air Magic from the mana in the necklace to send the message to his friend. Rayne stumbled for a moment before his shadowy visage turned to face Arthur.

"It's not over yet. I'll get to you!"

Arthur could only manage a weak smile.

"I name Rayne as family and my heir to the Kingdom of Fire." Arthur whispered.

Rayne has become the heir to the Kingdom of Fire. He will inherit the title of king when Arthur Firebrand passes away as long as he controls territory within the kingdom.

Arthur pulled on every ounce of mana left in the pendant. Dark energy swirled all around him and sparks of purple lightning flashed in the room. Reality warped as his vision shifted. Not knowing how he'd pulled himself out of the dimension last time, he just let his instincts work and dumped in power.

More stone fell as the roof finally gave way in the corner and Calfuray entered the room. She lunged forward and grabbed two guards in her jaws, crushing them instantly.

Get them out! Arthur pleaded.

She turned to look at him. Sadness overtook her expression when she noticed the Dimensional Magic warping around him. A fiery red tear ran down her face before she nodded and jumped toward Rayne. She wrapped a claw around him and turned on her hind legs toward the opening in the ceiling.

"Let me down, Cal! I have to help them!" Rayne raged in her grip.

Balair shifted into dragon form and looked back to Arthur.

Goodbye, my friend. Balair said.

After a step, he paused and picked up Allendria's body with his front claw and launched into the air.

The energy swirling around Arthur snapped into place and he faded from existence as he saw Calfuray escape through the roof. All color faded and his vision went dark.

Epilogue

A consciousness floated through a vast white space. The being did not know if it was truly a being or not. No memory came to it as it floated through an infinite void of white.

A sound drew its attention, and it drifted to another portion of the emptiness.

"What have you done?" The voice yelled as it reverberated through the white space.

"Sister, there's no need…" Isabell began.

"Shut up! This was not the deal. I agreed to cooperate so you could remove Arthur. There was nothing in our deal about Allendria or the baby." Lianna fumed.

"I didn't give the order to take them out. My agent must've taken the initiative. I assume out of a grudge." Isabell waved off.

"Mark my words. You will never receive my help again. If you thought we had a rivalry before. You've seen nothing. Probably time you learn to put your dogs on leashes because I'm having my people hunt all of them and put them down like the rabid dogs they are."

"Calm down. You really think another Firebrand child wouldn't draw just as much attention as their father. It may delay the backlash for a handful of years, but history would repeat itself. This is probably for the best." Isabell said.

"Sounds like you did plan this," Lianna said. "This is officially war, sister. I've played on the sidelines for too long. Now you suffer for this act."

The two stared at each other as power reverberated through the space. Reality bent as the solid white space contorted with additional grays. The stray consciousness watched the confrontation with confusion and interest. The blank slate of its mind absorbing the details they said but having no context to tie it together.

"Prepare your forces," Lianna spat. "Mine are coming for them."

Lianna spun and walked away. The thud of her heavy footfalls accented by the power distorting the surrounding space.

***

Rayne ducked into the shadow of an alley. Guards raced past in all directions, but he wasn't sure what to do about it. *Arthur is dead.*

The thought echoed through his head. His anger at the action fueling him with the desire to burn everything to the ground. The sting of his failure cut deep as he cursed himself for not making it to his friend.

The notification he received as Calfuray carried him away stung him even more. Arthur had been a dear friend and his final act had been to show Rayne his trust. He'd been unable to acknowledge the notification and kept glancing at it.

You have been named the heir of the Kingdom of Fire by Arthur Firebrand.

You are now the king of the Kingdom of Fire. All hail king Rayne Firebrand.

Tears stung the corners of his eyes at the message. Not only did Arthur trust him enough to take his place, he trusted him enough to grant him his last name.

The city was in shambles as confusion reigned supreme. Rayne had to come back and see what was happening himself. The city council tried to calm the citizens, but it wasn't working. Seeing no end in sight, Rayne crept back through the city and headed for the wall.

Reaching the top and hopping over was an easy feat for him, and none of the guards caught so much as a glimpse. Much of the countryside was now restored, but everything of importance now resided inside the walls.

A small cottage sat roughly a mile from the city, and Rayne walked inside. The young man in the building growled as fire formed over his hand.

"It's just me, Balair." Rayne said.

The dragon grunted and Rayne slipped inside.

"Anything?" Balair asked.

"Nothing. All I know for sure is Arthur is gone. I'll try again tomorrow as things die down. Not going to take my chances. No telling how many agents are in the city."

"How could this happen?" Balair mumbled.

"Arthur should've killed that bitch instead of letting her go," Rayne said.

"In hindsight, yes. Had he done it, he would be labeled as an evil tyrant. There wasn't enough solid evidence to convict her to death." Balair said.

Rayne's shoulders slumped. He looked over at the still form under the cloak.

"How is she?" he asked.

"Stable. That potion saved her life. It'll take time for her to recover." Balair confirmed.

"And the baby?" Rayne asked.

Balair just shook his head.

Rayne sat with his back against the wall, raised his knees to his chest, and buried his head in his arms. The tears flowed as his shoulders shook. He tried to maintain his composure, but he couldn't.

"I'm so sorry, Arthur. I failed you just as I have everyone in my life," Rayne cried as he rocked in place.

www.ingramcontent.com/pod-product-compliance
Lightning Source LLC
Chambersburg PA
CBHW072033190726
48294CB00005B/1240